Second Nature

Also by Don Thompson

Stellar Woods

Islands of Light

Places Not Here

Second Nature

Don Thompson

Order this book online at www.trafford.com
or email orders@trafford.com

Most Trafford titles are also available at major online book retailers.

Printed in the United States of America.

ISBN: 978-1-4669-0237-4 (sc)
ISBN: 978-1-4669-0238-1 (e)

Library of Congress Control Number: 2011962029

Trafford rev. 12/06/2011

 www.trafford.com

North America & international
toll-free: 1 888 232 4444 (USA & Canada)
phone: 250 383 6864 ♦ fax: 812 355 4082

~ For Donna, Ben, and Gracie ~

Acknowledgments

I am so fortunate to have had such a large, interested, and diverse group of people read and comment on the manuscript for this book.

First, my wife, Donna, spent hours poring over the chapters as they came off the keyboard, offering kind but tough and constructive criticism, and then did the same many times later as the book coalesced. Even more than this, she encouraged me countless times along the way, especially when I needed it the most.

My two grown kids, Ben and Gracie, both read early manuscripts and made their Dad feel as though his work might even find some traction with the young adult set. They were very encouraging.

I also owe a great debt of gratitude to Katie Walter, Sue Daley, Teri Orella and Eileen Jennings who all provided detailed comments, asked key questions, and made me re-think certain aspects of dialog and plot flow. Byron Stoeser reviewed an early manuscript and was enormously encouraging, making my next steps that much easier. Bill Wood, Jim Stewart and Wade Bassi have been friendly sources of honest commentary and encouragement as well, and for that I am most grateful. Having been there herself, Karen Burns was most helpful about the writing and publishing process and offered both practical advice and a willing ear over coffee. Carol and Ed Morrison, both psychotherapists, provided extremely valuable insights into the therapy process and the treatment of DID in particular. Finally, Karl Marlantes spent a very generous amount of time between his own book tours on a tough and enormously helpful critique of the work.

ONE

ST. LOUIS, 1980

· ·

I t was an accident, one that could happen to anyone. But it didn't happen to just anyone.

Accidents never do, thought Marilyn Jamison. They happen to friends, coworkers, lovers, mothers. Marilyn stared bleary-eyed into the untouched cup of black coffee on the otherwise bare table in front of her. Her brown hair, normally tucked into a neat bun, hung limp on either side of the cup.

"Tragic" was the word of the day, and it had been repeated in a newspaper article about Kathryn's accident the next morning. But the adjective was woefully inadequate. It was just a bandage applied in a vain attempt to stop the emotional bleeding—to stop the bleeding so life could go on for everyone else.

Everyone else? What gives anyone the right to be in that group? The doctors didn't seem to ask such questions. They just made the diagnosis, performed the surgery, worked for the best possible outcome. No one cried behind a surgical mask.

But Marilyn did. Grief overwhelmed her without notice and the tears began again. She felt that accidents like this should never happen, especially not to a bright young surgical resident like Kathryn Johansen. Not to a compassionate young doctor who would befriend a lowly medical librarian like herself.

Marilyn's mind circled back through the events leading up to the accident, as if perhaps mere recall could change the outcome. She had arrived early at St. Louis University Hospital on that cold and snowy morning, hoping to catch up on overdue notices before the chaos of her day began. She would try to get a little work done before the doctors descended upon the library asking for a priority photocopy of this or that paper from the Journal of Bone and Joint Surgery, or demanding immediate access to the only copy of a monograph that had been checked out to the Chief of Pediatrics the day before. Marilyn always managed to work things out, to find creative solutions for the doctors, but there would be no solutions today.

She remembered pulling into the icy parking lot at fifteen minutes before six on that morning in January, just a few spaces away from Dr. Johansen's red Camaro. Sometimes it seemed to Marilyn that her friend never left the hospital. The Camaro was always in the same space when Marilyn arrived for work in the morning and was still there when she left at night. At least the snow hadn't completely covered the cherry red paint yet.

Marilyn knew there wasn't much reason for Dr. Johansen to be anywhere other than the hospital. She had no relatives left, her mother having died last year, and her father when she was a child. And, as far as Marilyn could tell, Kathryn's social life was practically nil as well, other than their own brief talks at work.

Well, yes, Marilyn remembered, there had been that *one* trip. A few days after her mother's funeral, Kathryn escaped on a last-minute flight to Cabo, but even that was cut short by a reorganization at the hospital. When she returned, Kathryn confided in Marilyn about a fiery but ill-fated fling with a man at the resort. But now Kathryn's entire world once again seemed confined to patients, board certification study, her research on frozen section analysis, and a challenging team of interns.

Maybe I can pull her away for a quick cup of coffee before rounds, thought Marilyn. She smiled at the idea of chiding Kathryn, yet again, about her overdue issue of the New England Journal of Medicine.

Carefully bringing her VW to a stop on the slippery pavement, Marilyn stepped out and walked flat-footed across the ice toward the hospital. She glanced back to see if she had managed to park straight, and from that new vantage point noticed that the rear passenger-side door of Kathryn's Camaro was open. That was odd. Had Kathryn gone around to retrieve something from the back seat and then neglected to close the door? It wasn't like her to leave a door open, even if she was in her usual hurry.

Marilyn shuffled back over the ice toward the vehicles and made her way around the front of the Camaro, placing a hand on the hood of the car for stability as she made the turn to her right.

Her mind was set on closing the car door, so it took a moment for Marilyn to absorb the new context. There, on its back on the ice, with its head in a frozen pool of blood, lay a snow-dusted body. It took another moment for Marilyn to understand that this body was Kathryn's. She could see the marks in the snow where her friend had apparently slipped and fallen backward. Maybe the car door had been frozen shut and yielded all at once.

Marilyn dropped to her knees and instinctively brushed the snow from her friend's face. The lips were parted and had a bluish tinge but there was the barest wisp of air moving through them, creating a thin, ephemeral fog. The blue-green eyes were open but one pupil was fully dilated and neither one blinked. Marilyn heard herself scream.

Her vision came back first. Marilyn could see young doctors, two of them, moving quickly, bringing oxygen, a stretcher. Interns. Kathryn's interns. "Kathryn!" Her hearing popped back into operation at the sound of her own voice and people were talking all at once. Someone was helping her to her feet. She slipped back down and wanted to stay there. No, she couldn't do that. She had to get up.

"She's alive, barely," she heard Dr. Munoz say. "The cold may have actually been her best friend. Sorry, I didn't mean it that way. I know you two are close. Your screaming—it brought us out."

"Oh." Marilyn rubbed her eyes in a vain attempt at clarity.

"Here, let me help you up," Munoz continued. "We need to get Dr. Johansen into surgery right away."

"How bad?" was all Marilyn could manage as she struggled to her feet.

The second intern, whom Marilyn recognized as Steven Weingate, hesitated as he and Joe Munoz carefully slid their resident onto a flattened trauma stretcher. Then he spoke. "Whew, she's put on a few pounds. Sixth and seventh cervical vertebrae and a skull fracture. Her fall must have been just wrong."

Yes, wrong, thought Marilyn as she struggled to keep up with the interns hustling her friend toward the Emergency Room. She shouted after them, "Get Dr. Stinson!"

There was no response and Marilyn didn't want to delay Kathryn's care so she picked up her pace across the icy parking lot. Once inside the ER, she tried again as the young doctors moved their patient into an empty surgical suite. "You've got to page Stinson. He needs to be here for the surgery."

Finally, Weingate turned and gave Marilyn a look of exasperated condescension. "Stinson's an obstetrician."

"I know that. I may not be a doctor but I'm not an idiot either. Just get him and do it now."

Marilyn never knew whether it was just the extra few years she had on these new doctors or if they were actually responding to the authority in her voice, which even she was surprised to hear. Or maybe it was their own shame at not recognizing Kathryn's condition right away. Whatever it was, they both ran to the paging telephone. Munoz got there first and made the call.

Twenty minutes later, Marilyn found herself watching her first surgery, wishing it wasn't Kathryn's. She had seen the journals, read the clinical accounts of various procedures, heard the doctors discussing such things, but this was the first time she had ever actually witnessed an operation. She had asked to be allowed into the observation booth and, to her surprise, there had been no objection—just a nod toward the door from Dr. Weingate.

She was alone in the booth, looking down at her friend, now reduced to the status of patient, prepped and ready. *Ready for what?* There were four doctors in the room below, including Markhov, Chief of Surgery. Marilyn saw that they had positioned Kathryn laterally—not optimum for head and neck surgery. *They're favoring the baby,* she thought. *They would only do that if...*

It didn't take long for the doctors to make a decision. They examined Kathryn's injuries again. There was an EEG printout. Quick discussion. Shaking of heads. Then they gently moved Kathryn onto her back. That, Marilyn knew, marked both the end and the beginning. Stinson entered the room, masked and gloved. He made a low abdominal incision and Marilyn looked away.

Two

Seattle, Present Day

· ·

A llison Walker tilted her head back and sniffed the air as she stepped into the dimly lit salon. Just the usual boat smells: oiled woods, a little salt, the mildest hints of styrene and diesel. She checked her watch. It was 7:15 and, as always, she had arrived a little before the agreed time to set things up. Her prospect would be along soon.

Allison sometimes showed yachts early in the morning before typical work hours, but only when she knew enough about the potential buyer to feel safe being alone in a marina with little or no activity. This guy seemed fine, at least from his online corporate profile and the two short phone conversations they'd had. A little odd maybe, but no threat.

Allison opened the blinds along the starboard side of the salon and glanced out. Still gray and drizzly. She walked forward and up to the pilothouse to bring the vessel to life. Warmly glowing electronics always seemed to encourage buyers, she felt, and her own live-aboard experience reinforced this. Unless she was trying to sleep, Allison found a dark, quiet vessel a bit unnerving, even ominous at times. *Dead in the water.*

A shiver ran through her body as Allison leaned across the cold ship's wheel to toggle a few switches. She turned to the port side to flip on the diesel heat, and hugged herself against the damp cold. A few seconds later, the reassuring sound of the furnace's blower breathed comfort into the air.

Music or ship's radio? Allison knew that her prospect was already a yacht owner. He was also a mid-level exec in a local software company and probably a techie at heart, so she opted for the radio. That would have been her personal preference anyway, as its low chatter worked like a mental balm to mask the intensely competing trains of thought which sometimes steamed through her head. She reached up and turned on the VHF radio, tuning it to Seattle Traffic where the controller was logging in a container ship heading south through Admiralty Inlet.

Having satisfied herself that all systems were working, Allison looked forward through the pilothouse windows at the sky which was straining to take on a morning glow. She loved her own cozy little marina on Lake Union with its covered slips, but she had to admit that Elliott Bay Marina had its perks, for those who could afford them. From her vantage point in the raised pilothouse, Allison could see southeast through several other rows of boats, over a stretch of Elliott Bay and on to the city itself. Seattle's blue-green reflections on the water rippled smoothly in response to the wake of a ferry inbound from Bainbridge Island.

Allison gazed through the window for several more minutes, savoring the January morning calm as the yacht warmed around her. The occasional creak of the boat pulling against its dock lines, and the little ticks that came from the heating ducts, gave Allison the distinct impression that the yacht was stretching its muscles, slowly joining the morning with her.

Gradually, though, Allison's mind returned to the task at hand. She let her focus change from the distant view of Seattle to the reflection of her own face as the glow of the instruments revealed it in the window. She leaned forward to check her minimal makeup, ran a finger gently under each turquoise eye, and shook her head to position a swoop of medium length chestnut hair across her forehead. She pursed her lips and allowed that crooked little smile to appear, the one that her friend Margaret called her Meg Ryan smile. "Not too bad for thirty," she whispered to herself.

"Anybody home?" came a muffled voice from behind her.

Damn, I forgot to put on the coffee! thought Allison as she hurried down through the galley to meet her early client. "Be right there!" she called back.

Allison opened the aft salon door to find a pudgy middle-aged man with dark curly hair, graying around the edges. He was wearing a yellow rain slicker and his eyes moved constantly, as if searching the vessel for something interesting or dangerous. Thick glasses seemed to magnify the effect of his shifting eyes. Allison moved slightly to place herself in the focus of his attention.

"Good morning, I'm Allison Walker," she said, smiling and extending her hand. "You must be Mr. Terpin."

"Josh Terpin, good to meet you," said the man, breathing heavily, as if he had run down the dock. His eyes met Allison's for only an instant as he shook her hand, then resumed their darting. Terpin ran a hand along the teak woodwork.

"I was just about to get some coffee going," said Allison. "Care for some?"

"Twin diesels, right?" asked Terpin, glancing around the interior.

I guess that's a no on the coffee, thought Allison. "Yes, twin Cummins 370Bs, turbocharged. 370 horsepower at 3000 RPM." Allison felt some pride in her memory for this kind of detail. Even though her memory plagued her in other ways, it did help sell boats.

"Mmm. Thrusters?"

"Just bow thrusters. Hydraulic, though."

"Hours on the engines?"

"About four hundred, I believe."

"Okay, not bad."

This kind of exchange went on for several more minutes as Allison followed her prospect through the various spaces aboard the 49-foot motor yacht. She noticed that Terpin's breathing hadn't slowed much as he puffed around the boat, opening storage areas, inspecting wiring, flicking lights on and off. His eyes always seemed to be a half second ahead of his hands, moving constantly.

Allison tried to make some sales headway. "So, is this boat something like you had in mind?"

"Yeah, it's in the ballpark."

"What kind of boat do you have now, if I could ask?"

"It's a Bayliner, a 3988."

"So this would be a nice step up for you," Allison smiled.

"Hey, don't give me that bullshit about Bayliners," Terpin shot back. "They make a good boat."

"No, no! I just meant the size. Ten feet is a nice jump up, and with the extra beam, you'd have so much more interior space. And the pilothouse is a real plus here in the Northwest, don't you think?"

"I guess. So what's up top?" asked Terpin with a glance up the steep wooden stairs leading to the flybridge hatch.

"There's a nice upper helm, tons of space for a dinghy and seating for at least six. Here, let's go take a look," Allison smiled as she gestured upward toward the hatch.

Terpin grabbed the handrail and took a step up. "Ooh," he muttered, reaching back to massage a leg.

"You okay?" Allison asked.

"Yeah, happens every now and then. It's nothing." Terpin took another slow step up and winced.

"Why don't I just send you some photos of the bridge," offered Allison. "Besides, it's still raining out there. Here, let me give you a hand," she said, reaching up.

Terpin brushed her hand aside.

"Is it a cramping kind of pain, even burning sometimes?" Allison asked.

"Yeah . . ." Terpin looked at her sideways.

"Could be intermittent claudication," said Allison. "Restricted blood flow in the arteries of your leg, basically. It manifests as a temporary symptom, but often reflects a more permanent underlying condition. Can be a serious indicator . . ."

Terpin, having reached the bottom again, turned and stared at Allison. She noted that this was the first time the man had actually looked directly at her for more than a fraction of a second. *Flushed appearance, a light sweat. Hypertension too?*

"When was the last time you had your blood pressure checked, Mr. Terpin?"

"What are you, a yacht broker or an MD?" said Terpin as he backed away. "I've gotta get to a meeting."

Terpin stepped onto the dock, and with an irritated glance back, was gone.

Allison sat down heavily and pounded the seat of the couch with her hand. *What is wrong with me?!*

This wasn't the first time Allison had let one of the Teachers get in her way. They were usually helpful, almost always interesting. But sometimes, like now . . . *Just because she's a doctor doesn't mean I should let her jump in when I see someone in trouble! I mean, shit, it's my life!*

My life? Right, more like our life, or their life. Just in the last year or so, she had to admit that things had gotten more intense. And the headaches were more of a bother, too.

As far back as she could remember, Allison seemed to know things that she shouldn't know, to learn things much faster than her peers. Not everything, just things that the Teachers knew about: dry, skill-related things, nothing personal. Like that crazy journal reference that had been stuck in her head like an annoying song since childhood, long before she had any clue about its meaning. Just a string of words and numbers: *American Journal of Surgery, Vol. 134, August 1977, No. 2, p. 136.* Over the last few years, she'd read the paper several times, had no trouble understanding it, but failed to see how it could possibly be relevant to her life. Her life? What was that, anyway?

Allison slumped forward and put her head in her hands. Had it finally gotten bad enough to talk to someone about? No one could possibly understand. They would just send her away. No. She shook her head slowly from side to side, as if to reinforce the decision she had made and re-made hundreds of times before.

She hadn't breathed a word to anyone about the Teachers since she'd made that mistake when she was a little girl. On her fifth birthday, just a few days after Allison left her last foster home and was finally adopted, she had tried to make some inroads with her new big sister, Beth. The adoption hadn't been easy for either girl. Allison never knew her birth parents and had no experience with a real sibling; and Beth, for her part, saw little Allison as a foreign invader. So when Allison tried to share something about her Teachers in an attempt at intimacy, Beth shut her down. She said that Allison was broken and told her that only broken babies had imaginary friends. Imaginary teacher-friends were even worse. Not only that, she said, but if Allison ever did anything Beth didn't like, Beth would tell Mom and Dad all about the Teachers, and they would send Allison back where she came from. *Send you back. Broken.*

Allison still felt the pain of that moment. She knew it was juvenile, this crazy thought of abandonment. Why even allow it mental space? No one was going to send her anywhere. She was a grown woman, for God's sake! She'd made it this far in one piece, more or less.

Maybe her friend Margaret would get it. Maybe it would be safe to tell her. It would be an enormous relief, and there really wasn't anyone else. But Allison couldn't bear the thought of losing her only real friend; and that could happen, couldn't it? *Send you back. Back where you came from. Broken.*

THREE

· ·

The wee hours of the morning. *Where did that description come from?* Dan Gunnison often explored such seemingly random topics as he drove across the 520 bridge toward Seattle in the pre-dawn hours. There was almost no traffic and the lights around Husky Stadium winked at their floating twins in the calm waters of Lake Washington. *And what provoked me to consider the question in the first place? Ah, the meta-question, inevitably generated by the convoluted mind of the psychotherapist.*

Dan smiled, dismissed the second question, and let the first one hold its place a moment longer. Sure, wee numbers, but the morning itself felt small at 4:45, maybe because so few people visibly occupied it then. He felt as if he owned a piece of the day that was uniquely his. A small piece, but a treasured one.

The dark quiet of the car and the nearly effortless drive helped Dan start his day on a meditative note. He never listened to the news during these morning drives and rarely even played music; those things he reserved for the drive home when the world was much bigger.

The deep water of Lake Washington rippled on the left side of the floating bridge deck, but formed an unblemished mirror on the right as Dan cruised across. *A south breeze this morning. Maybe rain later.*

Passing the dimly lit covered slips of the Seattle Yacht Club, Dan soon found himself faced with Interstate 5, and the morning expanded a bit. It grew even larger as Dan merged with the south-bound traffic, fought his way across four lanes, and took the Union Street exit. By the time he pulled into a parking space at the Seattle Athletic Club just uphill from the waterfront, the morning was fully grown.

Once a week, Dan and his old college friend, Skip Hanover, met for racquetball at the club before work. Dan checked into the brightly lit club and made his way toward the locker room where a new thought intruded. With a shake of his head, it occurred to Dan that he'd known Skip now for nearly fifteen years. Had it really been that long since their undergraduate roommate days at UCSD?

The two of them had used that time so differently, he reflected. When they first met—Dan the surfer, medium height but wiry, tan and strong, with sun-bleached light brown hair, and Skip the lab rat, taller, but a bit on the chubby side with curly blond hair, glasses, and a ready smile—it was hard to imagine how they would get along, living in such close quarters. Between glassy, near-perfect waves at Black's Beach, Dan slogged away on his psychology degree while Skip worked diligently in the pre-med program, buried half the time in the bio labs and the other half, it seemed, in the library. In fact, Dan chuckled to himself, maybe that's how they managed to get along so well at first; Skip was hardly ever in the dorm.

But it wasn't just that. There was a certain complementary nature to their friendship, almost a symbiosis. By the Spring quarter of that first year, Dan had managed to pry Skip away from the labs and onto the beach, and then to the mountains east of San Diego for rock climbing. Skip, for his part, patiently helped Dan with experiment design and statistics. Skip's passion for learning and discovery had been contagious, and Dan wondered sometimes if he would have ever graduated had it not been for his friend.

Since then, their lives had taken radically different paths but their friendship had survived it all. Dan had moved on to earn a Masters in Cognitive Psychology from the University of Colorado in Boulder, and Skip had gone to medical school at Stanford and from there to Johns Hopkins for post-doc work in genetics, an internship and a residency.

Skip had married during his internship and, unlike many who tried that, he and Emily had made it work. They now had an eight-year-old son and were enjoying life together in the Northwest where Skip was a Clinical Geneticist and Professor at the UW School of Medicine.

Dan, on the other hand, had taken decidedly haphazard paths along both career and relationship lines. In fact, he often recalled with a pang, those two jagged lines had crossed once, but not as positively as Skip's. They crossed in a woman named Natalie. She had been a client in Dan's new psychotherapy practice and Dan had made a classic and damaging mistake.

Natalie was a brown-eyed dark beauty of a young woman, soft spoken, vulnerable following a breakup, and exuding sexuality without effort or any apparent awareness. She never overtly displayed her physical attributes through her choice of clothes but, during emotional points in the therapy sessions, she seemed to forget where she was. Dan couldn't help but notice the smooth curve of her breasts as she leaned over to pull a tissue from the box on the coffee table, or the inward sweep of her bare thighs as she adjusted her skirt and relaxed her position on the sofa. There was always something in the air during sessions with Natalie. Pheromones? Just the clean smell of her skin? Whatever it was, the entire sexual milieu began to feed Dan's fantasies. And the fantasies began to feed on him, first like a playful kitten on catnip but later with increasing ferocity.

When Natalie tearfully asked for a hug at the end of a particularly difficult session, Dan threw professional ethics out the window. This was just part of her therapy, he numbly reasoned. Probably even necessary. After all, this was just the benevolent therapist providing a little reassurance to a troubled client, wasn't it?

But Dan didn't try to hide his own urgency as he slowly pressed up against Natalie, breathing in her scent as his hands stroked her hair. When the tears stopped and her dark eyes met his, he let himself be swallowed up in their wide and wet space. When their lips met, Dan let his hands fall slowly from her hair, down her neck, across the sides of her breasts, to the hem of her skirt, then back up along the suppleness of her thighs.

Dan had never been able to shake the remorse he felt when he surveyed the state of his office after Natalie left that day. He had even cancelled the rest of his appointments. Natalie had been a trusting client, and he had violated that trust. Some of his clothes still lay on the floor, a lamp lay on its side, the shade broken, and the couch stuck out from the wall at an odd angle. Earlier, he and Natalie had joked uneasily about not being able to find her bra, but Dan didn't laugh when another client pulled it out from under the sofa a week later.

There had been an investigation and Dan's license was suspended for a year, Natalie sought therapy elsewhere, and the incendiary relationship ended almost as quickly and intensely as it had begun. Once Dan's license was reactivated, he had been required by the State of Washington to have all of his therapy sessions recorded for two years, a humiliating and invasive process.

That had all been nearly six years ago and Dan's practice had almost recovered, but he had not. At least not fully. He hoped that Natalie had.

There had been no further lapses, *nor would there ever be,* Dan vowed. Now his career was moving in the right direction again, but his self-respect and confidence still suffered at times.

At least I can still beat Skip at racquetball most of the time, Dan thought with a smile as he saw his friend approaching. "Hey Skipper, how's it going?"

"Good, good. How're you doing, buddy?" asked Skip with his engaging smile.

"Oh, not bad. Looking forward to whuppin' your sorry ass this fine morning!" Dan smiled back and clicked his locker shut.

"You think so? Hey, I've been down here practicing during my workout days, you know," Skip announced.

"Really?"

"Well, not actually every time, but yeah."

"Okay then, let's see what you've got." Dan enjoyed this light banter. It stood in welcome contrast to the seriousness of therapy sessions.

They played three good games that morning, with Skip taking the first one and Dan the other two. Later, as they walked out to the lobby, Dan congratulated his buddy on the first game and mentioned that he seemed to be shaping up, losing some weight.

"Thanks," replied Skip. "I don't think I'll ever get to the shape you're in, but hey, I feel good. By the way, how's the therapy practice coming along?"

"It's okay, could be better. I've got three more slots I'd like to fill during the week, but I'm almost back where I want to be."

"Been kind of a long haul, hasn't it."

"Yeah, story of my life in a lot of ways. But I've seen good progress in a few clients and that keeps me going. Think I need a new challenge, though."

Skip nodded, held up a finger and fished through his pockets for his ringing phone. "Sorry, I've gotta take this. See you next week, buddy."

Dan walked back to his car alone, wondering about his last remark. Did he really want a new challenge or was that just something he said to convince others he was moving ahead with his career? Maybe both.

FOUR

. . . .

A llison stepped off the stern platform of her boat onto the dock and breathed in the fresh morning air. It was a beautiful Saturday in late January, cool but sunny, with just the slightest breeze tickling the surface of Lake Union. She watched as an early float plane circled and landed, making its way to the passenger terminal at the south end. From her covered slip on the west side, Allison could see across the lake to Chandler's Cove on her right and all the way up to the delightfully eclectic grouping of floating homes on her left. In between were a series of marine facilities, including her own small yacht brokerage office.

Margaret would be along soon, and that would make the day even better. Five years earlier, Margaret Yee had helped Allison set up her new business, Rain City Yachts, and the two had become friends in the weeks and months that followed. Margaret's main line of work was marine environmental law and she rarely dealt with individual clients or other areas of the law, but she had made an exception for Allison. There were many yacht brokerages in the Seattle area, but until Allison walked in the door that day, none were owned and operated by women.

The early morning sun sparkled off the water, and Allison squinted against it. *No headaches today, please. Not today.* She pulled sunglasses from atop her head and put them on. Across the lake, Allison could just make out the docks where she kept her featured listings near the office. She had a completely clear schedule, which was unusual for a Saturday after the big January boat show. Not a particularly good sign, she reflected, but then again, she had plenty of active clients and little free time. So why not take some time on a day like this? Especially when Margaret's calendar was open, too.

She turned away from the water to walk up the dock to the marina restroom and was surprised to see her friend arriving early. Margaret was rarely late for anything but neither was she usually this early. She was dressed in light blue sweat pants, white boat shoes, and a black fleece pullover with blue trim around the neckline. She carried a small cooler in one hand and had a camera case slung across her other shoulder. Her shiny black hair was pulled back into a short ponytail that bobbed as she walked down the ramp from street level.

"Hi, beautiful!" she called to Allison, smiling broadly. "Sorry I'm so early. Guess I'm used to the weekday traffic around here."

"Oh, no, I'm just glad we could get together today, the earlier the better! Oh, look at you—aren't you cute!"

Margaret put down the cooler and the two friends hugged.

"I'm heading up to the restroom. Make yourself at home and I'll be right back," said Allison.

When Allison returned, Margaret was stowing sandwiches and a bottle of Oregon Pinot Gris in the galley's refrigerator. Allison busied herself with various system checks and started up the single Volvo diesel. She loved living aboard her forty-one foot American Tug and had recently sold her condo on Queen Anne Hill to buy it. A partnership of two doctors had owned the boat previously and, as Allison had seen happen with joint owners before, the docs eventually found that they couldn't see eye-to-eye about its use and maintenance. Allison had it professionally surveyed, found only minor problems, and picked it up for less than she knew it was worth.

Several friends had given Allison their "are you crazy, girl?" looks when they heard she was living aboard a tug. She had to explain to them that, while the boat's styling was evocative of the famous workboats that plied the waters of Puget Sound, it was actually a small luxury yacht. But that didn't really describe it adequately, either. Like its cousin and competitor, the Nordic Tug, this boat had a salty, unpretentious look about it, but inside it had two nice staterooms, two heads—one with a shower—a small but comfortable salon, a full galley, a fine entertainment system, and a fully instrumented pilothouse. The interior finish was all cherry wood and looked brand new. After this explanation, most of Allison's friends and acquaintances from Queen Anne had smiled politely and asked to see it someday. Others still looked dubious. But Allison hadn't cared; this boat was exactly what she wanted.

Only Margaret had followed up. She had arrived unannounced with a bottle of champagne the day after Allison took possession of her boat. By the time the sparkling wine was gone, the two women had talked and laughed through several dozen names for the vessel, almost as if it were a new baby, and had settled on one: *Far and Away*. Here she was, living in the heart of a fast-paced big city, but when Allison stepped aboard her boat she felt wonderfully removed and cozy. And if she wished, this boat was quite capable of carrying her to Alaska and beyond. On top of all that, Allison felt that this was far and away the best place, and the best way, she had ever lived.

With the diesel warmed up, Allison removed the shore power cable and then walked forward to untie the bow line. When she returned, Margaret was ready with the stern line.

"Let's go to Manzanita Bay!" Allison said as she made her way up to the pilothouse. She signaled to her friend and slowly backed the tug out of its slip.

There was little traffic on the ship canal that morning and the women arrived at the Ballard Locks just in time to make the next trip down to the lower tidal waters of Puget Sound. A salty tang spiced the air as a light west breeze rippled the water and brought the scent in from the sea water beyond. A harbor seal surfaced, took note of the approaching boat and dove again as *Far and Away* sliced smoothly ahead.

Allison and Margaret relaxed in the pilothouse after setting the autopilot on a course across the Sound to Port Madison at the north end of Bainbridge Island. The day was clear but Allison still kept one eye on the radar while the other moved between the scene outside and her friend inside. She'd learned to do that after being surprised once by the nearly invisible conning tower of a surfaced submarine ahead of her in Hood Canal.

"So, you seeing anyone special these days?" Allison asked with raised eyebrows and a crooked little smile.

"Well, maybe . . . I don't know if he's special, really. Not yet anyway."

"Really? Hmm, what's his name, what's he like, what's he do?"

"His name is Rick and he's an ER doc at Overlake."

"And . . . ?"

"And he's from England, actually, and he looks really hot in a white coat with a stethoscope around his neck, or any coat, or no coat. He's about your height, a couple inches taller than me, brown hair, blue eyes and doesn't speak a syllable of Chinese."

"Go on, go on," prompted Allison as she steered around a log in the water and got back on course.

"Well, I really, really like him. We talk about all kinds of things—not just our jobs, you know. We've been out to dinner a bunch of times."

"So what's the problem? You sound like there's some kind of problem."

"I think it's just that everything feels so nice and uncomplicated. It's kind of like being around you, like being with a really good friend."

"So you're not physically attracted to him?"

"That's the weird part; I am. I think I just don't want to wreck it, you know what I mean?"

"Maybe, yeah."

"It's like, once you go to bed everything changes. All of a sudden there's all kinds of stuff that comes up. Then there's that first fight and you have to start talking about where it's all going and blah, blah, blah . . . you know?"

"Uh huh, I know."

"I just don't want to wreck it. Everything's so nice right now. It's even kind of sweet and romantic, just like it is. So do you think I'm crazy or what?"

"Yes."

"Allie!! Come on, help me out here!"

"Well, look," said Allison. "You're telling me about a smart, great looking young doctor with an English accent who likes to talk with you about everything. Has he asked you about sex?"

"No, not really, not directly."

"That's even better, unless he's gay I guess."

"He's definitely not gay."

This conversation continued all the way across the Sound for the next four nautical miles or so, without resolution, until they reached the north end of Bainbridge and Allison changed her mind about the destination.

"Have you ever been inside the inlet here at Port Madison?" she asked Margaret, nodding to her left.

"No, I went to Manzanita Bay once with Charles years ago, but we never stopped here. I can't even see the opening. You sure this is it?"

"Oh yeah, look here on the chart, and it's worth it, too. It's only about two hundred yards wide at the entrance but once you get in, there's room to anchor. It's beautiful, trust me. Great bottom."

"Beg your pardon?" Margaret asked with a smile.

"Mud bottom. Good for anchoring."

At a nod from Margaret, Allison turned the helm hard to port and throttled the engine down to avoid creating a wake for the waterfront residents. Five minutes later, she slowly eased the fifteen ton vessel through the narrow Port Madison entrance.

"Ooh, this is gorgeous," said Margaret. She took out her camera and snapped a few pictures. "I want to live here."

There were several boats scattered around the wider section of water inside, with gracious northwest waterfront homes along most of the shoreline, some with verdant lawns stretching from the residence down to a dock or beach. Everywhere else was heavily wooded with Western Red Cedar, Madrona and Douglas Fir.

Allison brought *Far and Away* to a dead stop, then used the bow thruster to pivot the boat a few degrees into the light wind, aligning it with the others in the bay. She noticed Margaret watching her with keen interest as she performed this little maneuver, and then pushed a button to activate the windlass, lowering the anchor. She let out about forty feet of chain and reversed the boat, setting the anchor firmly. Allison smiled and shut down the engine.

"You know, I'm totally in awe of you," Margaret said. "That was magnificent. I mean, I was just thinking: we've been chatting this whole time, and you just sort of magically took us through the locks, navigated across the sound and set us down here in this amazing spot, all without breaking a sweat. Who are you, anyway?"

"Sometimes I'm not sure," said Allison with a sigh. "Anyway, I'm hungry. What about you? Open the wine?"

And they did. Margaret had made her famous turkey sandwiches on sour dough with mayo, cranberry sauce and thinly sliced apples. The friends sat on chairs high above the water on the upper deck by the dinghy and soaked in the view, enjoying the sunny fifty-degree weather, the food, and the Pinot Gris.

As the wine eased the conversation, Margaret tried again. "So, Allie, where'd you get your training? Or were you in the Coast Guard and never told me?"

"I didn't, and no I wasn't." Allison shaded her eyes and looked out over the water.

"So, what's the deal? I mean, you really know this. It's kind of like, in your bones. Second nature, right?"

"Yes, that's sort of the problem," Allison said, looking at her friend again for the first time in the last several minutes.

"Problem? What do you mean?"

"I mean, I know things, Margaret, things I don't think I ever learned. I haven't talked to anyone about this since I was a little girl." Allison shook her head sadly and her eyes misted over. She looked down.

"Well, sure. You've got some natural abilities. That's a good thing. Oh, why're you crying, Allie?" Margaret reached out and covered Allison's hand with her own.

"I don't know; I'm worried you'll think I'm completely crazy. Then you'll, you'll just . . ." Allison couldn't continue. She reached up to wipe her eyes.

"I'll what, Allie? What are you talking about?"

"You'll send me . . . no, I mean you'll go away. I'm sorry, Margaret. I don't . . . I don't know what I mean."

"Look, it's okay, Allie. Hey, come on, let's go back below and talk some more. I'm not going anywhere. You know I can't swim, right?"

That brought a little gasping laugh from Allison through her tears, and it helped. Margaret always seemed to know just what to say. She brought some toilet paper from the guest head and handed it to Allison. "Here, blow your nose. You'll feel better."

Once Allison had settled down a bit, she looked up at her friend and tried again. She could trust Margaret; that seemed pretty clear now. She felt almost safe. "A couple of weeks ago, you know, before the boat show?"

"Uh huh."

"I totally blew a sale that was looking good." Allison said.

"Yeah, but that happens sometimes, right?" Margaret reached over and gently brushed a few strands of loose hair out of Allison's face.

"Sure, but it shouldn't happen this way, and this was like the second or third time."

"What do you mean, this way?" Margaret cocked her head to one side and wrinkled her brow.

"Will you promise not to get on the radio and call Mayday if I tell you?"

"I don't even know how to work the radio," Margaret smiled.

"Okay, I'm sorry. This is kind of hard for me." Allison paused and daubed at her eyes with the remaining toilet paper.

Margaret waited and then said, "Look, Allie, I'm your friend and nothing's going to change that, alright? Nothing."

That was exactly what Allison needed to hear.

"I gave him some medical advice," she said, and winced.

"Him? Your buyer? Medical advice?"

"Yes. He was clearly suffering from some peripheral artery issues."

"Peripheral artery issues? But how did you.? I mean . . ."

"I know, I know. It's just all so nuts. But I'm sure that it was the right diagnosis."

"Okay, but how . . ."

"How did I know that?"

"Well, yeah."

"I knew it because, um, because Kathryn knows it."

"Kathryn?"

"Yeah, this is sort of the part where I hope you don't go for the radio or grab a life jacket," Allison looked up and tried to smile.

"No radio, no life jacket. I'm not going anywhere," said Margaret.

"Kathryn doesn't exist," said Allison. "She's just in my mind. She's a doctor and I know some of what she knows. It was almost like Kathryn was the one making the diagnosis. I was just trying to help."

There. The worst part was out.

"Well, okay, that is pretty weird but it's not like serial killer weird or anything."

"Thanks, I guess."

"So, is Kathryn the only one?"

"No, there are others, a few. None quite as strong as Kathryn, though."

"Is there someone who knows a lot about boats, navigation, and stuff like that?"

"Yeah, that would be Molly; she's a skipper. She knows a lot about large boat handling, particularly in rough weather." Allison was still wincing as she made these improbable statements.

"How long, Allie? How long have you known this stuff and . . . these people?"

"Oh I've known the Teachers—that's what I call them—ever since I was little, but it feels like I understand more about the things they know as time goes on."

"Can I ask one more thing about this, Allie?"

"Sure; I probably can't seem much crazier than this anyway."

"Do you ever feel like these other people tell you what to do? I mean, do they sort of like, take over?"

"No, I don't think so. At least I don't remember if they do. I'm always me, if that makes any sense. It's not like one of those things you read about where somebody wakes up in their car and can't remember how they got to New Jersey. Sometimes it's hard to resist using their knowledge, like the other day with the medical advice, but it's never like they take over or anything."

"Well, I'm no psychologist, but the way you talk about this stuff it doesn't sound dangerous. It's not like you're hurting anyone, right? Have you ever talked to a shrink about it?"

"I don't think I could do that," said Allison, looking down again.

"Yeah, I get that but . . ."

"But what?"

"Well, I think everybody needs to talk with someone objective and knowledgeable now and then. In fact, I saw someone years ago for a few months after Charles and I split. I think it helped a lot."

"But I'm talking with you and that's more than I've ever done."

Margaret placed her hand gently on Allison's knee. "Allie, I'm not objective when it comes to you. I'm your friend; I love you. Why don't you let me dig up that name for you. And if he's not the right one, he can probably recommend someone who is."

FIVE

· ·

The alarm went off at four, but Dan had been awake for at least a half hour. His mind had been moving in semi-productive circles around work and how his practice had seemed to plateau, not only in client load but also in terms of professional challenge. Things had gotten uncomfortably comfortable.

But Dan knew one thing was about to change: he would see a new client today. What was her name? Addison, or something like that. When he got to the office he would reread the email that she had sent a week ago. Dan hoped that she wasn't very pretty. It would just be easier that way. It bothered Dan that he would even have to consider such a thing, but this was part of his post-Natalie reality.

Dan propped himself up on one elbow, ran a hand through his hair, thought about scheduling a haircut, and looked out the bedroom window across Lake Washington and toward the lights of Seattle. Nice to be able to wake up to this view, but how had he managed to get to this point? It felt like such a random, stumbling journey. Then, to counter these thoughts and ready himself for the day, Dan did what he did every morning: he consciously and deliberately assumed the role of psychotherapist, talking himself back into semi-confident professionalism. He recognized this as a form of self-treatment, and so, he reflected as he stepped into the shower, at least he wasn't completely deluding himself. He gave himself some credit for that—a form of reinforcement—and the recursive nature of his thinking fed on itself. He smiled.

Dan used the quiet early morning drive across the bridge to review the day ahead. Including the new client, who had accepted the empty eight o'clock slot, there would be five other regulars, most of whom were making good progress and would be fun to work with. Then there was sweet old Mrs. Markel who presented a different kind of challenge. It seemed obvious that she was just there for the conversation, the companionship. After seeing her for a few weeks it had become clear to Dan that there were really no issues he could legitimately address. She was simply lonely. Dan would have to ease her out of therapy soon, maybe starting today. He would try to help her find other outlets.

Dan parked under his old building, tucked between two newer and taller ones in the redeveloping South Lake Union area. He climbed the stairs to the fourth floor where his office still had a nice view across the street to the marina in Chandler's Cove. A few weeks ago, Dan could barely see the water because of the massive Seattle Boats Afloat show that took over the area twice a year, but now things had settled down again and the lake was beginning to wake up to a more or less normal-looking day. After starting a fresh pot of coffee in the waiting room, Dan settled in to review his calendar and check email.

There it was: the mail he vaguely remembered from his new client. *Allison, that was it. Not Addison. Allison Walker. Oh, yes, referred by Margaret Yee. Seems intelligent,* he thought, on reading through the email again. *Talks like she might be a little skeptical about therapy, though. Not unusual. Very businesslike in her writing style. Wants some help with focus and direction. Sounds pretty straightforward. Probably just a few life-coaching sessions.*

Between clients, Dan forced himself to catch up on insurance paperwork, something he disliked intensely. So, when he heard the outside door to his waiting area open, he was relieved and ready to switch gears. He stood up, did a quick scan of the office to make sure everything was in place, adjusted a chair, and walked in to meet his new client.

Standing in his waiting room, pouring a cup of coffee, was a strikingly beautiful young woman, about five foot seven, wearing a teal sweater and faded jeans. Her reddish brown hair was tied back in a ponytail. She was slim, exquisitely feminine, and her iridescent turquoise eyes reminded Dan of a color he had once seen while diving on a coral reef. He silently vowed full professionalism.

The woman looked up from pouring and splashed a stream of the hot liquid off the lip of her cup, down the left leg of her jeans and onto the carpet. She froze. "Ow."

"Are you okay? That's pretty hot," said Dan, wincing at the inanity of his remark.

"Yes, I'm fine." She pulled a tissue out of her purse. "Just embarrassed." She knelt down and began sopping up the brown stain.

"No, no, don't worry about that. I've got it," said Dan. He spun around toward his office to get more tissues and clipped the edge of a wicker waste basket with his foot. It toppled and dumped its contents, including a half-used can of cola, onto the carpet. Dan bent over to pick up the can as it emptied itself.

"Shit! Sorry, I'll, uh, be right back."

When Dan returned, he found Allison kneeling on the carpet, laughing as she worked on the coffee. Dan quickly blotted up his own mess and then sat down across from Allison and offered his hand.

"Kind of takes the formality right out of the process, doesn't it? Nice to meet you, Allison. I'm Dan Gunnison. Oh, sticky hand." He withdrew his hand and nodded to his new client.

Allison daubed at her tears of laughter and then at her jeans. "Actually, Dan, . . . oh, can I call you that?"

"Hey, after that little performance, you can call me anything you like."

"Okay, Dan, you don't know how much I was dreading the session this morning. I mean, I almost didn't show up. I had this embarrassingly stereotypical image of a stuffy, detached, old Freud-like guy and his couch. You know what I mean?"

"Well, as you can see, that's not exactly me." Dan smiled and finished wiping up the carpet. "But I guess we *should* move into the office." He stood and offered Allison his other, dry hand.

Allison got up, refilled her coffee cup and followed Dan into his office. The preliminaries went quickly and the flat topics of insurance coverage and contact information helped Dan shift back into a more serious mode. In spite of the session's beginning, or maybe because of it, Dan was finding it a little easier to look beyond the beautiful woman in his office to see a fellow human with real concerns. Still, he would need to concentrate.

He began to search for the issues at hand. He could sense that Allison was losing some of the initial comfort that she seemed to have taken from the waiting room incident. Or maybe it was boredom. She was shifting her sitting position and picking at a fingernail.

"So, Allison, tell me a little about why you're here. In your email you mentioned trouble with focus."

"Yes, I have a lot of different interests and it's been hard for me to concentrate on any one of them long enough to do anything with it."

"I hear that you're a successful yacht broker here on the lake. That's something."

"Yes, I guess. I'm happy with that and it's fun because I love boats, but it allows room for other distractions, too."

"Such as . . ."

"Well, I'm fascinated by all things medical, particularly what's happening with surgical techniques these days. I read a lot, in that area and others. Before the boat business, I actually went through most of the pre-med curriculum at UW, but couldn't stay focused and dropped out. I finished a BA in sociology, though, at Western. A little later, I started grad school in marine biology back at UW, then sociology again, then Russian literature, of all things. I couldn't stick with any of them."

"That's quite a range of subjects."

"I suppose so."

"So, talk a little about where all those interests come from."

"Okay."

Silence. *Good. Let it sit there. Maybe there's something here,* thought Dan. A few seconds went by.

"What do you want me to say?" Allison finally asked.

"I don't want you to say anything at all if you don't want to. This is your time."

"I think I'd rather talk about something else."

Dan nodded and made a mental note to try this subject again next time. There was clearly something here.

"Okay, let's talk about your family. What was it like growing up?"

"Well, I didn't have a family at first. My mother gave me up for adoption at birth. I never knew her or my father. I don't even know their names."

"So then, you were adopted by another family?"

"Yes, but not 'til I was five."

"What about before that?"

"I was in a couple of different foster homes in the St. Louis area, but I remember almost nothing about that time."

"Anything at all that comes to mind?"

"Hmm, I remember when I moved from the first home to the second."

"And what was that like for you?"

"It was kind of . . . hard."

"It must have been *very* hard."

"Yes . . . I'm sorry." Allison reached for a tissue.

"Not at all, Allison. This can be difficult stuff. How old were you at that time?"

"I was three, I think."

"Only a couple of years before you went to your adopted family, then."

"Yes, that's about right."

"A lot of change, I'd say."

"It felt like things were never settled."

"Of course. Would it be alright to talk a little more about the other things you might remember feeling then?"

"I really don't remember much more."

"Okay."

And so the conversation went for the next ten minutes. As Allison skimmed the surface of her early life, Dan listened, took a few notes, and thought about how to get to the next level. There was something there, he felt sure, which Allison was reluctant to talk about.

SIX

. . . .

The Carver Research Institute sat atop a piece of prime real estate in Bellevue, Washington. It occupied the top two floors of an imposing steel and glass structure overlooking Meydenbauer Bay and had been the subject of some controversy when it was first built a decade earlier. Since then, tall buildings had become the norm as Bellevue had grown to rival Seattle as a center for commerce and the professions. But, as Dr. Seth Carver liked to remind others frequently, his was still the finest unobstructed view in the city, and would remain that way unless someone got a permit to build a floating skyscraper.

Dr. Carver was just finishing a phone conversation as he exited the elevator, ducking his head slightly to clear the door frame. He closed his phone, made his way toward the double glass doors of the institute, and glanced at his watch. 7:48 AM and the receptionist was already at her brushed nickel and ash desk, reviewing the day's schedule. Everything in place, as it should be. It would be a busy day.

"Did you cancel my three o'clock, Cyndi?"

"Good morning, Doctor Carver. Yes, I did."

"Good. And, did my ten o'clock confirm yet?"

"No, not yet."

"Then go ahead and set up the UW conference call for that slot."

"Yes, doctor. But what if Mrs. Roth does confirm in the next hour or so?"

"*She's* my ten o'clock? Damn. Keep her in there and find another time for the conference call. Work with Julie on that. I can stay as late as seven if need be. Dinner with Carolyn's not until seven-thirty and I can meet her at the restaurant."

"Doctor Carver?"

"Yes?"

"Um, isn't this your anniversary dinner? Would you like me to look for a gift while I'm out at lunch today?"

"Gift, yes, that would be excellent. Thank you, Cyndi. Saved my ass again."

Carver brushed past the reception desk, strode down a gently lit taupe hallway adorned with original art, passed several examining rooms, and placed his hand against an indented surface in the wall. The lock clicked and Carver entered his office.

He put his thin silver PDA down on the corner of his clean desk and allowed himself a moment at the floor-to-ceiling windows which formed the corner walls behind his desk. *Best view in the city, and it's mine.* Far below, the calm waters of Meydenbauer Bay opened to the riffled surface of Lake Washington. Carver looked farther west, across the lake to the city of Seattle and the snow-capped Olympic Mountains beyond. A commanding view: that's what the real estate broker had called it years ago. Carver had liked the description then and he loved it now.

A gentle tone from his PDA told Dr. Carver that it had finished synchronizing with the integrated office system. He sat down and his desk's sub-surface display lit up. It covered the entire expanse of the trapezoidal desktop, revealed several layers of depth, and was visible only from Carver's viewpoint. From the visitor's side of the desk, the surface appeared to be nothing more than opaque black granite.

From his desktop, Carver chose five items to be displayed by various framed screens subtly embedded in the walls and bookcases around the office. He liked to vary these from time to time, depending upon the mix of patients and colleagues on the schedule. On this particular day, he chose three stunning images of his favorite Haida carvings, his Stanford MD, and his American Board of Psychiatry and Neurology certificate.

Two quick knocks came from the side door and Julie Moore entered, carrying a glass mug and her PDA. She wore a tailored black business suit over a simple white blouse. Her medium length dark hair and blue-gray eyes completed the impression of elegant efficiency. She set the mug down on the desk and sat across from her boss.

"Double tall nonfat white chocolate mocha, quarter inch foam?" Carver asked.

"Of course. It's Monday. How was your weekend?" asked Julie.

"Busy. Spent most of it here working on the paper. Yours?"

"Oh, fine. Nothing special. Which paper? The DID treatment one?"

Carver smiled thinly and nodded. "Yes, that paper." The paper, entitled *Remediation of Dissociative States via Closed-Loop Non-Invasive Unilateral Amygdala Stimulation*, was to be the culminating piece representing years of work involving a novel treatment protocol for Dissociative Identity Disorder and related mental illnesses. He just needed one more patient—preferably a woman—who was symptomatic and would agree to undergo experimental treatment as a part of his study. Based on Carver's previous papers, the American Journal of Psychiatry had all but guaranteed publication in an upcoming issue focusing on DID. The trick was to complete the work in time. The deadline was in six months.

"Well, here we are on Monday morning, Doctor, and you've got a full day starting at nine with Terrence Oliver, the patent attorney, then Mrs. Roth at ten, followed immediately by Charles Taber at eleven, Stephen James at noon, and you can see the rest, I'm sure, there on your desk. Oh, and the UW conference call will have to be at six, I'm afraid. Dr. Severson won't be out of surgery until then."

"No problem. That'll be all for this morning."

"Thank you, Doctor," Julie said as she stood and walked back toward her door.

"Oh, and Julie?"

"Yes?"

"Let's run that ad again in the Times. The one seeking patients for the trial, free treatment, etcetera, etcetera. And can you work some of your contacts on this, too? A lot of people don't feel comfortable answering those ads."

"I'll get on that this morning."

"Thank you."

Precisely at nine o'clock, Julie returned with Terrence Oliver and introduced him to Carver. Mr. Oliver stood about five foot five, had wavy short dark hair, and wore a gray suit and glasses. Carver towered over his visitor as he stood to shake hands.

"Dr. Carver, this is Mr. Oliver from Schmidt and Gaines, here to begin the patent discussion."

"Thank you, Julie. A pleasure, Mr. Oliver." Carver extended his hand as Julie nodded and made her exit. "Here, have a seat. Care for some coffee or tea?"

"No thank you, Dr. Carver," said Oliver with a nervous smile. "I appreciate the offer but I think I'm sufficiently caffeinated for the morning."

"Fine. So, tell me how we go about getting this patent process started."

"Yes, of course. Today I'd just like to get an overview of your work. I'll take some notes, ask a few questions, and then, if it looks like we've got something patentable and you still want to proceed, I'll come back in about a week with a draft of the application."

"Okay, but wait a second. What do you mean *if* it looks patentable and *if* I still want to go ahead?"

"Well, if a medical process can be shown to be truly novel, then it is probably patentable, but . . ."

"Oh, there shouldn't be any problem with that. There's nobody else out there doing this kind of work. I mean *nobody*," interrupted Carver.

"That's great. So I don't expect we'll have much of a challenge there. But here's the real issue: since 1996, what we call Medical Process patents—patents on specific medical procedures—have become essentially unenforceable in the U.S. Naturally, that makes them pretty much worthless from a commercial standpoint."

"What the hell is that all about?"

"Well, I'm sure you can understand the concern. If a process is owned by an individual or a corporation, that entity can profit from its use and controls its improvement for a period of time."

"So? What's wrong with that?"

"It drives up costs for patients and limits their access to potentially life-saving procedures."

"And drives down the incentive to innovate, right?"

"Maybe, Dr. Carver, but listen, I understand part of your process has something to do with a new medical device, also. Is that true?"

"Yes, that's true."

"Good, because patents on medical devices are generally still enforceable."

"Excellent. Okay, so let me give you the thirty thousand foot view of my work and just let me know where you want more detail. Did we sign a non-disclosure agreement, by the way?"

"Yes, Julie handled that with me last week, but there's really no need. It's implicit in what we do as patent attorneys."

"Just the same."

"Of course, no problem."

"Okay, first of all, my focus for this particular process is on something called Dissociative Identity Disorder, or DID. Have you heard of it?"

"No, but it sounds like a multiple personalities kind of thing."

"Right. Until a few years ago, we called this condition Multiple Personalities Disorder. There's always been a cloud of skepticism hovering over this particular diagnosis and there still is, to a large extent."

"Why is that, if I may ask?"

"Some practitioners regard it as a consciously invented crutch. Others feel that it may actually be induced by the therapist, unintentionally, of course. And on top of all that, it has a sort of "woo-woo" aura about it, if you know what I mean. Have you ever seen the TV movie, "Sybil," the one with Sally Fields?"

"Yes, is DID really like that?" asked Oliver.

"The movie's definitely on the extreme end, but other than that it's pretty much on target."

"So what causes people to develop multiple personalities?"

"Well, in virtually all cases, people with DID experienced or witnessed severe trauma as children—usually some form of sexual or physical abuse. Sometimes serious emotional neglect is enough. The theory is that these people—the majority of whom are women, by the way—are trying to protect themselves from their deeply disturbing past. In effect, they dissociate themselves from the traumatic experience by unconsciously inventing another self which had the experience. In addition to that self, there are usually several more. Five to fifteen are not uncommon and there have been cases involving over a hundred. Almost everyone, by the way, is dissociative to some extent, but as the degree of dissociation increases, we start to label people with dissociative disorders of one kind or another. DID is just on the extreme end of the dissociation continuum."

"So these personalities," began Oliver.

"We call them 'alters' or 'parts' actually," interjected Carver.

"So these parts, what role do they play in all this?"

"Protectors, mostly."

"Protectors?"

"Yes, they protect the 'host,' the primary personality, from having to consciously remember, re-experience, or deal with the painful past. They do this in a variety of creative ways and in most cases they seem to regard the host as a child, one very much in need of that protection."

"And people actually function this way?" asked Oliver, looking up from his notes over the top of his glasses.

"Well of course that's the real problem. In some cases they barely function. Relationships are difficult and life is confusing, to put it mildly. The parts can emerge or 'come out' when the patient is exposed to triggers in the environment, things that might go completely unnoticed by you and me, but that have some significance relative to that patient's past. Say, for example, a picture of a man in a magazine underwear ad. The patient herself might not even notice such a picture as she flips through the magazine, but it might trigger the emergence of a personality, a part, that works to protect her from memories of abuse."

"So these triggers cause patients to remember?"

"No, not really. In most cases, patients have no conscious memories of the details of their abuse. The memories are there, but not anywhere near the conscious level. The parts emerge primarily to keep those memories from surfacing. At some level, we think that DID patients hold a very strong unconscious belief, if you can call it that, that they will suffer immeasurably or even die if they have to re-experience their repressed trauma in any way."

"Miserable. So can therapy actually help these people?"

Dr. Carver shook his head slowly and produced a sad smile. "Today, the best answer we can give to that question is 'sometimes and to some extent.' That's where my work comes in."

Mr. Oliver looked puzzled, pushed his glasses up to rub his eyes. "So, wait a minute, before you tell me about what you're doing, help me understand one more thing. Is the idea to somehow get rid of all of these parts, except the host?"

"Originally, yes, in a manner of speaking. The idea was to attempt to re-integrate all of the parts into a functioning whole."

"Originally?" Oliver's puzzled look hadn't changed.

"When therapists first started dealing with DID, they worked with patients over periods of years, usually, to help them remember their trauma in a way that felt safe enough to allow them to eventually let go of these protective parts. Only in rare cases, though, did this seem to actually allow patients to feel and behave like a single person again. So, today, for many therapists anyway, the goal is more like cooperation."

"Cooperation between . . . ?"

"Cooperation between the parts. In some people, the parts can be argumentative, accusing, or belligerent. They may be horribly distracting, often causing the patient to miss therapy sessions, work, or other appointments. Even so, the goal of the parts always seems to be to protect the host from what they perceive as re-exposure to trauma. The idea behind cooperation is, through therapeutic intervention, to help the parts work harmoniously with the host to the point where the patient can function more or less normally in society."

Oliver scratched his head and looked up. "Well, that sounds like progress but also kind of like a compromise."

"Exactly. That's my position," smiled Dr. Carver. "I believe that the original goal of complete integration is sound. But up until this point, we haven't had the tools that allow us to achieve it. With my work here at CRI, I hope to show that full integration is not only possible but that it should be considered the *only* desirable outcome. We need to move DID treatment out of the coddling hands of questionably trained psychotherapists and into the hands of board-certified psychiatrists, specifically those trained in the use of my treatment protocol and equipment."

"Okay, that helps clarify some things for me," said Oliver. "I think I'm ready to hear the details."

Carver smiled and began. "Here's my core assertion: DID patients cannot experience integration until they have consciously confronted the underlying trauma and deeply understood that they are no longer in danger. Once they reach this level, we, or even a therapist, can work with patients to help reduce or eliminate any sense of shame which might remain. So, you may ask, why isn't this a fairly straightforward process? The answer is that the complete DID mind, the 'system' as we call it, with all of its created parts, is incredibly good at resisting attempts by the practitioner and the patient herself to expose the trauma. After all, this whole thing is about survival, the strongest of all instincts."

"What about the use of drugs or hypnosis?" asked Oliver.

"Both have been used with limited efficacy. Zoloft and similar anti-anxiety compounds have been used in attempts to either help patients cope with anxiety or to lower barriers to conscious memory. Various forms of hypnosis have also helped, but again, just to a degree. However, I believe I have found a method which not only brings down barriers to the conscious experience of traumatic memory but also allows these memories to be processed with little or no fear. Once that is done, we have essentially dealt with the core problem. The need for the separate parts disappears and the patient becomes whole."

"That almost sounds too good to be true, Dr. Carver. Too simple."

"Well, the process is not instant. It takes time, many sessions. But we're talking about weeks or months, not years. And while it may sound simple, that's because most of the complexity is hidden in the specialized software of my proprietary system."

"Amazing. So, drop down to the five thousand foot level and describe this whole thing to me, if you would."

"Okay. Imagine a perfect doctor, if you will, who is able to tell, within less than a hundred microseconds, when his DID patient is switching— that is, allowing another part to emerge. Now, also imagine that perfect doctor being able, at that very moment, to perform some kind of magic that eliminates fear in the patient related to the triggered memory. That is essentially what my system does. If the patient's switching was caused by a trigger in her environment which is related to her past trauma, she is now in a state which allows the doctor to guide her into a fearless exploration of her suppressed memory."

"Got it, I think. Now take me down to a thousand feet."

"Right, well, now replace this perfect doctor in your mind with an automated system. In real-time, the system monitors the patient's brain activity via a very specialized EEG device. Using a high-speed digital signal processor with special firmware, it watches for certain brain wave patterns associated with switching behavior in this specific patient (which the system has 'learned' during prior training sessions). Within microseconds of detecting such a pattern, it triggers another subsystem which then stimulates a key portion of the patient's brain—specifically her left amygdala—allowing her to process the memory objectively and without fear."

"Amazing," said Oliver, setting his notepad to the side. "But why not just administer a drug of some kind that reduces inhibitions and fear."

"It turns out, Mr. Oliver, that the repression of specific memories is so unimaginably strong in DID patients that any generalized approach would have to be so powerful as to render the patient incapable of any meaningful interaction whatsoever. On top of that, any such approach could be enormously dangerous. We have normal fears and inhibitions for good reasons."

"So you're saying that your approach is targeted at specific memories?"

"Yes, effectively. And limited in time, under precise control of the doctor."

"Wow. Okay, one more level down for today. The brain stimulation part of this—I've heard of things like that but they always seem to involve brain surgery. Are you talking about something as invasive as that?"

"No, no, that's another novel aspect of this, and one that probably deserves patenting in its own right, in my humble opinion. With the help of a couple of bright young engineers on staff, I've developed a system that accurately targets any area of the brain, not with wires but with converging low power radio beams."

"I'm sorry, but you've really lost me now."

"No problem. The idea is to be able to target a precise area of the brain without inserting electrodes. To do that, we have the patient wear a hat, if you will. It actually looks and feels like a hat so that patients are not terribly distracted by it. In addition to the EEG sensors, this hat contains two tiny directional antennas that are capable of transmitting extremely narrow beams of low-power, ultra high frequency radio energy. Neither beam, by itself, carries enough energy to trigger neural activity in the brain. But, when the two beams are directed to *converge* on a specific spot, the combination is just adequate to provide stimulation, and only at that specific location. Make sense so far?"

"Yes, actually, it does."

"Okay, then here's the final key element. The radio beams are simple amplitude-modulated carriers. The modulation is a phase-shifted version of the brain wave pattern which was identified with the dissociation trigger just microseconds earlier in time. Our signal actually arrives at the left amygdala just before natural neural activity associated with the trigger event occurs there. For all the incredible power of the brain, its data communication speeds are actually quite slow compared to rates we can achieve with high-speed optoelectronics today. So, in effect, we run a race with the brain and win. We get there just ahead of the signal which would naturally result in an acute fear and avoidance reaction, and, through the phase shift I mentioned, we cancel out its effect. When the phase shift and the speed of delivery are adjusted correctly, the result is an alert, calm patient who can deal rationally with an otherwise overwhelming memory."

"Amazing. And this actually works in real patients?"

"We're in clinical trials now and the results are extremely encouraging."

"Excellent. I assume you have some technical documentation I could take with me?"

"Absolutely. Julie has a packet made up for you."

SEVEN

. . . .

When Allison arrived for her next appointment, Dan was ready. He had just gotten back from a six-mile run, had showered in the office basement and felt refreshed. He had reviewed his notes from the previous session and found himself drawn to something on the second page. In that session, Allison had appeared so open and fluent at first. Later on, she had become guarded and hesitant as she tried to describe her early childhood. Dan hadn't found anything particularly unusual about that. He saw that kind of reaction all the time, especially with clients who had come from foster homes. No, there was something else, something in the middle of his notes that peaked his curiosity.

When Dan had asked Allison how she came to have such a diverse set of interests, she had shut down. It was a dramatic and unexpected reaction to what Dan had intended as an exploratory question right in line with Allison's stated concern about focus. And Allison's response, which Dan had written verbatim in his notes, seemed incongruous, to say the least. It was almost as though someone else had taken her place on the couch for a few seconds. Dan had drawn a little red flag in the margin.

The sound of his client pouring coffee in the waiting room brought Dan back to the present.

"Allison, come in. How are you today?"

"Fine. Great, actually. I just buttoned up a big sale last night."

"Congratulations. Here, have a seat and tell me about it."

Allison tossed her purse into one corner of the couch and sat down next to it. Her hair was down this time and she wore khakis and a brown sweater. She looked up and smiled. "It was that same boat I mentioned before. Different buyer, though."

"I don't think we talked about that last time, if I remember correctly," said Dan, feeling a little puzzled. He lowered himself into a chair across from his client.

"Oh, I'm sure we must have. You know, the one I've had some trouble with?"

Dan searched his memory. Was it possible that Allison had actually mentioned this and he hadn't been listening? Had he been distracted by her appearance? The sound of her voice? *Who's the one with focus problems here anyway?* He could sense his confidence ebbing, a feeling he hated under any circumstances but feared during client time. With an effort, Dan pulled himself back together.

"I'm sorry, Allison, but it just isn't coming to me. Would you mind going back over it again?"

"Actually . . . , now that I think of it, could we just skip it?"

"Yes, of course. But I'm wondering a little bit about why you'd feel that way. This seems like a pretty important event for you, this sale."

"Yeah, no kidding. When you depend entirely on commissions like I do, you need to keep things moving. But a sale like this one can take care of you for a few months."

"I bet it felt good to get that done."

"Yes."

Allison pulled a strand of hair back over an ear, blinked, and gazed out the window toward the lake. Dan noticed that her face had gone blank. He waited.

"You ever do any boating around here?" she finally asked.

"Me? Oh, I've done a little sailing on and off, with friends. Been at the helm of a powerboat maybe twice for a total of an hour or two, but I could never afford one of those things, at least not the kind of boat I think you're talking about."

"You might be surprised," Allison said, with a crooked little smile starting to show.

"Ah, well, I doubt it. But let's get back to you. Can you tell me anything about your comment a moment ago when you wanted to change subjects? Can you tell me how you were feeling just then?"

"A little headachy."

Dan nodded.

"And a little scared maybe," Allison added, looking away again.

"Okay, and how are you feeling now?"

"Headache's better, but still there."

"And the scared feeling?"

"Mostly gone, I guess."

"Did these things—the headache and the scared feeling—did they come and go just then? I mean, were they with you when you came in this morning or did they start when we began to talk about your sale?"

Allison slowly scanned the room, Dan noticed. It was almost as if she were looking for something. He could see her gaze move from the window, to something high on the wall behind him, to the office door.

Dan worked to catch his client's eyes again. "Allison, I want you to know that this, right here in this office, this is a safe place for you. And these times, when you and I talk? These are safe times for you."

Allison frowned. "You mean . . . that I shouldn't feel scared."

"No, what I mean is that if you *are* feeling scared, or feeling anything else, this is a place where you can be free to talk about it, to explore it. What you did by telling me, a minute ago, that you were feeling scared, was very healthy. I want you to feel good about being able to do that. And part of this being a safe place means that we will only talk about these feelings to the extent that you want to. You have control over that."

Dan paused. Allison was nodding, and so, after a moment, he continued. "Do you want to explore that scared feeling any more today?"

"No, I don't think so."

"Okay, that's fine. Where would you like to go with the rest of our time this morning?"

"I think I'd like to talk about my friend, Kathryn."

"Sure."

"I've been wanting to mention her because she's got the kind of focus in her life that I'd like to have. She's a doctor."

"That certainly takes focus. I remember you mentioned medicine as one of your interests."

"Actually, I think I get that from her."

"Is she your doctor? Is that how you know her?"

"Oh no, just a friend."

"Close friends, would you say?"

"Yes, I'd say we're pretty close. We talk all the time."

"Does she live in the area?"

"Oh yes, right here. In South Lake Union, I mean."

"Uh huh. It sounds like you really admire Kathryn."

"Yes, I guess you could say that. She's so knowledgeable, so competent."

"Things you'd like to say about yourself?"

"Well, yes, of course. Who wouldn't?"

When the session wrapped up forty minutes later, Dan ushered his client out and made some notes. He drew another red flag in the margin of the final paragraph:

> Allison Walker presenting with possible DID indicators. Not clear, however. Have not observed actual emergence of parts but suspect Kathryn might be one. Concerned about foster home background and recent experiences which A is avoiding. Also concerned about headaches. Might need help on this case. Another session may clarify.

EIGHT

· ·

Cynthia Roth waltzed into Seth Carver's office at 10:15 with a flourish, and draped her black wool cape across an empty chair. Tall and slim, she was the picture of established prosperity, her grey hair swept back into a form of French twist which had become trendy again among those in her sixty-something age group with similar status. The designer department at Nordstrom's had clearly shared some happy moments with her, and Carver immediately noticed the new diamond earrings which flashed as his benefactor moved under the ceiling lights.

"Seth dear, how are you? You look a bit tired. Were you out late last night with that adorable wife of yours?"

"No, actually I was working on the DID paper right here in the office until, I don't know, well after midnight."

"Well, God knows I wouldn't want to discourage anything related to the work that brought my Ethan back to me, but for goodness sake, Seth, you've got to spend some time with Carolyn now and again! How many times have I told you that? Now, I want you to promise me that next month when I sit down in this chair you'll have at least one date with Carolyn to tell me about."

"Promise. Psychiatrist's honor." Carver smiled and held his hand up in mock salute.

"Good. I'm glad that's settled. I want to hear all the details. Well, maybe not *all* the details if everything goes as it should. Now, tell me Seth, how are the clinical trials going?"

"They're going well, for the most part. Pretty much as we'd hoped."

"You're equivocating, Seth. I'm not a fool so please don't treat me like one."

"No, of course not, Mrs. Roth. I was just . . ."

"Seth, you know the funding is okay, so don't start going opaque on me. The treatment worked for Ethan, and I can't ask for more than that. I can *hope* for more—results for others with this affliction and a boost for the Institute's reputation—but I can't require it. However, I can, and will, require straight answers. Is that understood?"

"Yes, absolutely. I just didn't want to bother you with details that are probably irrelevant."

Mrs. Roth leaned forward and her eyes seared into Carver's. "Bother me," she said.

"Yes, well, as you know, I've had some concerns about side-effects."

"Yes, I remember you were worried about the brain stimulation part of things—the strength of it or something."

"That's right. The good news is that I believe we've found a very effective carrier frequency and a narrow amplitude range that produces focused deep structure stimulation in all subjects."

"And the bad news?"

"Out of our thirty nine subjects, one is showing some disturbing new symptoms."

"How disturbing?"

"Well, that depends quite a lot on whether we can find any more documentation on her psychiatric history."

"I'm sorry?"

"She's presenting with clear symptoms of paranoid schizophrenia." Carver brought his hand up to the bridge of his nose and winced.

"When? Is there a link . . . ?"

"We don't know yet. She presented rather abruptly following her treatment here last Tuesday."

"Symptoms?"

"All the classic DSM 295.3 stuff: delusions about one of our techs trying to kill her, hallucinations, acute irrational fears, you name it."

"This isn't good, Seth. What did you mean about her history?"

"It's interesting, in a clinical sense I mean. P-239, that's her ID, she's always been kind of the odd one in our trial. Coming in, her chart didn't show clear evidence of alter emergence but we observed it here."

"You, personally?" asked Mrs. Roth.

"No, Hamilton did the interview I believe."

"And that's when you let her into the trial?"

"Yes," said Carver.

"And what about the schizophrenia? Is there anything in her chart about that? Prior observations?"

"No, unfortunately."

"So, it's possible that the treatments have somehow caused this."

"No. Well, of course anything's possible, but no, I don't think so."

"Seth, you're equivocating again."

Carver sighed and looked past Mrs. Roth toward a depiction of a fiercely painted Haida warrior on the wall behind her. "There is a *remote* possibility. It's highly unlikely, but if our stimulation technique is somehow causing abnormally high dopaminergic activity in the mesolimbic pathway, then one might expect schizophrenic symptoms."

Mrs. Roth frowned and stared at Carver in silence until he returned her gaze. "Coarsely translated, I take that to mean that you could be in deep shit."

"Me?"

"You and your clinical trial. You *are* Dr. Seth Carver of the Carver Research Institute, are you not?"

"But . . ."

"Seth, let's hope nothing comes of this, but if anything does, I'll do what I can to help you. As you know, I have excellent connections."

Seth Carver had heard about these connections. The details had remained vague but they implied power, wealth, and frightening leverage. When he was an undergraduate at the University of Washington, Carver had overheard a conversation between his Microbiology professor, Dr. Richard Roth, and a few colleagues, about the professor's recent divorce. Seth was with a girlfriend at a restaurant on Eastlake Avenue, hoping to find some relative quiet at a dark table near the back of the dining room. Still, he couldn't help but hear snatches of alcohol-fueled conversation coming from two tables away.

The professor had left his wealthy wife of twenty years for reasons that had something to do with their son, Ethan. The details hadn't been clear then and had gained only a little clarity since. All Seth knew then was that Ethan suffered from some form of mental illness and this had played a key role in the divorce.

Only years later, after a PhD, an MD and a post-doc stint at Stanford, when he was approached by Cynthia Roth to start his own company, did Carver learn more. He had been working in the field of psychophysiology and Cynthia Roth had tracked him down through her ex-husband. Her son needed help and money was no object. But Seth understood even then that Roth also regarded him and his work as an investment opportunity, quite apart from Ethan's needs. Or were they *her* needs?

Carver had diagnosed Ethan with DID and that had determined the primary direction of the nascent institute—a direction that could never lead to financial viability on its own merits but had tremendous potential for extension. The diagnosis also told Carver that something traumatic had happened to Ethan and that it had probably been part of a pattern, possibly an incriminating pattern. Cynthia Roth needed all of this to go away, starting with her son's symptoms. Seth Carver had become one of her connections, one of her key resources. Only when the Carver Research Institute was established with assistance from a Palo Alto venture firm, when the prototype was complete, and when Ethan's treatment started, did Carver begin to understand the fundamental cause of Ethan's symptoms. But by then he was the CEO of a new Bellevue firm with a seven-figure salary and an even larger equity stake.

NINE

· ·

What an amazing day, thought Dan as he walked down the steps to the waterfront at Elliot Bay Marina. It was late April and the bright sunshine was making little stars on the fairways between the floating docks. Along with those, the reflected light from hundreds of white hulls reminded Dan to begin the seasonal search for his sunglasses. He thought that people who lived in the Northwest appreciated the sun more than others did, as they emerged from their homes and offices on days like this with a shared sense of relief and gratitude. It seemed a clear case of absence making the heart grow fonder.

Dan sat down at an outdoor table at the bistro-style restaurant in the center of the marina. He formed a visor with his hand against the bright light and gazed out over the breakwater toward Bainbridge Island across Puget Sound. Sea gulls called and circled overhead, having spotted some lunch of their own. The air smelled pleasantly of salt, and Dan breathed it in deeply, closing his eyes.

"Hi! Can I get you started with something to drink?" asked a smiling young waitress who appeared at Dan's side.

"An iced tea sounds perfect today, thanks," said Dan.

"And will someone be joining you?"

"Yep, there'll be one other."

"Awesome. I'll be right back with that iced tea."

Dan smiled. Was she really full of awe about someone taking the other chair across the table from him? Probably not, but it didn't matter. She seemed happy, and the day did have an unusual radiance about it. So, why not? Awesome it was.

Skip walked up moments later and Dan waved him over to the table.

"Skipper, hey, how's it going?" Dan remembered when he first started using that nickname. It was just after Skip received his M.D. and began his internship. For a short time, Dan had referred to his friend as "Skip the Doctor," then "Skiptor." Eventually, the moniker settled down to the easy tag he used today, and Dan felt that it fit. It sounded right and carried the positive connotation of a recognized leader.

"Good. How can it not be, on a day like this?" said Skip, raising his hands in a posture of sun worship.

The two friends settled into an easy conversation about the day and then ordered lunch. Later, between bites of a fresh halibut taco, Dan began a more serious discussion.

"So, Skip, I've got this new client . . ."

"Please tell me this is not an absolutely gorgeous babe," joked Skip, and then immediately thought better of it. "I'm sorry Dan; that was completely out of line." Skip squinted, and shook his head slowly back and forth. "I don't know why I said that. I'm sorry."

"No, that's okay. I still deserve some crap on that. Probably always will. And, actually, yes, she is an extremely attractive young woman, but it's not a problem. Maybe I'm just getting older, I don't know. Maybe wiser, although that's probably just wishful thinking."

"No, I'm truly sorry Dan. You *are* getting wiser. The last few years prove it. So tell me about this client."

Without revealing her name or other personal details, Dan described the situation he was seeing with Allison. He said he was considering a diagnosis of DID and gave his friend a quick tutorial on the subject. He felt grateful that Skip was such a patient listener, and an interested one at that. Dan would consult with others in his field, but there was a certain reflective freedom in trying out ideas with Skip first. Skip would keep him honest, ask probing questions, and help Dan frame his thoughts, all within the safe confines of trust and friendship. And Dan had done the same for Skip many times in the past, so the process felt balanced, symbiotic, and natural.

"So tell me again why you haven't actually settled on the diagnosis?" Skip asked.

Dan described the sudden intrusion of Kathryn into the therapy process, calling her "Kay," but pointed out that Kay might well be a real person. In fact, for all Dan knew, Kay might even be a colleague of Skip's over at the University. Kay hadn't "come out" in the classical sense; she hadn't explicitly emerged as a personality part. Instead, she was introduced into the conversation as a friend. But there was something about the *way* she was introduced, and the timing. It didn't quite fit the DSM diagnostic model and therefore didn't allow Dan to formally proceed down the DID path. But, at the same time, it seemed very odd that Kay would come into the conversation at just the moment when Dan's client had described her fearful state. But the other factors *were* classical: female, foster homes, nonspecific fears associated with early years, headaches.

"Shaky ground, sounds like," said Skip. "When do you meet with this client again?"

"Tomorrow morning."

"Any ideas about how to clarify things?"

"I don't know. I just have to let things unfold, I guess. I don't want to lead her too much. Can't let my suspicions become suggestions. At the same time, I need to help her approach her fears again. If there's a trigger there, maybe Kay will actually come out."

TEN

· ·

D r. Seth Carver guided his black 7-series BMW down old Main Street in Bellevue with Pearl Jam giving the car's ten speakers a good workout. Carver had slept well the night before, and things appeared much brighter this morning. And why shouldn't they? He was on the verge of publishing one of the most revolutionary treatment protocols—probably *the* most revolutionary—to hit the field of psychiatry in a century. And the patent process had started off well, too, portending a well-deserved financial future. Any speed bumps along the way would be handled.

Dr. Carver eased the car into his space below the CRI building and shut off the engine. Silence isn't golden, he thought. It's irritating. It connotes inaction, stagnation, cessation of progress. Carver stooped to extract his six and a half foot frame from the vehicle, ran a hand through his medium length blond hair, and strode to the elevator. This simple action was enough to eradicate the silence and get things moving again. Bring it on, he thought. Whatever the day has in store, it's no match for me.

"Good morning, Cyndi," smiled Carver as he entered his clinical domain.

"Good morning, Dr. Carver. I'll let Julie know you're here. She has your schedule ready, I believe."

"Thank you."

Carver entered his office, synced his PDA, quickly surveyed the state of Meydenbauer Bay, and, finding everything in order, sat down to digitally customize his office for the day.

An email icon was slowly rotating through three dimensions in the center of his desk subsurface display, vying for attention, but Carver ignored it as Julie entered through the side door.

"Good morning, Julie. And a fine one it is."

"Good morning, Dr. Carver. Well, aren't *we* in a cheerful mood this morning."

"As if I'm not always a ray of sunshine," smiled Carter.

Julie was the only person in the office who could get away with this kind of banter, and Carter thought of it as a kind of privilege which she enjoyed in her role. He wasn't exactly sure how she viewed it, and didn't much care as long as the line of professional respect was never crossed. And it never was. The relationship had evolved within implicit but pragmatic boundaries. These were never discussed; they just worked. Sometimes Carver wondered what Julie was like in her world, outside the office, in her kitchen, in her bedroom, but he never let those thoughts go too far. He certainly never asked about her personal life in any depth, and she never opened those doors. The line of professional respect was bilaterally maintained.

Julie smiled. "Just glad to see that you're doing so well. You've got a busy day ahead. Shall we have a look?"

The schedule was packed, as Julie had indicated: two new patients, the patent attorney with some draft material for review, staff meeting, lunch with a colleague, three long-term patients, and a quarterly budget review. After making a couple of minor timing adjustments, Carver dismissed his assistant and glanced back across the massive, black electronic desktop. He had a few minutes before his first appointment.

There were several new emails, but the one he noticed earlier was spinning rapidly now, demanding attention. When he selected it, the mail icon reversed its spin and rose to the surface like a trout to a fly. The mail was from Dr. Hamilton. Carver applied his fingertip to the surfaced image and a terse message appeared: *P-239 expired due to successful suicide attempt. Body at SMC morgue. Please advise as to trial protocol.*

ELEVEN

· ·

D an Gunnison held his coffee cup in both hands. He had driven to the office through a cold rain, and the warmth of the cup provided at least half the pleasure of the drink. The heat, the dark roasted taste, and the caffeine, provided the artificial sunshine he needed in order to begin the day. It had been a week since Dan's last appointment with Allison Walker, but before preparing for his early morning client, he allowed himself a few minutes with the Seattle Times. That, combined with a BBC news website and a local public radio station, provided him with most of the global context he needed to feel that he was reasonably well informed.

As he finished scanning an article about the growth of biotechnology in the Puget Sound region, a small advertisement in the lower right corner of the page caught his eye. Dan vaguely remembered having seen a similar ad before, but this time it caught his attention. It was a notice about an experimental treatment program for Dissociative Identity Disorder. It wasn't phrased quite that way; in fact, it didn't specifically mention DID at all, but it described the symptoms in a way that anyone experiencing DID would understand. Dan might have dismissed it out of hand, except for the fact that it was from the Carver Research Institute, which was a well-respected local company staffed by top psychiatrists recruited from around the world by Dr. Seth Carver, formerly of Stanford University. Dan jotted down the phone number and email address.

He returned to the paper, skimming the World and National sections. Finding nothing but discouraging news, Dan was ready to put the paper down when his mobile phone alerted him to an incoming text message. As a matter of economy, but at some peril to his own privacy, Dan used this phone as his sole business line, and the arrangement had generally worked out well for him and his clients. There had only been a handful of times when Dan found it to be seriously invasive, but these had been outweighed, in his view, by the security that even the knowledge of such a direct link provided to his most troubled clients.

The text message was from Allison Walker, who was due for a session in less than an hour. It said, "can't come to session at 8 but need help. headache bad. pls text or call back."

A quick check of his schedule told Dan that he had an open slot at nine that morning. He would have extra time to help, whatever that might mean. *But what am I getting into? This isn't really part of the client-therapist deal. I shouldn't be doing this.* He closed his eyes, took a deep breath, then composed and sent a reply: "will be glad to help. what do you need and where are you?"

Within thirty seconds, Allison's reply came back. "need aspirin and talk. must find out what's happening to me."

Dan repeated: "where are you?"

"at home on boat. slip B-7"

"marina name?"

Dan got his answer and ran out the door, remembering to snag a bottle of aspirin from the office supply cabinet along the way. Getting onto Valley Street at that busy hour in the morning wasn't easy, but once Dan managed that part, the rest of the trip to the marina took less than five minutes. *I shouldn't be doing this. Bad client precedent. Liability? Damn. But I can't just leave her in this condition. She seems desperate.*

Dan parked the car and ran toward the marina entrance, only to find a locked security gate. He ran up and down along the perimeter of the fence, looking for another way in, but this small private marina didn't appear to have a harbormaster's office or anything else that could offer the possibility of entrance. Dan grabbed his phone and dialed Allison's number. It rang six times before he hung up. *Not a good sign.* Just as he was about to dial 911, he spotted a young man in a blue rain jacket coming up the ramp from the docks. The man exited through the security gate and Dan slipped in before it closed again. The man looked back and gave Dan a disapproving look but didn't try to stop him. Dan hated doing such things, but . . . *the situation demands creative solutions.*

Dan made his way down the ramp to the docks, all of which were covered, protected from the Northwest weather. The place looked like one large communal boathouse. *B-dock. Must be the second one, right there.* Dan walked as fast as he could down the dock to slip number seven. A newer looking tug-style trawler was tied up there: dark blue hull, white deck and superstructure, high bow, and very well kept, from all external appearances. Dan could see a dimly lit interior through the raised pilothouse windows. He double-checked the number on the slip and then made his way to the stern where he boarded. He knocked briskly on the aft door and waited. No response. He knocked again and called Allison's name. Nothing. He peered through another window but saw no signs of life. Everything seemed orderly and in place. The only problem—*no Allison*.

Dan called out and knocked one more time, but again got no response from inside the quiet vessel. He walked along the starboard gunwale, peering into windows along the way. Nothing. *Could she have intentionally misdirected me*, he wondered. He dismissed the idea almost as soon as it made its appearance.

Dan walked back to the stern and tried the door. It was unlocked and yielded easily to his pull. He stepped into a small but warmly decorated salon, with a full galley forward and to port. A built-in sectional sofa wrapped the starboard aft section. Forward along the center line were wooden stairs up to the pilothouse. Dan walked up. Someone had been there recently. On the desk was a half-full coffee cup, two open books and a set of charts.

More stairs to starboard curved down to the staterooms forward and below. Dan called out, more quietly this time, not wanting to alarm Allison if she was asleep. "Allison, it's me, Dan. Are you there?"

Hearing no response, Dan ventured down the curved, dimly lit stairway to find two staterooms. He approached the larger of the two, presuming it to be the master, and immediately found what he was looking for.

There, sprawled face down diagonally across the bed, was Allison. Her open cell phone lay near her right hand. She had apparently been in the process of getting herself ready to leave for the morning but had not finished with some important details. She was fully clothed only from the waist up, and a pair of jeans lay crumpled on the floor at the foot of the bed. Dan stood stunned for a moment, his mind unable, or at least unwilling to accept the grimmest possibility. He had once been told by a CPR instructor that it was much easier than one might suppose to tell if a person was dead. Dead people just look dead, he was told. You just know.

TWELVE

. . . .

Seth Carver spun his chair around and stared out the window over the bay, slowly shaking his head and muttering to himself. "Great. Just what we need right now—a dead schizophrenic patient. Maybe even induced schizophrenia, induced by us. Shit."

Carver thought for a minute. He needed to talk to Hamilton. Had they over-stimulated P-239 for some reason? She was the one with the questionable symptoms. She might have been misdiagnosed. Even if she hadn't been, the mere possibility of that could be useful.

"Get Hamilton in here for me, please" Carver spoke while touching Julie's office intercom icon. *Calm, firm rationality is what's needed here. Speed bump, just a speed bump in the road. It's the road we need to concentrate on. Keep your eyes on the road.*

Dr. Hamilton, a heavy-set man in his late thirties, with receding and prematurely graying brown hair, walked into the office wearing his white lab coat. He wasn't smiling.

"Charles, sit down. So, I got your email," said Carver.

"Yes, sad situation, isn't it," said Hamilton, taking a seat across the black expanse of Carver's desk.

"Piss poor timing if you ask me."

"I'm sorry?"

"The trial, Charles. We needed her result for the trial."

"Well, yes, but with all due respect, Dr. Carver, we're talking about a young woman who died yesterday. A single mom with two teenage kids."

"I'm painfully aware of that."

"And, I might add," continued Hamilton, "that we do have a result—just not one we'd hoped for. But it *is* a result nonetheless."

"Not necessarily, Charles. Not necessarily."

Hamilton stared silently back at Carver for a moment, blinking. Then, "I'm really not following you; I'm sorry."

"Charles, I don't think that P-239 belonged in the trial at all. I think you misdiagnosed her."

Carver watched as Charles Hamilton's neck reddened, and he drew some satisfaction from the sight. He knew that Hamilton wasn't revealing anger; this was shame, and it was exactly what Carver wanted. The next few moments would be crucial in this game.

Hamilton was looking down at the desk. "No, I don't think so. She had all the symptoms. I followed the DSM all the way."

"Tell me about the emergence of the alter you observed," probed Carver. "Was there just one?"

"One alter, or one emergence?" asked Hamilton.

"Either, both; tell me everything."

"I observed one alter on one occasion. The part was an older woman named Sarah, I believe. She claimed to be an accountant."

"Not P-239's profession, I assume."

"No, P-239 was a marketing executive."

"Okay, so, when Sarah came out, tell me about that."

"Well, I was asking the patient about a childhood incident—a rather harsh punishment she received from her adopted mother for a very minor shoplifting incident. She might not have even stolen anything, from what I could gather. She might have simply forgotten she was holding the item. Anyway, in the middle of telling me this story, the patient stopped abruptly."

"And then?"

"And then she told me that she wanted to talk about her friend, Sarah. I could see a definite shift as she told me about this friend. The patient brightened up for the first time in my experience with her. Her entire facial structure seemed to shift subtly as she began to tell me, almost with glee, about the satisfaction of dealing with hard numbers—things that can't be refuted."

"But Charles, listen to yourself describe this! What I hear is simply a patient forcing a radical change of subject. I don't hear Sarah coming out. I hear P-239 talking *about* Sarah."

"Perhaps, the way I just described it, but . . ."

"No. You had a specific objective to sign up a trial patient that week. You were under pressure. It was a Friday if I recall correctly."

"Yes, but that had nothing to do with my diagnosis. I had a named alter who emerged after an obvious switching episode."

"No, Charles. You had an anxious patient with other problems. And you were anxious, yourself. You were anxious about failing to meet that objective and so you let yourself become convinced that you had a genuine DID patient."

"I . . ."

"Look, it's understandable. Here's what we do: P-239 was never a patient in the DID trial. She was here for treatment of non-specific anxiety."

"But, Dr. Carver, that is at the very least unethical."

"Charles, look at your situation rationally if you can. You misdiagnosed a patient, admitting her into an experimental program; you then treated this patient for a condition she did not have—and I want to come back to that in a moment—and then the patient exhibited clear schizophrenic behavior, in your office no less. The next day she is dead by her own hand. Now, if I were you, I'd want to carefully weigh the relative merits and consequences of my actions at this juncture."

"But I'm an employee of CRI, acting under the direction of the Institute."

"Read your contract more carefully, Charles. Individual physicians are individually culpable at this institute. We are all professionals and we are all expected to exercise that professionalism in our choices, particularly those which involve the lives of our patients."

"No, you can't do this Seth. Think about our commitment to the science."

"I can and I will, Charles. Think about the value of this new treatment protocol to actual DID patients. We can't let this small incident dampen the beneficial impact this work can have."

"Look, I want this thing to succeed as much as anyone here. You know that! But we can't just alter the data, Seth. We do that and we cease being scientists."

"I don't want that either, Charles. If there was an adverse effect here—if you inadvertently caused the death of a patient by inducing schizophrenia in an otherwise only mildly disturbed patient—then we need to understand the mechanism so that the unfortunate situation isn't repeated. When this treatment becomes widely adopted, there are going to be other misdiagnoses—it'll just happen, statistically—and if there is even the slightest possibility that the treatment can induce schizophrenia in such situations, we need to change the treatment protocol so that it can't happen. Are you following my reasoning here?"

"Yes, so what exactly are you proposing?"

Carver knew he was close. He just had to tie up the loose ends. "It's more than a proposal, Charles. You do understand that."

"Go ahead."

"As I said before, P-239, this particular P-239, was never part of the trial. She was here for other reasons. You will make sure that this is well documented. Then, you will change your focus here at the Institute for as long as it takes to do three things: first, determine if the treatment was adjusted in any way because of the lack of full symptoms and if that altered treatment could have resulted in a significant dopamine release or in any other event which could cause or mimic acute schizophrenia; second, if you reach that conclusion, and I think you will, then recommend the necessary procedural changes which will eliminate this unfortunate result even in the event of future misdiagnoses; and finally, find a replacement for P-239 with similar symptoms, if possible, in order to verify the effectiveness of your changes and preserve the integrity of the trial."

"Integrity?"

"Charles, you need to be with me on this."

"I am my own man, Seth."

"No, I mean you *really* need to be on board, and not just because your career could be destroyed."

"I can't believe I'm hearing any of this from you. I don't need to hear any more." Dr. Hamilton rose to leave.

"You love Carol and the kids very much, don't you?" said Carver with a feigned sigh.

"What are you talking about!?" Hamilton turned back at the door.

"Well, this could be disastrous for them, too, you know."

"You underestimate them as badly as you underestimate me. They'd stand by me through any of this."

"But would they stand by you if they knew about Nancy? I have very good sources, Charles, and I know all about Nancy and you."

"Oh, God."

THIRTEEN

· ·

E ven though Dan could only see part of Allison's face from where he stood, it was obvious that she was alive. A second later, Dan remembered to breathe as he saw Allison slowly draw breath herself. Her shoulder blades rose just slightly with the vital action.

Dan glanced around the room, and finding a comforter folded across the dressing table, he quickly but gently covered Allison. He was surprised at his reaction to the near nakedness of her sublimely feminine form. It was not an erotic moment, but one of compassion. Dan's vision was momentarily blurred by unexpected tears as he finished covering her feet, thinking that they must be cold.

He moved to the other side of the bed, to her head, and tried to understand if she was just deeply asleep or unconscious. He gently brushed a lock of auburn hair from across her eyes and spoke her name, once, twice, and a third time before he saw some flickering movement under her closed eyelids. This relieved him greatly because he suddenly realized that he had absolutely no plan in mind to cover any other outcome. *Why didn't I call 911 right away?* he thought. *Was I afraid of being found here with her? Screw that!*

Dan reached for Allison's phone to make the call. But before he hit the second "1" Allison opened her eyes and, looking startled to see someone there, tried to prop herself up. Dan put down the phone.

"Allison, are you okay? It's me, Dan Gunnison."

"Oh . . . yes, ow . . . I think so. This has happened before. I'm alright. Headache's bad, but I think I'm okay." She started to get up and then seemed to realize that the comforter hadn't been there before. "Oh, thank you. I'm sorry I was . . ."

"It's okay, Allison. It's okay. You're safe," said Dan in an awkward attempt to regain some therapeutic distance. He blinked and brushed at his eyes. "Can I get you some water or something?" he asked.

"Please, yes, and some aspirin if you brought any." Allison sat up slowly, bunching the comforter up over her hips and legs.

"Here. Here's the aspirin." He handed her the bottle. "And I'll be right back with the water."

When Dan came back from the galley with a glass of water, Allison had pulled on her jeans and was sitting on the edge of the bed, two aspirins in hand. "Thank you," she said, with the slightest hint of a smile.

"Oh sure, here you go," said Dan handing her the glass.

"No, I mean for coming here. I'm so sorry to have put you through all this trouble."

"Oh, no trouble at all," replied Dan.

"Well, I know that's partly a lie—a nice one though. Speaking of lies, there's something I haven't been totally honest about."

"Okay. Want to talk about it for a few minutes? This is actually your time you know."

"No, but I think I need to. Can you give me just a couple of minutes to splash some water on my face?"

"Sure. I'll be up in the salon. You have a coffee maker?"

"Yeah, oh sorry. Coffee's in the cabinet just above the stove. Make yourself at home. I'll be right up."

When Allison reappeared, Dan pushed a cup of coffee across the table to her and tried to assess the situation. Allison had brushed her hair and looked surprisingly fresh. *How could she have recovered so quickly?* Dan wondered. Sometime in the last half hour, Allison had apparently passed out while getting dressed. Now she seemed okay. *What is going on here? What is she hiding?*

"So, how're you feeling?" Dan asked.

"Not too bad, actually. Headache's better. Not gone entirely, but better."

"You said something earlier about this happening before. How often, would you say?"

"Oh, maybe four of five times, this bad. Usually I don't pass out."

"So, it's been more frequent but usually milder?"

"Yes, actually, this is part of what I haven't told you about," said Allison. She stood and walked over to the galley, as if to escape the situation, Dan thought.

"And," Allison continued, while loading last night's dishes into the dishwasher, "it sort of has to do with PMS."

"Oh, okay." Dan said with some relief and a touch of embarrassment. "That doesn't sound too unusual."

"No, but here's the situation." Allison finished up in the galley and was walking back to the salon, pen and notepad in hand. She sat opposite Dan, crossed her legs, and began to speak. Dan noticed a distinct change in his client and made a mental note of it. She no longer seemed ready to flee. In fact, she seemed very much in control.

"Dan, it's well known that PMS and PMDD symptoms include such things as headaches, dizziness, fatigue, irritability, et cetera, but loss of consciousness is decidedly atypical. The presence of that symptom clearly argues for a parallel pathology, probably something exacerbated by hormonal shifts."

Dan was shocked at the change in his client's speech and demeanor. This was not the warm, friendly, but sometimes tentative and fearful client he was beginning to know. This was a woman in command: objective, knowledgeable, even cold, dispensing medical information to a patient or a student. Dan simply nodded and watched with amazement as Allison began sketching two curves on the same pair of X-Y axes and continued her lecture.

"Here is the idealized 28-day menstrual cycle. Of course the actual cycle varies a great deal from individual to individual, but most women experience something at least qualitatively similar to this. You can see that here, in the latter half of the cycle, typically called the Luteal Phase, estrogen levels are beginning to fall while progesterone levels are rising. Right here." Allison pointed with her pen and looked up as if to check on Dan's level of comprehension. "Somewhere around day 22 to 24, you can see that estrogen is near its minimum at about the same time that progesterone hits its peak. If a woman experiences premenstrual symptoms, this point in time is roughly when she can expect the onset. Are you with me so far?"

Dan nodded again, finding himself at a loss for words.

"Alright, here's the important part. *Our* patient doesn't usually report much, if any, difficulty with PMS. In fact, her symptoms occur at a different point in the cycle."

"Okay, go on." At this point, Dan was nearly certain that he was in conversation not with Allison, but with Kathryn—a part of the Allison system of identities. He was now intently listening on two levels, trying to understand the literal information that his client was communicating, while also attempting to apply his observations to a diagnosis of DID.

"Her headaches and apparent hypotension that occasionally results in loss of consciousness appear at approximately mid-cycle, much earlier than PMS or PMDD symptoms typically manifest."

"Isn't that point usually associated with ovulation?" Dan asked, hoping to prolong the conversation.

"Yes, that's true. And this is also the time when progesterone levels come off their minima and begin to rise. In most women, the rise is gradual, but I suspect in this case that the rise is steep and sudden. It has been shown, at least in studies with sheep, that acute doses of progesterone can produce a drop in mean arterial pressure, and thus, potentially, can result in fainting."

"That's fascinating, Doctor," tried Dan.

"What? Oh, I wish. I know a few things about medicine, but I'm far from being a doctor."

"Could have fooled me, Kathryn."

"I beg your pardon?" Allison shot back.

"I'm sorry. It almost seemed as if I'd been talking with your friend, Kathryn."

"What? What are you saying?"

Allison looked stricken and Dan tried to think through the situation, but no clarity emerged, just more questions. *Did I just witness a switching episode in which Allison's Kathryn part was present for a few moments? Did my direct mention of Kathryn somehow cause a switch back to the host identity? Or is this all just theoretical bullshit and I'm missing something obvious? What am I doing here anyway?*

"Look, Allison, I'm sorry. I really should be going. I think you're okay now and we really shouldn't be having this conversation here anyway."

Dan stood up and slowly turned toward the salon door. When he glanced back over his shoulder to suggest an off-schedule meeting at his office, what he saw shocked him. Just moments before, he had been in conversation with a self-assured, highly competent individual. Now, Allison had pulled her knees up to her chest as she sat in her chair, slowly rocking. Quiet tears were streaming down her face and her eyes were pinched shut. She was hugging herself desperately, as if she were freezing or in some deep internal pain.

"I . . . I knew it. You're doing it, aren't you?" she squeaked, her eyes still shut tight.

"Doing what, Allison? What am I doing?" *What am I doing?*

"Please don't . . . please don't . . . please don't." Allison rocked herself with each plea.

Dan turned back and sat down across from his client. "Allison, tell me. Tell me what it is." *What am I doing?*

"You're going to send . . ." Allison couldn't form the last words as her mouth twisted in apparent agony and she shook her head slowly from side to side.

Dan reached out and put a hand on her shoulder. "Allison, tell me what you're feeling, what you're thinking. What am I going to send?"

"Me."

Allison was still rocking, holding her knees in tightly, as if she'd fly apart without the self-imposed pressure.

"You? I'm going to send you? Where, Allison? Where am I going to send you?"

Allison did not respond; she just continued her rocking. Her eyes were pinched shut so hard that it seemed to Dan she might cramp the muscles in her face. Dan let her silence stand for a few moments longer. Then he reached out and placed a strong hand on each of her shoulders and said, "Allison, look at me, please."

Allison continued to look down. She slowly shook her head and Dan felt loose strands of her tear-soaked hair brush his arms. She looked and felt so beautiful, even in her twisted distress. So vulnerable. So in need.

Distance. Professional distance. She is not your friend, certainly not your lover. She is your client. She needs your help.

Dan slowly pulled away from Allison, removing his hands from her shoulders. He felt a little shudder go through her body as he released her.

What now? What do I do now? "Allison, please look up at me. I'm here to help."

"You're still here?" she asked the darkness behind her eyelids.

"Yes, I'm still here. Do you want me to leave?"

"No, no! Please don't go, please!" Allison said through sobbing gasps. She reached out and grabbed Dan's arm, pulling him toward her in three weak attempts. She looked up with red, begging eyes.

Like a child, Dan thought. Just like a child needing a parent.

"No, I'm not going anywhere, Allison. I'm right here. You're safe. It's okay."

FOURTEEN

· ·

O
n the drive back to his office, Dan wrestled with the things he had just observed, the things he had done and the things he had left undone. He hadn't been able to leave Allison in her vulnerable condition and had stayed with her through his next appointment time. But his phone call with the displaced client hadn't gone well. *Pushing boundaries, bending rules; that's what I seem to do best. Maybe I'm in over my head here.*

On impulse, Dan pulled into an espresso drive-through and picked up an extra-hot nonfat mocha.

"And how's your day starting out?" asked the young and darkly pretty barista over the hiss of the milk steamer.

Dan took pleasurable notice of the fact that she hadn't used the word "sir." He laughed and shook his head. "Different," he finally said, still chuckling. "Very, very different. Yours?"

"A little slow, I guess, but it'll pick up. The rain always helps."

"Yep."

Dan accepted the hot drink and fifty-seven cents in change. He kept the coins and tossed a dollar bill into the girl's tip jar. That won him a warm smile and he savored the easy simplicity of it all. *A nice break from real life. Real?*

Back at the office, Dan made some notes about the morning's encounter with Allison and then carefully reviewed Section 300.14 of the American Psychiatric Association's Diagnostic and Statistical Manual of Mental Disorders, otherwise known as the DSM.

Refreshing his memory on the subject, he found that a diagnosis of DID requires several factors:

- The presence of two or more distinct identities or personality states, each with its own relatively enduring pattern of perceiving, relating to, and thinking about the environment and self.
- At least two of these identities or personality states recurrently taking control of the person's behavior.
- Inability to recall important personal information that is too extensive to be explained by ordinary forgetfulness.
- The disturbance is not due to the direct physiological effects of a substance or general medical condition, including brain injury, medication, sleep deprivation or intoxicants, all of which can mimic symptoms of DID.

The first two conditions seemed clear to Dan at first, while the third and fourth remained largely unknown. Then he began to wonder a bit more about the second one. *Does the doctor identity really take control? It seemed so obvious while she was discussing "her patient's" endocrinology as if Allison wasn't even there. And yet, what is it about the Kathryn part that doesn't seem quite right?*

Dan took another sip of his mocha and reflected back on Kathryn's lecture. Kathryn's manner had been confident, even arrogant, clinical, pedantic. That certainly distinguished her from Allison. But, at the same time, Kathryn had been fragile in some way—ephemeral. Dan had been able to toss in a quick comment or question during Kathryn's monologue, but the moment he tried to personally engage her in conversation—calling her "Doctor"—she simply vanished. Instantly, Dan had found himself speaking with Allison again. Or had that really been another part of the Allison system? A child part. Clearly afraid of abandonment. Emotionally raw, exposed, needful.

Dan made a few more notes, ending with, "Two parts may now be in evidence, in addition to the primary: Kathryn and a child (call her C). Must conduct SCID-D interview at earliest opportunity."

FIFTEEN

· ·

Allison decided to take the dinghy into work. This was her option of choice whenever the weather cooperated, which, for her, meant anything above freezing with better than ten feet of visibility. On this particular morning, it was hard to distinguish between sky and lake. The water in both seemed to merge into a gray continuum, which would have been a depressing scene for many—even some die-hard Seattleites—but not for Allison. She found that the early morning trip across Lake Union calmed her and set a positive tone for the day, even on a morning like this. Maybe especially on a morning like this. There was no other lake traffic and the otherwise still water was punctuated with millions of little droplets making it look like a vast unmarked chess board populated solely by pawns.

Allison liked the gray consistency of the scene and the regularity of the rain pattern. By the time she tied up at the brokerage dock, she felt ready for the day ahead. The visit from Dan earlier that morning had been unsettling on the one hand but an enormous relief on the other. Although Allison remembered only parts of the encounter, the parts that surfaced gave her solace. *He showed up, and he stayed. He could have run but he didn't. I even have another appointment with him in a couple of days. He made extra time for me.*

Allison walked up the dock, unlocked the front door to Rain City Yachts, and flicked on the lights. She remembered to make a pot of coffee—more for her clients than herself—and sat down at the computer to check the day's schedule. *Dan McGaw at noon. Dan? Weird. Oh well, doesn't mean anything. Lots of Dans out there.*

At five after twelve, a neat, casually dressed man with a light complexion, seemingly in his fifties, strode into the office, glanced at the photos of the various yachts for sale and turned to Allison.

"Allison Walker?"

"Yes, and you must be Mr. McGaw."

"Please call me Dan." He reached out to shake hands.

Immediately Allison noted the hard and corded feel of the man's hand, and the fact that it didn't seem to reopen easily after the handshake.

"So, why don't you have a seat and tell me a little about what you're looking for, Dan," said Allison. "Coffee?" *I know that condition! What is it called? Hardened tissue in the palm. Slight clawing of the hand . . .*

"Yes, thanks, I'd love a cup."

"Good. Cream, sugar, both?" *I know that condition. Patients over forty, northern European descent . . .*

"Black's fine."

"Well, that's easy. Here you go. What do you think of this day of ours? Almost dark at noon." *What the heck is it. I know this. Maybe if I ask him about it, it'll come to me.*

"Oh, I don't mind it really. Just part of the experience here, isn't it? I actually like being aboard a boat in the rain."

"Me too. I know what you mean." *No! Don't do this, Allie. Don't screw this up.*

Allison resolved to get back on track. "So, Dan, do you have a boat now?"

"Yeah, but it's time for a change. I've got an Ocean Alexander 440. You know, master stateroom aft, sundeck, good for cruising around the sound, the San Juans, stuff like that. Now I'm looking for something with more range, lower fuel consumption, more of a passage-maker, I guess. A pilothouse would be nice. My wife and I want to make a cruise up the Inside Passage to Alaska. We've always looked forward to having enough time to do it and now it looks like that's going to happen."

"Good for you. That sounds fantastic. I've actually got three vessels right now that might be interesting to have a look at, just to get you started in your search, and one of them is here on my dock. Did you want to stick with twin engines or are you open to a single?"

"Single would be okay, along with thrusters. I don't think I want to go down to the really low horsepower range though. You know, like those 135 Lehman diesels you see on some of the older trawlers? I like cruising at eight or ten knots but I also want to be able to crank it up to fifteen if I need to get ahead of the weather or handle a heavy current."

"Okay, no problem. And I'm guessing that you want something that you and your wife can handle by yourselves, without more crew?"

"Yes, absolutely. It's got to be just us," said Dan McGaw, raising his hands in front of him to emphasize the point.

"That helps. So we'll probably want to stay below fifty-five feet." *That right hand is almost clawed. Tissue is hardened under the palmer fascia along the tendons for the third and fourth fingers.* "In fact, the boat out on the dock here is a great example of an early but updated Selene 53. Might be worth a look."

"For sure. I'd love to see one of those. I don't know that it'll be in the price range, though."

"Would you mind giving me some idea of where we are with that?" asked Allison. *Wow, this is going well. That right hand . . . Kathryn would know.*

"Well, we're probably looking at around 800K tops."

"Okay; would that be including funds from the sale of your Ocean Alexander?"

"Yes, it would have to be. How much do you think I could get for that boat, if you were to sell it for me?"

"It depends a lot on its condition and age. How would you describe it?" *Dupuytren's Contracture! That's it! Got to be.*

"Bristol. It's five years old, has only 350 hours on the Cat diesels, and I updated the electronics just a few months ago."

"Excellent." Allison tapped a few keys on the computer. "A quick estimate would put us . . . let's see . . . just north of three hundred thousand, I'd say. Would you mind if I had a look at your right . . . I'm sorry, I mean, I'd like to have a look at your boat right away if that would work out for you. I have a buyer who's actively searching for something in that range." *Damn it Allie. Keep it together here. Definitely Dupuytren's, though.*

"Sure, that'd be great. It's down at Shilshole Marina. Maybe we can find a time later in the week." Dan McGaw chuckled and held out his right hand, palm up. "It's okay, I can tell you're curious about my hand. It's pretty obvious, you know—your curiosity. Here, have a look. Doc says it's nothing to worry about but it does seem to be getting worse."

Allison's mind raced. *Come on Allie. Don't screw this up. Don't be the doctor here. You can get a sale, maybe two, if you're careful. And he's being so nice about it.* She found a convenient and benign lie.

"Oh, I'm so sorry. It's just that my Dad . . . my Dad had something that looked just like that and it brought back memories. I think he said it was called Dupuytren's or something. He had surgery and it fixed him right up. I'm sorry; I didn't mean to intrude."

"No, that's okay. Most people notice and I find it easier just to bring it out in the open. Doopwitren's you say? And the surgery worked?"

"Yes, actually he regained full use of his hand. I don't think there was much pain involved either." *Whew!*

"Hmmm, interesting. Maybe I'll go get a second opinion on it then. Let's go have a look at that Selene."

SIXTEEN

. . . .

"Mrs. Roth, to what do I owe this early morning honor?" Dr. Seth Carver stood as Cynthia Roth, the institute's original financial backer, strode past Julie, seemingly unaware of her presence and function. She tossed a small black leather purse onto one of the guest chairs. Julie stood in the doorway and held up both hands as if to say, I'm sorry but there really was nothing, I mean *nothing*, I could do.

"It's not that early, Seth." Mrs. Roth spun around. "Julie? Be a dear and get me a black coffee." The matron of CRI glanced around. Carver imagined that she was checking to be sure everything was in place and that the office continued to meet her high aesthetic standards. She seemed more or less satisfied on that point and positioned herself directly in front of Carver's desk. "Sit, sit; we need to have a little talk." Mrs. Roth glared at Carver and waited for him to take a seat before doing so herself.

A little talk. This is not good. I don't have time for this. What an incredible pain in the ass. "Yes, of course, Mrs. Roth. What's on your mind?"

"The fact that you even have to ask, Seth—that's why I'm here. Sometimes I think that if I didn't keep my eye on the ball, you'd let it sail right by. Or worse, get hit right on the top of your head by a high fly to center because you were contemplating the color of the turf. The big picture, Seth! Look up every now and then."

"Thank you, Julie," said Dr. Carver as his assistant reentered the room and placed a steaming cup of coffee in front of Mrs. Roth. *I hope it burns her lips off.* "So, I assume you would like an update on the trial," Carver said to The Presence across the desk.

"Shouldn't take an assumption, Seth, but yes, of course I would like an update on the trial. Is there anything else that matters right now?"

"No, of course not."

"Well, alright then. Where are we?"

"We've, uh, uncovered some new history on the former P-239."

"New history. Interesting choice of words. And?" The Presence raised a carefully crafted eyebrow.

"And, it appears that P-239 had several documented episodes of paranoid schizophrenic behavior over the last decade."

"Fine, but shouldn't the institute have known about this? Isn't it your responsibility to review the medical records of all potential trial subjects and screen them accordingly?"

"These weren't medical records."

"Oh?"

"No, they were criminal records. Misdemeanors, nothing too serious, but clearly indicative of paranoia."

"And these records were discovered . . . how exactly?"

"Hamilton. Let's just leave it at that, if you don't mind."

"Okay, fine. But what about the question of admission into the trial. How could we have allowed someone like that in?"

"Well, it turns out that we didn't," said Carver with emphasis on his last word. "We were seeing her on a pro bono basis related to complaints about general anxiety and mild hallucinations—nothing to do with the trial. Our records clearly show her two visits with us, a consult with someone at the UW Medical Center, and two days prior to her death, a prescription for medication which she never filled."

"Poor woman," said Mrs. Roth with a compressed smile.

"Yes, unfortunate."

"Can we trust Hamilton on this? He strikes me as pretty black and white."

"Believe me, there's more to him than meets the eye. He and I have an understanding."

"One with teeth?"

"More like fangs, I'd say. We're fine."

"Excellent. I might have misjudged you, Seth."

Carver felt himself relax just slightly in his chair. He noted the faint praise, experienced a mild wave of revulsion, and controlled it successfully. He smiled at The Presence.

Mrs. Roth continued. "Now that we're clear on that, what about the trial? There is a new P-239, I hope?"

"Not exactly yet, but we're on it."

"Equivocation, Seth. Doesn't suit you. Hamilton on this, too?"

"Yes, we need a borderline case, one that we can use to verify our protocol modifications. Hamilton's on it."

"We don't have a lot of time, Seth. The FDA's clock is ticking."

As if I didn't understand that particularly obvious fact. What a bitch. "No, we don't, but we need the right subject."

"Now, let me ask you one more thing. What if this new P-239 reacts the same way? What if the new protocol fails?"

"It won't."

"Come on, Seth, you're still a scientist at heart. There's some probability of failure, right?"

Still a scientist? "We have a contingency plan, of course."

"Don't make me drag it all out of you, Seth. What is it? It had better be different from this last after-the-fact cleanup."

Dr. Carver found himself standing up, towering over Mrs. Roth, clenched and enraged. "Yes, it *is* different," said Carver, his voice barely under control. "We have arranged for an accident, if necessary."

"Fatal and far away from here in all respects, I hope. Don't screw this up, Seth."

Carver glared down at his desk, his hands splayed out over the cold, dark surface.

"Seth, are you listening to me? Hello? Anyone home?" Mrs. Roth rapped loudly on the desk with her knuckles.

Carver's head jerked up. "That's enough! If you can't trust me then go find another outlet for your fucking money! Find somebody else who'll deal with your shit! Get out!" He thrust a shaking finger toward the exit.

Mrs. Roth rose from her chair calmly, picked up her purse, smiled thinly, and headed for the door. She touched the doorframe with a fingertip, turned around and said, "I can see you're angry, Seth. That's good. It's about time you showed a little passion on this. I'm proud of you."

The Presence left the room and Seth Carver sank back into his chair.

SEVENTEEN

· ·

"Good morning, Allison. Have a seat." Dan Gunnison motioned across a small coffee table toward the couch in his office. He smiled and waited for his client to speak. He noticed that she wore a short lime green skirt and a simple white top. Her legs were tanner than he remembered from the week before.

Allison smiled back and quickly looked away. She sat down on the couch and carefully adjusted her skirt. "Good morning."

Dan sat in his chair across the table. He continued smiling but kept his silence for several long moments.

"Aren't you going to ask me something? Are you angry with me?" Allison asked, looking back toward Dan.

"Why would I be angry with you?"

"Um, I don't know . . . maybe because I totally messed up your schedule earlier this week, made you come out to the boat to deal with my stuff? Stuff I should've handled myself?"

"Is that how you feel about it, Allison? That you should have handled everything on your own?"

"Yeah, maybe. Yes, I should be able to take care of myself."

"Okay, sure. But I'm wondering about that particular day, that particular time. Would you have preferred it if I hadn't come?"

"I don't know," said Allison, slowly shaking her head.

"I seem to remember you feeling pretty strongly about it at the time. I think you really wanted me to stay . . . that you might have felt abandoned if I had left. Do you remember feeling that way?"

Allison stood up and walked to the window. She stared out over Lake Union, back in the direction of her marina. "Yes, I guess I asked you to stay, didn't I?"

"Yes, you did. Do you remember anything else about that time?"

"Of course. Why wouldn't I?"

"Just wondering. What stands out for you the most?"

"Well, I remember you covered me up when I was half naked. Okay, maybe like three quarters. I feel strange about that. I hope you don't think I was trying to, you know . . ." Allison continued to gaze over the lake.

"Trying to what?"

"Trying to seduce you, I guess. Because I wasn't. I just passed out right in the middle of getting dressed."

"No, of course not. I know that, and you don't have to worry. What about other things you remember from our session on your boat?"

"As if that wasn't enough!" Allison turned away from the window, walked toward Dan's wall of books, and seemed to examine a few of the titles, including some of the ones down on the lowest shelf. When she bent down, Dan noticed that Allison's skirt wasn't doing its intended job. Or maybe it was.

Dan forced himself to look aside. He waited.

Allison slowly turned back toward Dan and he noticed a change in her face—a younger look, but with an edge. She placed one long, tan leg, slightly bent at the knee, in front of the other. "So, you're saying that you don't find me attractive?" she asked.

Dan struggled to control his response, to stay with his therapeutic goal, to appear unaffected. "No . . . no, I'm not saying that at all, Allison. But I *am* wondering if it's important to you that I do."

"What?"

Dan leaned forward. "Stay with me on this for a moment and try to answer me honestly, even if it's hard, okay? Do you feel that it's somehow important, for this relationship," Dan moved his hand back and forth between the two of them, "that I find you attractive?"

"Relationship?"

"Yes, the client/therapist relationship. It's a different type of relationship, but a very real one and often quite an intimate one, but not in a sexual sense of course."

"Okay, so no . . . yes . . . I don't know! Yes, maybe it *is* important to me somehow. Is there something wrong with that?"

"No, there's usually not. We all want to feel that we're attractive to others. That's a natural, healthy thing."

"So then why are you so interested to know whether I feel that way?" Allison asked, with her head cocked to one side.

"Because I think it might be one of the keys to your therapy. Would it be okay if I reflected a few things back to you? Things that I've noticed during our last few sessions that I think might be important?"

"Sure, I guess." Allison looked puzzled, and then slowly smiled. "But you never told me whether you think I'm attractive. I think I deserve an answer." She sat back down on the couch and crossed her legs.

"Okay, fair enough. As your therapist, keeping in mind what I said about that relationship, I will tell you exactly what I think. I think anyone would say that you are an exceptionally beautiful woman, Allison. Does that answer your question?"

"Well, no, Mr. Therapist, not exactly. That was nice to hear but it was more like an impersonal physical observation, I'd say. My question was whether you, personally, find me, personally, attractive—me, *all* of me."

Dan felt himself reddening. Had he jumped to a bad conclusion about what Allison meant? Had he automatically gone to the physical, sexual implication of the question when she had meant something much deeper? *Come on, man. Get it together. What kind of a therapist are you, anyway?* But then there was her almost teenage flirtatiousness, that very short green skirt, that darker-than-northwest tan, the episode on the boat. *You're okay, you're okay. You're a fine therapist. Just keep your focus. There's something else here.*

"Well, Allison, I really don't know you well enough to give you an answer. And even if I did, that wouldn't be something I could discuss with you as a client. But, it's a very interesting question and I'd like to explore some of your feelings behind it. Could I tell you a little about what I'm noticing and then see where we go from there?"

"Jeez, you can be so frustrating sometimes! Why can't you just talk to me like a normal human being?!"

Dan waited for Allison to collect herself. Finally, she tossed a lock of hair out of her face and said, "I'm sorry."

"That's okay, Allison. It's just that, in order to truly help clients, therapists need to maintain certain boundaries, even when their clients might feel that crossing those lines would be helpful. Believe me, in the end it never is. But, at the same time, it can be very useful to talk about the thoughts and feelings that push us in that direction. Does that make sense to you? It's kind of a subtle distinction."

"Yes, I guess I see that."

"Okay, good. Then let me take a minute to be a sort of mirror for you. I'd like to reflect back to you some of the things I've noticed and then explore them with you for the rest of our time here today."

"Alright." Allison found a throw on the couch, placed it over her lap, kicked off her shoes and tucked her legs under her to the side.

"When you called me earlier this week, asking for help, I stretched a therapeutic boundary to come out to your boat. I felt it was a big stretch, but not a crossing. And I'm glad that you called because I think it helped me to see and understand some things about your situation that might not have come out here in the office."

"Such as?"

"Well, as you mentioned earlier, when I arrived, you were missing some, well, some major items of clothing. Now, I don't think this was something you arranged consciously before you collapsed, and believe me, there is absolutely no blame here, but I wonder, if I had been a female therapist if that situation would have been different."

"How could it have been? I was unconscious, for God's sake!"

"Now again, Allison, I truly don't think this was something you thought about or planned explicitly. But I do wonder, on another level of consciousness, a deeper level, if was an effort to make me stay. To keep me from leaving."

Dan noticed a slight quiver in Allison's lower lip as she nodded. He continued. "And then, when I gave you the aspirin and determined that you were okay, I think you sensed I was ready to leave. And I *was* about to go at that point. But you offered to talk about something you said you hadn't been totally honest about. When you mentioned that, I was drawn back in because I felt I might otherwise miss a very important therapeutic moment with you. Do you remember?"

"Uh huh. But I wasn't trying to trick you, really."

"I know that, Allison. I don't think that you were. But I think that this was a way for you to deal with a very deep need: a need for attachment; a need to *not* be abandoned."

Allison nodded once.

"But then, instead of telling me something that might have been helpful but very painful for you, you delivered an interesting, and medically informed, lecture on the endocrinology of PMS. Do you remember that, too?"

"Yes." Allison looked down and slowly shook her head.

"It's okay, Allison. This could be very helpful. Besides, you give a good lecture. It was fascinating."

This brought a small smile from Allison as she looked up and grabbed a tissue from the low table in front of her.

"Do you mind if I go on a bit further?" Dan asked.

"No, go ahead, I'm okay." Allison blew her nose loudly into the tissue.

"Alright. Now, can you talk a little about that lecture? Can you tell me where all that medical knowledge comes from?"

Allison took a deep breath, pursed her lips and stared down at the coffee table in front of her. Dan waited for what seemed like nearly a minute while Allison put her head in her hands and rubbed her temples. Finally, she looked up and peered at Dan through her fingers.

"It comes from Kathryn."

"Yes, you've mentioned Kathryn before. Can you tell me more about her now?"

"It's hard to."

"I know. But remember, nothing you say here will hurt our relationship. That's one of the things that's special about the client/therapist situation. It's not fragile."

Allison exhaled as if she had been holding her breath for the last several minutes. "Kathryn doesn't exist. I mean, not in the physical sense. She's kind of like, in my head."

"Does her voice intrude on your daily life sometimes?"

"No, not really her voice. But her ideas, yes. I just somehow know her."

"Okay. What does it mean to know her?"

"Well, it might seem strange to you, but she's been around for as long as I can remember, so for me she's just part of my life."

"No, it doesn't seem that strange to me."

"Good, because here's the part that I just took for granted as a kid but has seemed less normal as I've grown up. I know Kathryn. I mean I know what she knows. That's where the medical knowledge comes from."

"So, did you have this knowledge even as a little girl?"

"No, not exactly. I mean, I think it was there but I only gradually began to understand it. Does that make sense?"

"Sure, I think that we can have factual knowledge without necessarily integrating it, relating it to other knowledge, using it in practical ways. I think we can 'know about' things without fully understanding them."

"Yes! That's what it was like. But then, over the years I've become more interested and I've read a lot. I'm probably the only yacht broker in the world who subscribes to the American Journal of Surgery. So now it's harder for me to tell where Kathryn's knowledge ends and mine begins. Is this making any sense at all?"

"Actually, yes, quite a bit."

"Oh, good. But, . . . what does this make you think about me?"

"Well, it makes me think that we're getting somewhere. This is good, Allison. You're doing an excellent job."

Allison smiled and looked down.

"Can we shift gears here for a moment, Allison, and talk about your childhood for just a bit?"

"I guess; sure."

"I think it was in our very first session that you told me you were adopted after several years in foster homes. Is that about right?"

"Yes, I was five at the time."

"And what would you say about how the world felt to you then, when you were finally adopted?"

"How the world felt . . . Well, I remember feeling so relieved, so grateful to have parents, and a sister, and an actual place to come home to—a place that wasn't going to go away. But . . ."

Dan noticed that Allison had just pulled a section of blanket around her shoulders and was hugging her knees up to her chest.

"But what, Allison?"

"But one day I told Beth about Kathryn."

"Who was Beth?"

"She was my adopted sister."

Dan nodded. "And what happened when you told her?"

"She . . . she said that only babies have imaginary friends."

"That sounds pretty typical of a child that age. Do you think that Beth might have been a little jealous of Kathryn? I mean, it might have seemed to her that you already had a sister and didn't need another one."

"I don't know. Maybe. But she was so mean about it."

"What made you feel that she was being mean?"

"Beth said if I ever mentioned Kathryn again she would tell my new Mom and Dad and that they would send me back where they got me. She told me that she was the only real girl, that they just bought me at the store. That they would just send me back if they ever found out that there was something wrong with me. That I was broken."

"That must have been very hard for you. Did Beth ever mention this again?"

Allison took another tissue and wiped her eyes before replying. "Yes, many times. Anytime I got on her nerves. Anytime after Mom or Dad gave me any special attention. Like birthday parties."

"That must have been awful for you. Did you ever discuss this with your adopted Mom or Dad?"

"No, of course not. How could I? I needed a home."

"So you believed Beth—that your parents would actually send you back?"

Allison nodded. "I know it must seem strange to you, but yes, I had no doubt. I knew that I was broken and that Beth would tell. I knew it."

Dan looked up to the ceiling, closed his eyes and let out a long sigh. "And you lived with this. Were you ever able to feel close to your new parents?"

"We went through the motions, you know. But I could never really believe they were permanent somehow. They really tried, at least my stepmother did. I just couldn't let them in."

"And why do you think you couldn't let them in?"

"Haven't you been listening, Dan? Don't you get it?!"

"Yes, I have been, Allison, and I think I do. I just want you to have an opportunity to talk about it."

"Yeah, well, I think I'm done talking about it today." Allison tossed the blanket on the couch and stood up.

"Then maybe we can continue next time. Our time is about up for today anyway."

"Okay, next time."

When Allison left, Dan made a few notes.

Clear history of attachment deficit now coming out. Interesting background about K and adopted sister's issues with same. Not classic DID presentation, but some possible switching to child, maybe teenager, during session. Didn't seem to stick, though. Very transient. No apparent gaps in memory. Concerned that A would not deal well with end of session today but was surprised at how secure she seemed. Possible progress? Need to continue with childhood discussion. Ultimately, SCID-D interview still seems a good path forward.

EIGHTEEN

. . . .

When Allison arrived back at the boat later that day, her phone's ringtone told her that a text message had arrived. She touched the display and found a note from Margaret: been a long time. early drink & dinner tonite?

Allison smiled and immediately keyed back: sure. chandlers @6?

It was already 4:30 and that gave Allison just enough time to get changed and take the dinghy across the lake to Chandler's Cove. She tied up at the guest dock and climbed the ramp to find Margaret waiting for an inside table at their favorite restaurant on the point. The women hugged and chatted as they were led to a window booth overlooking the marina. Allison ordered a Cabernet-Shiraz blend from Australia and Margaret asked for a Cosmo.

"So, tell me about your guy. Rick, right?" asked Allison.

"Oh he's great. Hard to find much time that's good for us both, with him working nights at the ER, but yeah, he's wonderful."

"Wonderful? Oh, that sounds good. So are you two . . . ?"

"No, not yet. We're just like really, really good friends."

"Sounds like more than that to me," said Allison.

"Well, yeah, maybe. But what about you? Did you ever go see that therapist?"

"Oh, I didn't tell you? Wow, I guess it *has* been a while. I'm sorry, yes, I did. I still am, actually. Been several times."

"And?"

"And I think it's a good thing for me."

"No need to thank me or anything," said Margaret with a faked scowl.

"I'm sorry. Yes, I *do* thank you. Thank you *so* much. I never would have gotten into therapy if you hadn't told me about Dan."

"Dan, hmm, sounds like you guys are fairly familiar."

"He's pretty informal; said I could call him that."

"So you like him?"

"Uh huh." Allison gazed out the window.

"That's all? What going on, Allie?"

"Nothing. It's just that I feel better when I'm around him."

"So? Isn't that what therapy's all about?"

"Yeah, but I hate when I have to leave. Dan really seems to understand me, you know. He gets me."

"Well, that's good, being that it's his job and all," said Margaret with a quizzical look at her friend.

Allison took another sip of her wine and then, "No, I think I might like him just the tiniest bit too much." She held her fingers together as if pinching salt.

"Oh. Okay, yeah, that could be a problem, couldn't it."

"Maybe, but I don't know. At least I don't think it's mutual."

"You pretty sure about that?"

Allison glanced around, leaned forward and whispered, "Yeah, pretty sure. He saw me naked and it didn't even seem to faze him."

Margaret's mouth dropped open and she nearly spilled her drink. "What?! What kind of therapy is this, Allie? *I* haven't even seen you naked, and I've known you for what, five years? And we've been to the gym together!"

A waiter passed by at that moment and his head jerked back. "It's not like it sounds, really," said Allison, more for the waiter's benefit than her friend's.

"Whoa, girl. You got some 'splainin to do. What are you talking about?"

"It's kind of a long story."

"I've got all night." Margaret flagged down the waiter. "Could you bring me another Cosmo, please?"

Allison told her friend everything, except the part about the short green skirt. That part just didn't seem relevant. No, maybe the issue wasn't relevancy. *When did I start lying to myself?*

Allison looked at Margaret, hoping for some sympathy, some encouragement, some exoneration, something. But Margaret was just smiling sadly.

"Margaret, what? What are you thinking? Talk to me."

"I just think you should be more careful."

"I know, I know. I must be crazy."

"No, Allie, that's not what I mean. There's something about Dan I need to tell you. I wasn't sure it was really important, but after what you just said . . ."

"Oh?"

Just then the waiter reappeared with an awkward smile. "And what can I bring you two for your entrées this evening?"

"I'll have the house salad with the raspberry vinaigrette, and a cup of the crab bisque," said Allison, closing her menu and handing it back.

"Same here, except make mine the chowder, please," added Margaret.

"Very good. Can I get you anything else while you're waiting? Another drink for you . . . Miss?" the waiter smiled at Allison.

"No thanks."

"I'll be right back with more bread." The waiter departed.

Allison giggled. "That's what I call a 'Near Miss'. But I'll take it over Ma'am any day. So, what's this about Dan?"

Margaret laughed, but then quickly became serious. "Okay, yesterday, after I hadn't heard from you for a few weeks, I decided, just on a weird hunch, to use my connections at the office and do a quick background check on Dan Gunnison. I guess I was a little worried about you and wanted to make sure that Gunnison was still around and that he was really a good place for you to start."

"Okay . . . thanks for thinking about me like that but it's working out just fine so far."

"Here's the thing, Allie. It turns out that just a month or so after I stopped going to him, Dan Gunnison's license was suspended. He had a fling with a young female client. After his license was reinstated, his practice was monitored for a couple of years and no further infractions have been reported. Legally, he's clean, but when something like that happens, I don't know about you, but I always worry."

"Oh," was all Allison could manage at first.

"Yeah, oh. And it's not just an abstract legal worry. I worry about you, Allie. You. Especially after what you just told me a few minutes ago."

"Oh, my. But it wasn't rape or anything was it?"

"No, it was apparently consensual, but she was a client and that's an absolute no-no. And they did it in his office."

"Oh, wow, what should I do? Shouldn't he have said something? Isn't he required to?"

"No, there's no requirement like that, and, to Gunnison's credit, it does seem like he's learned something from this, at least if his record is any indication. Still, though, I worry."

"Yeah, me too . . . now." Allison shook her head slowly. "What should I do, Margaret? I feel like a total idiot."

"Well, of course that's completely up to you, but if I were you . . . ? If I were you, I guess I'd at least think about finding someone else. I'm sorry."

Allison nodded. She was no longer hungry.

Nineteen

. . . .

It seemed to Allison that she had barely slept an hour. All night long, between fitful dreams, she had wrestled with the dilemma of Dan. Could she trust him? What about her therapy? Could she face starting over with someone new? Go through all that stuff again? In the wee hours of the morning, nothing seemed clear.

Finally Allison got up, made coffee, and sat out in the cockpit of *Far and Away*, watching the sun come up red across the water between broken, blowing clouds. The morning itself seemed unsettled and the boat moved unpredictably with the heavy chop on the lake. *Red sky in morning, sailor take warning.*

I've got to quit, she thought. *I'll call him a little later. No, I'd better leave a message now while I'm feeling resolved. Shouldn't he have told me? I'm not sure I can trust him anymore.*

Allison got up and walked back inside to find her phone. She finally located it on the chart table in the pilothouse and dialed Dan's number.

"Dan, this is Allison Walker. I'm sorry to be leaving this message so early but I couldn't sleep. I hope your phone wasn't set to ring. Listen, I've decided to stop therapy and wanted to let you know now, while I still have the guts to do it. No need to call me back. I'm fine. Just send me your latest bill and I'll take care of it. Thanks. 'Bye."

Ouch. That was kind of harsh. Maybe I'd better call back and explain. No, don't do it. He didn't tell me; why should I tell him?

Allison gathered her things and walked up the dock to shower at the marina restroom. She felt an odd mix of relief and anxiety as she thought about both the clean break she had made and the uncertain road ahead.

He had gotten her to think about her situation in terms she had never considered before. She dared to think that she might someday be free of her past. From Kathryn and the other Teachers. But how and where would she go from here?

The warm water of the shower soothed her, and the soapy slipperiness felt good on her breasts. *At least he never saw these.*

Allison dressed, dried her hair, put it in a ponytail and drove to the office. The water was just too rough to take the dinghy. It wouldn't really have been dangerous, just a little unpleasant. Why go through that?

Traffic was all but nonexistent on this Saturday morning, and Allison made it to the office in record time. She busied herself with paperwork: a contract on the Selene—*a good commission if that one actually closes*—some insurance stuff, whatever lay on her desk. She had successfully buried her anxiety beneath the pile of details when the office phone rang.

"Good morning, Rain City Yachts, this is Allison. How can I help you?"

"Allison, this is Dan Gunnison. I got your message. Couldn't reach you on your cell so thought I'd try here. You okay?"

Oh shit!

"Hi, Dan. Yeah, I'm fine. Listen, I'm in the middle of a few things here. Can I call you back?"

"Sure, no problem. But Allison?"

"Yes?" *How could I have ever let you see me in that skirt, or **out** of it for God's sake? What an idiot I am!*

"Of course it's completely up to you to decide what to do with your therapy, but if you really decide to stop, there are some things about your condition that I need to discuss with you. Just so you'll be better equipped to go from here. Okay? It's really important."

My condition? "Sure; I'll call you back in a few minutes when I get free."

Allison hung up the phone and stared at her desk, unable to move. *My condition? What the hell is he talking about? Is he just trying to get me to call? He sounded so concerned. But how can I possibly trust him?*

She glanced at the clock. 8:30. On impulse, she picked up the phone and called Margaret. It rang three times before her friend answered.

"Hello?"

"Margaret, did I wake you? This is Allie."

"Allie? Oh, what time is it? Is it Saturday?"

"Yes, eight-thirty. I'm sorry. I did wake you, didn't I?"

"It's okay. What's up? You alright?"

"Not really. Can I talk with you for a minute? I really need some advice."

"Sure, and I really need to pee. Hang on; I'll be right back."

"Yeah, sorry. I'll hang on."

What do I really want to know? What can she do to help, anyway? I've got to do this myself . . .

"Allie, you still there?"

"Yeah, I'm here. Thanks, Margaret. I'm so sorry to get you up."

"No problem. What's going on?"

"I left a message for Dan telling him I'm going to quit therapy."

"Okay, that sounds like a reasonable decision, under the circumstances."

"But then he called me back."

"And?"

"And I just couldn't talk to him. I told him I'd call him back in a few minutes."

"When was this?"

"A few minutes ago."

"Oh, okay, so . . . ?"

"So now I've got to decide whether or not to do it. He told me that if I quit he needs to give me some information about 'my condition' so that I can decide what to do from here."

"Your condition?"

"Yeah, that's the word he used."

"He didn't say what it is?"

"No. I'm scared, Margaret. What should I do?"

"What's your gut telling you?"

"I guess I feel like I need to find out what he's talking about. The rat!"

"Rat? Aren't you being a little hard on him? Wait, he hasn't done anything to you, has he Allie?"

"No, no. It's just that I feel like I've been such an idiot with him. And now that I know about his past, I just feel dirty and weird. You know?"

"Uh huh, yeah."

"I don't know, maybe *I'm* the rat," moaned Allison.

"No, you're not a rat, Allie, but I get what you mean. You wanna know what I think?"

"Yes, I do."

"I think you should call him back. You can feel whatever you feel about him, but just get the information you need. For you. Okay?"

"Okay. Thank you, Margaret. I don't know what I'd do without you. You're such a good friend. Now go back to sleep."

"Sure, like I'm really gonna do that. Just call him."

"I will. I love you, Margaret. 'Bye."

TWENTY

. . . .

Allison stared at the phone. *I can do this. Just get the information and get off the phone. Just like Margaret said. Okay, I can do this.* She dialed the number and waited.

"Hello?"

"Hello, Dan, this is Allie, Allison." *Shit!* "So, there were some things you wanted to talk with me about?"

"Yes, that is, if you really have decided that stopping therapy is in your best interest."

"I really have decided. Yes."

"Allison, I have to say that I'm a bit surprised at your decision. Can I ask what brought you to this point? It seemed to me that we were making some pretty good progress."

"Maybe, yes. But I have my reasons. You said something about my condition on the phone. Could you explain that please?"

"Allison, you sound angry with me. Are you?"

"I don't know. Maybe a little."

"You seemed okay, just a little upset at the end of our last session when we were talking about your adopted parents. You actually wanted to end the session early. Was there something about that conversation that bothered you?"

"No, it wasn't that. It's something else that I really don't want to discuss right now. Could we just talk about this condition thing?"

"Allison, this is something that we really need to talk about in person— face to face."

"Why?"

"Well, mainly because it's very important for you to understand everything I need to tell you and I really don't trust the phone for this kind of conversation. You know what I mean? I've got a pretty free day. Could you meet me at the office in, say, twenty minutes?"

"I don't think so. No, I really don't think that would be a good idea."

"I'm sorry? I must be missing something here."

"Maybe, yeah, it's complicated."

Silence.

Allison continued. "Okay, look, Let's meet over on the Eastside, Bellevue Square Starbucks at eleven."

"But there'll be a ton of people over there and it's at least a twenty minute drive for you. You sure you want to meet there?"

"Yes, I'm sure. I've got to be over there for a boat showing anyway. Eleven at Starbucks, Belle Square."

Allison hung up. She couldn't remember the last time she'd hung up on someone. *What's going on with me?*

The next two hours went by slowly as Allison tried to get some work done but found herself entirely too distracted by worry and confusion to be productive. *Do I have some kind of disease? A brain tumor? Maybe it's 'just' some form of psychosis. That would be better. Why can't I diagnose myself like I do everyone else in the world? That's actually a symptom of whatever this is, isn't it? I need to see a medical professional, not a therapist.* Eventually, she stopped all the mental flailing, locked the door to the office, sat down at her desk and cried.

At 10:30, feeling a little steadier and even more resolved, Allison got in her car, drove out of the city and across the 520 floating bridge to Bellevue. She walked into Starbucks five minutes late. Parking was much tougher than she expected. She hated being late for anything, but at this particular moment it seemed irrelevant. Dan could wait.

Allison found Dan seated in a corner. She ordered a coffee and sat down across a small circular table from him. He smiled and Allison tried to reciprocate but avoided eye contact by putting her purse down on the floor under the table.

In spite of her confused feelings, Allison found herself saying, "Thanks for coming all the way over here. I appreciate it."

"Hey, no problem. It's actually more convenient for me, anyway. I live over here in Kirkland."

Great. I really don't want to know where you live. "Oh, good, then this is okay. Good. Uh, look, I don't have a lot of time this morning," Allison lied. "Could we just talk about whatever it is you think is going on with me?"

"Sure, but would you let me know about how much time you have, so I can adjust accordingly? I want to do the best I can to help you with your next steps."

Allison searched her mind for a reasonable number, one that she thought she could tolerate but that would also allow time for her to get the information she needed and to ask any questions that occurred to her. She didn't want to have to endure another session after this one. "A little less than an hour now."

"Okay, we can do this. Now, Allison, I want you to know that you can call me anytime, even after we're officially done with your sessions, if you need to talk or want to get back into therapy. As I've told you before, I'm not going anywhere."

Terrific. "Thanks, but I don't think that'll be necessary."

Dan put down his cup and Allison could see that he was trying hard to catch her eye, to engage her. "Allison, look. It would help me to help you in this last session if I just understood why you seem so upset with me. Maybe you could just give me a hint?"

Allison took a long sip of coffee and struggled with the decision. If she told him, it would sound so minor, she suddenly realized, even though it didn't feel that way to her. If she didn't tell him, she might not get everything she needed today. She could lie, but that seemed a bad option too, because it would probably lead to more lies and pointless discussions. She made her decision.

"I can't tell you, I'm sorry. I just can't." Allison stared past Dan at a hanging lamp beyond.

"Okay, I have to respect that. We'll just have to try and work around it, whatever it is."

"Alright, thanks. Now, can you tell me about this condition you mentioned?"

"Sure. We didn't get far enough along in your therapy for me to make an actual diagnosis, so what I'm about to tell you is just my current state of thinking—my best guess right now. Is that clear? You can't take this as anything more than that. I shouldn't even be telling you this much, but I want you to be equipped to make the best possible choices about your own care going forward. Okay?"

My own care? That sounds serious. "Yes, I get it. Please just tell me."

Dan sighed and began.

"Allison, I think it's possible, maybe even likely, that you are suffering from a condition which psychologists call Dissociative Identity Disorder, or DID for short. I'll tell you right now that this is a controversial diagnosis, so not everyone in the field is even willing to explore it. But, I have to say that your background and some of your symptoms point to DID."

"I've never heard of DID before. What is it? Is it serious? For some reason, Kathryn doesn't have—I don't have—any special knowledge in psychiatry or psychology."

Dan nodded and went on. "DID is a condition in which a person exhibits more than one personality, often five or six, but sometimes upwards of a hundred. We call these distinct personalities alters or parts. Most practitioners prefer to use the term 'parts' because it implies something we believe to be true, which is that all of these personalities are actually parts of the individual, revealing themselves in different ways. All parts taken together form what we call the system."

"How does someone end up with DID?" Allison asked.

"Well, DID is fundamentally an effort by an individual to protect herself from re-experiencing past trauma. Almost all DID patients have a history of sexual or physical abuse in childhood, but occasionally, rarely actually, the abuse can take the form of radical neglect or abandonment. Allison, your childhood experience fits most closely with the latter."

"Yes, if anything. I wasn't abused, not that I remember anyway, and I think I would, wouldn't I?"

"Not necessarily, no. Not everyone remembers, and DID patients often hold the specific memories of abuse in one or more separate parts, kept away from the primary identity. It's all about protection."

"So . . . are you saying that I was abused in some way?" Allison asked, her coffee now forgotten and set to the side.

"Allison, I just don't know. I don't think so, other than neglect, but this is one of the many reasons I believe you should still be in therapy with someone, if not with me. Tell me, is Kathryn the only one, or are there others?"

"There are others, a few. I've always called them The Teachers."

"Have you ever had any memory lapses? Periods of time that you can't account for?"

"No, nothing like that."

"Hmm, okay. Still, we—or you and another therapist—should explore this. It's very important. And, even though your situation doesn't fit the classic model, I still think you'd be better off with a specialist, someone with specific DID training and experience."

"You're kicking me out?" Allison asked, surprised at her own words and the tears forming in her eyes. She looked away. "I'm sorry. I don't know where that came from."

"Allison, I believe you were the one who insisted on leaving therapy. Isn't that why we're meeting here today? I would never kick you out."

Dan gently touched Allison's sleeve and she recoiled.

"Yes, no, you're right. It's my decision. I'm sorry, I do need to leave. I mean, like, right now. I'm sorry. Thanks for everything." Allison stood up.

Dan stood with her. "Look, Allison, let me do one last thing before we formally wrap up our sessions. There's a group in town, in fact right here in Bellevue, called the Carver Research Institute. It's headed by Dr. Seth Carver who just happens to have a DID research initiative. The Institute works in several other areas, but right now Carver himself is running a clinical trial focusing on a new treatment for DID. If you'll let me, I'd like to consult with someone at the Institute and see if maybe you'd be a good match for this work. Would you let me do that? And then, of course, it would be entirely your decision about going forward with this, or not."

"Sure. Thank you. I've got to go."

Allison turned and walked toward the door.

"Are you sure you're okay to drive?" Dan asked.

Allison nodded but left without another word.

She walked back to her car in a daze. Dan didn't deserve this kind of treatment, even if he had screwed a client. Or maybe he did deserve it. But that was so long ago and he seemed like such a good man, a kind man. Dan hadn't ever come on to her, even when she . . . . oh it was so embarrassing now, and so confusing. Why was she behaving this way, as if she were the perfect one? Hah! The perfect one, right.

Allison got into her car and absently watched a young mother in the parking space ahead of her fitting her toddler into a car seat, guiding those active little legs into position as she set her gently down. The woman buckled her daughter safely in place and kissed her on the forehead before walking around the car to the driver's side. Allison smiled wistfully and thought how she had never had that experience, how she had never felt that warm, caring, protective presence when she was a toddler. In fact, it occurred to her that she never thought of herself as having been that age at all. She desperately wanted to miss her mother, to feel something for her mother, but she had no mother to feel for. This left a hollowness somewhere deep inside, an emptiness that her adopted mother, Dolores, had never filled, even if she had tried. Had she tried?

There were birthday parties, walks in the park, things like that, but Allison's adopted sister, Beth, was always there too, constantly demanding attention. Allison could not remember one special occasion that was hers alone. And yet, she had a permanent home, and that seemed to compensate for everything else.

But she remembered other things quite clearly. Her face grew hot, even now, as she recalled a particularly painful moment when she was probably six years old, which would have made Beth seven and a half. She and Beth were getting dressed one Saturday morning, preparing to go to the playground with their mother, and Allison had selected a dress which Dolores had found for her recently at a garage sale. But she could not find any underwear in her drawer. That seemed strange to her because Dolores washed almost every day and always made sure that the girls had plenty of clean clothes. There were lots of socks and little white undershirts in her drawer, but no panties.

She turned to Beth and said, "I don't have any underpants. Do you know where they are?"

Her sister giggled, said no, and then mumbled something about it not being her problem.

Allison looked in the dirty clothes bin and found it empty, too. So she turned back to Beth. "Could I . . . could I please borrow a pair of yours, just for today? Or some tights maybe?"

"Eeew, yuck!" said Beth, pretending to throw up in the corner of the room. "You don't share panties. You don't do that, ever! Didn't any of your other parents ever tell you? It's dirty. If you ever ask me to do something like that again, I'm going to tell Mom and she'll be so ashamed of you that she'll . . . well you know what she'll do."

Of course Allison did know. She was convinced by that time in her adopted life. She would be sent back. Dirty little Allison, sent back where she came from. So she walked back to her dresser with her head down, trying to hide the tears of shame that welled up in her eyes. She tossed her new dress aside and quickly tried to pull on a pair of jeans, but Beth came up right behind her.

"Uh, what're you doing?"

"I'm wearing jeans."

"No you're not. Mom got you that dress and she expects you to wear it. Look, I'm wearing mine." Beth smiled primly and executed her best pirouette, the black tights under the dress making her look like a chubby ballerina.

"But, what about . . . okay I will."

Allison put on the dress and smoothed it down to make sure it covered her. It did, but it felt strange and airy.

When the girls and their mother arrived at the park they played tag with some other boys and girls from school while the moms chatted on nearby benches. Then everyone's attention turned to the playground equipment and they ran back as fast as they could, racing for first place. Allison won easily while Beth took third or fourth place and stomped around shouting that Allison had cheated, but no one seemed to pay any attention to her. They were all laughing and giving Allison high fives.

Then, abruptly, Beth seemed to perk up and came over to the rest of the group. "Allison, let's see who can hang from the bars the longest, you or me!" She jumped up to grab one of the higher bars and held on. "Come on!"

Allison felt she had no choice and even felt a little badly about beating her sister in the race, so she jumped up. The two of them hung here for what seemed like minutes on end until Allison decided that maybe she could make peace by letting her sister win, so she dropped to the ground, feigning exhaustion. Beth dropped after her and held up her arms in triumph. "I win!"

Allison noticed that no one else seemed particularly impressed, and maybe that was why her sister did what she did next.

"Hey, wait! Bet you can't do this, you looser!" she shouted. Beth jumped up, grabbed the bar, swung up and hung by her knees, then swung back and forth and let go, doing a little flip and landing nicely on her feet. "Do it! Hey everybody, it's Allison's turn!" she yelled, with a glance over her shoulder toward her mother.

Without another thought, Allison jumped up to imitate her sister, this time intending to show her up. It wasn't until she was hanging upside down and everyone was laughing and pointing that she remembered her lack of panties. Just before she crashed awkwardly to the ground, she heard Beth say, "Mom, look! Allison's naked!"

Allison's left ankle hurt from her fall, but that seemed like nothing compared to the burning anger and shame she felt. She pulled her new dress around her, buried her head in her hands and sobbed.

She kept her eyes tightly closed against the world, even when she felt herself being yanked to her feet.

"Get up and come with me, young lady! We're going home now! What in the world did you think you were doing!?"

That Monday Allison pretended to be sick. She just couldn't face the kids at school. But when Tuesday morning arrived, Dolores was no longer convinced by her adopted daughter's manufactured symptoms and she forced Allison to go back to school.

The day was a nightmare for little Allison. By then her story had made the rounds and the whole school seemed to know what had happened. Some kids laughed, some turned away from her, and a few of the fifth and sixth grade boys sneered and call her horrible names she had never heard before. She cried almost all day.

But then, when she was desperately waiting for the school bus at the end of the day, a boy named Tommy who wasn't in Allison's class but had been part of the awful Saturday playground group, came up to her and she braced for more insults and shame. She closed her eyes and turned away from him, as if that could make either him or her disappear—she didn't care which, as long as one of them ceased to be. But she was shocked by the words he spoke. They were the only kind ones she heard that day, and they saved her life.

Now, as she sat in her car some twenty-five years later, she cried as she recalled those words with absolute clarity: "Allison, I'm sorry about what happened to you and I know it wasn't your fault. You're nice, not like your sister. And . . . I didn't look, honest. I covered my eyes for you . . . even though you are really pretty. I hope you feel better. Bye."

Allison never spoke with Tommy after that day, as much as she longed to, and he moved away within a month or two. They had exchanged shy smiles once or twice at school but that had been all. She thought then, and still thought now, *maybe that's what love feels like.*

TWENTY-ONE

. . . .

D an walked into a dumpy little bar along Alki beach, just as the sun broke through the clouds and highlighted the Seattle skyline across Elliott Bay. He and Skip occasionally hung out there. It wasn't the kind of place Dan would ever take a date, but it was perfect for having a couple of beers with a friend on a Saturday night. The interior had a dark, cheap nautical look and smelled vaguely of creosote pilings, one of which graced a corner of the bar. Dan often wondered why the health department hadn't insisted on its removal years ago. A one-legged stuffed seagull was perched unsteadily on the piling and an ancient yellowed life ring hung from one side. But the view out the large windows over the water was what made the place work.

"Hey, Skipper, how's it goin'." Dan gave his buddy a slap on the back and sat down.

"Not bad, you?"

"Bad, actually. Yeah, pretty bad. The week from hell."

"Here, I already ordered you a Corona. That okay?"

"Perfect, thanks."

"So, tell me what's happening. Can't be that bad. I don't see any blood or bruising."

Dan gave a half smile, squirted a small wedge of lime into his beer, and took a long swig. "Yeah, well, if you could see my brain right now you might reconsider."

"I'll order an MRI along with the fried calamari."

"Calamari? Sounds good. Hungry, actually."

"That's a positive sign. See, things are looking up! So, what's going on with you?"

"Remember that possible DID client I told you about? The one I called 'A'?"

"Yep, I do. Things not going well with her?"

"Could be a hell of a lot better. She decided to quit therapy."

"Oh?"

"Yeah, and just when it seemed like we were starting to make real progress. Frustrating."

"Sure. I can imagine. Seems like an odd time to quit, doesn't it?"

"Well, not really. If a client starts talking about quitting, it's often when we're just beginning to uncover some really important stuff. That's also when things tend to get the most painful."

"Okay, makes sense I guess."

"But usually it's just talk, you know. Well, not just talk—I shouldn't say that. It's more like the client is trying to tell me, 'Hey, can we go a little easier here? I don't know if I can take much more of this right now.' But they usually don't flat-out quit. You know what I mean?"

"Sure. So what usually happens at that point?"

"Well, most of the time I take the hint, back off a little, change the pace or the topic for a session or two. Then circle back around to the sore spot and try again, but from another angle. The clients usually hang in there."

"But, I take it that didn't work this time."

"I really didn't have much of a chance to try. She's showing some anger which seems directed at me. Could easily be transference, though. Might not have anything directly to do with me at all. It probably points to something else we need to explore, but now it looks like we won't have the chance."

"So, did she formally quit then?"

"Yep. Got up and walked right out of the coffee place."

"Coffee place?"

"Oh, that's the other thing. She refused to meet in my office for the last session. It had to be Starbucks."

"Hmm. What do you think that's all about?"

Dan paused for another sip of beer, frowned and said, "You, know, that's a great question, Skip. I've been so caught up in the rest of this that I really haven't given any thought to that. And I *should* have. Probably too late to worry about it now, though."

The calamari arrived and the two men dug in.

"So, Skip," said Dan between mouthfuls, "what're you up to in the lab these days?"

"Interesting stuff. At least *I* think so, which is a good thing since I spend so much time at it. Most people just mentally go to sleep when I try to tell them what I do. You ever have that experience? You try to explain something to someone, like at a party, and you can almost watch them float away. You just lose 'em."

"Huh? Oh, sorry. I was just thinking about that tug going by out there."

"Hey!"

"Sorry, bad joke. You were saying?"

Skip quickly recovered and explained that he and his team were exploring certain aspects of what was once called "junk DNA." Dan was surprised to hear that, at one time, it was thought that as much as ninety-eight percent of the human genome might be non-coding, and therefore non-functional, snippets of genetic material. Today, Skip continued, that number is thought to be considerably lower but still very significant. While some of this genetic material has been found to be useful in repairing sections of damaged DNA, and other portions of it are likely to be involved in regulating gene expression, most of it still appears to be superfluous. Some chromosomal regions have been designated "pseudogenes"—essentially the remains of ancient genes which have lost their protein coding ability—and other regions appear to hold retrotransposons of Human Endogenous Retroviruses, the remnants of ancient viruses which managed to infect the human germ cells and have therefore been passed through the genome from generation to generation.

Skip waved a hand in front of Dan's face to check if he was still in attendance. Dan nodded, finding himself more interested than he had expected to be, and Skip continued.

"But, to me the really fascinating part is that this vast pool of neglected DNA might well be the genetic basis for our future evolution as a species. That's what we're studying."

"Wait a second. How is that?" Dan asked.

"It turns out that mutations tend to accumulate faster within this pool of apparently unused DNA because they aren't selected out as rigorously, if at all. In other words, since most of these genes are non-coding, it doesn't matter if they're damaged. In fact, animal experiments have shown that damage done intentionally to these genes has no effect on the viability of the organism. The other side of that coin is that it's also possible for beneficial mutations to accumulate more rapidly in these areas and become functional. And so, my friend, you just might be the vehicle for the next jump in human evolution."

"I seriously doubt that. And if I am, God help us all."

"Hey, don't kick yourself around so much, man. You're really worried about this A thing, aren't you."

"I guess I really am. The thing is, during one session it seems like I'm seeing clear DID indications. But then next time it all turns to crap and it isn't clear at all. If anything, she's borderline dissociative. Her background, at least the part I've been able to get to so far, just doesn't fit with a typical DID patient, if there is such a thing. You ever heard of CRI over on the Eastside? The Carver Research Institute?"

"I've heard of it. Don't know anything about it, though."

"Turns out they're running a clinical trial right now around a new DID therapy. It uses some sophisticated new non-invasive brain stimulation technology to allow patients to constructively explore the traumatic past without fear, without switching."

"Sounds like it could be useful here, with A."

"Maybe. I don't know. I just have a basic distrust of shortcuts like this. Everything about my training and experience tells me that patients need to work through the pain, to take time with it. Still, in A's case, I don't know, maybe it's worth a shot. Doesn't look like I can help her anyway."

"So what're you going to do?" asked Skip.

"I called over there this afternoon and actually got a real person. Hamilton, I think it was. Dr. Hamilton. I've got a consult with him on Monday. Ever heard of him?"

"No, but that doesn't mean anything. I'm not really in touch with the psychiatry crowd."

"Sure. We'll see how it goes. I was starting to feel out of my depth, anyway."

TWENTY-TWO

. . . .

O n Monday morning, Dan Gunnison walked through the tall glass doors of the Carver Research Institute. He glanced around and saw more glass, polished chrome, light woods, and a sparkling view of the bay behind the reception desk.

"Can I help you sir?" came a voice from behind the desk.

"Oh, yes, sorry—caught up in the scenery. I'm Dan Gunnison, here for an eight o'clock with Dr. Hamilton. A consult, actually. I'm not a patient."

"Certainly, Dr. Gunnison. Just one moment." The receptionist paged Hamilton through her headset.

"No, I'm not . . . never mind. Thank you," Dan mumbled.

A few moments later, a stocky man in a white lab coat strode down the hall. He extended his hand and Dan noticed a slight tremor. The man's graying hair was thinning on top and it seemed strange to Dan that there would be tiny beads of sweat on his brow. The office was a bit cool, if anything.

"Dan Gunnison? I'm Charles Hamilton. Come on in. Coffee?"

"Yes, please. That'd be great."

"Cyndi, would you mind? Thank you."

Hamilton led Dan down a long, tastefully decorated corridor and ushered him into a small, dimly lit, and well-appointed office with a couch, two chairs, and an exotic hardwood desk. Cyndi appeared moments later with two coffees on a silver tray, along with cream and various types of sweeteners.

"Thank you, Cyndi," said Hamilton with a nervous smile. So, Mr. Gunnison . . ."

"Call me Dan, please."

"Sure. Dan, first of all, thanks for taking the time to meet with me this morning. I'm sure you're quite busy, so let me get right to it."

"Oh, glad to be here. Quite an amazing facility you've got."

"Yes, it is, isn't it. And, we've got some of the best psychiatric minds in the country right here, too, not to mention a state-of-the-art lab and our own pharmacy." Hamilton had picked up a pen and was tapping it lightly on a notepad as he spoke.

Dan glanced around as if he could see the lab and pharmacy from where he was seated. He nodded and waited for Hamilton to continue. Dan had an odd, out-of-context feeling, as if Hamilton were one of his clients in a first session. He tried to resist analysis but the man's nervousness was so palpable. *Why is this guy so uneasy, or is it impatience. Fear? Why around me? Maybe that's how he is around everyone.*

"So, please, tell me about your DID client. How certain is your diagnosis?" asked Hamilton, the pen still tapping.

"Well, that's kind of a big issue, actually. She decided to terminate therapy before I could formally make the diagnosis. Her background doesn't seem to fit the model very well. I don't believe there's true abuse or any major trauma. But there is abandonment and neglect. I just didn't get far enough with the therapy to dig further."

"Hmm, and what about alter emergence? Was that clear?" Hamilton had transferred the pen to his mouth and was nibbling on the cap.

"It seemed clearer than anything else, but even that, I have to say, wasn't definitive."

"How many?" asked Hamilton. He dropped the pen, grunted and bent down to pick it up.

"I'm sorry? How many what?" Dan asked.

"How many alters?"

"Oh, that's hard to say with any certainty, but I think I've observed three: an older doctor, a child, and possibly a teenager."

"And the patient herself, how old is she?"

"Thirty."

"Her name?"

"Her name is Allison Walker. She's a yacht broker in Seattle. Owns and operates the business. Single, smart, engaging, angry—at least right now she seems a bit angry; that's new."

"Is there a particular part that's showing the anger?" Hamilton laid the pen down and had folded his hands on the desk in front of him.

"It seems to be right there on the surface, coming from the host identity. I didn't detect any switching when I observed it."

"Do you know what it's about. Think it's significant?"

"No, I don't know. Again, there wasn't time. It appears to be directed at me but I suspect transference."

"Yes, of course." Hamilton was smiling now and Dan wasn't sure how to interpret this change in demeanor. "What about the usual diagnostic tools? Have they been of any help?" asked Hamilton, returning to the central topic.

"I was planning to do the SCID-D interview. That would've been my next step."

"But you didn't have time, I'm assuming, given your client's decision."

"Right. So, I'm guessing that Allison doesn't really fit your profile for the trial," said Dan. "That's no problem, really."

"To the contrary, actually. I think she might be an ideal candidate."

Dan was surprised, not only at Hamilton's response but also at his own reaction to it. He was prepared to be relieved because it was hard to imagine Allison in this environment. It just didn't seem right for her. But, Hamilton apparently felt otherwise.

"Why is that?" Dan asked.

"Oh, it's really quite technical and I won't bother you with the details, but I think having her in the trial would be mutually beneficial. Could we extend our meeting for an hour or so? I'd like to get a more detailed history and assessment from you. Can I have Cyndi help you with any rescheduling you might need to do?" Hamilton appeared to relax.

"Uh, sure, I can stay for a while. I don't have a client session until eleven but I do have a haircut scheduled for nine-thirty. Maybe she could cancel that for me."

"Absolutely, let's take care of that right now. I really appreciate your flexibility, Dan."

When Dan left Hamilton's office a little over an hour later, he was confused. He felt good about having a concrete plan to present to Allison, something that had a chance of helping her move forward. But at the same time, he felt uneasy about her acceptance into the trial. It bothered him that the borderline nature of Allison's condition was the thing that seemed to have tipped the scales in her favor. If anything, it should have tipped them the other way. Are they really in her favor? *Am I doing the right thing for my client here?*

As he drove across the bridge to Seattle, Dan continued to wrestle with this apparent contradiction. Allison was in, but why? Did it really matter? She would get help. But he wouldn't have anything to do with the outcome. As long as she gets help. *I need to let go. She's not even my client anymore.*

As traffic on the bridge slowed to a stop, Dan made a call to Allison and was relieved when it went to voicemail. He left a detailed message with the news that she had been accepted into the trial at CRI and that she would hear from the institute soon. He urged her to join the trial and wished her well.

She was just a client, Dan thought, as he swallowed against a dull ache in his throat. Cars began moving again and Dan followed them into the city.

TWENTY-THREE

· ·

Three weeks later, on her cruise to work across the smooth surface of Lake Union, Allison checked her voicemail. She glanced back over her right shoulder at the towering Space Needle and the residential hump of Queen Anne Hill, and, as she did, Allison found herself hoping that Dan would call to check up on her. But, at the same time, she always felt relieved when there were no messages from him; this time was no exception. *Dissociation. That's what Dan had called it. Being of two minds about something. Everybody does it, right?*

There was another message from Dr. Hamilton at CRI. Allison had ignored the other four and did the same with this one. Hamilton sounded insistent, almost desperate, she felt, and there was something disconcerting about that. Besides, this was a clinical trial. Allison knew that she wouldn't be guaranteed real treatment. She might be put on a placebo protocol. So, what was the point?

Allison swung the dinghy deftly into the dock and walked up the ramp to her office.

The first half of the day passed quickly. She showed two boats, both at the brokerage dock, made some follow-up calls, and reviewed a closing document. Buried in the day's stack of mail, Allison found a letter from the Carver Research Institute. She tossed it in the recycle bin, grabbed her purse, and headed out the door to find some lunch.

She found it on Eastlake Avenue, just a short hike up and away from the water, at her favorite sit-down deli squeezed in between a tiny maritime bookstore and a noisy bar full of noontime celebrants. The whole street was like that: an eclectic and bewildering mix of small businesses, restaurants and espresso bars. Allison stepped up to the counter and scanned the menu on the chalkboard. She already knew what she wanted but looked anyway, thinking that maybe she'd force herself to go for something different this time.

But it never happened. The place made a simple sliced turkey sandwich on freshly baked sourdough with homemade cranberry mayonnaise and the crispest lettuce; Allison just couldn't switch to anything else. It was almost as good as Margaret's and would have been if the deli had added thin slices of green apple to the recipe.

"Hey, Doc," smiled Randal from behind the counter. "The usual?"

Allison nodded, paid for her lunch and quickly glanced around to see if she knew anyone. No familiar faces. Randal's "Doc" reference had come from a time when Allison had performed the Heimlich maneuver on a choking customer and probably saved his life. In the process, she had said something which indirectly led Randal—and everyone else in the deli—to believe she was a doctor; she had never attempted to correct the impression. The longer the misunderstanding persisted, the harder it became to undo, and so, reluctantly, she let it stand.

Allison took her meal to an outside table and sat down. The day had turned out to be unseasonably warm, and she breathed in the fresh air, enjoying the ever-changing street scene as she savored her sandwich. She was having a very pleasant time up to the moment a scream came from inside the deli and she turned to see Randal running toward her.

"Doc, help! It's Hannah!" He ran back to the kitchen and Allison followed without a second thought, leaving her handbag on the table.

Hannah, the deli's baker, was on the floor of the kitchen, clutching her stomach and moaning, her eyes as wide as silver dollars.

"Has anyone called 911?" Allison shouted.

No one responded.

She barked at Randal, "Do it now!" Then she knelt down and tried to get her patient to focus.

"Hannah, look at me. You're going to be fine. I'm here to help you, but I need to know exactly where it hurts. Can you show me?"

Between keening moans, Hannah pointed to her lower right abdomen.

"Good. Now I'm going to apply a little pressure here and I want you to tell me what you feel, okay?"

Hannah looked up at Allison with panic in her eyes, then over to Randal."

"It's okay, she's a doctor. You're going to be fine. Just tell her what you feel," said Randal, between answers to the 911 dispatcher.

Hannah nodded once and then closed her eyes. Allison pulled up Hannah's top enough to expose her belly and placed two fingers firmly on her lower right abdominal area and began to gently press. She noted a small mass and Hannah yelped with pain. When Allison removed the pressure, Hannah cried out again. *Both primary and rebound tenderness. Some form of parietal involvement, probably appendicitis.* "I'm sorry, just one more quick check."

This time Allison moved to Hannah's left side and palpated again. "Ow!" Hannah involuntarily clutched at her right side and Allison nodded.

"Okay, that's all, Hannah. No more pressing. We're going to get you to the hospital where they can take care of you.

Hannah moaned, rolled to her side and vomited on the floor. Allison immediately noticed that her patient's eyes had rolled back and she was now motionless. Allison cleared Hannah's mouth and checked for breathing.

Just then, two EMTs rushed into the room with a stretcher, scanning for their patient.

"Over here!" shouted Allison, waving them toward her. "Patient is female, mid-twenties, acute appendicitis. Rovsing's sign is positive. Let's get her loaded up and start pushing antibiotics on the way. Rupture seems imminent."

"And you are?" asked one of the EMTs over his shoulder as he and his partner slid Hannah onto the stretcher.

"Dr. Johansen. Kathryn Johansen."

"Okay, good enough for me. Let's get moving."

"I'm coming with you," decided Allison on the spot. Hannah did not look good.

Once in the ambulance, An EMT set up an IV with antibiotics as Allison had ordered, along with the usual monitoring gear. Allison, meanwhile, kept one eye on her patient as she scanned the equipment around her. She tried to identify everything, to remember as much as possible. To remember. *What the hell am I doing?*

Siren screaming, the ambulance raced toward Harborview Medical Center. As Allison thought about their destination, it suddenly occurred to her that she didn't know what to do when they arrived. Would there be paperwork? Allison tried to contain the panic and concentrate on her patient. Hannah had just regained consciousness, her pale face once again contorted with pain. Allison reached out to hold her hand. It was hot. "It's okay, Hannah, we're almost there. You're going to be just fine."

Then the ambulance came to an abrupt halt and Allison heard other sirens. She grabbed the intercom microphone. "What's going on? Why aren't we moving?"

"Doctor, I'm sorry, but there's an accident ahead," the driver said. "Checking alternatives now."

Allison kept holding Hannah's hand and reassuring her as they waited. "I know it hurts. It won't be long now. Just stay with me, Hannah. We're going to get you through this. Just stay with me."

Allison picked up the mic again. "Alternatives?"

"Hold on a sec . . . I'm sorry Doctor, but it looks like there's been a pileup behind us too. It's bad. There's cars on the sidewalk. Wait, maybe there's . . . No, sorry, I just can't move until they . . . I'm hearing emergency calls on the radio for . . ."

Allison tuned him out. She whispered to the EMT in the back with her. "We need to find a way out of this mess. The antibiotics can only do so much. The peritonitis has probably been at it for a while. Internal bleeding's likely, too, from the look of her."

"You want my input, Doctor, uh, I'm sorry, I forgot your name?"

"Johansen. And yes, I would like your advice."

"We've been stuck right around this area before, and we always managed to get out within five or six minutes, but that was without accidents on both ends. I think we've got three options: airlift; walking her out on a stretcher over to another street where we can get picked up; or field surgery. Airlift is unlikely, and even if we could get a chopper close by, it would be a least twenty, thirty minutes. Walking her out? Even more time. I think you should open her up right here, Dr. Johansen."

Allison felt as if she'd been kicked in the stomach. *Here? Now? Me? Get it together, Allie. You're deep into it now.* "Right. Do you have a surgical kit onboard?"

The EMT gave Allison a quizzical look. "Yes, of course, the usual. You'll have to handle it the old fashioned way, though, if that's what you mean. No laparoscopic equipment. You okay, Dr. Johansen?"

"Yes, yes, I'm fine. Sorry, just not used to working this way. Okay, can you help me prep her?"

"I'm on it, Doc. What do you want for the general?"

General? What's he talking about? Come on, Kathryn! Oh, God, yes, anesthetic. Uh . . . , okay, what was that common non-barbiturate? "Propofol. Start a Propofol drip please. Uh, I'm sorry; I never asked your name."

"Gerald. Call me Gerry."

"Okay, thanks Gerry. Here we go. BP?"

"One forty-two over ninety. On the high side but stable."

Gerry spoke to the driver, letting him know what they were doing and telling him not to move the vehicle, even if the blockage cleared. Allison felt grateful for the man's expertise and felt, for a instant, that they just might get through this together. They had to.

When Hannah was clearly under, Gerry prepared the sterile field, exposing the lower right abdomen. Allison watched and searched her memory. Kathryn knew this. It was a common emergency surgery. *Just have to be careful of the muscular structure. Sure glad Hannah's so slim.*

Allison scrubbed up, donned a mask, nodded to Gerry, and examined the area, palpating it gently. She noted the position of the mass again, making a small mark on the skin. She then checked herself by spreading her hand across the abdomen from the umbilicus to the anterior superior iliac spine. One third the distance up: McBurney's point.

"Base of the appendix should be right about . . . here." Allison made another mark, a couple of inches from the first one.

"Scalpel, please." *I can't believe I'm doing this. Kathryn, what about the musculature?*

Allison closed her eyes for a moment, trying to get a good image. *Okay, slit the External Oblique Aponeurosis. Just deep enough, no more. Good, not much bleeding. Now, at a right angle, the Internal Oblique . . . oh, more blood here.*

"Suction, please, Gerry. Thank you."

"Okay, here we are," said Allison when she could get a clear view through the incision. *Incredible! Look at that—the appendix, right there on the end of the cecum. Definitely distended and infected but not burst—that's what's causing her pain and it extends down lower than it should.*

Allison palpated the organ, checked its position, and verified that it was indeed the mass that she had felt from the surface.

"Ligature, please, Gerry," she said, with her left hand extended.

Gerry was ready with the material and Allison quickly tied off the appendix at the base and completed the ligation, much to her own amazement. Allison tried as hard as she could to mask her incredulity at the result. She inverted the tiny stump and pushed it into the cecum.

Carefully removing the inflamed appendix from the abdominal cavity, Allison dropped the organ into the stainless steel tray which Gerry held ready.

"Thank you, Gerry. Excellent work."

"You too, Doctor. You saved this girl from a lot of anguish."

Allison nodded, accepting the praise outwardly, but inside she was torn. She was a yacht broker, not a surgeon. *I could've killed that poor girl.* But she hadn't, this time, and she needed to be a doctor for a few more minutes.

Allison turned back to Hannah and forced herself to concentrate. She sponged up the small amount of blood in the incision and disinfected the site. Her hands were shaking and she tried to maintain control over her voice. "Are you an RN, Gerry?"

"Yes."

"Good. Surgical?"

"Yes."

"Would you please close her up? I'm feeling a bit shaky." *I could've killed her. She could still die. What have I done?*

"Sure, Doctor. No problem. Why don't you have a seat."

Allison watched through a mental fog as Gerry skillfully stitched up the Internal Oblique with dissolving suture material and then dealt with the external musculature and skin. He applied a topical antibiotic and covered the wound with a bandage.

"Excellent," said Allison, forcing herself back into physician mode.

"Thanks, Doc. Should I bring her back out?"

"Yes, and let's give her an analgesic. That Propofol's not going to help with the post-surgical pain."

"Will do."

Allison pulled her phone from a pocket and glanced at the screen as if she had just received a message. "Gerry, sorry, I've got to go. Looks to me like you've got everything under control."

Allison pushed open the back door of the ambulance and stepped out into the brightness of the street. Her stomach rebelled and she fought down the urge the vomit. *I could've killed her!*

"But, Doc, what about the admitting forms and all the rest?" Gerry shouted after her.

"Sorry, another emergency. Please handle it for me. I've got to go!"

Allison closed the door and scanned the chaotic scene around her. She was breathing rapidly and tried to control it, to no avail. Her stomach lurched again. Three cars were up on the sidewalk and medics were working to free trapped motorists and treat the injured. An old gray pickup truck was on fire, having hit a lamppost and severed its fuel line.

Allison felt Kathryn's pull toward the victims and pushed back. She tried to turn and run in the opposite direction but her legs felt like heavy columns of water contained only by thin membranes. This slowed her progress to a dragging walk and a part of her consciousness made a confused attempt at self-diagnosis. Her whole being felt sluggish, and Allison's world began a bewildering rotation. She reached out for the arm of a storefront bench as it lazily swept through her narrowing field of vision.

Everything's so quiet now. What does this mean, Kathryn? Pressure falling. Maybe just a little rest. Just a little . . .

TWENTY-FOUR

. . . .

Voices. There were voices in the dark. Strange voices. Except one. That one she had heard before. It was asking questions but there just wasn't enough room to answer. No space to speak into. Best to be quiet and crawl back into the corner where it was warm and dark. Safe.

But eventually the voices found their way in, even to that remote corner. At first, it wasn't hard to ignore them and go back to sleep. But later—days, hours, minutes?—it became much harder. And later still, the voices became an annoyance. So she crawled out of her dark corner to investigate, to silence the voices so she could crawl back, curl up, and get some rest.

What are they doing yelling like that at this hour? thought Allison through her dark haze. She remembered something her adopted mother used to say and she tried to use it politely against the intruders: *Indoor voices, please! Indoor voices!* But they didn't seem to hear. Or maybe they were just ignoring her. She began to feel foolish for even trying.

Allison winced at the sudden presence of a bright pinhole of light ahead, and it made her want to go back to the corner. Not safe out there. But the voices were getting clearer and she was able to pick out a word or two. That got her attention, even against her will. She didn't want to hear the words, let alone make the effort to interpret them. And yet, there was something important going on.

"Still non-responsive . . . Seventy three over forty two . . . Falling . . . Pulse erratic."

On the way back to her cozy corner, Allison thought about these words. Some patient was in trouble; that much was clear. Could it be . . .

oh, what was her name? The girl at the deli? I should help her but it's too dark to work here, and I'm too tired. Much too tired. Get an intern to go check on her. Is there a blanket here somewhere? I need to cover up. It's getting cold.

Allison huddled in her corner, hugging herself against the chill. At first she rocked back and forth and then it felt better just to sit, not to move at all. It wasn't so bad, really. It would be nice to go to sleep now. Just let go and fall into the softness below. But, wait, Kathryn didn't think much of this idea. In fact, there was a warning there, somewhere in that Kathryn space. *Don't do it. Don't go down there, Allie.* But it was so hard to resist. It would be quieter down there—softer, warmer, peaceful. No voices down there. No lights. Quiet. It sounded so good to her. She argued with Kathryn's ideas in a confused fog. But the warnings were persistent.

Later, there were outside voices again. *Why can't they just leave me alone?* Allison thought. But the words kept coming in and Allison tried to discard each one as it arrived, so as not to trouble herself with its meaning. Then, a few words began to stick together in phrases. These were harder to throw away, as much as Allison tried. And then, one phrase leapt up at her like a predator: " . . . can send her back now."

Send her back? Send *you* back.

"No!" Allison heard herself shout from her little corner, through the haze, through the barrier. The sound of her own voice startled her into the raw, noisy physical world. She found herself lying on her back, unable to move, seeing a light green wall moving quickly along beside her right side, a door passing by every few seconds, a ceiling sliding by above.

And the voices. The voices were there again, but clearer this time.

"Looks like our Jane Doe's back," said someone behind Allison.

"I keep telling you," said a familiar voice, "it's *Doctor* Kathryn Johansen."

"Hey, Gerry, I keep telling *you*, she's got no ID and until we can talk to her, doctor or no doctor, her chart says Jane Doe and that's who she is for now. Come on man, you know the drill! Now let's get her to Recovery. We've got a bunch more in the ER worse than she is."

"Yeah, you're right. You go on back. I'll take her from here."

"You sure, man?"

"Yeah, no problem. Go ahead. I'll catch up with you in a few minutes."

The doors kept going by and Allison tried to tilt her head back, raising her eyes far enough to look behind her. *Gerry. Yes, the ambulance. Hannah. Surgery. Oh, God, no.*

"Oh, there we are. How are we doing, Dr. Johansen?" asked Gerry.

"Head hurts, can't tell much else yet," muttered Allison. "How's Hannah doing?"

"She's fine, thanks to you. She's in good condition, recovering up on the fourth floor."

"Oh, what a relief. That's great."

"But you, you had us pretty worried there for a while," said Gerry, still pushing Allison's gurney down the hallway. He leaned over so that she could see him better. "Quite a smack on the head. Just came back from Radiology. They weren't going to do the MRI because you didn't have your insurance card, but I vouched for you. Do you know where it might be? Your ID and all?"

"I think I left my bag at the deli."

"Okay, good, we'll get all this cleared up soon. I'll have someone go pick it up for you."

"Thanks, Gerry, but . . ."

"Don't worry; you just rest. Just rest. I'll take care of everything."

In spite of her efforts to stay awake and correct Gerry's misapprehensions, Allison did rest. When she woke again, she was in a private hospital room with mauve colored walls and a window looking out onto a dark sky. The room lights were dim, the TV was off, and the only sound Allison could hear was her own pulse faithfully repeated by the cardiac monitor to the left on the wall behind her. She thought about silencing the monitor, but when she raised herself high enough to see it, she quickly realized that it was a much newer model than the ones she understood. And anyway, her temples throbbed so badly that she was forced to lie flat again. She reached up to hold her aching head and felt the heavy bandage for the first time.

I must have hit something when I went down. There was a bench. Maybe that was it. The metal armrest. Ouch.

Sleep came again, involuntarily, and when Allison next awoke, sunlight filtered in from the window. Her head felt a bit better but she had to pee, badly. When she tried to sit up, Allison realized that she was hooked up not only to the cardiac monitor but also to an IV. She fumbled around, found the nurse call button and pushed it.

Please, someone. I really, really need to get to the bathroom.

But no one came. She hit the button again, then again. On her fourth attempt, a nurse finally answered over the intercom.

"Someone will be with you in just a few minutes, Miss Walker."

Walker? Oh, no.

As if in parallel defeat, Allison's bladder released. She felt the wet warmth spreading between her legs and onto the bed, but she could no more stop the flow of urine than she could reverse the events of the previous day. She lay in the bed, helpless, weak, wet and humiliated.

TWENTY-FIVE

· ·

In the quiet moments before his staff arrived, Dr. Seth Carver sipped a latte while scanning the Seattle Times on his PDA. He felt a momentary pang of guilt at using valuable time for such a pursuit but successfully quashed the feeling by rationalizing his behavior as necessary. How could one make sound business decisions without being generally well-informed about the state of the world? Besides, he was Seth Carver, wasn't he? And Seth Carver had earned the right to do anything he damn well pleased. He clicked through to the local news.

A headline immediately caught his eye: "Seattle Yacht Broker Does Surgery Too." He clicked on the link and read the short article.

Times staff and news services
SEATTLE — Yesterday, in a small deli on Fairview Avenue, a young woman collapsed. A regular patron, claiming to be a Dr. Kathryn Johansen, stepped in to help and later accompanied the victim in an ambulance to the hospital.

"She knew exactly what to do—just took over and did what was needed," said Randall Harris, owner of the Eastlake Deli. "And this wasn't the first time either. She saved a life here a few months ago. Nicest person you'll ever meet."

According to sources at Harborview Medical Center who asked to remain anonymous, Dr. Johansen carried no ID with her and was later identified as Allison Walker, a yacht broker and owner of Rain City Yachts in Seattle.

The story might have ended there, but it took an even more bizarre twist when the Times discovered that Ms. Walker had actually performed an emergency appendectomy aboard the ambulance when the vehicle became stuck in a major traffic accident en route to the hospital. After the surgery, Walker reportedly left the ambulance abruptly and became a victim herself, sustaining head injuries from a fall near the traffic accident site.

Walker and her "patient" were taken by a second vehicle to Harborview where she was treated and regained consciousness several hours later. Walker's unidentified patient is in good condition, recovering from the apparently successful emergency surgery.

Walker's patient is not pressing charges but, according to the District Attorney's office, Walker may still face felony charges involving the practice of medicine without a license.

Carver tucked his PDA into a coat pocket and smiled. He pressed an icon on his desktop and left a message for his assistant. It simply said: "Get Hamilton in here ASAP."

A half hour later, Dr. Charles Hamilton walked into Carver's office, his white coat wrinkled and his face flushed. His prematurely thinning hair seemed to wander over his head, not able to find a suitable resting place.

"You wanted to see me?"

"Yes, it's about the trial and the patient you haven't been able to enroll."

Carver did not invite his employee to sit, but Hamilton didn't seem to care. He sat anyway, heavily, legs sprawled out in front of him. He let his head sink into his hands and then looked up with reddened eyes.

"Look, Seth, I've been here all night trying to find another patient, another way, something. Okay? I'm exhausted, so if you're going to fire my ass, just do it now and get it over with."

"Actually, I intend to save your sorry ass, against my better judgment. Have you seen the Times this morning?"

"Are you kidding? I haven't had time for the newspaper in weeks!"

"Well, if you'd taken the time to stay better informed, you might have run across this little article." Carver slid his PDA across the smooth surface of his desk.

Hamilton scanned the article listlessly. And then, "Oh shit! It's her. It's Walker. Now we'll never get her." His head sunk back into his hands.

Carver slowly shook his head. How could anyone be this dense? Why had he hired Hamilton, anyway? There must have been some reason, other than the Harvard degree. He decided to take a different approach. *Focus on the clinical trial, not the barriers like this idiot. Leverage the barriers. Use them to your advantage.*

"Charles, Charles, look at me. If you weren't so exhausted, I'm sure you'd see the opportunity here. I know you've been working hard at this. It's been a tough slog, but look, here's your big chance. It's almost being handed to us. Just go down to the hospital and convince them that this is a medical issue, not a legal one. Work with the Seattle police, the DA's office, whatever. Make a deal. Get Roth involved if you have to, but just get Walker in here."

Charles Hamilton lifted his head and nodded slowly. He stood up, turned, and walked to the door. Before opening it, he reached down and tugged on his coat, as if to straighten out some of the wrinkles. He ran a hand through his hair, straightened his back, and walked out.

TWENTY-SIX

· ·

T he next morning, Dr. Charles Hamilton walked into Harborview Medical Center feeling better than he had in weeks. He had conferred with Mrs. Roth, which had been less painful than he'd feared, then actually gotten nine hours of sleep, felt rested, and was ready to take advantage of the opportunity before him. He was wearing a freshly cleaned gray suit, a crisp white button-down shirt, and a classic red silk tie. Even his thinning hair had seemed rather distinguished in the mirror that morning. Dr. Hamilton took an elevator to the third floor, where a receptionist at the Adult Medicine Clinic greeted him.

"Good morning. How can I help you?"

"Yes, good morning. I'm Dr. Hamilton from the Carver Research Institute, here for a meeting with Dr. Archer."

"Oh, yes, just a moment Dr. Hamilton." The receptionist picked up the phone, spoke a few words, and put it back down with a bright smile. "Just have a seat. Dr. Archer will be right with you. Can I get you anything?"

"No thank you, I'm fine," replied Hamilton.

And he felt fine. Even fine enough to deal with the tall, self-assured figure of a doctor who appeared moments later with his hand extended.

"A pleasure to meet you, Dr. Hamilton. Sam Archer. I've heard nothing but great things about the Institute. Here, let's walk back to my office and we can talk about this interesting patient of ours."

Hamilton smiled and chatted easily with Archer as they made their way down a sterile, white hallway. Archer's office was plain but efficient looking, with a newer light oak desk, a small table in the corner with a flat screen display and keyboard, and two wooden guest chairs. Some unassuming artwork graced the walls and two small family photos sat on a neat credenza behind the desk. Dr. Archer motioned for Hamilton to take a seat and then lowered his own athletic frame into his desk chair.

"So, you think our Ms. Walker may be DID? What an interesting case, don't you think?" asked Archer. "And a surprisingly nice, intelligent young woman."

"Yes, fascinating. Sounds like she may be looking at some legal trouble though. Any news there?"

"Maybe, yes. A Seattle detective showed up yesterday and spent a few minutes with her. The girl Walker operated on isn't pressing charges but the DA seems keen on prosecuting anyway. I'm sure I don't understand all of the legal and political issues but my main interest is the wellbeing of the patient, as I'm sure yours is," said Archer with a smile.

"Absolutely," replied Hamilton. "And, as I'm sure you know, we're in the midst of a clinical trial involving a new treatment protocol for DID and related illnesses. Allison Walker was actually accepted into the trial a few weeks ago but she never showed up. We'd pretty much given up hope and actually restarted the recruiting process. Then this happened. We'd like to be of help, if we can. Maybe explore some kind of arrangement with the DA that involves mandatory treatment in place of jail time or a fine. Something like that."

"That's good of you, but I think that Walker's attorney may already be working on some kind of a deal."

Hamilton's heart sank. "Really? I didn't know she'd gotten a lawyer involved. What kind of a deal?"

"I don't really know, but I'd be happy to put you in touch with the attorney."

At a nod from Hamilton, Archer walked over to his computer and tapped a few keys. "Let's see. The attorney is . . . just a second. Yes, it's Margaret Yee, here in Seattle. I'll get you her number."

While Archer was working on that, Hamilton asked, "What about Walker's head injuries? How serious are those?"

"Actually, not nearly as bad as we first thought. She has one fairly nasty laceration, just back of her hairline above the left temple, apparently from an encounter with a park bench. We closed her up without complication. She had a concussion and was unconscious for a couple of hours and her MRI initially caused quite a stir."

"Oh? What was that all about?"

"The etiology is confusing, but Allison Walker's cerebral cortex shows some abnormality. Volumetrically, her frontal lobes are approximately six percent larger than normal, but there is no evidence of swelling, hemorrhaging, or any other pathology. The size differential is completely symmetrical. Initially we thought that we were looking at something related to her recent trauma, but I'm convinced that this is a congenital abnormality. Actually, abnormality is too strong a word. Put simply, Allison Walker just has a larger brain that most of us."

"Interesting," said Hamilton, without feeling much real interest. He was worried about the lawyer and how she might impact his ability to get Walker into the trial, or more to the point, how she might disrupt the plan to save his own career.

"Yes," continued Archer. "Interesting enough that we obtained Walker's permission to send some tissue samples from her head wound over to the UW for analysis. I've got a colleague over there who's doing some fascinating work in genetics. Oh, here's that number for you."

Archer gave Hamilton the phone number for Margaret Yee, they discussed a few more details about Walker's medical status, and then the meeting came to an end. The two doctors shook hands and Hamilton found his own way out as Archer took a phone call.

On the way over the bridge to Bellevue, Hamilton punched in the number for Margaret Yee. *I've got to work this carefully*, he thought as the call was answered.

"Good morning, this is Margaret Yee."

"Yes, good morning. This is Dr. Charles Hamilton of the Carver Research Institute in Bellevue. I believe we may have a mutual client in Ms. Allison Walker. Do you have a moment to talk?"

"Yes, can you hold on for just a moment?"

"Certainly."

"Thanks. I need to put you on hold for a few seconds. I'll be right back."

Moments later, "Dr. Hamilton, thanks for waiting. I was just on a call with Ms. Walker so I took the opportunity to get her permission to speak with you about her case."

"Oh, excellent. How did she respond?"

"She's okay with us having a discussion about her situation—a little reluctant at first, but she agreed. She seems to know who you are."

"Good. I'm hoping that you and I might be able to work together to Ms. Walker's benefit."

"Well, I suppose that depends upon what you have in mind."

"Ms. Yee, are you aware that Allison Walker has been accepted as a patient in a clinical trial at CRI for the treatment of Dissociative Identity Disorder?"

"I know that she's been involved in psychotherapy, but this clinical trial that you mention, no, I'm not specifically aware of that."

Hamilton sensed the upper hand and smiled inwardly. "Yes, she was referred to us by her therapist, a Mr. Dan Gunnison. It turns out that she's a good match with our criteria and we offered her a position in the trial."

"Okay . . ." said Margaret.

"But she never responded."

"Oh, I see. Maybe that's why she never discussed this with me."

"Perhaps, yes. But here's what I'm thinking, Margaret. May I call you Margaret?"

"Yes, of course."

"Good, please call me Charles. Here's what I'm thinking. If it looks like there may be an indictment in the works, perhaps we can head things off and avoid a lot of unpleasantness for our client. Is that of interest to you?"

"Naturally. Go on."

"Good. I believe that we might be able to convince the DA that felony charges aren't warranted in this case."

"That would be a good thing," said Margaret. "But how would you imagine doing that? Campbell's a tough guy, not known to bend easily once he's made up his mind to proceed. In fact, I've spent the better portion of today racking my brain trying to find the right angle for a discussion with him."

"Well, this might just be the angle we need then. I've been told by very reliable sources that Dick Campbell is worried about reelection. He's generally viewed as a heartless bastard, which I guess isn't necessarily a bad quality for a district attorney, but apparently it's starting to turn some voter sentiment against him. We can give him a way to change that image but without looking too soft."

"Okay, how?"

"Well, you and I both know that it would be pointless to deny the fact that Walker performed a serious, even life-endangering, medical procedure without a license. There's just too much evidence, and it's very public."

"Yes, I don't think Allison, I mean Ms. Walker, would try to deny that. But, there is some room for discussion on technicalities. For example, there was never any attempt at personal gain. Walker's actions appear to be based purely on some misguided but altruistic motive—nothing more. When you add to that the fact that this appears to be an isolated incident, it becomes very difficult to claim that there was any real form of 'medical practice' involved here."

"Exactly. And if we were faced with anyone but Campbell in the DA's office, I don't think we'd even need to have this discussion. There probably wouldn't be any charges at all—at least not at the felony level. But, as things stand . . ."

"Right, I agree," replied Margaret. "Which brings us back to finding some kind of compromise with Campbell."

"Yes, and the way we do that is to argue for some form of mandatory psychiatric treatment for Ms. Walker's unfortunate affliction. And, since she has already been accepted into the CRI trial, all we need to do is to add some enforcement, some oversight, to the situation."

"Meaning what, exactly?"

"Well, meaning that we would have to agree to full-time care for a period of time."

"Confinement, you mean?"

"Let me assure you, Margaret, that her situation would be very comfortable. At our facility in Bellevue we have two special patient rooms—actually more like studio apartments—which are much nicer than the ones most people call home. They even have Lake Washington views. We would agree to put her up in one of those for the duration, approximately six weeks."

"Okay, look, Charles, I have to ask you, why are you so eager to do this? What's in this for you, for CRI? Oh, and another thing, this is a clinical trial, right? So how could you guarantee real treatment and not placebo?"

"Fair questions, Margaret. Let me address them for you head-on." Hamilton pulled into the parking lot at CRI and turned off the engine. He took a deep breath and continued. "First, you have to understand that finding suitable candidates for this trial is extremely difficult. DID is not as uncommon as we once thought, but it still relatively rare in the population. It is not a disease in any classical sense, but a result of serious psychological or physical trauma in the patient's past. But even more significant—and a big problem for us—is that DID sufferers often try to deal with their situations on their own. The very nature of the condition involves self-protection, and personality parts will often resist any attempt to get the whole system, the patient, into therapy. So, the bottom line is this: it is very, very tough to find candidates for this work, and that makes Ms. Walker, to be frank, a highly valuable commodity for us."

"A commodity? Come on!"

"I'm sorry, a poor choice of words, but I'm trying to help you understand our motivation here."

"Okay, I get that. Now, what about this issue of the trial itself?"

"Yes, of course. This trial is not at all typical in the sense that it involves both a medical procedure—painless and non-invasive as it may be—and traditional therapy sessions. The therapy is still the biggest factor in determining success or failure, and the variables involved with that are almost impossible to control. The medical procedure is the controllable and truly novel element. It is designed to make the patient open to therapy. It temporarily reduces or eliminates fears specifically associated with the patient's traumatic memories that must ultimately be the subjects of therapy. Am I making sense to you?"

"Yes," replied Margaret. "But I still don't see how you can guarantee that the real treatment will be provided in Walker's case. Isn't this a classic randomized double-blind trial?"

"Yes, it is. Sorry, I was getting to that point. All patients in this trial are given the same opportunity for therapy and all are fitted with the equipment involved in the medical procedure during therapy sessions. The difference is that this equipment is activated for some patients and not for others. The therapists remain unaware of the equipment's status during sessions. The equipment itself responds to a schedule that is pre-determined by random selection so that it is always activated for one set of patients and is never activated for the other set. Only at the conclusion of the trial is any of this made known to the therapists, the other researchers, and the patients themselves. If the trial is successful, then those patients who were randomly selected for placebo treatment will be given the opportunity to obtain the actual treatment at no cost."

Hamilton noticed that he had no trouble with the subtle lie involved in this description. He had to hide some of the truth in order to protect the integrity of the trial—or the perception of integrity, he reminded himself. In Walker's case, the situation was far from random. Walker would definitely get the full treatment. They needed to understand her reaction to it because she represented a marginal case, like P-239, whose schizophrenia might have been induced by the formerly un-tuned treatment protocol. He wondered why he was not more bothered by this lie, then decided that it was because he was so sure that the protocol changes made Walker's risk minimal. He could live with that.

"So, what you're saying is that Ms. Walker is guaranteed treatment only if the trial succeeds," asked Margaret.

"Basically, yes, but that's really the situation in which one would want treatment. And, from a legal perspective, you get the result you want: no felony record for your client, right?"

"Uh, yes, of course. But I have to be able to convince my client as well."

"Forgive me please, Margaret, but I feel like I'm missing something here. Your client basically gets off the hook legally, and in addition gets the best possible shot at the most advanced treatment available for her condition. It would be hard to imagine a better situation for her, don't you think?"

"Yes, you're right. It's not a bad plan. Let me confer with the client and I'll get back to you."

"Sounds good. I think we have a true win-win here, Margaret. Thanks for your time today."

"You're welcome. I'll call you back by the end of the day."

Hamilton ended the call, inhaled deeply, closed his eyes, and let out his breath in one long hiss through his front teeth. The conversation had gone almost as well as could be expected, but something bothered him. Why had Margaret Yee seemed so concerned about the treatment part of this deal? It almost sounded personal. Would she waver? He didn't think so, but still, there was a nagging possibility. If this was to work, he and she would need to present a completely unified front when meeting with the DA.

TWENTY-SEVEN

· ·

D an Gunnison put his feet up on the desk and took a moment to
enjoy the warmth of the coffee cup in his hands. The day promised
to be an eventful one, with two new clients filling empty slots and little
breathing room in between. And so, in an attempt to prepare himself, Dan
was beginning the day with some quiet reflection. He closed his eyes for a
moment, savoring the rich coffee. But when he re-opened them, something
in yesterday's newspaper on the desk under his crossed feet caught his eye
and distracted him. It was just two words, peeking out from beneath a
folded page: Yacht Broker.

He reached up, feeling the stretch in his leg muscles, and lifted a
page, exposing the small article which had ended his reverie. It took no
more than the first two sentences to alarm him. Dan yanked his feet off
the desk, spilling his coffee in the process, and focused on the rest of the
article, oblivious to the fact that the hot liquid had stained through his
khakis and was scalding his right knee.

Kathryn, Allison, surgery—it was all there. She was in deep trouble this
time. This was no longer just a social and professional inconvenience.

Ignoring the pain from the hot coffee, Dan quickly checked his
schedule on the computer. As he had feared: full until noon, starting in
ten minutes, then packed again after lunch until four-thirty. Dan felt
trapped. What would he do, anyway, even if he could get away? He had no
idea, but the adrenaline jolt from the article made him want to break out of
the office, run down to the parking lot, race to the hospital, and . . . then
what? Would Allison even be there? Then, as the endocrine surge began

to release him, Dan realized that he did have another option; he could call the hospital.

Getting the general number from Harborview's web page, Dan keyed it into his phone and waited.

"Harborview Medical Center. How may I direct your call?"

"Uh, yes, I'd like to speak with one of your patients—a Ms. Allison Walker."

"Just a moment sir; I'll connect you with the third floor nursing station."

"Thanks," said Dan. As he waited, he tried to construct an approach to the conversation. Allison had stopped returning his calls weeks ago and he wasn't sure that she'd take this one, either. But he had to try.

"Adult Medicine. This is Kathy."

"Hello Kathy, my name is Dan Gunnison and I'd like to speak with one of your patients, if I might. Her name is Allison Walker."

"Oh, I'm sorry Mr. Gunnison, she was discharged early this morning."

"This morning? But it's not even eight yet."

"Uh huh. She was already gone by the time I started my shift at seven."

"Do you know how I can get in touch with her?"

"No, I'm sorry, sir. I really can't say anything. Privacy, you know."

"Yeah, I know how that goes. I'm a psychotherapist—Allison's therapist, actually." Dan winced as he intentionally omitted the word 'former' from his identification. "And I'm very worried about her current state of mind."

"Yes, well, I'm sorry, but I still can't help you. The only thing I'll say is that I think you're right to be worried. I'm sorry. I wish I could be of more help."

When Dan hung up he was even more frustrated and concerned. Had she been moved to another hospital? Arrested? The article had implied that she had legal troubles. Was she home on the boat? He tried her number, got no answer and left a message. He tried Rain City Yachts, with the same result.

Then, as Dan re-read the article for other clues, he heard his waiting room door open and knew that he must compose himself. The day had officially begun. He quickly worked on the coffee stain in his pants and went to greet his first client of the day.

Four hours and as many clients later, Dan once again had time for Allison. Lunch could wait until dinner, and another coffee, maybe with extra cream and sugar, would do in the interim. Dan walked out to the waiting room and filled up his cup. The room was blessedly empty and Dan paced in a small circle with his cup, allowing himself to work through his frustrations out loud.

"Okay, so why should I even let this bother me? She isn't my client anymore. Right, I should just let it go. Maybe she got into that clinical trial in Bellevue a few weeks ago. But then, what that nurse said . . . Damn."

Dan made a few more circles around the small room, sipping coffee, and occasionally shaking his head as if he could make Allison fly from his thoughts through centrifugal force. But she would not be shaken loose.

He could call the Carver Research Institute but they probably wouldn't tell him much, even if Allison had joined the trial. And anyway, they might not know anything about her current mess. Maybe that one doctor, though . . . what was his name? Hamilton. Maybe he would know something. Maybe he would talk.

Dan walked back into his office, found the number for CRI, and punched it in.

"Good afternoon, Carver Research Institute. How may I help you?"

"Yes, Dr. Hamilton please? This is Dan Gunnison, calling about a mutual patient."

"Oh, Dr. Gunnison, yes, you were here a few weeks ago."

"No, yes, right, I was."

"I'm sorry, but Dr. Hamilton is out for the day. Would you like his voice mail?"

"No chance of reaching him on his cell?"

"No, I'm sorry."

A lot of people are sorry today. "Okay, voicemail is fine. Thanks."

Dan hated voicemails but did his best to sound professional, objective and helpful. He offered his assistance, if any was needed.

When Dan finished, he hung up and turned to stare out the window. He tried to see anything positive in Allison's apparent situation and came up with one weak candidate: at least her symptoms were becoming more clearly defined. According to the article at least, Allison actually identified herself as Dr. Kathryn Johansen. That might allow her therapy, *if* she is working with someone, to proceed more effectively. She needs help now more than ever, and she would probably be more receptive in the light of recent events—that is, if she remembers her own actions.

But, Dan thought, what is it about Allison's history that's so traumatic? Neglect alone just doesn't account for her behavior. And even if there is something darker hidden in her past, how do "Kathryn's" bizarre actions now serve to protect her from that trauma? As hard as he tried, Dan simply couldn't make the pieces fit. Eventually, the clock forced a temporary end to his struggles and he began the latter half of his client-filled day.

TWENTY-EIGHT

· ·

That evening, Dan tried to let the sunset over Lake Washington take him away. The view from his balcony, along with two bottles of Hefeweizen, were working their combined magic, and the spell was proving to be effective enough to dampen his anxiety but not potent enough to keep Allison out of his thoughts altogether.

Her smile, the one he had seen at their first meeting when she was on the floor of the waiting room, coffee-soaked and dissolving in laughter, that smile—and the bright beautiful turquoise eyes that went with it—appeared in Dan's mind against the backdrop of a reddening sky, and the image would not go away. Dan knew that it persisted only because some level of his consciousness willed it to persist.

The simple fact, he admitted after another pull on the Hefeweizen, was that he missed that smile. No, it was much deeper than that.

She's not my client anymore. So why . . . For the first time, Dan smiled and relaxed as this recurring thought intruded once again. *She's not my client, and that's a good thing. A very good thing.*

Wanting to clear his mind for further thought about Allison's situation, Dan rose and went inside. He popped a frozen chimichanga into the microwave and poured a glass of vitamin water. When the food was ready, he took it back out to the balcony and sat down to enjoy the last rays of the sun as it made its exit behind the peaks of the Olympic Mountains a hundred miles away. As he ate, he felt his mental acuity returning but, thankfully, the anxiety he had harbored all day did not return with it.

Dan allowed himself to think about Allison's plight in psychological terms because he hoped to help her with the skills he possessed, but now he allowed himself a decidedly personal slant. As he thought back on Allison's sessions, he tried to remember if he had truly witnessed the emergence of separate personality parts.

Oddly, it wasn't the Kathryn part that came to mind. He could not honestly say that he had observed any definitive switching to the Kathryn part. Instead, Dan's thoughts went immediately to the day that Allison had asked him, point blank, if he found her attractive. Now *that* felt much more like switching. That felt like a flirty, teenage part emerging. Was she chewing gum that day? He couldn't remember, but that would have fit. It did not feel at all like the more mature, intelligent, even sweet personality he had come to associate with Allison. So what was that all about?

The evening had passed into night and the rapidly cooling air drove Dan inside. He settled down on the couch, vitamin water in hand, and continued his mental exploration. He remembered the note he had written following his observation of Allison's teenage behavior. He had written that she had a "clear history of attachment deficit." That was the same session, he recalled, in which he and Allison had discussed abandonment issues, which she had not been able to confront in previous sessions. Could it be that she had developed enough trust in the client/therapist relationship that she had simply let her inhibitions down for a few minutes? Could the flirty behavior have been just an awkward overreaction to her normal but long-repressed need for attachment, for intimacy? Yes, it was not only possible, but likely.

Then there was Allison's recent and very evident anger. Could that have been a reaction to what she might have perceived as rejection from Dan during her awkward and inappropriate plea for intimacy? It was possible, because it became evident only after that last session; but still, the intensity and persistence of her emotion seemed out of line. Did this mean that Allison's anger emanated from another personality part? Not necessarily.

Given Allison's history, it seemed to Dan that it would be relatively easy, even natural, for Allison to move rapidly and irrationally from feelings of mild rejection to deep fears of total abandonment. If she had developed a form of trust with Dan and that trust had subsequently been violated, then she might not only feel abandoned but she might feel betrayed as well, leading directly to anger. But where was the violation of trust? Dan felt that it was there, somewhere—at least as a perception for Allison—but he could not identify it, unless it sprang out of his rather clinical answers to her intimate questions that day.

And what about the whole Kathryn thing? Was it related? Dan began to feel that it was not. He began to see a clear distinction between that and the flirtation episode. He was seeing two different and completely unrelated issues, of that he was almost certain now. And neither one pointed decisively to DID. Not even Kathryn. Allison seemed to possess knowledge—knowledge that this "person" named Kathryn had—but Allison never seemed to take on a fundamentally different personality, at least not in Dan's presence. Well, yes, there *was* the lecture on female endocrinology aboard her boat that day a few weeks ago. *That* felt like a switch, but even that could simply have been a retreat behind a defensive wall of knowledge following her embarrassing exposure. Allison herself— in her very first session—had referred to her interest in medicine and her extensive reading, not to mention her pre-med studies at the University. And, Dan recalled, Allison had reacted strongly against his trial reference to her as "Doctor" during her recent lecture. She denied being a doctor and seemed taken aback, even hurt, when Dan later tried addressing her as "Kathryn."

Dan found himself creeping up slowly, uneasily, but inexorably upon a conclusion he'd been resisting for weeks: *This is not DID. This is something else entirely.*

TWENTY-NINE

· ·

Allison sat quietly as Margaret drove her across the floating bridge toward Bellevue. It was early May, and Allison looked ahead through a light fog to see the land across the water washed with pale green leaf buds revealing themselves on the deciduous trees which had hidden all winter among the evergreens.

I just wanted to help, she thought. *And now, here I am.*

Allison had always felt a bit different from everyone around her, but most of the time she saw this as a distinctively positive thing and she had certainly never considered herself to be mentally ill. That was a label reserved for the bedraggled old man who mumbled curses at the sea gulls on the dock, or the pale, blank-faced woman pushing a shopping cart full of empty bird cages. Now Allison had been officially placed alongside these people. She was a patient, and not only a patient but a mental patient about to enter mandatory treatment. *Mandatory. No choice. Trapped. Run aground.* These words framed her emotional state, and no matter how hard her friend tried to buoy her up that morning, Allison would not rise up from this dark, fatalistic place.

"And it's only six weeks, Allie. Think of it—in a month and a half, you'll be back on your boat, life will be good again, and you'll probably be free of your Teachers, too. You'll be free. And in the meantime, I'll make sure your business stays afloat. And don't forget that trip we've got planned to Sucia Island in the fall. That's gonna happen, girlfriend!"

Allison nodded, even turning her head slightly toward her friend, but no crooked little smile emerged. She realized that Margaret was trying her best, but the words just sailed by her, sucked out the window and swept under the car as it made its way inexorably, mile by mile, to the Carver Research Institute on the edge of Meydenbauer Bay.

When they arrived, Allison remembered that she had seen the building before, but from the water. It had looked impressive then, with the bay's reflection on its glass, but now, from the vantage point of the patient parking area and the perspective of her situation, the word "oppressive" seemed a much better match. This glass and steel building was to be her home, her prison, for the next six weeks. If it had been ringed with razor wire and fortified with guard stations it would not have seemed any more dismal or felt even the slightest bit more terrifying than it did in that moment.

Margaret turned off the car's engine and the silence shouted at Allison. It shouted finality, darkness, and defied the spring sunshine that was beginning to burn through the fog. She felt as if she were being delivered in the back of a long black hearse to her own gravesite.

When Allison made no move to get out, Margaret sighed and walked around the car to open the door for her. Even then, Allison sat numbly, feeling herself moving slowly to a point of empty resignation. *Mandatory, no choice, trapped, run aground.* And what do you do when you run aground? Wait. Wait for high tide. But were these even tidal waters? Allison did not know.

She took Margaret's outstretched hand and stepped out of the car. She was grateful for her friend's presence by her side but still could not shake the feeling that she was not moving up the walkway toward the entrance on her own volition. She was being taken. The tall glass doors ahead felt to Allison like the entrance to a modern mausoleum and she walked slowly through them, looking neither right nor left for fear that she might see row upon row of somber body-sized drawers holding the barely living remains of other patients.

The check-in process was a blur as Margaret handled the paperwork, asking Allison for information only once or twice, Allison answering as needed in a voice that sounded strangely distant and monotonic to her own ear. Then there was an argument of sorts, a discussion between Margaret and the receptionist about whether or not Margaret could accompany Allison to her room, but Margaret seemed to win quickly and easily, asserting her role and responsibilities as Allison's attorney.

A graying man in a white coat appeared, greeted Margaret as if they were old friends and introduced himself to Allison as Dr. Hamilton; he led them through a security door and down a long quiet hallway to a door on the left at the end. The tastefully painted and decorated hallway looked to Allison like one she had seen in a high-end hotel, with its pleasant sconce lighting and deeply padded carpet, but it had the clean alcohol smell of a hospital. The juxtaposition was confusing but not entirely unpleasant.

When the group arrived at the end of the hallway, Dr. Hamilton smiled and held out his hand toward the door on the left. Allison looked up and saw her name embossed in an antiqued brass plate at eye level on the heavy five-panel oak door. A nice touch, she had to admit, but the aura of permanence was disturbing. The brass plate appeared to be crafted into the door and was clearly not one of the sliding removable kinds which Allison had seen many times on office doors—the kinds that moved with their occupants as they climbed their way up the corporate ladder.

For six weeks? It didn't seem to make much sense. And when Dr. Hamilton pushed the door open, the scene inside just added to Allison's incredulity.

"Pretty nice, isn't it, Allie?" said Margaret with a sad smile. "I hear they even stock the kitchen for you."

"Uh huh," was all Allison could manage. She scanned the room and the five-star impression returned, dominating her senses. To her left was the bathroom door through which she could see a large walk-in granite tiled shower, a designer pedestal sink, a heated towel rack with several plush beige bath towels, and a toilet with accompanying bidet. To Allison's right was a closet door, and straight ahead, against the backdrop of an enormous floor-to-ceiling window, was a beautifully decorated living area with a queen sized bed, a desk with a notebook computer, and a small couch. A tiny kitchenette lay in a nook off to the far right.

Allison walked slowly into the room, drawn by the window. Outside the fog had lifted and she saw the sweep of the bay, opening out into Lake Washington with the Seattle skyline in the distance beyond. A Grand Banks trawler was slowly turning to enter the marina below. *Coming home or just visiting?* Allison wondered.

Her thoughts were interrupted by Dr. Hamilton. "Allison, I'll let you settle in while I have my assistant bring your things up. Margaret, good to see you again." Then, turning back, as if with an afterthought, "Oh, and Allison, I'll be back in about an hour to help you get oriented and set up for treatment." Dr. Hamilton nodded to the two women, backed out and closed the door.

Allison turned back to the window and watched the trawler head into a slip. She heard Margaret walk up behind and felt her friend's hands rest lightly on her shoulders.

"Allie, I do think this will be a good thing for you, I really do."

Allison nodded and reached up to place a hand upon one of Margaret's, but she still did not speak. The room seemed so incongruous with captivity. The pleasure her accommodations seemed to promise and the actual facts of her situation created such cognitive dissonance that Allison found herself in a dizzying state. Her mind sought resolution and imagined a bare concrete-walled room with a single light bulb hanging from a frayed wire in the center of the ceiling, and a cot. That seemed preferable and provided some momentary relief. She slowly shook her head with the absurdity of it all.

After Margaret said her goodbyes, promising to return the next day, Allison was left alone with her thoughts. She wandered numbly about, exploring the boundaries of her plush cage, looking in drawers, checking kitchen supplies, testing the bed. Then it occurred to her with clinical detachment: *they must not consider me a suicide risk.* She went back into the kitchen and, sure enough, there was a full complement of utensils, knives and all.

It didn't seem right. It wasn't how she would handle things if she were running this clinical trial. But, of course, she wasn't. She was a patient. A mental patient. Not a doctor.

She continued her examination of the room, and as she was checking the door—it was locked from the outside, something she was not surprised to discover—she looked up and in the process resolved her question about the suicide risk. There, blending in with the ceiling just above the door was a very small circular object: a miniature fisheye lens, a digital video camera undoubtedly behind it. She immediately checked the ceilings above the bed, in the bathroom, and in the kitchen. Cameras everywhere. *Great, zero privacy. I'm being observed. Wonder if they planned on telling me?*

Allison walked back to the desk in the living area and sat down in front of the computer. Absently, she checked her email account. Nothing new. *I bet everything I do here is monitored—probably every click and keystroke. The only thing I have left to myself is my thoughts.* She sat at the desk for several minutes, just staring at the screen in front of her.

THIRTY

· ·

A llison jerked awake at the sound of someone knocking at the door and found herself sitting at her new desk. Automatically, she said "Come in," and then quickly ran a hand through her hair. Dr. Hamilton entered.

Allison stood and faced her physician/jailer. She skipped the usual conversational pleasantries and dove right in. "So, were you planning to tell me about the cameras?"

"Of course, Allison. I was going to bring that up as part of your orientation, but let's talk about it now."

"Yes, let's."

Hamilton reddened but continued. "Well, it's all part of our safety protocol. We certainly don't expect any problems in your case, but we occasionally do have patients who have demonstrated self destructive tendencies in the past and we want to be sure they're protected."

"From themselves . . ."

"Yes that is, unfortunately, the point."

"But, since you don't expect any such problems with me, why don't we dispense with the surveillance?"

"I'm sorry Allison, but we have no experience together and, until we do, we need to be as careful as possible—again, for your sake."

"Experience together, hmmm. Can we at least get rid of the bathroom camera? I mean, come on!"

"I'm sorry."

"Yes, me too."

"Can we move on to more important matters?"

Allison sensed Hamilton's impatience with her and tucked away the small victory. "Yes, of course."

"If you're ready, let's walk down the hall to our Healing Center."

Healing Center? Interesting euphemism. "Yes, I'm fascinated to see what CRI has come up with."

Allison followed Charles Hamilton down the hall, through the security door, and down another hall to a room that, to Allison, looked like a bizarre hybrid between a therapist's office and an operating room. It was dimly lit, tastefully appointed and comforting on the one hand, but subtly infested with technology on the other. In that sense it reminded Allison of her own quarters.

"Please have a seat wherever you wish," said Dr. Hamilton with a wave of his hand.

Allison sat at one end of the couch and listened intently to Hamilton as he took her through the details, from a "patient perspective," he said, of the treatment process. He showed her the equipment, including the hat apparatus used for non-invasive targeted brain stimulation, and when he was done, he asked Allison if she had any questions for him.

Allison nodded and said that she did have a few. "So, I'm curious about your Phase One results—both efficacy and safety. I assume that we are now involved in Phase Two of the trial, at the very least."

"Yes," replied Hamilton, seeming surprised by Allison's question. "We're in Phase Two and the earlier results were very encouraging."

"Quantitatively, please?"

"Uh, yes, we found that seventy-three percent of our phase one patients demonstrated integration of personality parts by the end of the trial."

"Impressive. That, I'm assuming, is seventy-three percent of those patients on full treatment—not placebo?"

"Yes, that's correct."

"And what percentage of those on placebo protocol demonstrated integration?" asked Allison.

"Four point five percent, actually."

"Kudos to your therapists in those cases, I'd say, or to the patients." Allison knew she was in control of the discussion for the moment and relished the experience, knowing that it would be temporary.

"Yes, well, our therapists are some of the best in the country, if not the world," replied Hamilton.

"What about the rate of spontaneous integration in DID patients?"

"That's actually not known with any confidence, but for this study it's assumed to be near zero."

"Probably a decent assumption, given the timeframe of the trial," noted Allison. "So how does the study measure integration?"

"Excellent question, Allison. In this study, we define integration as the absence of switching during three consecutive one-hour sessions involving stress stimuli which have been demonstrated in the past, in that particular patient, to produce switching episodes with a probability of greater than zero point six seven."

"But, as I understand your protocol, the treatment itself suppresses specific fears and therefore temporarily minimizes or eliminates associated switching. So, under what conditions do you measure integration?" Allison noticed that Hamilton was now pacing the room and a light sweat was beginning to form on his brow.

"Well, obviously, we do that in the absence of brain stimulation," he replied.

"Obviously. But what about follow-up work? Have you shown persistence? Do patients in your seventy-three percent group *stay* integrated?"

"Uh, well, of course the study is still in its infancy in many ways. We don't yet have much history, but all indications are good at this point. We like to see three solid months of integration in a patient before we claim persistence. And, if you don't have any other questions, maybe now would be a good time to get started."

"Actually, I do have one more. You've talked about efficacy; now, what about safety findings? How well do patients tolerate treatment?"

At that moment, the door to the room swung open and a tall, handsome, and impeccably dressed man entered with an engaging smile and outstretched hand.

"Ah, you must be Allison. So good to meet you. I'm Dr. Carver and I just wanted to stop in for a moment to welcome you to the program. I trust that Dr. Hamilton has answered all of your questions and helped to make you comfortable with the process?"

"Yes, we were just . . ."

"Good," Carver interrupted. "You're in excellent hands, let me assure you. And now, let's walk on down the hall and introduce Allison to her new therapist, shall we Dr. Hamilton?"

"Of course. Right this way, Allison," said Hamilton, indicating the open door.

THIRTY-ONE

· ·

Allison was ushered into a room remarkably similar to the one in which Hamilton had conducted her aborted orientation session. Rising from a chair to meet her was a short, thin, mole-like man with dark, slicked-back hair and an exceedingly pale complexion. He peered up at her through a pair of black glasses and she could have sworn that his nose twitched. He looked as though he spent his entire waking life in a basement lab, far away from natural light. His smile was thin but seemed sincere.

"Allison," said Dr. Hamilton, "this is Dr. Kane. He'll be working very closely with you for the next six weeks."

Allison extended her hand slightly downward to shake with her new therapist. "Good to meet you," she said, wondering whether it was, in fact, good, and whether it would even be possible to discuss her personal life with this . . . this person.

"A pleasure," said the little man.

Allison tried to conceal her shock at the sound of Kane's voice. It was a deep resonant baritone and jarringly incongruous with the rest of his physical characteristics—so much so that it left Allison speechless. Dr. Hamilton took his leave and Dr. Kane nodded toward the couch with another thin but not unpleasant smile.

"Please Allison, have a seat and let's get started. It's okay, by the way; you don't have to try to hide your surprise. I used to dread first meetings. People just don't expect my voice. God's little compensation, or joke, I don't know which. But now I find that it serves as a pretty good icebreaker."

Allison let out her breath, surprised to find that she'd been holding it in for a while, and a little laugh escaped with it. "Thanks, I guess I was somewhat taken aback. You have a wonderful voice," she said.

"Thank you," said Kane with a slight bow. He seated himself in a low chair across a coffee table from Allison's couch and brought his hands together in prayer-like fashion with the tips of his index fingers touching his lips. He paused for a moment, seeming to be formulating an approach, then looked up.

"I've had a chance to study your rather remarkable file, Allison, and before we begin your actual therapy, I have to say that I'm very impressed— in many ways. I guess there is no "typical" DID patient, but you do seem to stand out, and I had to ask myself why. What is it that makes your background, makes you, different from the other people we see here? When I thought about that, two major things came to mind. First, you not only hold a steady job but you own a business, and a successful one at that. By the time patients come to us, most of them are so fragmented that doing anything with consistency, let alone running a business, is nearly impossible for them. And second, you do not seem to lose time."

"I'm sorry Dr. Kane, but what do you mean by that?"

"Losing time?"

"Yes."

"That is a strange term, isn't it." Kane sat back in his chair, appearing comfortable with the discussion. "Yes, it means having memory lapses, leaving time which can't be accounted for. Virtually all DID patients report episodes like this. A woman will wake up one morning, for example, and discover three new dresses hanging in her closet. She has no memory of buying them. They are her size but not a style that she would normally wear. She finds a receipt in her purse for the dresses, dated yesterday and with a signature in her handwriting."

"Things like that actually happen?"

"Yes, in almost all cases we see. You've never experienced anything remotely like that?"

"No, nothing like that. I know things, say things, even do things sometimes that surprise me, but I don't think I lose time. How would I know, by the way? I mean, how do you know if you've forgotten something? Sort of a paradox, isn't it?"

"Yes, exactly. So people only know because they discover the evidence, like the dresses in the closet. Or maybe a friend brings up something in conversation that the person did but can't recall. Things of that nature."

"That must be very frightening and enormously disorienting," observed Allison.

"Yes, to the extent that some patients will make up stories to explain such things, and then fervently believe those stories themselves, all in an effort to avoid the frightening truth."

"I don't think I've done that. I mean, the whole reason I'm here is because I performed an appendectomy—an appendectomy, for God's sake! And I *know* I did that. I remember doing it. I even remember thinking, at the time, how odd it was that I would even try. But I knew what to do and the girl was in trouble, so I did it. It was like, I don't know, second nature to me."

"But you did use another name while you were having that experience, didn't you?"

"Yes, I did. Kathryn, yes, that is the weird part of this whole thing, I know." Allison looked down at her feet.

"So, let me ask you, was it Kathryn doing the surgery?"

"No, it was me! And no, I don't have classic psychotic episodes either. I don't hear Kathryn's voice, or anyone else's. She doesn't tell me what to do. Okay, sometimes I do actually ask her questions, but that's just my way of tapping into the knowledge in my own mind that I think of as hers. Do you get what I'm trying to tell you? Dan understood it."

"Dan?"

"Yes, sorry, my previous therapist."

"Ah."

Allison took a deep breath before continuing. "Dr. Kane, do you mind if I ask you something about this clinical trial before we really get going?"

"No, please do."

"Am I really a good candidate for this treatment?"

"How do you mean that, Allison?"

"I mean, we've just been talking about how atypical I am and it's making me wonder if I'm really in the right place."

Allison watched as Kane went back to his prayer-like pose before answering.

"Allison, I'm not involved in the trial design process. In fact, like most of the other therapists here, I'm a contractor—not actually part of the Institute—and we're all intentionally kept in the dark about many aspects of the trial. That's just part of the double-blind protocol. It's the way these things work. But I do know that patient pools are generally designed to be broadly representative, even sometimes to the extent that a very small number of borderline patients are included. You may be one of those."

"Oh. Should I be concerned about that in any way?"

"I shouldn't think so, no."

Allison thought she detected another nose twitch but preferred to concentrate on Kane's voice. It seemed steady and reassuring.

"Okay, good. Look, I'm feeling really tired and was wondering if we could start tomorrow? Today has been a big transition for me, if you know what I mean."

"Of course, Allison. No problem. Let's get you back to your room."

"Oh, one other thing, and I hope you can give me a straight answer on this," said Allison. "I'd like to be able to conduct business and personal communications via the computer in my room and I'd like to think that my business is private. Many of my big clients insist on this. Is my computer usage being monitored?"

Dr. Kane laughed. "No, I can tell you honestly it is not. Well, with one caveat, I guess: those pesky cameras. If you're sitting at the computer the way it's oriented now, it's in view of the living room camera. So, I guess in theory, if someone wanted to, they could try to see what you're up to, but even then I don't think they could see much, if anything, because the cameras are strictly infrared devices monitored by special software looking for patterns. The cameras basically just track body movements by detecting heat. They can't resolve details."

"I know the gentleman who runs the IT department and deals with all of the security systems," Kane explained. "I've known Tim for a long time and I trust him. I was a software architect before switching to psychology and met him during the latter part of that career when he was just starting out. He's followed me around since then."

"But back to your question about privacy. If you want to be really sure, just move things around in the room a bit. If you do something that triggers one of the pattern profiles then you might get a visit from security, but that would be the worst of it."

"Oh, I should mention," Kane continued, "and you've probably already noticed this, that your phone won't work in this building."

"No, I hadn't actually tried it yet."

"Well, don't bother. We can't allow the radio frequency interference. It would be much too risky for our patients, given how our equipment works. So we actually send out controlled signals, which our equipment tolerates, that disable your phone's transmitter, making it useless while you're here."

Once settled back in, Allison did move things around a bit. In fact, after pulling the desk away from the wall and flipping the computer around, she went straight to the bathroom carrying a chair, climbed up and placed a nice healthy glob of amber-colored hair gel over the lens of the camera in the ceiling.

"Analyze *this* pattern," she said. Then she took a nice long, hot shower and felt much better.

THIRTY-TWO

· ·

T he next morning, Allison woke just before dawn and watched the pink light of morning creep across the bay below. She got up, dressed in the relative privacy of her bathroom, put on her minimal makeup, and made her way to the kitchen. There she fixed a bowl of cereal and brought it back out to the computer where she intended to do some research. It frustrated her that she'd not been able to diagnose her own condition and she wanted to become as knowledgeable as she could, as quickly as possible.

On the internet, several search engines quickly did Allison's bidding and she began to devour material about DID. Some of it was clearly sensational garbage and speculation which she quickly recognized and dismissed, but she ultimately found the core research she hungered for. She read with the mind of a physician, trying to correlate results from several international studies with her own experience as the patient. Everything that Dan had told her seemed to ring true, including his hesitation about her symptoms, or lack thereof.

During her reading, she ran across several references to the DSM, the manual that psychologists and psychiatrists used to arrive at formal diagnoses. Finding excerpts from the DSM online, Allison discovered that the portion of the manual dedicated to DID was just three or four pages out of nearly a thousand in the complete book, but in those pages she found the four fundamental requirements for a DID diagnosis:

- The presence of two or more distinct identities or personality states, each with its own relatively enduring pattern of perceiving, relating to, and thinking about the environment and self.

- At least two of these identities or personality states recurrently taking control of the person's behavior.
- Inability to recall important personal information that is too extensive to be explained by ordinary forgetfulness.
- The disturbance is not due to the direct physiological effects of a substance or general medical condition, including brain injury, medication, sleep deprivation or intoxicants, all of which can mimic symptoms of DID.

In examining this list Allison tried to put herself in the dual role of psychologist and patient as she struggled to objectively assess her own state of mind and experience against the standard criteria. The first one seemed to fit, and the second, with a broad interpretation, could be considered a match, but the third felt distinctly foreign. Allison did not feel controlled and was quite certain that she would naturally rebel against such a thing if it were present. She used Kathryn's knowledge, and yes, she did tend to take on a different persona when she felt driven to use that knowledge. Did that amount to being controlled? Maybe, but she didn't experience it that way. And, thankfully, she felt certain that she had not suffered any form of amnesia. Drugs and brain injury were not factors, so the last item fit for her, but it fit for the majority of the non-DID population as well.

Allison also discovered that a diagnosis is almost never made without strong indications emerging from something called the SCID-D interview and, as far as she knew, neither Dan nor anyone else had conducted such an interview unless it had been hidden somewhere within the therapy sessions. Further reading confirmed Allison's tentative conclusion. The SCID-D was much more structured and formal than anything she had experienced during sessions with Dan. The intent and direction of Dan's questions seemed in line with it but the interview itself had never happened; that much seemed clear.

When Allison finished her rapid survey of the literature three hours later she found herself in the frustrating and dichotomous position of being well informed but still very much in the dark. She understood much more about her supposed condition, felt a great deal of compassion for those who had suffered enough to develop such elaborate defenses, but was also convinced that she was not among their ranks.

This was both a relief and a source of new anxiety. If not DID, then what? And even more relevant to her immediate situation, if not DID, then why was she here at the Carver Research Institute?

Allison shut down the computer, placed her fingertips on her temples and searched for some rational scenario, something that would explain her presence in this place, something other than DID and a modified jail sentence. Perhaps it was as simple as Dr. Kane had suggested: that she was just a fringe case rounding out the trial population. The explanation was compelling if not entirely convincing, and in the end Allison suppressed her fears, not wishing to add paranoia to her list of ill-defined symptoms. She decided to follow, or at least to begin, the therapeutic path that lay before her. If she was careful and observant, she reasoned, she could stay in control of the situation and learn a great deal in the process. It could be fascinating, from a clinical perspective.

Allison moved back to her window feeling better armed and calmly resolved. She watched a Hatteras yachtfisher back out of its slip, pivot in place, and slowly make its way out to deep water. She could see someone on deck hauling in fenders and stowing them away and she wondered about the boat's destination for the day. *I'll be back on the water in less than six weeks*, she thought. A little smile crept across her lips for the first time in days.

When the knock on her door came at 9:30, Allison turned and said, "Just a moment. I'll be right there." She walked to the bathroom and took a few moments to brush her hair and check her makeup. Then, when she was ready, she returned to the door and opened it.

"Good morning, Allison," said Dr. Kane through a thin smile in his incongruous baritone. Allison thought that Kane looked something like a small, friendly vampire, as if there could be such a thing. His dark suit, black slicked-back hair with a widow's peak, and unnaturally pale skin seemed quite the caricature and it made Allison smile.

"Good morning, Dr. Kane. And how are you today?"

"I'm well, thank you. It's good to see you smiling, Allison. Shall we?" Kane nodded toward the hallway and Allison walked with him to the Healing Center.

Allison covered a laugh with a dainty cough as she watched the little man with the big voice setting up equipment and tapping information into a keyboard.

The process took only a few moments and when he was done, Kane looked up and said, "Alright, Allison, we're ready to outfit you with this lovely headgear. It shouldn't take but a few minutes and then we'll be ready to get some baseline information from you. As Dr. Hamilton I'm sure has told you, the whole process is absolutely painless and completely non-invasive. Are you ready?"

"Yes, I'm ready." Allison sat quietly while Dr. Kane gently placed what appeared to be a soft, pink fabric hat, not unlike a large version of a winter wool cap, on her head and adjusted it to fit symmetrically. The hat had no wires attached and felt slightly snug but otherwise not unpleasant.

"Does that feel too tight?" asked Kane.

"Maybe just a little," replied Allison, reaching up to adjust it.

"Here, let me take care of that for you," said Kane. "It's got a headband inside that I'll loosen just a bit. When we have it right you shouldn't even notice it after a few minutes. There. How does that feel?"

"Much better, thanks. So, Dr. Kane, is this basically a wireless EEG device?"

"Yes, basically, but it's a bit more complex than that. I don't want to bore you with the details."

"Try me," said Allison with the slightest touch of irritation.

"Certainly." Kane nodded deferentially and seemed to recognize Allison's need for information and her capacity to absorb it.

He sat down across from Allison and began. "This whole approach falls into an area called psychophysiology—the study of the bi-directional relationship between physiological and psychological states—but ours is one of the very few systems created for treatment rather than pure research."

"So the system manipulates the brain in order to effect a change in the mind," observed Allison.

"Yes, very astute of you, very well put. We use an approach related to something described in the literature as Event-related Potentials in which we record certain tiny voltage fluctuations or 'potentials' emanating from the brain and use those as indicators of the patient's mental state, particularly fear-related states, that arise during the recall of traumatic events."

"And then I assume that you use that information during treatment in some way."

"Yes. For each individual patient we obtain a custom set of readings over the initial sessions, both for the quiescent state and the agitated state. From those readings we derive what we call the Baseline Profile and the Event Profile. Then, over a period of some weeks, we work with our patients in therapy sessions with the aid of our system, to help them deal calmly and constructively with key events in their histories."

"So the treatment involves a kind of synthesis between traditional therapy and neurological intervention," Allison noted.

"Exactly. It is just such a synthesis. Special software and hardware uses the Event Profile as a trigger to stimulate a brain structure located in the medial temporal lobes called the amygdala. We focus particularly on the left amygdala. With precise pulse timing, frequency and amplitude, our system creates just the right amount of stimulus to dampen the natural fear response and it does this in a highly selective way associated with specific fear-inducing memories. The patient is then in an otherwise completely normal, alert state which allows her to deal with her memories calmly and constructively as the therapist guides her through the process."

"Dr. Kane, I'm sorry but I'm just wondering why one would go to all this trouble when drugs or hypnosis could be used to achieve a similar result."

"No, that's a very reasonable question. Both techniques have been used—hypnosis probably being the most effective of the two—but not everyone responds well to hypnosis and the use of drugs in dosages sufficient to deal with the intensity of fear that many patients experience leaves those patients almost non-responsive, making therapy impossible. And, of course, all drugs have side effects which we'd prefer to avoid. So, we like to think of our approach as a gentle, highly specific catalyst that enables traditional therapy to proceed rapidly and effectively."

"Well, I'm impressed, I really am. So what now?"

"Actually, Allison, we're done for this morning. While we've been talking, the system has obtained our first Baseline Profile. Pretty painless, wouldn't you say? We'd like to have you come back this afternoon at three for another short session."

THIRTY-THREE

· ·

D an Gunnison took two stairs at a time, running down to the underground parking lot below his office. He was going to be late for lunch with Skip at the University.

Skip had left a message that morning asking if Dan could meet him, adding that he had something interesting to discuss. Skip didn't usually need a pretext for lunch and Dan was curious. In any case, interesting information or not, it was good timing because Dan wanted to pick Skip's brain about the dilemma he faced with Allison. He wanted to find her and to resolve the tension that had so abruptly developed in their short relationship. But he could not figure out how to proceed without violating confidences. Dan suspected that Allison was being treated at the Carver Research Institute but Dr. Hamilton had not returned his call. He reminded himself that he was only Allison's friend and no longer her therapist, and probably only a unilateral friend at that, so a call-back from Hamilton, while he wanted one desperately, wasn't necessarily warranted.

Dan sped down Eastlake Avenue and took the bridge over Portage Bay to the School of Medicine on Pacific Street. He felt lucky to find a parking space quickly and ran up several flights of stairs, bypassing the crowded elevator, and found himself in Dr. Skip Hanover's office just five minutes late.

The two friends shook hands and Dan collapsed into a guest chair, out of breath.

"Come on, Dan, get your butt out of that chair. We're heading down to the lab."

"You mean down all those stairs I just ran up?"

"Yup, those would be the ones—unless you'd rather join the heart patients on the elevator."

Dan grimaced and followed Skip out the door and down the hall to the stairway. He so rarely saw his friend in what Skip called his "natural habitat," and the white coat, the highly-charged academic environment, the easy greetings with other doctors along the hall, all contributed to make Dan feel both proud of his former roommate and a little jealous of his success. He smiled, remembering how often he saw the same juxtaposition of emotions in his own clients.

Down in the lab, Skip introduced Dan to three of his residents who were finishing up some work before heading off to lunch and then took him back to a corner where he sat him down in front of a large high-resolution screen. "Look at this," he said.

Dan studied the pattern of color-coded letters displayed in bewildering configurations and shook his head. "Okay . . ."

Jealousy, he noted, was now being joined by its close friend, Sense of Inadequacy. Together, they formed quite a pair and he didn't like either one, much less the combination. He pushed them aside and tried to focus on what Skip was saying. Skip was going on about something related to the human genome. It sounded like a lecture and it was hard for Dan to keep his own agenda and his growing hunger in check as he tried to listen.

" . . . and it takes less than two percent of our genome to create all of the proteins necessary for life. The remaining ninety-eight percent are only vaguely understood. For example, eight percent are thought to be the remnants of ancient retroviruses which managed to make themselves part of our heredity. I think I mentioned that to you the other day. Some of the rest seems to be involved in regulating gene expression, but a huge portion remains a mystery and that's where I've been looking for patterns with the help of some sophisticated software. And there *are* patterns present but their meaning is elusive. Now, here's the thing, my friend."

Skip waved his hand in front of Dan's face to check for signs of life, a habit which had annoyed Dan since their undergraduate days, but about which he had never spoken because he felt he actually deserved it. He found it hard to pay attention to detail like this, but he knew from experience that Skip wouldn't put him through it unless there was something truly important at stake. Dan felt honored, in spite of the hand-waving, that his friend would want to share key moments with him.

"Yesterday, I stumbled across something that just blew me away. A colleague from Harborview sent me a tissue sample that he was curious about. He was curious because the woman it came from has substantially enlarged frontal lobes—that's part of the brain, not . . ." Skip was smirking. He was clearly enjoying himself.

"Hey, man, give me a *little* credit."

"Okay, sorry, couldn't resist, but this enlargement is not pathological or deforming in any way. It appears to be normal, for her, and that's why Dr. Archer was so interested in her genetic makeup. Well, what we've found here in the lab is that this patient's non-coding DNA appears highly atypical. In fact, the patterns suggest that it *is in fact* coding for proteins with a very interesting structure. I think that this DNA is coding for neural proteins."

"Brain cells?" Dan found himself instantly engaged.

"Yes, perhaps. But it's even more interesting than that. I think—and this part is highly speculative right now—that a huge percentage of this new coding determines not the construction of neurons per se, but *intraneural connections*, coded in a very compact fashion, almost like there is some highly evolved compression algorithm at work."

"Wait, you can't be talking about . . . I mean, you could get your ass kicked out of the academy so fast for even suggesting . . ."

"Yeah, I know. That's why I'm talking with you about this. Not even my students know what I'm doing with the data they've collected for me and I intend to keep it that way until I've done a lot more work."

"So, just so I'm clear, you're talking about memory," said Dan, eyes wide.

"Yes, as heretical as that sounds, yes, I'm talking about long-term memory coded within the genome itself," confirmed Skip, swallowing hard. Dan noticed that Skip's hands were shaking and it appeared hard for him to control the cursor on the screen as he spoke.

Skip collected himself and finished. "Inherited memories. Passed from generation to generation, but only for those individuals with this class of genetic coding."

"But," said Dan, now concerned for his friend's reputation, "Wasn't all this Lamarckian inherited-traits stuff proposed and tossed out the window over two centuries ago?"

"Yes, and several times since Jean-Baptiste Lamarck. I think it's just possible that we keep circling back around to the general idea of transgenerational memory not just because it's so temptingly fascinating but because there's some actual truth to it. And I believe that the reason this phenomenon has been so elusive is that it applies only to a very select group of individuals. I know it seems highly improbable and even arrogant of me to suggest that I might be lucky enough to be looking at the DNA of one such highly evolved person. I mean, who knows, there may only be a handful of these people in the world today, but I suspect, if this all proves to be true, that we will find many more."

"Skip, if you pursue this, you know you're either headed for Stockholm or the unemployment line. You know that, right?"

"Yeah, I know it but I don't really know it."

"Man, you've got to have *so* much evidence before you even hint at this stuff. You've got to be really careful. You don't want to end up like one of those perpetual motion 'free energy' nutcases you hear about every now and then. I mean there are tons of questions that jump to mind right away—even *my* mind! Like, for example, how would new knowledge ever get introduced into this process? Wouldn't we just expect to see the same ancient memories reproduced again and again through the generations? What kind of evolutionary value would that have? And how would that original knowledge have been captured in the first place?"

"I've been thinking about that very thing, Dan, and in fact there is other evidence here in this data that suggests a truly dynamic system—not a static one like you describe. I even hesitate to mention this part to you because it sounds even more bizarre than what I've already said."

"I promise not to run to the Times with it."

Skip produced an uneasy smile and continued. "The thing is, static, eternally reproduced ancient memories would seem to have little evolutionary value, but knowledge accumulated over many generations and passed on genetically? Now *that* would have survival value. We humans have succeeded in our ecological niche primarily by outsmarting competitors, not necessarily by being physically stronger. Think about it even in today's terms, just within our own species: most of us succeed or fail in our careers based on our abilities to acquire and apply knowledge. Each of us, after we are born, must start from scratch with this process, learning most things our parents learned, and more, storing our knowledge in artificial memories like books and databases including the new collective consciousness of the Internet so that the next generation can start over from that base. But what if we didn't need to start from scratch? What if we could begin from a higher base and go from there? Wouldn't that be an evolutionary leg up?

Now, I'll admit that it's hard to imagine a baby understanding quantum physics. Okay, but what if that baby possessed the information but was only able to discover it, truly integrate it or really understand it as he or she matured into adulthood? What if it was all there as information but not usable as knowledge until the brain matured sufficiently and acquired other knowledge necessary to fill in the gaps?"

"Yes, I get that but how the hell could it ever work? I mean, a woman's eggs, with all of their genetic hand-me-downs are already formed by the time she's born! Any knowledge she acquired after birth would have no chance of being encoded and passed along."

"Unless that whole mechanism was changed, too, or augmented."

"Oh, come on Skip. That's ridiculous. Even more than the rest of this. I'm sorry man, but it just is."

"I know, I know. But think about it for a minute. It's possible to at least imagine a reverse transcription mechanism that produces genetic information from protein structure. If that mechanism existed—say in these individuals we're talking about—then all we would need is some kind of cycle that would trigger such 'updates'."

"This isn't the first time you've thought about this, is it?"

"No, I told you my research involved new evolutionary potential embedded in this vast pool of "unused" DNA, right? Well, these ideas have been percolating for a while. And when I got this sample and began to see the anomalies in it, some of the pieces began to fall into place."

"So this update mechanism you mentioned—what about that?"

"Well, females have the perfect mechanism if we imagine it overloaded with new properties: the menstrual cycle. The twenty-eight day cycle is the perfect trigger for genetic update and the creation of real-time eggs. I know that this is beyond radical, but I am starting to believe that some of the women among us represent the next major step in our evolution."

Dan's mind was spinning in ever-tightening circles as he listened, trying to incorporate what he was hearing with the ill-fitting puzzle pieces of his own recent experiences with Allison. The unexplained knowledge, the monthly headaches and loss of consciousness. Could it be possible?

"Skip, could you tell me a little more about this particular patient? Like her name?"

"All I know is that this tissue sample came from a female, age thirty, admitted to Harborview with head trauma following an accident downtown a few days ago. That's it, and even if I had her full chart I'd be bound by privacy laws."

"Sure, I understand. I think I really do."

THIRTY-FOUR

· ·

Allison Walker reached up to adjust the pink hat. It was only slightly heavier than one might expect for an actual fashion accessory and not at all unpleasant to wear as long as one ignored its odd appearance and didn't think too much about its purpose. Allison was successful on both counts and settled into the couch for her second session at the Carver Research Institute.

Dr. Kane glanced at a screen on his desk, hit a few keys, picked up a small tablet device and then took a seat opposite his patient. He brought both hands together in his usual prayer-like posture and paused to think for a moment before looking up to begin.

"Allison, this afternoon I'd like to talk with you about your experience with the appendicitis patient the other day. Would that be alright with you?"

"Yes, I have such mixed feelings about what happened that day, but sure, go ahead."

"Good. Let's begin by thinking back on the moment you first encountered your patient. Do you recall her name and what she looked like?"

Allison noticed Kane touch an area of the screen on his tablet and then look up expectantly.

"Her name was Hannah. I don't know her last name, but she was a baker at the deli where I sometimes have lunch. She had blond, medium length straight hair; she was rather thin, probably in her earlier twenties."

"Had you met her before? Did you know her at all?"

"No, she worked in the back and I'd never seen her until that day."

"Okay. Was she in some kind of obvious distress when you first saw her?"

"Oh, yes, she was on the floor, writhing in pain. It didn't take a doctor to tell she was in trouble."

"But it apparently did take one to diagnose her specific illness," Kane probed.

"Well, yes, in a way. I guess so."

"So how did you proceed?"

"Well, I located McBurney's point, palpated the region and the patient presented with both primary and rebound pain. Also, Rovsing's Sign was positive, so at that point I was quite certain."

Kane touched another area of his screen. "Could you explain Rovsing's Sign, Doctor? I'm not familiar with that."

"Come on Dr. Kane, you know I'm not a doctor. Please don't insult my intelligence by baiting me like that."

"I'm sorry, Allison. I'm simply trying to understand your situation better, that's all. But I am sorry. Would you please tell me about Rovsing's Sign."

Allison sighed. "Okay. In many cases of acute appendicitis, palpation of the lower left abdominal area—just over the left Iliac Fossa—will induce a symmetric pain on the right side. Palpation produces pressure in the descending colon which in turn results in pain on the right side if the appendix is sufficiently inflamed."

"Thank you. That was very clear. Now let's move on to a slightly later time that day, when you were actually performing the surgery. I understand that you had some help from someone else in the ambulance."

"Yes, there was a surgical nurse there. Very nice guy and knowledgeable."

"Did he do the actual surgery, then?"

"No, I did the surgery and he assisted."

"And you knew how to do the incision and actually remove the appendix? All of that?"

"Yes, well, Kathryn knows so I do, too."

Kane made another change on his screen. "I've read about Kathryn in your chart, but could you please tell me about her in your own words?"

"I don't like talking about this."

"Yes, I know. It's a difficult subject for you, isn't it?"

"Uh huh." Allison nodded and looked aside, watching Kane in her peripheral vision. She wanted him to move on to something else but he just sat there with his thin smile and waited.

Finally he broke the silence. "Let's not talk about Kathryn then, at least not directly. Could we explore these feelings that come up, though? These feelings that make it hard for you to talk about her?"

"I guess so. I'll try."

"Very good. Can you talk a little bit about how you feel when you're doing something like that surgery, when Kathryn is there."

"First of all, Kathryn isn't there. I mean, she's someone I know about. Well, that's not exactly right either. I only know about what she knows about. I guess I don't really know much about her, personally, except that I think of her as a doctor."

Kane nodded his head and continued. "So, maybe a better way for me to ask the question would be: how do you feel when you're working on something medically-related, something that Kathryn has knowledge of?"

"Oh, I feel fine when I'm in the middle of it. Not so much later when I have the time to reflect—then I have doubts and sometimes feel stupid about it—but at the time I actually feel great. I feel like, um, I feel useful I guess. I feel like I'm doing something positive. It feels natural, if that makes any sense."

"Does it make sense to you?"

"I hate those kinds of psychotherapy questions! Yes, of course it makes sense to me. I'm just trying to see if you understand what I'm telling you."

Kane just nodded and went on. "So now let's move back to Kathryn herself for a moment. You don't have to tell me anything about her, or the others, but I want you to think about all of them right now, in the privacy of your own mind. I want you to imagine telling someone about them: when you first noticed them, what they mean to you, times that you might have tried to tell your friends or relatives about them, things like that. I'd like you to try to concentrate on those things right now, please. I'll just sit here and be quiet for a few moments while you do that, okay?"

"Okay." Allison closed her eyes and tried to concentrate on Kathryn, then on Molly, and all of the other vague unnamed ones that occupied areas of her mind. Doing this was relatively easy because it mainly served to reinforce the positive self-image she experienced when she operated in one of her areas of expertise. It did seem a bit odd though, thinking about all of this more deeply now, that aside from the names of the first two, she knew almost nothing about these people, even though she clearly thought of them as people. What she knew consisted of things they knew, not things about them. That seemed exceedingly odd as she allowed herself, perhaps for the first time in her life, to question this phenomenon which she had taken for granted since she could remember anything at all. She had the odd sense that she really did know more about The Teachers, personal things about them, but that she just could not drag that knowledge up to the surface. She thought back on times in school when a teacher or professor had asked a question of the class and Allison knew that she knew the answer but just could not dredge it up. Sometimes it would come to her later when she had given up trying to think of it, and sometimes it remained hidden, but even then she *knew that she knew*. This situation was very much like those times.

Allison set that dilemma aside and tried to move on to some of the related topics that Dr. Kane had suggested. She thought back on the first time she tried to take Beth into her confidence concerning The Teachers. It was only slightly less painful to think about that time than it had been to actually speak about it with Dan or Margaret. *Oh, Margaret said she'd visit today, didn't she? I wonder if she still will. She's such a good friend and she's put up with so much from me in the last few days. I really need to see her.* Allison's mind wandered down that path for a moment before she turned back to the task at hand.

She again forced herself to concentrate on the first experience of harsh rejection by her adopted sister and the many painful events that followed. She was a grade school kid again: broken, defective, worthless, naked, laughed at, shamed. She tried to stay with the pain, the shame, and the fear of being sent back, but she could only stand so much. She squeezed her eyes shut tighter in an effort to continue, but then the tears came and shut it all down.

Allison wept into her hands. "I'm sorry. I'm sorry, Dr. Kane. I'm sorry I'm such a mess."

She felt his hand on her shoulder and looked up to see him smiling and reaching across the table. His voice was deep and reassuring.

"Allison, you can stop thinking about these painful things now. You did very, very well. I'm proud of you for working so hard. I think we've got all of the baseline information we need to begin your actual sessions. Here, take a few tissues. You're okay. You're safe."

"Thank you," said Allison. She dabbed at her eyes and blew her nose. "I feel so stupid. Sometimes I get so angry at Kathryn and the others."

"Angry at them?"

"Yes, if it weren't for them I'd never have to deal with all of these stupid emotions."

"Your emotions are anything but stupid, Allison. They are very real and spring from real experiences. And The Teachers aren't really at fault. No, they are there because you are trying to protect yourself from the pain. When we work together to find the real source of that pain, it will slowly begin to subside and The Teachers will fade away. You will be free."

"I want freedom from the anguish. I want it so much, Dr. Kane. But I don't want to lose Kathryn and Molly and even some of the other ones. Does that sound crazy? Does it make any sense? And *please* don't turn it around and ask if it makes any sense to me."

Dr. Kane smiled and said, "Oh it makes perfect sense. Many people feel that way. Don't worry about that right now. We can talk more about it later."

Kane looked down as his tablet produced a text message alert tone. "But now, I believe you have a guest waiting in the visiting area."

"Oh, that's wonderful! I was just thinking about that a few minutes ago and was hoping she'd drop by today. That's so great!"

Kane smiled again and showed Allison out the door. He directed her to a small, semi-private visiting room with a window to the hallway, and turned back, saying that he would see her tomorrow at nine-thirty.

Allison was beaming with joy when she opened the door but was shocked when she saw who was standing inside the room.

"Dan, what are you doing here? I thought you'd be Margaret. I mean, I thought Margaret was here. I'm sorry, I need to go back to my room."

"Wait, Allison, wait. Just give me a minute. Please."

There was something about Dan's voice that managed to get through the barriers that Allison had erected against him. She tried to keep moving, to back out of the door and disappear, but something about Dan's manner, along with his tone of voice, made her stop.

"Okay, I should thank you for coming to see me, I'm sorry. So, thank you. But please, can we make this short?"

"Yes, of course. Can we just sit down here for a moment, Allison? Just for a moment?"

"Okay. Just for a moment. Margaret will probably be here soon anyway."

"Okay, thank you. Look, Allison, there are really two reasons I'm here. One is that I was hoping we could resolve whatever it is that has caused you to be so angry with me."

"Why do we need to do that? I'm not your client anymore."

Dan looked down at his feet and then back up into Allison's flaming eyes. "Because I care about what happens to you. I . . . I care about you."

"Oh, like you cared about that client you fucked in your office? The girl you lost your license over?"

"Oh, my God, Allison, no, not like that at all. Is *that* what this is all about? Is *that* all this is?"

"Isn't that enough? I mean shit, Dan, I felt like such a fool when I found out about that, especially after some of my own stupid behavior. How could you have done that? How could you have taken advantage of her when she trusted you to help her? And without any remorse!" Allison shook her head and buried her face in her hands.

Dan stood up and Allison could see through the cracks between her fingers that he was pointing at her. His hand was shaking.

"Wait, Allison, stop right there. Now you've got *me* pissed off! You don't know anything about that situation! What do you mean, 'no remorse?!' What gives you the right or the special insight to even imply something like that?! You don't know anything about my life. Not a single day goes by that I don't hate myself for violating Natalie's trust, for undoing months of her therapy! Not a single goddamned day!"

At these words, Allison found herself covering her face with her hands, hot tears threatening to emerge. She wondered vaguely if Dan was able to read something into that—the only way she could communicate at the moment—because she noticed him lowering his voice just slightly. But he kept throwing his words at her.

"I got caught up in an emotional moment with her and I made the most profound mistake of my life. I damaged a life, a beautiful life, and it kills me that I can't go back and reverse my stupidity and save that poor girl from even more misery than she came to me with. I've been trying to atone for my mistake ever since, as if that even makes any sense, and I don't have any idea if I'm making one shitty little bit of progress, but I keep trying every day. And then you come along and accuse me of not caring! I'm sorry, but I just can't take that. So there it is. A few weeks ago you said you wanted me to stop talking to you like a therapist, so there it is, damn it! That's the baggage I'm carrying around and now you get to deal with it too! So now I've wrecked another client. Ex-client. Shit!"

Dan spun around and gave the couch a hard kick, but his foot went under its skirt and his shin slammed into the hard wooden surface just above. "Ow!! Goddamnit!! Fucking hell!!" He limped around the room muttering more obscenities.

Allison looked up and managed to say, "Oh, I'm sorry Dan; is your leg okay?"

Dan collapsed onto the couch and pulled up his pant leg to look at the damage. He was grimacing with pain. Allison knelt down to examine the wound and found that Dan had managed to cut through the epidermis almost to the bone. There was blood everywhere. She grabbed a box of tissues from a nearby end table and gently began to daub up the blood to get a better look at the wound.

"Ooh, I'm sorry, I know that must hurt something awful, Dan. But at least you didn't shatter the bone. You'll be fine in a few weeks. Let's get a proper bandage on that, though." Allison made a move toward the door."

"Wait, Allison, there's more I've got to tell you and I'm afraid if you go out there and they find out what happened in here, I'll be ushered out the front door before I can say another word. So, could you just wait for a second?"

"Yes. Here, let's just put another couple of tissues on that to stop the bleeding. There, that's better." She looked up into his eyes which were still squinted in pain. "Dan, I'm so sorry. Not just about your leg but about what I said. I don't know why I said that about remorse. I guess I've just been assuming some things I had no right to assume. After listening to you now, I feel like an idiot again, for a completely different reason this time. I'm so sorry."

Allison gently patted his knee above the injury as she said these things. She left her hand there when he reached down to cover it with his own.

"Apology accepted, and I'm sorry I yelled at you like that. I let my own shit get the best of me and took it out on you. If I were a better therapist I would have understood your anger long ago. I should have guessed that you heard about Natalie and felt a parallel sense of betrayal and exposure. Naturally you would feel that way. Your childhood puts you on the edge of abandonment all the time. If I'd been sensitive enough to understand the connection then, I would have told you about everything. I'm sorry."

"Apology accepted here, too, Dan. Thank you."

Dan let out a long sigh. "So there's one other thing I want to talk to you about, Allison. It's much easier than the first one, I think, but just as important, probably more so."

At that moment, the door opened and a CRI security man entered. I'm sorry, sir, you need to come with me. And ma'am, please go on back to your room with James here." The man nodded over his left shoulder toward his partner in the hallway.

"He needs a bandage for that leg," said Allison, looking back at Dan.

"We'll take care of that on the way out. Now let's go."

Allison glanced back at Dan, just as James firmly gripped her arm to take her back to the room.

"Allison," he said. "You're not DID. The Teachers, they're not just in your mind. They're . . ."

Allison desperately wanted to hear more of what Dan had to say but she was hustled down the hall before he could continue.

THIRTY-FIVE

· ·

B ack in her room, Allison paced back and forth from her door to the window then, overwhelmed, sat down on the edge of the bed. In the course of the last ninety minutes she had experienced intense emotional pain, shame, anger, relief and confusion. She was confused about Dan's final words to her but even more confused about the abrupt change in her own feelings for him. All of this made her want to sleep for a week.

But before a nap she wanted a shower. She wanted to feel the soothing flow of warm water on her body, that feeling of being in and with the water that she so cherished. So she entered the bathroom and checked the ceiling camera for her hair gel lens cap. She was surprised that "they," whoever "they" were, allowed it to stay in place. Maybe they knew she wasn't at risk. *Maybe they don't care.* That was a new and chilling thought. She put it on hold. There were just too many other things vying for attention.

Allison warmed up the shower and slid out of her clothes. She looked at herself in the mirror, noticed a few small worry lines around her eyes, and made a mental note to try the new cream that she had recently purchased but had left on the boat. She turned and examined her profile. Her breasts still looked young, full and nicely upturned. She smiled and stepped into the shower.

The luxurious and strong stream of warm water was as soothing as she'd imagined, and it lulled her into a sleepy state. She gave in and knelt down on the large tiled floor in a yoga "child's pose" letting the water fall onto her back as if it were a warm embrace. She felt it trickle down behind and between her legs where it awakened repressed longings. She welcomed the exquisite stretch in her lower back and the relief it brought to tensions she had unconsciously stored there for days. She let her neck muscles relax as she thought of Dan.

Dan didn't deserve her hurtful words. He had more than admitted his mistake and clearly felt horrible about what he had done. He was a good man, a man with deep feelings. But none of that was really her business or her concern anyway, was it? Why had she felt so strongly about it all then? Why did she now feel so much relief? *I want to be close to him. Is that okay? He's not my therapist anymore. I guess it's okay, but I'm not really sure how he feels. But if he hadn't felt something, he wouldn't have come to see me. To see me. I want him to see me.*

Allison's body responded to her thoughts and demanded attention. She was surprised at the erotic intensity brought on by the simple, warm thoughts of Dan. *The warmth of Dan.* She brought her chest up off her knees and felt the edges of the spray make her nipples stand up; then she slid herself back and opened her legs to the intense center of the water's flow. She let her head fall back and imagined Dan standing before her, strong and erect, watching her, smiling with something warm and wonderful in his eyes. She opened her legs wider and arched her back. The water became Dan as it warmly and firmly stroked her private softness and flowed into her. She arched again, hard this time, and gave herself fully to the fantasy, pushing her hips forward in smooth but insistent thrusts. The climax stole upon her slowly at first but then took her strongly and irrevocably with one, two, and three peaks of ever increasing ecstasy. At last, Allison collapsed back to the tile and curled up like a contented kitten. She imagined Dan curled up with her, behind her now, holding her, stroking her hair, his breath warm against her neck.

THIRTY-SIX

· ·

A llison awoke with a smile. How long had she been asleep? Five, six minutes? All she knew was that the warm water had not run out. It still rained down upon her, making her feel covered, warm and safe. She rose and shut off the shower, stepped out and dried herself off.

She put on a terrycloth robe, went back into the living room and stood by the window. Below she could see the early evening sun reflecting off the glassy bay, calm in the waning windless warmth of the day. There were several boats out in the broad waters of Lake Washington, all heading for their nighttime moorage, Allison imagined, but no vessels moved within Meydenbauer Bay itself. She gazed far to the west toward the Montlake Cut, picturing her own moorage hidden in Lake Union beyond, and longed for the day she would once again be aboard *Far and Away* and life would be full again.

She stood by the window for fifteen, twenty, thirty minutes, watched the changing light and noticed the bank of dark clouds building in the distance over the Olympic Peninsula but chose to ignore them. Allison's temporal sense was dulled by the new environment and she found it less and less important to know the exact hour and minute. There were two appointments a day, and unless she had visitors, nothing else really demanded her attention. But in spite of that, the thought of returning to her home, and now the vague hope that Dan might be included in that life in some way, kept Allison focused.

At the thought of Dan, Allison moved to the desk and sat down to mull over the words he had spoken before they were so rudely and abruptly separated. For some reason he had evidently become convinced, as had

Allison, that she was not DID. The confirmation, the second opinion, was good to have but it still left open the question of her involvement at CRI. *Why am I here? If I'm a patient on the edge of the target population, I must be way out on the edge.*

But Dan's other message to her was considerably more cryptic. What had he been about to say? Was he simply trying to affirm her experiences in some way in order to make her feel better? That did not seem like something Dan would do. He was in the business of delving deeply into issues, not skimming the surface, not treating symptoms without regard for underlying causes. No, he meant something else. *Not just in my mind . . .*

Allison stared at the computer screen on her desk as she thought more about Dan's words. What in the world had he meant? As she pondered this, Allison idly keyed the name "Dan Gunnison" in a search box on the home page. After a few irrelevant references, she found a link to a site for a Daniel Gunnison M.S., LMHC in Seattle. The site was very basic, but there was a nice picture of Dan's smiling face, a description of his therapeutic approach, and an email address. She quickly memorized the address.

Next, feeling a bit foolish, she went back to the search page and keyed in "Kathryn Johansen." Within two seconds the screen was filled with references. There was a third grade teacher in Omaha, an author of historical fiction, a craft shop owner in Pensacola, and several more, none of which seemed at all relevant. Allison laughed at herself and walked back to the window, attracted by the rays of the evening sun streaming through gaps in the distant clouds.

She hadn't been at the window more than a couple of minutes when she heard a knock at the door. Allison didn't have another session until morning, and dinner wouldn't come for another hour or so, so she was curious and a little wary. She walked to the door and peeked through the security hole.

"Margaret!" Allison pulled the door open and flung her arms around her friend. "Come in, come in! Oh, I'm so glad to see you."

"Me too, Allie, me too."

"Hey, how'd you rate, getting to come up here instead of using the visiting area? This is great! Here, have a seat."

"I didn't even know there was a visiting area. Maybe it's because I'm your lawyer, I don't know. Anyway, I'm here, and I brought this." Margaret pulled a bottle out of her bag.

"Wow, wine?"

"Well, not exactly. They're pretty careful around here. No alcohol allowed, even from your lawyer. This is sparkling cider, but hey, we can pretend, right? Have you got a couple of glasses in that nice kitchen of yours?"

Allison pulled two wine glasses off the shelf and came back to sit with her friend on the couch.

"So tell me, Allie, how's it going so far? Are you okay? You seem so much better than when I left you here before. I mean, I felt like I was dropping off a puppy at the pound."

"I feel a lot better, I do, even though the actual therapy hasn't started yet. There's just one kind of big thing that I'm concerned about."

"Oh?"

"Yeah, I'm convinced that I don't have the condition that this clinical trial is designed to treat."

"Oh, that *is* kind of a big thing. Why are you convinced of that?"

"I did the research, read all of the clinical and research literature I could get online. And, Dan agrees. He told me before I could even tell him."

"Whoa, girl, what? Dan? You still seeing him?"

"Not professionally, no. He stopped by earlier today."

"Wait, wait, wait!" Margaret tucked her legs under her on the couch, flipped some hair away from her face, and turned to face Allison directly. "The last time you and I talked about him you sounded like you were ready to toss him into the nearest pit of fire—a little unjustly, I thought, by the way."

"I know, I know. I was being impulsive and stupid. I was letting my own insecurities crawl all over me."

"You're not, uh, letting *him* crawl all over you, are you?"

"Margaret! No, although . . ."

"Although what?"

"Although, who knows what could develop in the future. I like him very much."

"But, wait a minute. I'm still completely confused here. What about his affair with the client?"

"Natalie?"

"Oh, you even know her name?"

"Yeah, well, I sort of confronted Dan with the whole thing, we had a big fight, and he mentioned her name somewhere along the way. Actually, that was one of the things that convinced me that he was sincerely sorry and that he didn't take it lightly at all. It wasn't just some girl, some client. It was Natalie. He used her name."

"Oh. So you two must have had quite a talk."

"I'd say eighty percent of it was more like a shouting match."

"Was he trying to defend himself, Allie? 'Cause if he was, I think you still need to be careful."

"No, it wasn't like that. I accused him of having no remorse."

"Ooh, ouch."

"Yeah. I had no right to do that—which he also told me in no uncertain terms—because I didn't really know anything about what had happened or how he felt about it. He was totally pissed with me, and with himself all over again. Talk about remorse! I was completely off base. He never once said anything about losing his license or the damage to his career or anything remotely like that. It was all about how he had harmed Natalie, how he had undone her therapy in that one stupid emotional moment, and how he wished he could go back and change everything."

"Wow."

"Yes, I think he's a good man who made a bad mistake years ago, one he freely and painfully admits."

"Sounds like it. So how did you leave things with him?"

Allison laughed. "Well, the part of our conversation was very sweet, but then he got hauled out of the room by CRI Security, so we couldn't really finish."

"Wait . . . you're just full of zingers tonight. Hauled out by Security?"

"Yeah, well, our fighting was pretty loud, I guess. And then there was all the blood."

This time Margaret just stared with her mouth open.

"No, no! He kicked the couch and hit part of the wood with his shin. It was a real mess." Allison produced a guilty little smile and held her hands up to her lips. "I think he was pretty frustrated with me."

"Allie, you've lived a whole life since I've been gone, and it's been only, what, a little over a day?"

The two friends talked for another hour and finished off the bottle of cider. Margaret promised to visit again soon and left Allison feeling tired but happy. She dropped down in her chair at the desk and stared at the screen full of Kathryns. Irrelevant Kathryns. Allison was accustomed to getting high quality results from online searches and rarely looked past the first ten or so. But this evening, she let her mouse stray to the "Next" button. She clicked, and up came a new page of results. Her tired eyes scanned the page and she almost gave up and closed the browser, but one result stood out for its terseness. It read:

> Johansen, K — Am J Surg — Use of frozen section analysis in the treatment of hepatocellular carcinoma — 01-Oct-1979 — 112(4): 232-245.

And once it caught her eye it became even more interesting. Clearly, it was a reference to an old paper concerning the analysis of liver cancer cells from the American Journal of Surgery, and the author was one K. Johansen. A doctor, no doubt. It wasn't the same paper and it wasn't authored by the same doctor, but it was published in the same journal that had lodged in her mind for so many years.

THIRTY-SEVEN

· ·

D r. Kane walked down the hall after a long day and hoped to find Hamilton still in his office. He was bothered by some anomalous baseline data and wanted to alert his boss. He knocked on the door.

"Come in."

Kane walked in and found Hamilton awash in paperwork. The surface of his desk looked like one from a 1950s detective movie, and Kane wondered where Hamilton had even found that much paper, let alone how he knew what it all was. No one worked with paper forms and memos anymore.

Kane tried to hide his incredulity but Hamilton must have seen something on his face because he immediately offered an explanation.

"Damn government agencies. I'm looking at old approval case studies and this is the only way you can get some of the material. I can't believe it. Anyway, it is what it is. What can I do for you, Nathan?"

Hamilton propped his feet up on the paper-covered desk and put his hands behind his head.

"Look, Charles, I can come back in the morning if you like. You look like you're buried, literally."

"No, have a seat, please. I'd welcome the break. Carver's got me busting my ass over this stuff so we'll be ready to file the minute the trial's over. I can't blame him though. He and the investors have an unbelievable amount of money riding on this thing. So, what's up?"

"It's about Allison Walker, our resident patient."

"Yes?"

"I finished her baseline assessment today."

"Good, that's great. So she's ready to go tomorrow?"

"Well, I'm not so sure. I'm somewhat at a loss actually, Charles. I was able to lead her into difficult territory without much trouble, but there was no switching, at least none that I could detect. And that's not terribly unusual—I understand that—but the EEG and derived results were quite odd. I've never seen anything like it. Would you mind having a look? They're up on the system under P-239 slash Baseline."

"Sure, no problem." Hamilton turned away from the pile of paper to his screen. In seconds he was examining the EEG and its analysis.

"I thought the P300 component of the ERP section looked a tad low, for one thing," offered Kane.

"Yes, a bit. But I wouldn't worry too much about that just yet. It's barely below normal, possibly even in range for this part of the population," said Hamilton.

Kane noticed that his boss was reddening around the face and that there were small beads of perspiration forming on his brow. Even without psychology training, he thought, anyone would wonder about that.

"Are you feeling alright, Charles? You look like you're running a fever or something."

"Oh, no, I'm okay. A little overworked, that's all. Is there anything else?"

"Well, I hate to bother you any further, but I'm having a hard time interpreting this . . ." Kane stood and pointed at several rows of data on Hamilton's screen. "This was during a line of questioning regarding her masquerading as a doctor."

"Yes, I see what you mean. That is odd. Are you sure that you haven't superimposed two separate data sets here? I mean, it looks like some form of parallel cognition, but of course it can't be. I think we're looking at an artifact of the system software. Write up a bug report and get it down to engineering tomorrow. They're working on a new release for next week and there might still be time to get a fix in before they freeze the code base."

"Will do. Sorry to have put a kink in your evening, Charles."

"Not a problem. Like I said, I welcome the break. Just get Walker started tomorrow. She'll be fine."

Dr. Kane walked back down the hallway to his own office and sat down, trying to decide if he would write up the report or wait until morning. He decided that it could wait. He would tackle it first thing.

But he continued to be bothered by Hamilton's reaction to the P300 line. Hamilton's appearance clearly indicated anxiety and yet his response was casual, unconcerned. The dichotomy was worrisome, almost schizophrenic, which was ironic, thought Kane. Low P300 was a well-understood indicator of latent schizophrenia.

THIRTY-EIGHT

· ·

Allison peered at the screen, wondering how to dig deeper and whether she even wanted to. The reference to the journal article was not an active link and it left her with no immediate path to more information about this particular K. Johansen. In fact, she realized, it was quite possible that the K stood for something other than Kathryn. It could be Kara, Kaitlin, Karen, or even Karl for that matter. Allison was so tired that she was having trouble making even the simplest of decisions: to dig a little further or go to bed. To her beleaguered mind it seemed a nearly intractable problem. In the end she decided to take one more step and then quit if it failed to lead anywhere interesting.

She went to the home page for the American Journal of Surgery and found the archives section of the site. Full text versions of articles from the oldest issues were not available but abstracts were, so she pressed on. It took mere seconds for Allison to locate and display the one she was looking for. She skipped the paper's summary and went right to the short blurb at the end about the author.

And there it was: Kathryn Johansen, M.D. A sudden chill ran up her spine and she shivered involuntarily. *This is crazy.* The rest of the blurb fell below the bottom edge of the screen and Allison hesitated. *So what if there's a doctor out there named Kathryn Johansen? So what? It doesn't mean anything. There could be ten or twenty doctors with that name. Why should I even care?*

But she did care, in spite of her reasoning. Allison scrolled down the page and found these words:

Dr. Johansen is Chief Surgical Resident at St. Louis University
Hospital in St. Louis, MO.

Allison shook her head. Another connection, but what did it mean?
St. Louis? Is that it? She lives in my home town?

Did she know this person, maybe even learn from her, and then forget
the actual events? *Losing time!* Could she be doing that? Maybe she really
was fully symptomatic. Maybe there were even more dreadful things in her
past. She knew about one, but . . . *No, there aren't any pieces of my history
I can't account for. But . . . would I know if there were?*

For a few terrifying seconds, Allison felt as if she were a stranger in her
own body and she experienced a wrenching, irrational desire to run away
from herself, to split up, to dissociate. Just when life once again seemed
to offer bits of hope, here was this impossible possibility, this portent of
darkness. *Do I even know who I am, or was?*

Then the familiar light-headedness came over her. Allison recognized the
symptom and knew she should protect herself but felt distant, lethargic, and
strangely ambivalent. *What if I fall and hit my head again? It might be a big relief
not to wake up, to just go away. Like they always said I should. Send me away.*

But some small reserve asserted itself and Allison managed to slide off
the chair and onto the floor before the darkness came.

Hours later, Allison woke to a tickling sensation in her nose. She
opened her eyes and a fuzzy beige forest appeared, gradually resolving
into carpet strands. Allison sneezed and slowly crawled back onto her desk
chair. She rubbed her eyes, pulled back her hair, and checked the time on
her computer: 4:37 AM. Her light-headedness was gone but an uneasiness
remained. She made a trip to the bathroom and returned.

Deciding whether or not to further pursue the Kathryn Myth, as she
began thinking of it, was too difficult in her sleepy state so Allison let it float
and checked her email instead. That didn't take any mental commitment.
Somewhere in the back of her mind she knew that she would eventually
compose and send something to Dan but she wanted to think things through
before doing that. Still, just checking email was innocuous enough.

There were a couple of simple questions from potential yacht buyers
and Allison answered them quickly, bringing her mind back into focus in
the process. There was another email from a client who wanted to know if
Allison was indeed the person mentioned in the recent Seattle Times article.
There goes that piece of business, she sighed. *I wonder how many more will*

follow? Allison keyed in a carefully worded response that answered her client's question in the affirmative but also implied that there had been a basic misunderstanding which she expected would be cleared up in the coming weeks. *Hey, this whole thing is full of misunderstandings,* she rationalized as she hit the Send icon. Too late, she realized that she should consult with Margaret before taking a position that could conceivably find its way back to the court system. She vowed to keep email silence if any other clients asked that question, at least until she could talk to Margaret about it.

Allison scrolled down through a mass of commercial email, deleting them all without opening a single one. Then, with those off the screen, another small batch appeared, one of which caught her eye immediately. The sender was Daniel Gunnison. She opened it.

Allison,

I think I'm probably persona non grata at CRI (but I hope no longer with you) after all the commotion I caused in the visiting room yesterday, not to mention the bloodstains. I noticed that texting to your phone doesn't work—tried that last night—so I'm hoping you can get email. Would you please send me a reply so I'll know?

I'd really like to continue our conversation via email, if you're willing. As I said just before CRI's Finest suggested I take a hike out the front door, I'm convinced that you're not suffering from DID. I don't have much more detail to offer you yet, but I'd suggest looking more closely at your Teachers and your own personal history. I no longer think they are the classic "parts" that we talked about at Starbucks. I'd also strongly urge you to talk with your doctors there at the Institute about this. I'm a little concerned that you're even in this trial now, and I feel largely responsible for the fact that you are.

I'm getting some help from a good friend and doctor named Skip Hanover at the UW on your case. No, that doesn't sound right. I don't think of you as a case. You're no longer officially my client, anyway. I think of you as a very interesting, intelligent, and yes, beautiful, woman (but please don't take that in the context of my regrettable past) whom I want to get to know better if she'll let me. And, if I can help along the way, I very much want to.

Wishing you nothing but the best,
Dan

Allison let out her breath, realizing she'd held it while reading Dan's email twice. Without a second thought, Allison composed and sent a quick reply.

Dan,

Thank you so much for the email. I'm sorry I've been such a rat. I think I go on some kind of mental hyper-alert with these kinds of things. I know, you'd probably say it has something to do with my childhood and you'd probably be right. Anyway, thank you for understanding. And yes, I'd love to continue on email with you, at least until I can see you in person again.

Your non-client,

Allison

Allison leaned back in her chair and sighed. *So much for thinking things through. I hope I'm not being an idiot.*

Allison went back and re-read Dan's mail again, this time from the Kathryn Myth point of view. It was encouraging to think that she wasn't alone in her quest for understanding. When she finished, she did a search for St. Louis University Hospital and went immediately to their website and then to the Physician Search section. She keyed in "Kathryn Johansen" and got no results.

Well, she thought, that paper was published decades ago, so she could be anywhere now. Maybe not even in St. Louis. Allison noticed a link to the St. Louis Metropolitan Medical Society and followed it. A search there also came up empty. Probably moved to another city years ago. As a last ditch effort to rule out St. Louis, Allison went to the Contact Us page on the medical society site and found an email address. She composed a quick query, asking for any information, historical or current, on Dr. Kathryn Johansen. She cited the American Journal of Surgery paper thinking it might help. Finally, Allison went to the journal's website and sent them a similar query.

She waited for a few minutes, hoping that someone might respond quickly, then remembered that even in St. Louis it was still early. So Allison decided to make some oatmeal and get ready for her first day of actual therapy.

THIRTY-NINE

. . . .

When the knock on her door came at 9:00, Allison was ready. Dr. Kane greeted her and led her down the hall. He was pleasant, as usual, but Allison thought she detected a certain clinical distance, like a doctor would try to maintain between himself and a terminal patient—an objectivity aimed both at patient care and self-protection. It was in his questions. There were more of them than usual and they seemed to be probing for something. Did Allison sleep well last night? Were there any troubling or confusing dreams? Did she eat breakfast and was her digestive system functioning normally? Was she overly worried or concerned about anything?

Allison provided answers that seemed to satisfy Kane, until the last one. That one just seemed absurd and insulting.

"Of course I'm worried! How could you even ask me that? How could any patient in this situation *not* be worried, Dr. Kane? So what is your definition of 'overly' worried? Am I more concerned about my situation than a rational person should be? Is that what you mean?"

"No, Allison, that's not what I meant to imply. Of course you'd be concerned about your situation. Perhaps I didn't frame the question well."

"Perhaps not." Allison sat on the couch and stared back at her doctor, using her silence to push Kane into further elaboration.

"I was thinking back to a comment you made yesterday, Allison. I believe you were wondering if this particular therapy was appropriate for you. That's what I was aiming at."

"You might have simply asked."

"Yes, of course. I'm sorry," said Kane with a slight bow of his head and a thin smile.

"Okay, well, yes I'm still concerned about that but you seemed confident so I've tried to put it behind me. But now you're bringing it up again and I'm not sure what that means. Should I be more worried?"

"No. I'm sorry I brought it up. Do you think we could get started?"

"I guess so. Sure."

Allison donned the pink hat and Dr. Kane adjusted it for her. Kane set up the parameters for the session on his tablet, made a few short notes, then leaned forward in his prayer-like pose before beginning.

"Alright. Good. Allison, I'd like you to start today by thinking of a peaceful time in your life for a few moments, a time when you felt whole and contented with life. Go ahead a take a moment to remember a time like that. It will help if you can remember a very specific experience. Then, just let me know when you have formed a clear image of a time like that in your mind."

Allison nodded and closed her eyes. It didn't take long for her to remember such a time. She imagined being in that moment again, and tried to feel the same deep-breath kind of contentment and ease that she experienced then. She nodded again, signaling to Kane that she was ready.

Kane spoke in his quiet, soothing baritone. "Very good, Allison. Now, keep your eyes closed if that helps you stay in that moment, and tell me as much as you can about what you see, hear, feel—everything you remember about that time. Just take it slowly and enjoy the experience all over again."

Allison kept her eyes closed and began. "I'm on my boat, alone, on my first solo trip to the San Juan Islands. It is late September and the early evening sunshine still has some warmth left in it. The water is like glass as I approach the entrance to Reid Harbor." Allison paused and let out a long sigh.

"It sounds beautiful, Allison. Where is that harbor and what do you see?"

"This is the south harbor on Stuart Island. There are a few rocks at the entrance but the channel is clean and the tide is nearly high. I move the throttle to idle and glide in. I notice only four other boats inside, one tied to the dock at the far end and the others moored to buoys off the eastern shore. Reid is a large harbor, so it feels empty. The sun is setting behind the trees on a hillside. I find a mooring buoy just off a little cove lined with

Madrona trees. There's no wind and I'm able to snag the buoy easily. I'm secure. I smell salt and a subtle ammonia-like scent, probably from the seals on the rock way off my starboard side. I turn on the anchor light and shut down the diesel. I hear the call of a tern and see the last small ripples of my wake lapping at the nearby shore."

Allison took another deep breath and could feel a crooked little smile forming as she visualized what happened next.

"I fix a hot cider and climb to the upper deck to watch the sunset. The forests around me are moving from green to gray as the sun sinks lower. There's a large three-masted sailboat moored across the harbor and I see a man walk out on the foredeck carrying something in his arms. There is barely enough light left in the sky to see the man's face, and at first I can't identify the thing he carries. But now, as my eyes begin to adjust, I notice that there are two things in his arms and one of them is a little girl whom he gently lowers to the deck. She sits down and looks back up at the man, who I assume is her father. I think that she is maybe five or six years old."

"The air is cooler now and I'm glad to have the warmth of my cider cup. I breathe in its steam and watch, still wondering about the other object which now seems to have a lower part and several pipe-like appendages above. It's only when the sounds reach my ears that I understand. It's a bagpipe. I hear the long, haunting, Scottish tones as they drift across the water. The man is playing Amazing Grace and I cry with the beauty of it."

Allison took a tissue from the table in front of her and wiped her eyes. She could feel herself still smiling through the tears. She heard Kane sniff once and wondered if her narrative had affected him as well. She thought of asking him and then dismissed the idea and opened her eyes.

Kane was sitting opposite her with steepled hands under his nose. His eyes were closed and he kept silent for several more seconds. Finally, he looked up and spoke.

"That must have been a very moving experience, Allison. It felt that way to me."

"Yes, it was, and a bit sad, too."

"Could we explore that sad part for a few moments, Allison? I think it would be helpful for the next part of our work here today."

"I can try."

"Good. So, what was it about that experience that brought on the sadness?"

Allison thought it was obvious and wanted to tell Kane that he ought to know, but reined herself in. He was only doing his therapist job and his intentions seemed good. So she answered.

"It was the father-daughter part. It was unlike anything I'd ever experienced. I don't know who my real father is, and I barely remember my foster fathers. After I left the first home I never wanted to go through that pain again so I probably avoided it by keeping my distance."

"And what about your adopted father? Were you ever able to feel close to him? I don't see anything in your chart about him." asked Kane.

"He was hardly ever there. And when he was around, my sister Beth wouldn't let me near him. He was always traveling on business, and when he'd come back he'd always seem distracted or angry about one thing or another. He might ask me how I'd been, maybe even tousle my hair a bit before he'd go sit down with Beth. But then, later, when I was about ten . . ."

Allison looked up with surprise. "That's strange."

"What's strange, Allison?"

"I've never been able to even *think* about that time without getting physically ill, let alone actually talk about it. And now . . . I don't know, it just seems okay somehow. Not the things themselves, but talking about them. It seems . . . like history, dry old pages. You know what I mean?"

"Yes, I do. You feel that you can stand outside those events now."

"Yes, I do. It was a terrible time but I'm not afraid to think of it anymore. It's kind of like it happened to someone else, even though I know it was me. You must be an amazing therapist, Dr. Kane."

"Thank you, but I can't take all the credit. This is probably the Carver therapy working—the Amethyst System, as they've code-named it."

"Oh. I'd actually forgotten about that. I still think you're amazing."

Kane nodded, smiled and then continued. "Thank you. Do you feel like you can go on? Can you talk about what actually happened when you were ten?"

"Yes, I think I can. It was horrible. I was still in elementary school and Beth had just started junior high. I remember it was a Friday because my school had one of those teacher prep half-days but Beth's didn't. So I walked home and got there just before lunch time. Both of my adopted parents worked, so I thought it was strange that my father's car was parked in the driveway. I walked in the front door and yelled something like, 'Hi Dad, I'm home.' I didn't hear anything so I went ahead and fixed myself a sandwich and watched some TV.

About a half hour later I decided to go upstairs to get some homework done. I called for my father again but there was no answer. I thought, well, he must be out in the backyard or something, so I just walked up the stairs and headed for the bathroom. And that's where I found him. Actually, I smelled him first. I didn't know you could smell blood but I guess when there's that much of it . . . it smelled like rusty iron and I knew, even before I pushed the door open, that something was dreadfully wrong. I didn't want to go in. The combination of the quiet and the smell was terrifying. And I've never talked about this to anyone, ever. I can't believe I'm doing it now.

Thinking back on it, I remember knowing that it was blood, like I'd smelled it before. My mind was so confused. I remember thinking we're going to need five or six units of blood, at least. I even glanced around with the intention of ordering a nurse to get the patient's blood type and get the units here. I shook off that crazy thought and pushed the door open.

He was in the tub, fully dressed, shoes and all, but his shirt sleeves were rolled up and he had hacked away at both wrists. It was like he wanted to be sure. These weren't just slices, especially on the left side. He had nearly cut off his left hand. A serrated kitchen knife lay in the bottom of the tub, soaked in red like the rest of everything—the tub, the clothes, the body. His eyes were wide open. It was horrific. I thought about checking for a pulse but I knew it was pointless. He was so white, whiter than any person I'd ever seen. It wasn't even like looking at a real person. For a moment I felt removed, detached. I examined the body like a medical student would assess a cadaver. And then, I came to myself again. The reality of it hit me like a baseball bat to the gut and before I could turn away, I threw up, right on the body, not once, but three times. On the second and third times, I'm sure I could've turned away, but I didn't. I'm so ashamed now to even think of it, to admit it. Please don't tell anyone, Dr. Kane."

Kane leaned forward across the table. "No, of course not, Allison. Are you okay? Do you want to stop talking about this now? You don't have to go on. What you experienced that day was way beyond what anyone should ever have to deal with, let alone a ten year old child."

"No, I'm alright, amazingly. I'm okay. I think I need to finish, though. May I go on?"

"Yes, of course, but please stop at any time you feel the need to. These things hurt you deeply then, but they can't hurt you again. That was all in the past. You're safe now."

Allison continued. "There was a note. He had written a short note and left it on the sink. In a way, reading it was worse than finding my dead father drenched in his own blood. It said something like, 'Lori,'—that's what he called Delores—'the company went under today. I've been trying to save it for months but I just couldn't. I've been borrowing money to keep us going, lots of money. I'm so sorry to leave you with that, and with this. I can't do anything more. I've failed to take care of you and our daughter. I loved you. I'm so sorry.'

"The note actually said 'daughter,' singular?" asked Kane, his mouth hanging slack.

"Yes, it actually said that."

"I'm so sorry for you, Allison. That, with everything else, is unimaginably cruel and sad."

"There's one last thing."

"Okay."

"I was scared, I was shocked, and I was so angry. When I put down the note, I turned back to the tub and spit the last of my foul-tasting saliva on my dead father. Then I guess I passed out, right there on the floor next to the tub. I woke, I don't know how much later, to the sound of Beth screaming and the feel of her fists pounding on me. She was flailing at me, sobbing, and wailing, 'You killed my daddy! You killed him! You killed him! I hate you! Get out!'

As the reality of the situation flew back into my mind, the first feeling to return must have been anger because I pushed my sister away, hard. She slipped on the tile floor and hit her head on the side of the tub. I checked for breathing and a steady pulse. She was unconscious but her vitals were fine. I knew she'd be okay, probably just a minor concussion. You see, I knew a few things about medicine even then, but I only understood a little of it. I think Kathryn understood it all.

I remember thinking—and I know this is horrible—that at least I had shut Beth up, stopped that intolerable screaming. I went for the phone and called 911, or whatever we used then, probably the operator. Then I just sat down on the carpet outside the bathroom and waited. I didn't even cry. I remember thinking that maybe I *did* kill him; that maybe if they hadn't adopted me there'd be enough money; that maybe he wouldn't have done this if I'd never been born. I felt sure that Dolores and Beth would finally send me away and I knew that I deserved it."

"Allison, you didn't deserve any of that. Not any of it. None of that was your fault. Do you understand that?"

"Yes, I guess, but I rarely feel it."

"No, of course you don't. But perhaps starting today you'll be able to feel it more deeply and consistently. You were a little child, a good child trying to do your best in a bad home situation. It seems to me that the family system was deeply flawed and dysfunctional from the beginning, way before you came on the scene. You had nothing to do with this tragedy, Allison. Once you start to internalize that, you will begin to feel freer. And your anger? It seems to me that it is more than justified."

"Thank you, Dr. Kane."

"Yes, of course, Allison. If you don't mind, could I ask you one more thing? Did you stay with your adopted mother and sister after that?"

"I did, until I was eighteen. I left that very day."

"Then, it must have been extremely hard for you during your teenage years."

"After a while it was just gray. That's how I think of it, gray. After the first miserable year or so, we just settled into a routine and we never talked about the past. Not once. In some ways it was like nothing had ever happened, but in other ways it colored everything. It colored life gray. Nobody cried anymore, nobody seemed overly sad, but nobody was happy either. We just were. We did the dishes, we did homework, Dolores went back to work, Beth and I even went to our separate school dances. But she and I rarely talked, and never about anything of substance. We never left the safe, dull gray zone."

"I understand. You survived. All three of you survived in your own ways. Allison, I think we've gone far enough for today. You've made excellent progress. I hope you can feel very good about that. Why don't you take the afternoon off. Get some exercise in the gym right down the hall, do some reading. Whatever you want. We won't need another session today."

Allison nodded. She was feeling better, but drained of energy.

"But before you go back to your room," Kane continued, "I'd like you to try thinking back on that wonderful experience in Reid Harbor again. Close your eyes and try to smell the trees, the salt water, the hot cider. Watch the sunset. Listen to the bagpipe. Just take a few moments. You don't need to talk. Just relax and put yourself back in that quiet, soothing moment. Then open your eyes when you're ready to go. I'll be right here finishing up some notes."

FORTY

· ·

D r. Kane stayed in the office late that night, annotating data sets from the patient sessions of the day. This wasn't dry clerical work by any means. Quite the opposite, in fact. It took tremendous concentration: careful analysis of conversations based on notes, time-correlation between EEG signals and session audio, and interpretation of the EEG charts. But even so, Kane found his mind wandering back to Allison Walker's case time and again.

The day's treatment seemed hugely successful and Kane felt certain that Allison was not one of the patients randomly chosen for placebo. In fact, it was easy to guess who was and who wasn't, just based on patient behavior during sessions. So much for double blind experimentation. At least that was a positive indication of the effectiveness of the Amethyst protocol. And, of course, he didn't actually know. He was just reacting to what he observed.

And yet, there were several things about the Walker case that were troubling. She certainly had a difficult childhood. Traumatic would not be too strong a word. That fit her diagnosis. But there was apparently no direct abuse, or none that anyone had yet uncovered. That didn't fit. And then there was this very odd situation with her alters. Walker had actually made mention of one coming out—in an indirect sort of way—during her experience of the suicide. So if Kathryn truly is an alter, she must have arisen out of some other trauma that preceded the suicide. She would not have first materialized in that moment, fully formed with all of her medical background. Conclusion: either there is earlier hidden trauma or this is not a case of DID.

A knock on his door interrupted Kane's thought process. He could see through the large window in the top of the door that it was Dr. Hamilton. Kane waved him in.

"Nathan, have you got a moment. You look busy."

"Sure, no problem; I'm just finishing up. Have a seat." Kane motioned toward an empty chair across the desk. "What can I do for you?"

"Oh, nothing new to put on you Nathan. You're probably overloaded as it is. No, I just wanted to see how things are coming along with that patient of yours. What's her name? Walker? How's she responding?"

What an interesting coincidence. "Amazingly well, actually."

Kane proceeded to tell his boss about the day's session and how Allison had been able to face an exceptionally painful childhood incident—one she had apparently never been able to speak about before—with little or no fear.

Kane could see Hamilton's face brighten with the news. *Why is he so interested in her out of all the others in the trial? Why am I, for that matter? There's something special, something unusual about her.*

"Excellent. Glad to hear it, Nathan. Good work."

Kane nodded politely, acknowledging the compliment, as Hamilton got up to leave.

Then, just as he was about to close the door behind him, Hamilton turned around. "Oh, by the way Nathan, you haven't noticed any, uh, odd or paranoid behavior with her, have you?"

"You mean with Walker? No, nothing comes to mind. Why? Are you worried about that P300 waveform?"

"No, just looking after the patients, Nathan. You'll let me know if anything like that does come up though, won't you? With any of our patients."

"Yes, of course."

"Good. Thanks." Hamilton paused and Kane thought he had something more to say but he just patted the edge of the door, closed it, and walked away.

Kane finished up the evening's work. He had managed to keep his mind off the Walker case for the last half hour, but he finally succumbed to a temptation that had been nagging at him all evening. He punched in the number for the IT department and waited.

"IT, Tim Johnson."

"Hey, Tim, Nathan Kane here. I didn't think you'd still be around."

"Yep, still hangin'; what's going on up there?"

"Oh, just finishing up for the day. Say, Tim, is the infrared camera system still off in the Walker room?"

"Wow, that's freakin' weird."

"What? What's weird?"

"That you'd ask that right now. Dr. Hamilton was just down here about twenty minutes ago. He asked me to switch on that room for the first time since the patient's been here. One of the lenses was fouled so I sent maintenance up to fix it."

"Don't we have to tell the patients when we start monitoring, even though it's just software looking at them?"

"Yeah, Hamilton said he'd take care of that."

"Okay, Tim, thanks. You have a good evening."

"You too, Doc."

Kane hung up and stared at the wall.

FORTY-ONE

. . . .

Taking Kane's advice, Allison forced herself to do forty-five minutes on the treadmill in the gym down the hall from her room. It did feel good to get the blood flowing again, and by the time she got back to the room, she was hungry. She also felt more alert than she had in days. So she fixed herself a tomato and cheese sandwich and sat down in front of the computer.

There were three emails that immediately stood out from the rest: one from Dan, one from the Medical Society in St. Louis, and one from someone at the American Journal of Surgery. She opened the last one first and found a very short message indicating that the paper Allison cited was the only one ever published in their journal authored by Dr. Johansen.

Thinking that her Kathryn Myth research was likely to dead-end, she put off the Medical Society email and went straight to Dan's. It was short but encouraging:

Allison,

What a relief to get your reply. So glad to hear from you. You sound good. I've only got a few seconds before my first client arrives this morning so I'll have to send you more later, but for now I just want you to know that I'm thinking of you and wishing for the time, not too many weeks from now, when you'll be out of there.

In the meantime, could I have your permission to contact your friend and lawyer, Margaret Yee? I'd just like to have another way to stay in touch with you and to help in any way I can.

I'm here for you,

Dan

Allison smiled and thought about that time, "not too many weeks from now," as Dan had said. He made it sound like it was just around the corner but it felt like an eternity to her. It seemed such a long time to be cooped up in this velvet cage, to be analyzed every day, to be away from Dan. She wanted to be with him, to talk with him, to explore him, to let him explore her, not as a client but as a friend and maybe, yes, as a lover. She wanted to tell him about her breakthrough discussion with Dr. Kane and how she now felt as though she might be able to separate herself from her past, or perhaps even incorporate her past, integrating it positively, not fearfully, with her present and future. That seemed a better outcome if she could achieve it.

Allison rolled all these things around in her mind, mentally composing several versions of an email to Dan when the Medical Society email hijacked her attention. She had been staring at the unopened item the whole time but now it came back into focus. *Well, let's just get this over with. Let's just close the book on this myth and move on.*

Allison opened the email but had to read it three times before she could even begin to process its implications. It felt a bit like running into a favorite old elementary school teacher in a sleazy bar. The context is all wrong and recognition doesn't function normally.

It took a fourth reading before Allison's mind allowed itself to put together the pieces.

Dear Ms. Walker:

Thank you for your inquiry. As you may know, part of our function here at the Society is to maintain a public historical database of our region's medical establishments and physicians. To that end, I'm delighted to provide you with the following summary.

Dr. Kathryn Johansen was born in Manteo, North Carolina to parents Molly and Fredrick Johansen. She began her undergraduate education at the University of North Carolina but finished her premed work at

Washington University, here in St. Louis. She then went on to earn her M.D. from Johns Hopkins University, finishing in 1976. She returned to St. Louis the following year and did her internship at St. Louis University Hospital, followed by a surgical residency.

Dr. Johansen rose to the position of Chief Surgical Resident at SLUH before falling victim to a tragic weather-related accident. She died on January 7, 1980 from upper spinal cord injuries incurred during the accident while undergoing an emergency C-section to save her unborn daughter. Dr. Johansen left no living relatives other than the child, who was put into foster care.

Ms. Walker, please let me know if I can be of assistance again in the future.

Lillian Staples, MLS
Sr. Librarian
St. Louis Metropolitan Medical Society

Allison stared at the screen as a flood of conflicting emotions overwhelmed her. *January 7, 1980. That is my birth date.*

FORTY-TWO

. . . .

I am that child. Kathryn was my mother. I had a mother, a real mother. And Molly—my very own grandmother!

Allison cried quietly into her hands. She cried for the joy of identity, of connectedness, of family, of love. And she cried for grief. *My mother lived and died all in a single moment for me. I had her only for an instant. But I did have her and she had me. I'll take that. It's more than I ever hoped for.*

Allison cried steadily for a long time and it felt good. She had a real history, a real family. They were all gone now but they had lived in real towns, went to real schools, occupied real houses, ate dinner, had babies, lived. Little Allison did not just appear out of nowhere, destined to be shuttled around the foster care system. Her mother would have kept her if she'd lived; Allison felt sure of that.

But then new questions started to form. What of these strange memories? Why did she have them at all? They weren't even memories in the sense that most people spoke of family history. They were more like pieces of knowledge: medical and nautical knowledge, not personal in any way, other than the names Kathryn and Molly. And then there were the others, much fuzzier, older, unnamed and unclear.

And what about her father? Allison knew from the email that he was no longer in the picture. Was he dead too, had they divorced, or perhaps never married? And why did she not have any knowledge related to him, or to her grandfather for that matter?

All these questions lurked around the edges of Allison's newfound identity, threatening to move toward the center and bring new worries with them. But Allison decided to leave them all at the edges, at least for a while, so that she could concentrate on the matter of her own treatment which had now taken on new meaning.

Allison searched her mind for information about brain structures, especially those related to memory and fear. She found that she had a reasonably good grasp of brain anatomy and physiology—knowledge she had never had occasion to use in the past and was probably out of date—but no corresponding psychology to speak of, just basic Psych 101 survey-level information that she recalled from her own studies. Still, the combination was enough to build on and she felt that it would give her an enormous head start.

Hours later, finished with the day's research, Allison found that she was hungry again. She heated up a can of soup and sat back down, exhausted. She had started with basic Wikipedia articles to get some direction, and then quickly moved on to the key academic journals. These had required intense concentration and much re-reading but the work had paid off. Allison now had a much deeper understanding of the theory behind the treatment she was receiving. Based on other work in the field of psychophysiology, the theory appeared sound and, even better, it did actually seem to work for her. It had allowed her to process some incredibly difficult memories and had changed her self-image almost instantly.

But that immediacy itself bothered her. Personally, she wanted to accept the outcome without reservation or critique, but clinically she found it hard to believe that such an intense burst of unilateral amygdala stimulation would not produce side-effects of some kind. She understood that the stimulation was focused and precisely timed but nevertheless she had her concerns. Current research clearly supported the idea of hemispheric specialization, and targeting the left amygdala in particular made some sense in this situation, she had to admit. And yet, nature was, by and large, symmetrical, and the artificial introduction of intense unilateral stimulation raised questions in Allison's mind. She would ask Dr. Kane about this in the morning.

But what would she tell him about Kathryn and Molly? She needed to find a way to convince him that she had been misdiagnosed, but how could she offer any credible evidence? She didn't even understand it herself. She continued pondering the imponderable as she got ready for bed.

Sleep came easily as the day's effort overcame Allison. But somewhere in the darkness just after midnight, a strange dream began dominating her unconscious mind. It was a simple dream unlike anything she had experienced before and it repeated throughout the night. In retrospect, it reminded Allison of something a surgical patient might experience while coming off a poorly administered anesthetic.

There were no people in this abstract dream, if it could even be called a dream at all. There were just two identical, massive black stone spheres, separated by perhaps four or five meters of empty space. Allison had the impression that the spheres were each at least a meter in diameter and were of incalculable weight. In the dream she knew that it was her solemn responsibility—in fact, her *only* role in life—to keep these dark masses apart. It was absolutely critical that they never touch. She did not know why, but she knew this to be true and did not question it.

And yet these masses were in motion, moving slowly but inexorably toward one another as if drawn by their own considerable gravities. But Allison could not touch the spheres or physically intervene in any way. She had no direct way to stop their motion and yet it was her life's purpose to do so. And so she tried everything else she could think of. She willed them apart. She even prayed them apart. But they defied her every attempt, moving closer and closer together.

The relative proximity of the stones seemed to correlate not only with a deep sense of dread and impending personal failure but also with a hideously building nausea. As the stones drifted ever closer, Allison could feel excessive saliva squirting into her mouth, preparing her to disgorge the contents of her stomach. She summoned every last unit of psychic energy as the stones approached each other, demanding that they cease their evil progress. And then, the unimaginable happened. The two petro-spheres collided and fused in a massive explosion.

When the blinding light subsided, Allison miraculously remained, but so did the spheres. The hideous objects were once again three or four meters apart and had begun moving toward each other. The cycle repeated, reaching its dreadful climax several more times until Allison finally woke in a pool of cold sweat.

FORTY-THREE

. . . .

It took Nathan Kane three attempts before his patient answered her door the next morning. And when she did, Kane was shocked to see her hair in disarray and dark circles under both of her eyes. She was wearing sweatpants and a tee shirt. She mumbled something about a rough night and said she would be out in just a minute.

When she finally re-emerged, Kane saw that Allison had pulled her hair back into a ponytail but that everything else about her appearance remained unchanged. She followed him down the hall to the usual room and slumped down on the couch.

"Are you doing alright, Allison? You don't seem quite yourself."

"Sorry. Like I said, I had a rough night. Horrible repetitive dream."

"Do you want to tell me about it before we get started?"

"Sure," said Allison, with little conviction.

Kane listened as Allison told him about the two huge stones, her singular task, and the impossibility of that task as the two masses inevitably collided. She also mentioned the accompanying nausea and finished by saying, "I felt like Sisyphus, except horizontal. At least I didn't have to push the damn things up a hill all night. And, I guess one night beats eternity."

Kane thought he saw the beginnings of a smile on his patient's face and returned it. "Sounds like the epitome of frustration, Allison."

"Yes, you could say that. And so pointless."

"Perhaps, but let me suggest one possible interpretation, if I may."

"Sure, knock yourself out."

Kane smiled and nodded. "It could be that this dream is a response to your own mental reintegration. Here's how I see it: the first stone sphere is a symbol of you—your primary personality; the second one represents all of The Teachers, as you call them. You've lived with The Teachers for as long as you can remember, right?"

"Yes, from the beginning."

"Alright. Now, there are probably elements of your psyche that understand the potential for integration, for elimination of The Teachers as separate personalities, and those parts of you may even desire this, in a manner of speaking. But the majority of you resists. You still want to keep The Teachers as separate persons and to interact with them this way, simply because that is your normality. It's what you're accustomed to."

"And so I try desperately to keep the spheres apart," said Allison.

"Yes, exactly. But you also see the inevitability of the merger, and that is very distressing for you."

"Dr. Kane, can I ask you a question about this?"

"Of course."

"Are dreams like this common at the beginning of therapy?"

"Actually, no, not particularly. At least not ones this abstract."

"And resistance like this? Is that common?"

"Yes, but that's a bit more complicated," Kane began. "Sometimes the primary personality will express anxiety or fear at the thought of a part being pushed around or asked to leave. These emotions spring out of a deep unconscious concern about the potential loss of protection provided by that part. It isn't usually expressed that way, though. The patient usually says something to the effect that the part will be angry, or upset, or might do something embarrassing or harmful. And not all of the parts are always known by the primary, either. So in those cases, we might see different expressions of anxiety or fear, possibly coming out in dream form. But I have to say, I've never heard of a dream quite as definitive as yours."

"I think that might be because my situation is different," said Allison.

Kane could see that his patient's energy and focus was returning. She spoke with more conviction and re-worked her ponytail to tuck in some stray hairs.

"Oh? How is that?" Kane asked.

"Well, last night when I wasn't busy trying to keep two impossibly massive stones apart, I was wrestling with something else. I was trying to figure out how to tell you, or whether to tell you, about a discovery I made yesterday. Actually two discoveries."

Kane felt himself go on alert but tried not to show it. *Hamilton said to keep my eyes open. What is this?* "And did you decide what to do?" he asked.

"Yes, I did. I want to try to tell you about them, but I have to warn you; you'll need to keep a very open mind. This isn't going to sound particularly sane. It may be me against the whole medical establishment on this one, but just listen, okay?"

Kane smiled, nodded, and worked to control his own anxiety. *Me against the establishment? Damn.* "Of course I'll listen, Allison, go ahead."

"Well, let me just dive in then. Here goes. These parts of mine—Kathryn and Molly in particular—they are, or I should say were, real people." Allison looked back, wide-eyed at Kane, seeming to gauge his reaction.

Kane felt himself relax. He smiled and nodded his head. "That's a very normal and understandable feeling, Allison. They *are* real people in a meaningful way. They are parts of you. And when you say specifically that they *were* real people, that tells me that you are getting closer to accepting your reintegration."

"No, no, that's not what I'm trying to say at all, Dr. Kane. See, I'm not sure that you can deal with this right now."

Not sure that I can deal with this? Transference. Kane decided to push back a bit. "If you think so, Allison. But I'm wondering if this might be precisely the right time to move forward. Here, why don't you put on this lovely little hat and we can get started." Kane offered her the fuzzy pink apparatus.

"No, not now. That's not what I need. I need you on my side right now. *My* side. And I don't need this therapy anymore." Allison held up both hands, palms out.

Kane slowly put down the hat and pushed it as far away from Allison as he could. "Okay, that's absolutely fine. We don't need to do any more today. And I *am* on your side, Allison. If there are any sides to be taken here, I'm on yours."

"Okay, thank you. But I should warn you, there may not be any sides right now, but there will be, trust me. The Amethyst therapy has the potential for serious side-effects, at least for some parts of your patient population, including me." said Allison as she got up to leave.

After Kane delivered his patient back to her room, he went to his office and sat down with his hands steepled against his chin. *What just happened there? Choosing sides? The medical establishment out to get her? Side-effects threatening her? I've got to talk to Charles.*

Kane got up and strode down the hall toward Hamilton's office, but even from ten steps away he could hear Dr. Carver's booming voice coming from within. He stopped just short of the door and listened, trying to determine if the meeting was near an end or if he should give up and come back later. Carver could be a bit long-winded.

The conversation seemed heated, at least on Carver's end. Kane picked up a few fragments from Carver but could not hear Hamilton's responses.

He was about to turn around and walk back to his office when he heard, "Damn it, Charles, I hope you're right about that . . .

Yes, even something as little as that, absolutely . . .

What? No. We have her in my old suite for a very specific reason; you know that."

Kane glanced up and down the hall. No one there. He moved closer.

"Not just Big Red, no. And I hate that name. Who started that, anyway? Sometimes I wonder if you're focusing at all. We give her all the comforts of home, and more, so that we don't create extraneous symptoms . . .

Right, of course, and by the way, Red was indicating very disturbed sleep last night. Did you catch that? . . .

Then why the fuck didn't I get an email from you within milliseconds?! And remind me again, who's the rent-a-doc you've got on her case anyway?

You're kidding; that little bat-faced guy? Well, he might be good but he's expendable. Remember that. You know what to do: the moment you detect anything even *hinting* at induced schizophrenia, they both disappear. You know the stakes here, for you personally and for the company. You have no idea the kind of pressure I'm getting from the board right now and we've got that meeting tomorrow. This trial *will* succeed Charles . . .

No, don't give me that crap; the treatment works. Even if I didn't give a shit about the board there's an overwhelming ethical argument for making Amethyst available . . .

Yes, ethical! You've seen it over and over again. It's just the outliers. If we have to, we'll solve that problem another way, but it *will* get solved. We just need to push it into the future. We can't deal with it until after FDA approval and the money starts to roll in. I need you totally with me on this tomorrow in the boardroom. Don't fuck this up."

That sounded like a conversation-ender to Kane. He felt as though he couldn't move, as if he had leaden legs in an adrenaline-infused nightmare. But he had to move. He turned and walked as fast as he could back toward his office and entered his door just as he heard Hamilton's open and Carver fire off a couple of unrelated directives.

Kane closed the door behind him and sat in front of his computer monitor as if he were working diligently on session notes. He had not yet written anything about Allison's last session and now he didn't know what to do. He hoped that Hamilton wouldn't stop by his office next and ask him anything directly. How would he respond? How *should* he respond?

Kane was deeply disturbed. It wasn't just the personal insult; he had learned to deal with those long ago. It wasn't even so much the idea of getting fired, if that's what Carver had meant. No, as Kane reflected on the half-conversation he had just overheard, it felt like a shift in the tectonic plates of his naïve scientific idealism. Things were moving underneath him which were supposed to be foundational. Bedrock was turning to magma.

Carver had even invoked ethics, for God's sake! But power, fear, and greed were clearly in control. Ethics? What about the patients? It's just the outliers, he'd said, as if they were simply bothersome tails on a Gaussian distribution. They could be flattened out, made to fit, or eliminated. Parameters could be adjusted, evidence ignored, data faked, all in the service of success—success by someone's non-scientific, self-serving definition.

The real pity here, thought Kane, is that this therapy works in many cases and works extremely well. All it would take would be rigorous experimentation, careful refinement, and time—more time than was apparently available—to bring an effective and safe treatment into mainstream use. And it seemed clear that such a treatment could benefit not only the relatively small population of DID sufferers but also many others affected by lesser trauma. But much more work, probably years more, would need to be done before that would be safe.

Kane's thoughts next flew back to Allison Walker. *She mentioned side-effects. She knows something. How the hell does she know? And that EEG—that's worrisome. She's an outlier and she's in danger.*

FORTY-FOUR

· ·

D r. Nathan Kane made digital copies of Allison Walker's patient files, past and present, encrypted them, and placed them on his personal flash drive. He then sent an email to Hamilton, telling him that he was heading home early with stomach cramps and nausea. He said that he had no further appointments that afternoon and hoped to be back in the morning. He suspected food poisoning from the greasy café where he'd had breakfast but didn't want to expose anyone in case it was actually a virus.

Kane locked his office door, bypassed the elevator and took the stairs all the way down to the employee parking garage under the building. His excuse wasn't entirely fabricated. He *was* feeling ill but the reason had nothing to do with tainted food or pathogens. He was literally sick with the idea that power and money, or the fear of losing those things, could make otherwise brilliant scientists abandon their higher callings and respond to life at the level of the reptilian brain. Kane needed time to think.

He drove his Volvo up out of the parking garage, out of Bellevue, and east toward Woodinville where he lived alone in a small house on several acres fronting Bear Creek. He relished his privacy and rarely went out. Today, of all days, that privacy was exactly what he craved.

Pulling into his long driveway through a forest of cedar and fir, Kane breathed a sigh of relief. He parked in the garage, went inside and poured himself a single malt scotch. He then retrieved the laptop from his home office, sat down and decrypted Allison's files, copying them onto his computer. He searched the files for the name of her previous therapist. She had mentioned him once—Dan something—and the way she talked about him implied trust. He found the name: Dan Gunnison, along with his contact information, and transferred it all into his smart phone.

Kane refilled his glass and put the bottle away. He rarely drank, but this afternoon he needed something to calm himself, to keep himself from reacting too quickly or rashly. What was it that Carver had actually said? Had he directed Hamilton to fire Kane if Walker began showing symptoms of schizophrenia? No, he hadn't actually said that. It was much more ominous. He had said something like "they both disappear," referring to Kane and Walker. How does one fire a patient? One doesn't. Carver had clearly meant something else.

Kane looked out the window onto his forested property and considered his options. If he continued to treat Walker, he might induce schizophrenic symptoms. In fact, indications were that he already had. The amygdala stimulation was either too strong or the phase shift was wrong for someone without full DID-level fear responses. It might be optimum for the center of the population but not for the outliers. Walker had understood this, at least at some level, God knows how. And if he refused to treat her, he would have to provide some kind of explanation to Hamilton. Based on what Kane had overheard from Carver, either option could trigger both his and Walker's demise.

So what other options were there? Kane thought that he could simply leave—find some legitimate way to break his contract. There were plenty of loopholes. It wouldn't be too difficult and he could move on to other work without getting any deeper into this miserable quagmire, without appearing to know anything. But what would happen to Allison Walker under that scenario? No, Kane couldn't live with that option either.

What if he extracted her also—took her with him into therapy somewhere else? Would they be any safer on the outside if he could even get her out? Kane didn't think so. Anyone, either inside or outside the company, who knew that the Carver therapy was flawed, was a danger to the success of the trial and therefore to the fortunes of the key stockholders.

Could he go to the police, either alone or with Walker? That looked like a good option at first but then Kane realized that producing any convincing proof was currently beyond his means. And without proof they had no hope of receiving police protection during an investigation, if an investigation would even be launched. After all, Walker was essentially a convicted felon. They would be just as vulnerable as before. It would be riskier for Carver to make them 'disappear' if an investigation did indeed occur, but it would be far from impossible even then. His anxiety might even increase the likelihood.

Kane finished his second glass of scotch and stepped out onto the back deck of the house to listen to the creek below. *Who's being paranoid now? I could be inferring way too much from that conversation today.*

Kane thought that maybe it was the scotch but hoped it was just his good sense slowing him down. He decided to do a little more digging at CRI and then set up a back-channel before making a move.

The next morning, Nathan Kane packed a bag, grabbed his laptop, and locked up the house. If all went according to plan, he wouldn't be back for a few days, maybe longer. He drove into Bellevue at four fifteen in order to avoid traffic and get a start on his plan before too many people showed up at the Institute. He was counting on his friend Tim being there early, as usual.

When he arrived at the parking garage, it was empty except for a black Jeep Wrangler which Kane knew to be Tim's. *So far, so good.* He took the elevator to the IT level and stepped out. There, behind a gray smoked glass door, Kane could see LEDs and backlit LCD panels glowing on a forest of racked equipment in an otherwise dim room. A small lamp threw a pool of light on Tim's desk, and there was Tim himself huddled over his keyboard, his long brown hair hanging down almost to the desk surface.

Kane's keycard didn't allow him access to this inner sanctum of technology so he rapped on the glass and Tim let him in. Kane had to smile at the absurdity of security in most places like this. Long-term human relationships still trumped all, thank God.

"Hey, what brings you in so dark and early this morning, Dr. K?"

"Actually, Tim, something critical I need to talk with you about. Can you spare a few minutes?"

"For you, Doc—sure, no problem."

"Well, there actually may *be* a problem, possibly a large one. Is there any chance that our conversation could be monitored down here?"

"Uh, no."

"You're absolutely sure about that?"

"Yeah, absolutely. If there's any monitoring to be done, it's done through me and only me. This room's as clean as a whistle. Guaran-fuckin-teed. What the hell's going on?"

Kane took a deep breath. "There are some things going on here that you don't want to know about, Tim, you really don't. But, unfortunately, I found out about them, and now I need your help. I'm going to need some special access."

"Access to . . . ?"

"Email accounts and security."

"Holy shit, man! Do you know what you're asking? Okay, okay, I know you know. You're lucky we go so far back. That bastard Carver, whatever he's up to. He's like the living definition of asshole. Okay, talk to me."

Kane took another breath and continued. "Okay, I'd like you to put some code in the system to temporarily, like for fifteen minutes only, punch me a hole through the intranet firewall into our Exchange server that will let me manage email accounts. I'll need an administrator password too. I need to make one tiny change, look at a few emails, and then get out. I want to do this from my computer upstairs so that if it's ever discovered, you won't be directly implicated. Can you write something that does this, then re-plugs the hole and removes itself from the scene?"

"You got it. I'll write something that'll disable system logging, punch the hole, create a new password—it'll be n8, okay?—and will let you into the Exchange server for fifteen minutes. Sure you don't need a little more time?"

"No, that's all I want. I don't want to leave things exposed for too long."

"Okay, it'll open things up for fifteen minutes. After that, it'll invalidate the password, plug the hole, re-enable system logging and destroy itself. Something like that. I'll figure it out. I'll be out getting coffee when it all happens."

"Okay, good. Thank you. What time can I start?"

"Uh, let's see. It's five-fifteen now . . . uh, how's six-thirty sound?"

"Perfect. Just one more thing. I need the security cameras on the north end of the building and the parking garage off for five minutes starting at ten-fifteen this morning. Can you do a little time-stitching on the images and make that gap go away?"

"Kind of like Watergate for video, only effective?"

"Uh, well, I hate to think of it like that, but yes, that's the idea."

"You got it, Doc."

"Thanks Tim. I owe you."

"No, Doc, you made my career and saved my ass more than once. No, we're not even yet. Just be careful, okay?"

"I will," said Kane. He shook hands with Tim and walked out.

Kane got some coffee and was back in his office at five-thirty. He wanted to figure everything out before he put himself on a fifteen minute schedule. Fifteen minutes should be more than enough. He'd search Carver's and Hamilton's current and archived mail, looking for certain keywords, hoping to find something, anything to substantiate what he'd heard yesterday. Then he would set up an auto-forward script for each of the accounts which would silently forward all future incoming and outgoing emails with those same keywords to one of his own more obscure personal email accounts. He set up his login, minimized it off the screen, and waited, nursing his coffee and thinking about his very uncertain future.

When six-thirty finally came, Kane attempted his login. His first attempt failed and he waited a few more tense seconds before trying again. *Tim's script probably isn't active quite yet.*

His next attempt worked. He was into the server, then into Carver's account. It took him just seconds to set up the search. He used names he knew from the Board of Directors, he used the words Walker, Allison, Kane, P-239, schizophrenia, schizophrenic, and several others. Immediately, the search returned ninety-seven results. He was part way through skimming the emails and totally focused on his task when a sharp knock on the door injected adrenaline into his bloodstream. It was Hamilton.

FORTY-FIVE

. . . .

"**C**ome in." Kane waved his boss into the office and tried to control his racing heartbeat. He felt sure that the pounding in his chest would be visible.

"Well, you must be feeling considerably better to be in this early, Nathan," said Hamilton with a tone that Kane thought made the statement sound more like a question.

"Yes, a lot better, thanks. Rough night but I've regained the will to live." Kane forced a smile. "I wasn't able to get all the case notes done yesterday so thought I'd better get a head start today. What's on your mind?"

"Oh, just wanted to let you know how pleased I am about how Walker seems to be coming along. You know, sometimes I get lost in all the stress of the clinical trial and forget that these are not just subjects but real patients with real problems. You don't seem to lose that perspective and I admire that, Nathan, I do."

"Well, I don't know about that. I just . . ."

"Ah, no need to respond, Nathan. Just wanted to let you know."

"Well, thank you." Kane let his eyes drop to the clock on the bottom of his screen. *Eight minutes left.*

Hamilton nodded and went off about the Mariners' fading chances at the pennant, then something about one of the player's contract terms and the possibility of a trade. Kane felt himself getting more and more desperate to get his boss out of the office and mumbled something apologetic about not really following baseball that much, especially when he was so busy.

Hamilton nodded and Kane thought that perhaps freedom was within reach but then Hamilton regrouped.

"Right. Oh, speaking of work, would you mind letting me have a quick look at your notes on Walker's last couple of sessions?"

Adrenaline again. "Certainly; I should have something preliminary in say, two hours?"

"Nothing right now? Not even just something rough?"

Kane's mind raced for a credible response.

"No, I'm afraid not. I'm, uh, I'm quite the perfectionist; I don't know if I've ever told you. Pathologically so, actually. In fact, that has been at the center of my own therapy for some time. But it won't take me long at this point to have something I'll be happy to share with you."

Hamilton was frowning and Kane decided to try something risky. He decided to bet on an approach which he felt would have a better-than-even chance of getting Hamilton out of the office. He also knew that it could backfire with disastrous results.

"You seem awfully eager to get this, Charles. Is there something wrong?"

Immediately, Kane knew that his tactic had worked. Hamilton's neck began visibly reddening and within a second, other unmistakable signs of anxiety—perhaps even shame—began to appear. Hamilton looked away as the redness rose into his cheeks.

"No, everything's fine. Just interested in her well-being, that's all. There's a special Board meeting this morning at ten and I've been asked to provide an update on the trial. I'd like to include your results."

"I'll send you the session notes the instant I have them," said Kane, sensing closure.

Hamilton rose to leave and Kane stole another look at the clock. *Four minutes left.*

Kane smiled and nodded at his boss through the window after Hamilton made his exit, waited to be sure he was out of sight, and then plunged back into his work on the email server.

He scanned item after item with nothing particularly useful showing up until finally one stopped him. It was an email from several months back from Hamilton to Carver about a suicide, and the patient was identified as P-239. *There was another P-239? Those are supposed to be unique identifiers, never reused over the course of a trial. And yet, here is Allison Walker today with the same number. This was covered up.*

Kane looked at the clock. One minute remaining. There was no time to scan the rest of the mail. He selected all the filtered email and forwarded it en masse to his private account. He then raced to set up auto-forwarding scripts for both Hamilton's and Carver's accounts. He finished with two seconds to spare. Then he set up a delayed transmission from his private email account to Allison Walker's email address obtained from her patient records. The contents of the email included Kane's personal email account password with little explanation. He set the delay for three days and finished. If all went well, he would cancel the actual transmission within that period of time. If things didn't go well, then Allison would figure it all out, Kane was sure.

As an afterthought, Kane reset his computer to a restore point from the day before, erasing all local traces of his clandestine activity. Then he sat back and took several deep breaths.

Next on his agenda was the creation of Walker's patient notes based on his last session with her. Creation, Kane thought, was an appropriate term. *Loosely based on actual events. Inspired by a true story.* A little creative writing might help keep stress at bay, he felt, and pass the time until Allison's regularly scheduled appointment at nine-thirty.

Just under two hours later, when Kane completed what amounted to his first work of fiction since high school, he saved the file and emailed a copy to Hamilton. The positive essentials concerning Allison's breakthrough from two days ago were all there in great detail but Kane's observations about Allison's seemingly paranoid behavior and her startling mention of side-effects during yesterday's session were all missing, replaced by a rather lengthy, benign and reassuring discussion about a "transitional" and "stabilizing" session preparing the patient for another foray into the events of her traumatic childhood which would be attempted in sessions to follow. Kane did, however, include a description of Allison's disturbing dream but without interpretation. He was no longer sure that his original interpretation held water anyway, and besides, he wanted to make Hamilton a little uncomfortable without putting him on full alert. He also felt that it could lay some credible groundwork for his real notes, which he hoped to bring to light at an opportune future moment when both he and Allison were far away from the Institute.

After emailing his work, he wrote up those real notes, emailed them to his private account and deleted them from his computer.

Then Kane got up, stretched, and made his way over to Allison's room to begin what he hoped would be her last session at CRI.

FORTY-SIX

. . . .

The small but well-appointed CRI boardroom began coming to life at nine forty-five, and by ten all seven seats at the table were full. The Board was a high-profile mix of biotech executives, clinicians, and major investors, among them Mrs. Cynthia Roth. Along the back wall away from the table were four guest chairs, two of which were occupied by Julie Moore, Executive Assistant to Dr. Carver, and Charles Hamilton, Senior Vice President.

The front wall of the cherry-paneled room was a framed high-definition display that would normally have shown the meeting's agenda, but on this particular morning it rendered "La Grenouillere," a calming water scene by Renoir. The uninterrupted, subtly tinted windows along one long wall revealed the bay below and Lake Washington beyond. Coffee and water were on the table and conversations were winding down as Carver stood to bring the meeting to order.

"Gentlemen, ladies, thank you again for being here this morning, especially those of you who've traveled from California, Massachusetts, and particularly Beijing—thank you, Dr. Ling. Carver nodded to a man on the right side of the table. We'll try to use your time efficiently this morning, as I know many of you have other business in Seattle. Our purpose, as you know from the Board packets which Julie sent out last week, is to provide you with a review of our clinical progress as we prepare to complete the trial's final phase.

Dr. Hamilton has prepared a set of slides that will help move us through the topic this morning, so without further delay, let me turn the floor over to him. Charles?"

Carver returned to his seat at the table and began mentally assessing the mood of his Board. There was clearly some skepticism, some concern, many latent questions, but those things were endemic to any truly useful group of advisors. But how useful did he really want them to be? Months ago he had crossed a line which put him in a privately defensive role—well, semi-private; Roth was on his side of the line in most respects and, at least here in the boardroom, she would be a powerful ally as long as he continued to put on a good show. And Charles had been dragged across the line as well.

In some corner of his mind, Carver reflected, he still held to the altruistic long-term goal of patient wellness, and the positive results of the trial helped him to believe that. He'd convinced himself that he wasn't a purveyor of snake oil, but the reptilian metaphor still plagued him. There was a question—a very private question—of venom in the mix. Time and money would solve that. Time and money would solve many things. Let the show begin.

Carver smiled and nodded at his Senior Vice President as Hamilton took his place at the front of the room and the Renoir cross-faded into a title slide bearing both the code name and formal description of the trial:

Project Amethyst

Remediation of Dissociative States via Closed Loop Non-invasive
Unilateral Amygdala Stimulation

A Special Interim Update for the
CRI Board of Directors

Carver kept one eye on the participants and the other eye on the screen as Hamilton moved skillfully through his presentation. He seemed to be successfully masking whatever stress he might feel, and his points were clear and convincing. He walked the Board through several of the case studies, describing both successes and failures, being sure to underscore the point that the double-blind had not yet been lifted but that the percentage of clear successes predicted a very favorable outcome.

Dr. Ling raised a question about the SR status of the Amethyst device and, at a nod from Carver, Hamilton addressed it. The question of the device's Significant Risk status had been settled a long time ago, so Carver was confused but hoped that Hamilton would treat the investor's question with respect nonetheless.

"Yes, Dr. Ling, thank you for that question because it will allow me to give everyone an update and to ensure that we're all operating with the same context on regulatory issues."

Carver breathed a sigh of relief. *Good job, Charles.*

Hamilton continued.

"As you know, here in the U.S. the FDA is in the business of approving medical devices ranging from tongue depressors to implanted defibrillators. Our device, unfortunately for all of us from a timeline point of view, was classified by the FDA and our Institutional Review Board last year as a Class III device with an SR, Significant Risk, status. Now, this only means that the Amethyst device is classed alongside other useful and profitable equipment such as defibrillators and, closer to home for us, implanted intracerebral/subcortical stimulators for applications such as acute chronic pain relief. Even though ours is a noninvasive device, it does target the brain with RF energy and it does directly influence cerebral function. If it were simply a passive biofeedback device, it would fall into Class II and probably would also be given NSR status. But, neither would it be the breakthrough device we believe it to be.

The bottom line on all of this is that we are involved in the most stringent of the FDA processes for device approval. Those of you directly involved in medicine know that we are fortunate, however, not to be on the pharmaceutical side. That is a completely different approval universe and one that is immeasurably more complex and costly.

Our trial process actually exceeds all FDA requirements for obtaining Clinical Performance Data for devices, and its success should greatly increase the probability of getting PMA—Pre-Market Approval—from the FDA early next year.

Did I address your question, Dr. Ling?"

At a nod from Ling, Hamilton continued on to the next stage of his presentation involving technology and clinical results. He finished within ninety minutes.

Carver was feeling buoyant at the outcome. There were lots of nods and smiles around the table after Hamilton finished, and Carver himself was caught up in the ebullience. But one Board member, Jeremy Stines, a venture capitalist from Palo Alto and senior partner in his well-known firm, was frowning. Carver caught the look out of the corner of one eye and rose to attempt a meeting close. But Stines beat him to the punch.

"Just one other topic if I may, Seth," spoke up Stines. Carver groaned internally. *Shit. Here it comes.* The room quieted down and Stines cleared his throat. Carver sat down.

"Wonderful presentation, by the way, Charles," Stines began. It's very heartening to see the progress that your team has made here since we last met. I just wanted to hear a few comments, from both you and Seth, on a subject that's near and dear to me and I daresay to many of the other members here today. And that is Market Breadth. We've talked about this before and you've both been encouraging but, as investors, we always have an eye on mundane things like exit strategies, probable rates of return, and so forth. So I'd like an update. Are you still convinced that the market opportunity extends well beyond your core DID target? Are we still talking about extensions to the truly lucrative targets like, say, PTSD, depression or anxiety? I'd just like to hear your current assessment on that."

The room fell completely silent, and Carver could feel his carotid arteries pounding. He quickly organized a response.

"Sure, let me start off on that, Jeremy. An important question, and one that we concern ourselves with every day. As I'm sure you know, the degree of fear and anxiety experienced by DID sufferers far exceeds the levels we typically see from patients dealing with common depression or anxiety disorders. And the blocking signals we present to the brain reflect this difference. Now, having said that, we have a nearly infinite range of tuning potential with Amethyst and we are currently working with a number of what we might call 'fringe' patients whose diagnoses are not crystal clear, and this is where the flexibility of Amethyst is starting to provide hard evidence of efficacy in the kinds of cases you speak of. Dr. Hamilton has a particularly interesting case in point right now. Charles, would you speak to that for a moment?"

"Sure, be happy to," said Hamilton as he once again took center stage. The patient is female, age 30, with borderline dissociative symptoms. It seems that most of her struggles can be traced back to a traumatic incident in her pre-adolescent childhood in which she discovered a suicide victim: her adopted father. The patient had never been capable of discussing the incident and had probably repressed most, if not all, of the memory. She started treatment in our clinical trial and after the usual baseline acquisition time we began our first active session with her. Within minutes the patient was able to recall the event, discuss it thoroughly and rationally, and even begin dealing with her irrational and long-held belief that she was personally responsible for the suicide. Of course there will be extensive follow-up, but the immediate results were nothing short of astounding, I have to say."

Hamilton sat down.

"Thank you, Doctors," responded Stines. "I will bring that particular story back to my own Board on Monday. To be candid with all of you—and I've already spoken with Seth and Cynthia about this—there has been vigorous debate about continuing our funding of CRI and I think that this, along with the rest of your presentation, will help put us back on a more constructive path. One last request: Dr. Carver, I'd like to make a motion that we add the topic of Market Breadth to the permanent agenda for this Board."

The motion was seconded, voted upon, and approved. The meeting adjourned with the usual post-meeting socializing and side discussions following.

FORTY-SEVEN

· ·

At nine-thirty, just before the Board meeting got underway, Dr. Kane was at Allison Walker's door, and this time, to Kane's relief, Allison was dressed and ready to go. She looked much healthier than she had the last time they met. The dark eye circles were nearly gone, her hair was brushed and she wore jeans and a v-neck sweater.

"I'm guessing you had a better sleep last night; am I right?" asked Kane.

"Much, better, yes. And no nightmares. Thanks." Allison responded.

Kane and his patient took their usual seats in the Healing Center and Allison glanced uneasily at the pink therapy hat.

"No need for that today, Allison," said Kane as he switched off the session recorder. "Ours will be a very different kind of discussion this time."

"Oh?" said Allison, looking perplexed and relieved at the same time.

"Yes, you mentioned side-effects last time. You had something you wanted to tell me but my mind was too locked onto my own agenda and I wasn't listening well. Could you please talk a little more about that? I'm sorry I wasn't open to hearing about it before."

"Oh, that's okay. I understand. Sure, but in order to do that, I really need to tell you about my other discovery first. They're very related."

"Other discovery?" asked Kane. He was having trouble getting back into context.

"Yes, you might not remember, but during the last session I mentioned something about my supposed alters being real and you tried to reassure me that this was a normal feeling, that they were real parts of me, etcetera,

etcetera. You were being very sweet and reassuring about it all, but that wasn't really what I needed right then. I just needed you to listen to me."

"Yes, I do remember. I'm so sorry. If you feel you can talk about it now, please do. I promise to be a much more attentive listener."

"Thank you. What I'm about to tell you will probably sound pretty off-center, okay? I'm just warning you."

"Okay."

Allison pulled her legs up under her on the couch and began.

"On a hunch, and with some encouragement from my previous therapist, I started doing a little research from my computer in the room. I searched for information about Kathryn and Molly, just as if they were real people. And what I eventually found totally blew me away, but at the same time it began to explain some things I've never been able to understand about myself."

Kane saw Allison look up as if to gauge his openness.

"And what did you find?" he asked.

"I found two people, Kathryn and Molly Johansen, names that have been in my head since I can remember anything, neither one still living. Kathryn was my mother and Molly my grandmother."

"But, Allison . . ."

"Yes, I know, there have been many women with those names, even many mother-daughter pairs, I'm sure. But hear me out. As you know from my records, I never met my birth mother, let alone my grandmother. I never knew their names or their histories. But I've held these very names in my mind, along with a tremendous amount of knowledge of theirs from the very beginning of my life."

"Knowledge *about* them, you mean?"

"No. Knowledge, skills, information that these women held in their minds."

"I'm sorry, Allison, I'm really having trouble understanding what you're trying to tell me." Kane was feeling very uneasy about the direction this was taking.

"Yes, I'm sure you are having trouble. That's what I was trying to warn you about. I'm telling you that all my life I've been experiencing some form of trans-generational memory. I know much of what they knew. Not personal things, for some reason. Just skills, knowledge, even what you might call muscle memory. And this is going to sound really strange but one of those things that's always been lodged in my mind is a weird reference to an old paper published in the American Journal of Surgery back in 1977. I've looked the crazy thing up more than once because I keep thinking that it's got to be relevant to me in some way, but it just isn't. It's about some long-outdated kidney biopsy technique."

"Well, I agree that's very odd but I wonder if perhaps you've picked up some of this knowledge in your various studies or from your own reading and then repressed the memory of the original learning because of some traumatic event that occurred in your life at about the same time."

"Dr. Kane, believe me, these things have been rattling around in my head since I could form words. I just didn't know what they meant until much later. And then there's the whole crazy thing about the surgery I performed in the ambulance. I am absolutely sure that I had never done an appendectomy before last week. I'd never seen one performed or even read about the procedure. I just knew what to do. I knew how to diagnose it, where to cut, how to use a scalpel, what to look for, how to do the resection. I knew because Kathryn knew. It was scary, but it felt natural.

And I know a lot about boats. I know how to operate them, how to navigate, how to interpret radar signals, how to maintain diesel engines. I never had to learn any of that. Molly knew it. *Selling* boats is a different story. That I learned on my own. "

Allison paused and Kane caught her eye. "I'm listening, Allison. Please go on."

"Kathryn Johansen was Chief Surgical Resident at St. Louis University Hospital when she died. She had an accident and died on the operating table. One of the doctors apparently noticed she was pregnant and performed a C-section. Dr. Kathryn Johansen died during that C-section, on my birth date."

Kane wasn't sure how to respond. The story was so compelling, so detailed. But how could it possibly be true? He tried to form a reasonable question.

"But how can you be . . . I mean, is there anything . . ."

"I know. This is what I meant yesterday when I said I didn't think you were ready to hear this."

"No, you're right. I wasn't. I'm not sure that I am now, but please continue. I'm still listening."

"Most of this information I found by emailing the librarian at the St. Louis Metropolitan Medical Society. They keep records. Local medical history, you know."

"And Molly? What about her?"

"Her background was harder to get. It took me until last night to get much at all. Most of it ended up coming from the genealogical database that the Mormon Church keeps. It's amazing what they've collected. Molly Johansen was born in North Carolina and spent her entire life in the little waterfront town of Manteo. It's one of the gateway towns to the North Carolina Outer Banks. According to an old newspaper article from the Outer Banks Sentinel that I found in their online archives, she and her husband, Fredrick, ran a fishing charter business and she was the skipper—a very rare thing for a woman to do in those days, even these days. Hence the article. She and Fredrick had one child, Kathryn, who grew up and went to the University of North Carolina, then to Washington University in St. Louis, then med school at Johns Hopkins University in Baltimore, then back to St. Louis for her internship and residency at St. Louis University Hospital.

Here the genealogy is more detailed than the information I got from the Medical Society. Are you ready for this?"

"Honestly? No, but go ahead. I'm definitely listening."

"Okay, as I told you before, Kathryn died on the table. Her baby was several weeks premature and stayed in the hospital until she was strong enough to be put into foster care. Someone, there's no information about this, maybe a doctor or nurse in the neonatal unit or a foster parent, named her Allison. Allison Johansen. Five years and several foster homes later, Allison was adopted by Dolores and Carl Walker. She took their last name. I remember when that happened. It was strange getting used to a new name."

"Allison, I've got so many questions I don't know where to begin. But as much as I want to ask you about them, I need to hold those questions for now because we don't have much time."

"Why? Are we going to have a short session this morning?"

"No, there are some other things going on here that constrain our time. I'll explain in a moment. But for now, the side-effects you mentioned?"

"Wait. Do you believe me, about what I just told you?"

"Yes. I believe you."

"Good. Thank you. Okay. Well, here goes."

Allison closed her eyes for a second, let out a long breath, then continued. "I've got a pretty decent basic understanding of brain physiology. Most of it comes from Kathryn and some of that was quite out of date. So I spent a good deal of time online reading journals, catching up, filling in the gaps yesterday. I'm nowhere near a neurologist but I could probably pass a few tests."

Kane nodded encouragingly and Allison continued.

"Anyway, the psychophysiological approach you guys have developed here is amazing. It obviously works. I mean, look what I dredged up day before yesterday, and I could actually process it. Amazing."

"But, here's the problem, Dr. Kane. You're dealing with the mesolimbic pathway, and you're radically altering levels of the neurotransmitter dopamine. You may know this, so forgive me if I'm going over familiar ground, but the pathway begins with the ventral tegmental area of the midbrain and connects to the limbic system via the nucleus accumbens; then the amygdala, the hippocampus and the medial prefrontal cortex. The amygdala, of course, is your target. The left in particular. It is thought to be key in processing fear and anxiety, regulating responses to those strong emotions. Your intent is to selectively suppress fears surrounding events which the patient needs to process at a much higher cognitive level, and the way you've accomplished that is nothing short of brilliant."

"So far so good, but this also affects dopamine levels in ways similar to those implicated in the use of certain psychostimulants and opiates. In particular, it seems clear to me that in some patients—particularly those who are dealing with indirect trauma like mine, things that affected them deeply but weren't inflicted directly upon them—are at potential risk of developing schizophrenic or depressive symptoms over time, over multiple exposures to this treatment."

"Why just those patients?" Allison continued, rhetorically. "I don't understand the mechanism completely here. I doubt that anyone does, but I believe that it has something to do with the intensity and quality of fear levels. Dopamine is generally reabsorbed in the nervous system, but if the amount artificially produced is not commensurate with the fear, excess amounts remain and can produce a 'high' similar to that resulting from certain psychoactive drugs."

"For a while, and I don't know what the time period might be and how it varies over patients, the results appear excellent. The patient feels happier than ever before, she is able to deal with her life in new and positive ways, and the doctors are elated. And, even better, if traumatic memories are thoroughly processed during this period, with the help of a good therapist, the patient may enjoy permanent relief.

But, over time and repeated exposure to the treatment, the dopamine excesses may also induce schizophrenia. Probably not in all such patients, but how many is enough to matter? I'm one of them, I'm quite sure. My dream, the paranoia and depression I experienced the next day—they'll prove to be temporary, I'm quite sure. But I imagined what effects further treatment might have, and this prompted me to do the research."

Kane was stunned. Allison Walker, a Seattle yacht broker—or was it Kathryn Johansen or a blend of the two—had just described to him exactly what he had begun to suspect, but in more detail than he had considered before. He knew now that he had to act on his plan, but he was speechless for several seconds. He just stared at his patient. Finally, he was able to form words. "My God, Allison. My God."

"Dr. Kane, are you alright?" asked Allison.

"Yes. I'm just overwhelmed. You're making perfect sense to me and that doesn't make sense. Do you follow me?"

"Yes, of course. How do you think I've been feeling for most of my life?"

"I can begin to appreciate that. Listen, Allison, I need to tell you some things that might be just as hard for you to process as what you've just told me."

Allison smiled. "Okay, try me. I think I'm immune to incredulity."

"Okay, here's the situation. I'm convinced that Dr. Carver and Dr. Hamilton know about these potential side-effects. They suspect they exist, but I don't think they understand them, at least not at the level you do. Mainly because I don't think they want to. They want to ignore it all and they're hiding it from the Board of Directors. I overheard a very disturbing conversation between the two of them yesterday. Allison, there's more power, ego and money involved here than science. Do you know what I mean?"

"Yes, I think so."

"Getting this treatment into mainstream use could create enormous revenue for CRI or whatever spinoff Carver has in mind. I'm sure Carver must have patented the device, and if he has, he and his investors stand to make more money that Bill Gates ever did. Well, maybe that's an exaggeration, but probably not by much. And based on what I heard yesterday, there's no philanthropy in Carver's plan."

"So, what does all this mean?" asked Allison. She had shifted her position on the couch and was now sitting straight up, her eyes pinned on Kane's.

"It means that we're in danger, both you and I. You, because your results will invalidate the all-important safety criteria of the trial. The FDA will never approve the device and the treatment protocol if your results become known. And I'm in danger too because I'm not part of the inner circle here, nor do I ever want to be. I'd be the only one not in that circle to know about this."

"Do you have any real evidence?" asked Allison. "Because, I know I'm in no position to say this, but this all sounds a bit paranoid."

"I know. It does to me, too. But what I overheard yesterday convinced me. Carver called me 'expendable' among other things and then he said, and I think this is a direct quote: 'The moment you detect anything even *hinting* at induced schizophrenia, they both disappear. You know the stakes here, for you personally and for the company.'"

"Oh," said Allison. Now it seemed to be her turn for speechlessness but she recovered momentarily. "But that could mean anything, right? Couldn't it?"

"Yes, but I also found out something else. Your patient ID in the trial is P-239, and those IDs are supposed to be unique. They are never reassigned over the life of a trial. I discovered this morning that this particular one was. It originally belonged to another patient, a woman who began to present with schizophrenic symptoms and then committed suicide, or so they say. Her history has been erased from the trial records. You are no doubt her replacement. No, you *are* her for purposes of the trial because there can only be one P-239. They needed you here to prove to themselves that whatever adjustments they've made in the protocol have solved the side-effect problem. Clearly they have failed, and they're about to find out. I've hidden the session summary information for now, but it won't take them long to break through. I can't hide the underlying EEG data. It's part of another system nobody can alter until after the trial is completed and the results sent to the FDA. And . . . oh no."

"What?"

"Allison, I forgot about the session audio track from yesterday. It's still there, in that same system. This is not good."

"So what do we do?" asked Allison.

Kane could hear fear rising in her voice and he worked hard to calm her, to provide some direction.

"I have a plan. I've been sorting through all of the options that seem to make any sense, and there's only one that stands out, but it's a radical one and involves serious personal risks for both of us. I do believe it can work, though. Do you trust me, Allison?"

"Yes, I do,"

"Good, then here's what we have to do."

FORTY-EIGHT

· ·

"We need to get you out of here, and it has to be now," said Kane as he glanced at his watch. "The Board meeting is underway so circumstances are in our favor. No one of any consequence will be around."

"Shouldn't we go right to the police?" asked Allison.

"That was my instinct, too, but it's no good. We don't have any hard evidence yet. It would come down to our words against those of the prestigious Carver Research Institute. And, unfortunately, you have a police record and are basically serving time here. No, we wouldn't get any protection from the police. Chances are you'd be delivered right back here and even if that didn't happen, you and I would both be sitting ducks."

"But if we just take off, won't we be every bit as vulnerable?"

"No. We'll have a head start—at least a few hours—and Carver certainly isn't going to notify the police. That would cast a pall over the whole trial, and he'll try to avoid that at all costs. In fact, I'm almost certain he'll be bragging to the board this morning about the wonderful results he's getting on your case. And besides, we shouldn't have to hide long. I have a way to gather intelligence on CRI from wherever we can get email. Then, once we have what we need, that will be the time to go to the police."

"Okay, I'm scared, I'm really scared, but I trust you."

Kane nodded and tried to smile. "Of course you're scared. I am, too. If you can, try to think beyond this immediate situation toward a good outcome, which I'm sure will be there for us. That might help a bit. Do you think you're about as ready as you can be right now?"

"I think so, yes."

"Okay, we're going to walk back to your room and I'll drop you off there, like at the end of a typical session. Just respond as naturally as you can to any comments I make when we get there in case anyone's listening. Then grab whatever you really need, leave everything else, and be ready for me to come back for you at exactly ten-fifteen. I'll be there within a minute after that time. Okay?"

Kane delivered Allison back to her room and said goodbye, mentioning that she'd done well in her session and that he'd see her at the next one that afternoon.

At exactly ten-fifteen, Kane walked back to Allison's room, arriving at her door thirty seconds later. *Tim had better have surveillance down.* Allison was ready. Kane opened the door to the stairwell with his cardkey, listened for footsteps, and, hearing none, signaled to Allison to follow him. They arrived at the garage, scanned the area for activity, and walked directly to Kane's Volvo.

"Lie down in the back seat and cover up with the blanket I left there. Your things can go on the floor in front of you. That's great. Okay, we're off," Kane whispered to his hidden passenger.

As they left the garage and turned right onto Lake Washington Boulevard, Kane checked his watch. Ten-nineteen. If Tim had done his job, and Kane had little doubt that he had, their exit would be a non-event as far as building surveillance was concerned.

"Are you doing okay back there, Allison," Kane asked without turning around.

"I'm fine. Where are we going?"

"Two separate places. I think that's safest for you. I've booked a room for you at the Salish Lodge at Snoqualmie Falls. Your name for tonight will be Julia Henderson. Everything's been paid up front, in cash by your husband, Brian. That includes dinner tonight and breakfast in the morning. They won't ask for your ID. You're a teacher and you needed a little sanity break. All you need to do is check in and check out."

"That's incredible. Thank you, Dr. Kane, for this and everything you've done for me. You are a man of many talents, obviously, and very kind. Where will you be?"

"I think it's best you don't know that right now. When things settle out, I'll let you know. I'll get back in touch. But for now, is there anyone else out there that you absolutely trust?"

"Yes, there's Margaret Yee, my best friend."

"And lawyer, right?"

"Yes."

"Anyone else?"

"Dan Gunnison, my former therapist."

Kane merged onto the 405 and headed south.

"Okay, that's good. You need someone to help you over the next few days and keep you invisible. If I were you, I'd keep your lawyer out of the loop right now. The less she knows the better, until things clarify; but of course that's your call. I'd suggest that you get in touch with one of those two using the hotel phone tonight and arrange to get picked up tomorrow. Right now I'm nothing but a danger to you. You should be as far away from me as possible. And don't go home, whatever you do."

Kane took the I-90 East exit and was careful to stay within the speed limit. He wanted to avoid any special attention.

"Allison?" he asked, looking straight ahead. When I tell you, you can come out of hiding. Do you think you can crawl up to the front with me? I'll let you know when there aren't any cars near enough to notice."

"Sure, just give me the word."

A few moments later, Kane was able to find a dead zone over in the right lane and Allison moved up front.

"Do you mind if I give you another piece of advice?" he asked.

"No, of course not; please do."

"These memories of yours—there's obviously something very special going on there, something that people have speculated about in science and myth for centuries. I'd suggest being very selective about who you discuss this with. You probably know that such things have been debunked many times and the people who may seem most eager to work with you may be exactly the ones to avoid. Any scientist worth his or her salt will be highly skeptical."

Allison nodded and Kane continued.

"Also, if you haven't already, I'd suggest reading Carl Jung. In the first half of the twentieth century, he wrote about something he called the Collective Unconscious. This would be good background for you, ironically, because I don't think it has anything to do with what you're experiencing, and it would be good to understand the distinction if anyone tries to pull you in that ethereal direction. There may be a connection. I'm not saying that Jung was completely off base, just that your experience is infinitely more concrete. You're not perceiving some vague ancestral archetypes. If I were you, I'd look to the field of evolutionary genetics.

For all I know, you may have enough background in the field right now to serve as a basis for your own research."

"Thank you, Dr. Kane. I'll heed your advice."

"You're very welcome."

Kane exited the freeway and took Snoqualmie Parkway. In minutes they arrived at the lodge. Kane helped retrieve Allison's things from the back seat and, thinking it would be best not to show himself outside the car, reached across to shake her hand and wish her well. But Allison apparently had another notion, and Kane wasn't sure whether she was already playing the role of Mrs. Julia Henderson or wanting to express real gratitude. He decided to believe the latter. She ignored his hand and gave him one of her crooked little smiles and a short but warm kiss on the cheek.

FORTY-NINE

. . . .

T he next morning, Allison woke refreshed. She had slept better than she had in weeks. Perhaps it was the white noise of Snoqualmie Falls outside, perhaps it was the wonderful bedding or the warm ambiance of the room, but Allison thought it was more likely the simple release from her past. She no longer felt as though she had ill-defined, dark secrets that threatened to disrupt life and stifle relationships. She knew there was plenty of uncertainty ahead, but that seemed manageable by comparison. After all, everyone lived with uncertainty.

She had spoken very briefly with Dan before turning in last night, keeping the conversation as terse and cryptic as possible in the unlikely case that it was being monitored. He had promised to pick her up in front of the lodge at nine in a car which he described as "my old but faithful dark green Jeep."

Allison ordered room service for breakfast, checked out at eight-forty five, and sat by the window, thinking that she would scan the Seattle Times to keep herself occupied and inconspicuous until Dan arrived. But she barely had enough time to look at the front page when Dan pulled up in front of the hotel. She tucked the paper under her arm, grabbed her single small bag and went to meet him, feeling a tingle of excitement. Once out the door, she was no longer Mrs. Henderson, exhausted teacher.

Allison practically ran to the jeep and got in before Dan even had a chance to set the parking brake. Her smile was so wide that it squeezed tears from her eyes. She wanted to fall into Dan's arms and stay there forever. But she knew that this was not the time and wasn't even sure there would be such a time. Dan smiled back, but Allison could see that there was something somber, even tragic in it. So instead of thanking Dan profusely, Allison found her first words to be, "What's wrong?"

Immediately, she realized that this was a very strange question because there was still so much wrong. But she had not anticipated anything like Dan's response.

"Have you seen the paper this morning?" he asked.

"What? No, just the front page. Why?"

"Look at the Local News."

It didn't take long for Allison to find the short article with the caption, "Local psychiatrist found dead in Aurora motel." She scanned it frantically.

"Oh my God, my God no!"

Dr. Nathan Kane, heroin overdose, prostitution, it was all there, everything these horrible stories typically contained. But Allison knew that this was anything but typical. Kane's character was nothing like that implied by the article. And then there was the clincher: the article ended by mentioning that an anonymous source revealed that Dr. Kane had been in private practice out of his home in Woodinville and had apparently been struggling to make ends meet. There was no mention of CRI.

Allison felt a rage building inside her—a rage against the Carver Research Institute, a rage against the whole system of greed that lay behind it. Dr. Kane had brought her out of the darkness of her past. He had been insightful, kind and thoughtful. He had believed her. He had saved her life. And this is what he had received for his integrity and goodness. What kind of a world allowed, even encouraged, such an atrocity? Allison pounded the car seat with both fists and heard a growling animal-like cry spring from her own throat. Hot, angry tears leaked from her squinted eyes.

When she opened her eyes again, Allison noticed that Dan had moved the Jeep away from the front entrance to a spot at the edge of the parking lot away from the other cars, and was looking at her with warm, concerned eyes.

"I'm so sorry, Allison. I can't find any words. It seems so wrong." Dan handed her a tissue.

"That's because it is. Dr. Kane didn't do this to himself. It was done *to* him. Those *bastards*! If I could get to them right now, I'd string them up by their . . . I'm sorry, Dan. It's just so *fucking* wrong! I'm sorry."

"No, it's okay, you're right. But we've got to think of you now. We've got to focus on your safety."

That brought Allison back to the perilous present and she worked to bring herself under control. She nodded as she tried to slow her heart.

"And your safety too, Dan. I'm so sorry I've gotten you into this stinking mess with me."

"There's no one I'd rather be in it with," tried Dan with a sad smile.

Allison turned to him, and after an awkward moment, she put her arms around his neck and pulled him as close to her as the Jeep would allow. She wanted to stay there for hours, taking comfort from his warmth and scent, but she pulled away and looked into his eyes. She knew then that there would be other such moments but that they would have to wait. She needed to postpone both her grief and her passion.

"Allison, have you thought about where we should go now?"

"No. I had some ideas but now they seem absurd. What about you? What about your practice, your clients?"

"I've taken care of that. They're all being seen by my backup until I return from a family emergency. I'm going with you, wherever you decide, as long as you'll have me."

"Of course I'll have you. I mean I want you. Oh, I'm sorry! I'm such a mess."

Allison clamped a hand over her mouth and looked up to see Dan trying to hold back a smile, unsuccessfully. She laughed and cried at the same time.

After a few moments, Dan said, "Okay, we'll come back to that later. For now, I'm going to take the back roads down the mountain into Carnation and we can talk about where to go next."

Allison thought about their situation. Where would CRI expect her to go? Seattle? St. Louis? Her boat? She wished that they could go there. *Far and Away* seemed the perfect place in so many ways, literally and figuratively. But that would be suicide.

She watched the scenery flow by as Dan drove down the winding road through dense forest and then out onto the Snoqualmie River valley, green with spring trees and crops.

"Have you had breakfast?" Dan asked.

"Yes, about an hour ago. You?"

"Yeah, a scone at Starbucks. I'm okay for now. Anything else you need?"

"Some magic to undo the last twenty-four hours. I'm feeling sick about Dr. Kane, literally sick. We've got to clear his name, Dan. We've got to try."

"We will. I promise you."

They drove on for miles in silence, through Carnation, Duvall, and farther up the valley into Monroe. Allison wondered which way they should turn in Monroe. One way would lead to up into the mountains and then down into Eastern Washington. The other would take them west, back toward Puget Sound.

Puget Sound? That sparked a thought in Allison's mind and it developed rapidly. Soon it had the feel of a decent plan, or at least the beginning of one.

"Dan? I think I know what we should do."

"Yes?"

"Turn left up here. Let's go down through Monroe and take 522 into Bothell. Then across the top of the lake into North Seattle and down to the Magnolia area."

"Why, what's there?"

"Elliott Bay Marina."

FIFTY

· ·

The conclave took place in Seth Carver's office, but it was Cynthia Roth's meeting from the very beginning. All three participants, Carver, Roth, and Hamilton sat in guest chairs around Carver's desk with Roth facing the other two like a junior high school principal. She slowly shook her head and looked disdainfully at the two people she regarded as her chattel. She closed her eyes, took a deep breath, then opened them again like machine gun sites, took aim and fired.

"Charles, who the hell did you bring in to deal with this? Obviously he wasn't one of mine. Wait, I don't want to know. But what I *do* want to know is what in blazing hell were you thinking?! How could you be so *incredibly* stupid?! And you, Seth, you are ultimately responsible because you actually hired this imbecile." Cynthia Roth nodded toward Hamilton without actually looking at him.

Carver opened his mouth to respond, but Roth was not finished. She held up a finger to silence him, and that was all it took.

"Your people did less than half the job and cost me a quarter of a million. The money is nothing, but so were the results."

"How can you say that?" responded Carver. "Kane is gone, the story is solid. What more could you want at this point?"

"What more could I want?! What more could I *want*?! You tell me! Go back to your grade school days, boys, and tell me, what's wrong with this picture?"

"Mrs. Roth, I resent your tone, and your implications. We know that Walker is still at large. We *know* that. We're not fools. We have people at all the probable locations."

"And what about the improbable ones? I hope you're including the airports—and not just SeaTac, the regional ones, too. She is not going to end up anywhere nearby. She could be in South America by now."

"She's not in South America. She couldn't have gotten past our people."

"Oh, I'm so relieved," said Roth, her sculpted eyebrows raised as high as they could go. "And her boat? What about that?"

"Covered. Twenty-four seven."

"Her other therapist? What's his name?"

"Gunnison. We've got a guy at his office and his condo. And we've got other people all around the metro area."

"And that lawyer, the Chinese girl?"

"I've talked to her personally," said Carver.

"And?"

"She's in the dark, I'm absolutely convinced. She was shocked about Walker's disappearance. She cried, pitifully. I couldn't believe it. What kind of a lawyer is she, anyway?"

"And what kind of a CEO are you?' asked Roth through clenched teeth.

"What?"

"I rest my case. You haven't a clue, have you?"

"I . . ."

"That's what I mean. We had one good chance to get Walker and you blew it. Absolutely blew it."

"What the hell are you talking about?!" shouted Carver.

"Your people could have gotten the information out of that pale little bat-faced contractor of yours before they killed him and they didn't, did they? We could know, right now, where Allison Walker is, and we don't, do we? We don't have any *fucking* idea, do we Seth?"

Cynthia Roth held up her hands and shook her head in mock amazement.

"No, we don't. But not for lack of trying," tried Hamilton. He cringed in his seat like a beaten dog.

"Oh, great. Here come the good intentions. Wonderful. *Those* will get us out of this mess. Or pave the road to hell!" shouted Roth, refusing to look directly at Hamilton.

"Just listen to us for one single moment, Cynthia," said Carver.

"Stop. Don't you *ever* call me Cynthia. *Ever*! I cannot envision the day on which you will be worthy of that."

"Fine, your *fucking* royal highness! What Charles is trying to say is that our people literally tortured Kane, psychologically and physically. Are you happy to hear that? I think you are, you cold, heartless, ancient bitch! He never gave us a scrap of information, and he knew. He knew."

FIFTY-ONE

· ·

It was raining, and the mid-morning sky had already put on its dark afternoon overcoat as Dan drove west through Bothell on the back roads to Seattle. Allison sat next to him and privately revisited her anger and worked to manage her fears. Twenty-four hours ago, she had been concerned about the possibility of being forced back into semi-captivity at CRI. Her rescuer, in addition to taking care of her, must have also been worried about his illegal and potentially career-ending move to pull her out, although he never once hinted at it. Yesterday's anxieties seemed trivial today. Now Dr. Kane was dead. How had they tracked him down so quickly? Had he gone back to his house to get something? Why hadn't they found her yet?

And here she was, bringing yet another person into the void with her. She glanced over at Dan. Dr. Kane's death was intolerable. Dan's would be . . . Allison couldn't even finish the thought. It simply could not be. At that, Allison's anger crystallized into resolve. The personal risks she was about to take suddenly seemed of no consequence. She felt a sense of empowerment and knew it was not entirely rational, but chose to embrace it anyway. She would work to bring some meaning, however inadequate and incommensurate, to Nathan Kane's sacrifice.

Allison looked at Dan again and thought she saw a similar resolve in his face. He looked focused, strong and capable. It seemed a good time to tell him about her recent discoveries.

Tentatively at first, she began to talk about Kathryn and Molly, her newly discovered but long dead mother and grandmother, no longer just the Teachers. Then, as she saw belief and understanding in Dan's eyes, her confidence increased. She told him everything she had learned, and for the first time in her life it felt good to talk about them. Dan encouraged her by asking good questions—personal questions and not those of a therapist.

During one of those questions, Allison noticed Dan's eyes darting up to the rearview mirror.

"Problems?" she asked.

"Could be. I'm not sure but I think we might have picked up a tail. You should slide down as low as you can in your seat."

Dan glanced back up at the mirror again. "White van. It's been two or three cars back for a while now, taking all the turns with us."

Allison slouched as low as she could, her head below the bottom of the side window. She felt her heart begin to race.

"Hold on. We're about to find out," said Dan. He cut quickly into the left lane, earning a long, angry honk from a driver already there, and then made an immediate left through a small gap in the oncoming traffic. Allison peeked over the edge of the Jeep's yellowed plastic window and saw the white van. It had screeched to a halt along the main road.

Dan roared down the side road, made a hard right and then cut left through the middle of a weed-infested industrial lot, dodging holes and avoiding piles of cinder blocks. A freight train rumbled slowly along the back side of the lot next to an old warehouse. Allison popped back up, searching for a handhold to steady herself against the rough ride. As they rounded a corner at high speed, she spotted a dilapidated tin shed and pointed to it.

Dan nodded and blasted forward, skidding the Jeep around the back of the shed. The whole back side was open and Dan drove in, parking on a cracked concrete floor littered with beer cans.

"I couldn't even see this shed from the road back there. I think we're okay for now," said Dan. "It'll take the van a while to get across all that traffic and come looking for us. With any luck, they won't make the same turns."

"How do you think they tracked us down?" asked Allison.

Dan shook his head. "I have no idea. Oh, shit, I *do* have an idea. My phone's on. I wonder if that's how they found Kane. Is yours on?"

"No, I left it back at CRI."

"I think they tracked my phone as we moved between cells. Damn!"

Dan dug the phone out of his pocket and shut it down.

"Damn it! We're going to have to move. On foot—more agile that way. That old warehouse over there would be a good first stop . . . Wait, I've got a better idea. Follow me!"

Dan charged toward the railroad tracks near the warehouse and Allison ran behind him. For a moment, her heart sank as she thought he meant to hop the train but then she understood what he really intended. She watched as Dan turned his phone back on and jogged alongside an empty flatcar as it came by. Deftly, he tossed the phone up and onto the moving surface. Then, he pointed to the warehouse and ran.

From high up in the abandoned building, next to a dusty window, Dan and Allison stopped to rest. Allison was still breathing hard when she spotted the van. It cruised slowly down the street adjacent to the abandoned lot, paused, and then moved on, turning away from them, heading in the general direction of the train as it receded from view.

"Yes! That was brilliant, Dan!"

"Thanks. Let's go. We've got to keep moving. The Jeep's a liability now."

Allison followed Dan down the rickety warehouse stairs and back to the Jeep where they picked up their essentials and cautiously walked back out to the main road and a corner gas station.

Dan nodded toward the pay phone. "I'll call a cab."

Soon they were back on the road again, this time in the back seat of a beat up blue taxi with a white "Far West" sign on its side. Dan had directed the driver not to Elliott Bay Marina but instead to a residential area high above the marina on the Magnolia bluffs. When they arrived, Dan paid in cash and made a show of ushering Allison up a walkway toward the front door of a house.

As the taxi disappeared around a corner, Dan took Allison's hand and led her back out to the main road and into Magnolia Park. From there it was a straight shot, but not an easy one, down the steep, forested hillside and through a corner of someone's sloping property, to West Marina Place. Dan held out an arm, stopping their progress just before leaving the protection of the trees, and scanned for activity. Seeing none, they moved out into the big parking lot and down to the docks.

Now it was Allison's turn. She led Dan down G-dock and explained their opportunity more fully. This was a former client's boat, but he was in Argentina and would be there for the next three months taking charge of two newly acquired Malbec vineyards. He had asked Allison to operate the engines and generators periodically, even take the vessel out occasionally and run her around the Sound to keep her systems in shape. This was just one of those times when Allison would exercise *Grape Escape*. It might be a little longer than the usual cruise but hey, it was all in the line of duty, she explained. Her crooked little smile made a brief appearance.

Allison stopped at G-21 and watched for Dan's reaction.

"Wow. What *is* this?" he asked.

"She's a fifty-eight foot Ocean Alexander, a pilothouse motoryacht with twin C-12 Caterpillars. She's got satellite internet for the onboard computers, which we'll need. Best of all, she's not actually listed for sale right now—no traceable connection to me. Her name's a little cheesy, but I think she'll do, don't you?"

Dan nodded, open-mouthed, as he stared at the gleaming white vessel. "Can we, I mean can *you*, handle this thing?"

"Sure, no problem. I'll need a little help with line handling when we dock, but sure. The twins make her easy to maneuver, and on top of that she's got thrusters fore and aft. Molly would be ashamed of me. It's just too easy."

Allison took Dan's hand and led him around to the stern where she retrieved the keys from a lockbox and slid open the large glass door. She enjoyed watching Dan as he walked through the halogen-lit, cherry-finished salon.

"I take it you've never seen a yacht like this before?"

"Uh, no. This is like an upscale condo with a moveable water view."

Allison smiled.

"We'll have time to explore the rest of it later," she said. "Right now, we've got to get moving. I'll be down below for a few minutes. Could you remove the spring lines and loop the bow line once around the dock cleat and tie it off on the boat's bow cleat?"

"Spring lines?"

"The ropes that tie near the center and go to dock cleats at either end."

"Got it," said Dan with a nod.

Allison made her way down to the engine room. There she inspected both engines, checked oil levels, glanced at the fuel filters, checked the sea water strainers, looked for oil and water drips. Finding everything in order, she walked up to the pilothouse and started both diesels. The Nav systems, sounders, radar, VHF and single-sideband radios were next. Finally, she switched over to ship's power and went down to disconnect the shore power cable and stow it.

Allison was back in her element—or one of her elements—and it felt indescribably good in spite of the otherwise dark circumstances. She allowed herself just a moment to feel the rumble of the diesels below, to smell the salt air, and to anticipate the thrill of leaving the dock for places unexplored with Dan. She tucked all of these things into a corner of her mind for safekeeping, hoping there would come a time soon when she could pull them out and enjoy them again.

Once Dan helped her free all lines and was safely on board, Allison moved both transmission levers into reverse and backed the yacht slowly out of its slip and into the fairway. There she moved the starboard transmission lever forward and pivoted the fifty-eight foot vessel in place. With a couple of other turns, Allison took them out into open water.

FIFTY-TWO

. . . .

To Dan, everything about the day felt surreal. The twisty little passages of life had somehow converged for him and this beautiful, intelligent, resourceful woman who sat in the captain's chair next to him and guided them north toward the San Juan Islands. How had this all come to be? Just a few months ago, they had been complete strangers; then they became therapist and client; and now? Now it wasn't exactly clear. Two people on the run from the world.

The rain beat steadily on the pilothouse roof and brought the visibility down to no more than a quarter mile, Dan estimated. He could see that Allison was relying heavily on radar and he was once again amazed at her capability. He watched her reach over to adjust the settings.

"What's that all about?" he asked.

"Oh, just filtering out all the rain clutter on the screen. See? That's better. And there are a couple of new targets about . . . about four point two nautical miles ahead and closing. They're over in the shipping lane and won't be a problem for us. Probably a tug and towed barge because they're staying exactly in sync."

That was confirmed moments later when they heard the tug's captain contacting Seattle Traffic on the radio. A gravel barge bound for Olympia.

"So, we don't have to do that? Check in with Traffic Control?" asked Dan.

"No. We're under sixty-five feet, so we're exempt. That's another nice thing about this boat. We're small enough to be nearly anonymous."

"Yeah, just a little three-stateroom dinghy bobbing around out here," laughed Dan. "So, where to, Cap'n?"

"I'm thinking Fisherman Bay on Lopez Island. It's small, there are a couple of stores where we can stock up on supplies, and we can anchor in the bay without having to register with anyone. We should probably stay out of the more popular San Juan spots like Friday Harbor."

"Sounds good. How long a trip, do you think?"

"Somewhere between five and seven hours. We're only running at ten knots right now because of the visibility. If things clear up, we can push that up to fifteen or sixteen. We'll just have to see. The problem is logs in the water. They're all over the place around here and radar isn't much help with them."

"How's our fuel?" Dan asked, seeing no gauge on the panel in front of them.

"I keep the tanks full for the owner. About a thousand gallons, so we're set."

Dan nodded, sat back, and watched the southern tip of Whidbey Island approaching as they headed toward Admiralty Inlet. He had kept up this technical level of conversation because it was easy and he liked hearing Allison's voice. It was much easier than trying to deal with the big questions. Questions like, how will they gather evidence against CRI without Kane to help them, or how long will they need to remain invisible, or how to talk with Allison about Skip's research, or what the future might look like for himself and Allison.

This last question was beginning to become much more than a curiosity, and Dan allowed himself to sit with it for a few more minutes. He stole a glance at Allison's face, and she must have noticed because that crooked little smile appeared in profile.

"You're looking at me."

"Yes. Does it bother you?"

"Is that question coming from my therapist?"

"No, it most definitely is not."

Allison's smile grew but she continued to look straight ahead.

"Then who *is* it coming from?"

"A big fan of yours."

"I don't think I've ever had any fans before."

"I doubt that very much. But maybe you haven't had a fan quite like this one. I happen to know, on good authority, that he thinks your star shines brighter than the sun."

"Oh, my. He told you that?"

"Just now."

"Well, would you mind telling him something for me?"

"I'd be happy to."

"Tell him I'd like to meet him for dinner tonight if he's available. Say, eight o'clock? I know a cozy little place called The Galley. It's just steps from here."

FIFTY-THREE

. . . .

T he rain let up about half way across the Strait of Juan de Fuca, and
Allison was relieved to see patches of sun on the water in several places
where the clouds had parted. She was even able to discern the outline of
Lopez Island's southern shore ahead. There was a four to five foot swell in
the strait which had created an uncomfortable and relentless roll coming
at the vessel off the port side. Dan had gone quiet and retreated below an
hour earlier, having acquired a greenish cast not unlike the one Allison
remembered on the interior walls of her old elementary school.

The view of the island was welcome and Allison thought about calling
Dan up, but decided against it. He would emerge when he was ready.
She did feel sorry for him though, knowing first-hand how debilitating
sea sickness could be. Fortunately, it rarely afflicted her when she was at
the helm of a vessel. There was something about the mental attention to
navigation that helped keep the queasiness at bay.

Allison adjusted her heading and made for the waterway between San
Juan and Lopez Islands. The channel was only about three quarters of a
mile wide and Allison could not spot it from her current position. The
coastline looked like one continuous land mass with several small islets
and rocks guarding Davis Bay. Allison's course would take her west of the
shoals and into the channel.

Once in the lee of Cattle Point, the swell dropped to near nothing
and the ride flattened out. Ten minutes later, Dan reappeared, looking
somewhat more alive, if a little sheepish.

"Hi," he managed. "I didn't know that seasickness involved a serious death wish, until today. Whoo! I'm sorry I abandoned you up here. How're you doing?"

"I'm fine and glad you're feeling better. There's almost nothing worse, is there?"

"Almost nothing, including most forms of death, I'm convinced." Dan took a seat next to Allison and scanned the scene in front of them. "Where are we?"

"Right now we're running up the San Juan Channel between San Juan and Lopez Islands. That's Lopez over there to starboard."

"So we must be pretty close to Fisherman Bay."

"Just over a mile to go. The entrance to the bay is hidden behind that sand spit up ahead and it's very narrow—less than ninety yards. We've got a low tide right now so we'll only have a couple of feet of water under the keel when we first enter. And most of that ninety-yard channel is too shallow for us so we've got to stay right in the center. There's better depth once we get inside."

"So you've been here before?"

"No, just studied the charts."

Allison stood up and peered intently through the pilothouse windows. She could feel Dan's eyes upon her from behind. She liked the feeling intensely, but tried to stay focused on the task at hand. She pulled the throttles back and the boat glided smoothly toward the end of the spit. There, Allison turned hard to starboard and rounded the sand point.

"Red-right-returning?" asked Dan as the vessel moved slowly through the narrow opening.

"Yes; see, you're qualified for First Mate. We'll just leave the red marks to starboard as we go in. There's a green one ahead to port. See it?"

"Over there? Yes, got it. Wow, what a beautiful little bay." said Dan as the vista opened up before them.

Allison nodded in response as she scanned the area for a good anchorage. "Dan, are you up to going out on deck for a minute? I could use some help getting the hook down."

"Sure, the air would do me good anyway."

"Okay, if you could go out on the bow, pull the safety pin on the anchor, and make sure that the chain runs out smoothly when I start it, that'd be nice. I've never anchored this particular boat before so I'm not sure how well that windlass works. Just give me the cut-off signal at your throat if the chain binds or anything, okay?"

"Got it."

As Dan made his way out to the deck, Allison moved the boat around the bay, looking for an ideal spot. There were only three other vessels anchored so there were many possibilities. She chose a spot in just over a fathom of water, well away from the other boats, and let out about forty-five feet of chain—enough to compensate for high tide during the night and provide plenty of rode. She could see Dan watching as the chain rattled over the anchor guide; he seemed happy with its progress and gave a thumbs-up sign when Allison stopped the windlass. She backed the boat, setting the anchor to her satisfaction, then motioned for Dan to return to the pilothouse. He smiled and pointed down at the salt water wash-down hose.

Good to see him smiling again, Allison thought as she nodded her acknowledgment. He must be feeling a lot better. Looks a lot better without the green.

They had evidently picked up some seaweed and bits of shell during the rough passage across the strait and Dan washed it all overboard. Allison couldn't help but notice his solid shoulders and narrow hips as he moved purposefully around the foredeck.

Dan finished the wash-down, stowed the hose and stood on the bow taking in the view. Allison watched as the sun hung low in the sky behind him. When had she started trusting this man? She couldn't remember the exact moment. Maybe there wasn't a specific time. It had been a process, a series of events which had brought her to this point. But here they were, alone on a boat together, fleeing from the world.

Before Dan returned, Allison found a white tablecloth and a small candle in the galley. She set them on the table along with two wine glasses filled with apple juice—the only liquid refreshment she could find on board. The little store in Lopez Village would have closed over an hour ago so they would have to make do with what little they could find in the galley until morning.

"So much for the nice dinner," said Allison when Dan reappeared. She glanced at the table. "But maybe it's for the best. You're probably not that hungry anyway, are you?"

Dan admitted that he wasn't very hungry but wouldn't mind having a little something. Together they scrounged up some peanut butter and crackers to go with their faux wine. To Allison, the candlelight and the orange reflection of the sunset on the glassy bay made up for the lack of food. From Dan's smile and bright eyes, she guessed that he was feeling something similar. She noticed his eyes moving between the sunset and her face.

"You're looking at me again." She said.

"And again, and again. I'm sorry, I just can't help it. You're so beautiful, Allison. I'm sorry, you just *are*—your smooth hair framing your soft face and those bright, clear eyes."

"Oh, don't be sorry. I'm glad you're looking. I'm looking too, you know."

"You are?"

"I certainly am." Allison's crooked little smile was widening.

"And what do you see?" asked Dan.

"I see a strong, handsome, capable man, who's risking so much for me. I'm a little puzzled by that, I have to admit—the risking part."

"Puzzled? Why?"

Here Allison's smile faded and she looked down at the table, hiding from Dan's eyes. "I'm sorry, please don't take this wrong. You've been so kind to me and I do trust you, Dan, I do. And I love being with you. I love it so much, but I'm scared that you're here because, well . . ."

"Allison, no, don't worry. I've already put my things in the guest stateroom."

"Oh no, it's not that, Dan, not at all, but thank you. No, it's stupid, really."

"It can't be. If you're feeling it, it's important. Please tell me."

Allison paused, closed her eyes, and then looked up again. She tried to control her voice. "I see something wonderful in your eyes and I hear it in your voice, but my mind tells me to be careful."

"Careful about what?"

"When I look at myself with a doctor's eyes, with Kathryn's eyes, I see a fascinating clinical case. I worry that you see me that way, too. Even if you don't think you do, I worry that it underlies everything. Do you see?"

"Yes, I think I do, and it makes perfect sense. But please, listen to me for a moment. First of all, of *course* I think that your special memory is interesting. I admit that. It's fascinating. And I think it's incredibly important that we learn more about it, too. I want to do that with you. Your extraordinary memory is an essential part of you, but it is only one part."

Dan paused and Allison looked up to see that he was reaching both hands across the table toward her, inviting her to take them. She did.

Dan smiled and continued. "But there is so much more to you. You are smart, kind, capable, strong, wonderful to talk with, and beautiful. You have the most exciting smile. Your amazing turquoise eyes are bright and clear, and in spite of your past troubles you seem to have a certain balance that most people can only wish for. Your childhood may tell you that I will leave, physically or emotionally—that I will send you back, as you've said before. But please believe me, Allison, there is nowhere else I want to be but here with you, now and always. You see, over the past couple of weeks I've discovered something that no doctor can diagnose or explain. I've discovered that I'm falling in love with you."

Allison felt as though she would melt. It started with her wet eyes, flowed down and warmed her chest, tingled her inner thighs, traveled through her legs and out her toes. She moved over to Dan's side of the table, looked up into his eyes and saw the truth of his words. She had seen men look at her with passion before, but this was much more. In his eyes she saw physical longing, yes, but also caring, warmth, and something that looked like friendship. She had never seen that combination before and it made her move closer. She tilted her head back slightly, closed her eyes, and opened her lips to him.

Allison felt large, warm hands cup her face as Dan drew her closer. Then his lips were on hers, barely touching at first, then finding their place, exploring and loving. Slowly, he moved back, his hands still gently on her face, his eyes shining into hers.

"Dan, I don't think I've truly been in love before, except maybe with a little boy in grade school named Tommy who was kind to me when no one else was. But I think I am now."

Dan's eyes glistened as he smiled back at her and pulled her into his arms. She felt the breadth and strength of his chest pressing against her breasts. Hard and soft together, nature's marvelous pairing. She wanted nothing more than to invite Dan into bed with her, but she also loved Dan's thoughtfulness about the guest stateroom. She just held his gaze.

Dan spoke first. "Come on, let's get you to bed. You've had a big day, getting us all the way here, cooking this sumptuous meal." He laughed and offered a hand. "And no, I'm not going to ask to sleep with you—not tonight—as much as I want to. But I can't promise that I won't ask you sometime soon."

"Good, because that's a promise I don't want," said Allison.

Dan took Allison's hand and led her down to the master stateroom with its king-sized bed, cherry paneling, and burled wood ceiling. He sat her down on the bed, kissed her deeply, touched her face, and walked out.

FIFTY-FOUR

. . . .

D an woke to the sound of sea birds and the smell of fresh brewed coffee. It took him a few seconds to remember where he was, but when he did, the realization came at him from many directions at once. He smiled at the thought that Allison was nearby, probably in the galley just a few feet above him. He frowned with the uncertainty of their situation regarding CRI and the law. And he thought about how they would work together to reclaim their lives.

He used the guest head, ran a hand through his thick, light brown hair, and pulled on a pair of jeans and a sweatshirt. He followed the dark roasted smell of coffee up to the galley. There he found Allison with her back to him, pouring a cup, dressed in a long, white T-shirt and, he noticed with a jolt, absolutely nothing else.

"Good morning," he said quietly, trying not to startle her. It didn't work.

"Oh!" squeaked Allison. She spun around, spilling coffee down the front of her shirt.

"This seems to be our trademark," laughed Dan. "Here, let me get that."

Dan found two clean dish towels and, looking directly into Allison's eyes, moved one up under the hem of her shirt and one up the outside, soaking the hot liquid out of the shirt and away from her skin. He worked from bottom to top, the back side of his hand grazing her thigh, her hip bone, her right breast. He watched her eyes slowly close as he worked his way up.

"There, is that better?" he asked.

"Sooo much better," she moaned. "I'm going to pour some down the other side now."

Dan smiled and slowly removed the towels. "Later," he said. "And we won't need to bother with the coffee."

"I guess we do have work to do today, don't we," frowned Allison. "I'll just go below and slip into something less comfortable."

While Allison was busy getting into jeans and a sweater, Dan put together a list for the store. He thought it would be best if Allison didn't make an appearance on the island. If anyone were looking for them, they would most easily spot the pair of them, and next easily, Allison by herself. A lone man in a wool cap, baggy jeans and a sweatshirt wouldn't attract any undue attention on Lopez Island.

The distance to shore from their anchorage was only a few hundred yards so Dan decided to take one of the two kayaks strapped to the upper deck instead of learning the more complicated process of putting the yacht's powered tender into the water. It would be much quieter, too. When Allison re-emerged from her stateroom, Dan told her of his plan, got her input on the list, and paddled over to shore where he tied up near Lopez Village.

In the store, Dan picked up two tenderloin steaks, potatoes, mushrooms, peas, some breakfast and lunch items, and a bottle of an Argentinean Malbec in honor of their escape vehicle's owner. On the paddle back, Dan enjoyed the calm, clear water, but also searched for clarity on a plan for redemption.

Everything depended upon gathering enough evidence about CRI's involvement in Kane's apparent murder and the falsification of clinical trial data. The goal was simple enough, Dan reflected, but the means of achieving it were anything but simple. Allison had mentioned Dr. Kane's comment about his ability to gather intelligence on CRI from anyplace he could get email. But with Kane dead, how was that going to help? There had to be another way in. For Kane's comment to have made sense he must have had a trusted contact within the Institute. What about other resources? Dan thought about Skip. He might be helpful in gaining access but that would put him in potential danger, too. The same was true for Allison's friend, Margaret.

The situation seemed as dark and tangled as the patch of kelp under Dan's kayak as he approached *Grape Escape* from the stern. He tied up to a cleat and climbed aboard, bringing the supplies with him. He found Allison in the pilothouse bent over a computer screen. There were tears in her eyes.

FIFTY-FIVE

. . . .

Allison was seated in the captain's chair, staring at one of the monitors embedded in the ship's console. "Dan, It's like Dr. Kane died all over again. I'm sorry, it's just so sad. He was such a good man. Like you, in that way." Allison dabbed at her eyes with a tissue and pointed at the screen. "Look, I got an email from him this morning. But see what it says?"

Dan read the text out loud. "Allison, if you receive this email, it means that I was unsuccessful in getting to a computer in the two days after I dropped you off. I scheduled this message for delayed delivery, planning to cancel it once I reached safety. If you are reading this, I did not. I'm sorry that I could not provide more help, but perhaps this will give you a start. My email password is n8n8n8. Check my account. You are a very special person, Allison. Please use your gift wisely. Be safe, be happy. Nathan Kane."

Allison looked up at Dan, whose hands rested on her shoulders. She could see that his eyes were moist, too. His voice had faltered on Kane's last words.

For a while, neither spoke, then Allison felt Dan's lips on her cheek. He kissed her gently and said, "It looks like Dr. Kane is still helping us. But before we check into it, I think we should change our location. Do you know of another place we can go?"

"Yes, we should move. Stuart Island would be good. It's less than a mile from the Canadian border and about fifteen or sixteen miles from here. I'll plot the course."

While Allison warmed the engines and prepared the boat for departure, Dan hoisted the kayak back to the upper deck and secured it. Allison brought up the anchor and they were off. Their course took them northward through the San Juan Channel, passing Shaw Island, little Jones Island, and, in the distance, the southwestern portion of Orcas Island. Finally, a turn to the west took them between Spieden and Johns Islands and into Reid Harbor. At the entrance to the harbor, Dan pointed out several seals sunning on the rocks, their fur transformed to a golden coat as it dried.

Allison eased back on both throttles and idled into the harbor. It was near noon and there was a mere handful of boats scattered over the water. Allison chose a spot midway down the elongated harbor near the southern shore and anchored there.

After a simple lunch of fruit and cheese, Allison got ready to log in to Dr. Kane's email account. She glanced up at Dan just before making the final click. "Should I?"

Seeing a quizzical look from him, she explained. "It feels like such an invasion of privacy." Then she nodded and made the click.

The first thing she noticed was that there were over a hundred unread emails, all forwarded to Kane's address from Drs. Hamilton and Carver and a few other CRI people. There was also one from a Tim Johnson. That one stood out because it was encrypted and didn't originate from the CRI domain. After scanning a few of the other forwarded emails, it became clear to Allison that the original senders had not intended to include Kane. The forwarding addresses were those of the original senders but in most cases the content didn't seem relevant to Kane.

"Who's Tim Johnson?" asked Dan. "That's not a name I remember."

"I don't know. It's probably not related to any of this. Maybe a friend. Anyway, it's encrypted so we'll never know."

"Yeah, let's look at the others. What if we search for Kane's name in the contents?" offered Dan.

Allison set up the search, and within seconds she and Dan were presented with three emails that included his name. The first one was originally sent by Carver to Hamilton. It simply said, "Watch Kane carefully. He's getting too close to the patient. I don't trust him."

Allison noticed Dan raise his eyebrows. She said, "He was just very kind and understanding, that's all."

The next email was from Hamilton and read, in part, "Excellent results with W today. Kane's doing a fine job with her. Amethyst performing amazingly well. Good fodder for board meeting."

The final email from the search was more interesting. It was also from Hamilton but was more recent and the tone was distinctly different. It was an indirect response to something from Carver which wasn't included in the search results. It read, "Dream and Kane's session audio are worrisome, yes, but not enough to warrant action yet, imo. Need more time."

"Hamilton knew about my developing paranoia. He knew the treatment had negative side-effects," observed Allison.

"Yes, but there's nothing incriminating here," Dan said with a sigh. "Okay, let's start plowing through the rest of these. It'll take a while but we need to find something more useful."

They set to work, carefully examining each email. Most were innocuous: status reports, budget requests, routine business. Then there was one from Jeremy Stines, evidently a board member. It read, "Impressive results from Charles at last board meeting. I've met with the other partners and your funding is back on track. It's still fully contingent on FDA approval, but that should be a slam dunk given your recent assurances regarding safety and broad market applicability."

"There's a key pressure point," said Dan. "Let's keep going."

They read through the last fifty-seven emails with no further evidence emerging.

"That's disappointing," said Allison.

Dan nodded. "You feel like getting out and stretching your legs a bit?" he asked.

Allison welcomed the idea and worked with Dan to get both kayaks lowered into the water. They talked about the risks involved in public exposure but quickly decided that there was virtually no "public" on the island and that the chances of discovery were almost nil. They locked up the boat and paddled over to the northern shore where they tied up the kayaks and hiked up the trail toward the northwestern point of the island and the Turn Point Lighthouse. Allison had done this hike once before by herself and was excited to share it with Dan.

"Wait 'til you see the view from there, Dan," she said as they made their way uphill through a Madrona and Fir forest. They crossed over the top of the island and followed dirt roads down toward the point. The three-mile hike felt good to Allison and she noticed how effortlessly Dan seemed to handle the trails with her. He was clearly in great shape.

When they emerged at the lighthouse, the afternoon sun was sparkling off the water and the view was clear all the way to Vancouver Island. To the northwest, they could also see a few of the Canadian Gulf Islands: Moresby, South Pender, and Saltspring. A large container ship was making its way down Haro Strait, having just made its turn to port. Allison explained that Turn Point, where they were standing, was named because of that. It and the lighthouse marked the critical turning point for marine traffic passing between Canada and the U.S. The lighthouse had been built and put into operation in 1893 by an Act of Congress at a cost of fifteen thousand dollars.

"Fifteen thousand? Hard to believe anything could be done for that. Different times," said Dan.

"Different times," Allison agreed. "I guess people will say that about our times, too, in another century or so. Even twenty years from now, things are moving so fast."

"Too fast for you?"

"Not as long as I get to hide out in places like this from time to time."

"Can I hide out with you?" asked Dan. He took Allison's hands in his and she felt him search her eyes.

"Yes, but sometimes a hideout is only made for one."

Dan looked away, out across the broad stretch of water.

Allison could feel a light breeze blowing her hair back as she looked at Dan. There was no one else in sight. She smiled, squeezed his hands to bring his eyes back to hers and said, "Most of the time I think I'm pretty transparent, but I suppose there are times when I'm not so obvious." She squeezed his hands again and placed them low—very low—around her back and looked up into his eyes. "I was just letting you know that there are times when I love being alone. It's centering for me, rejuvenating. I want you to know that about me."

"Of course, Allison. That's good, that's . . ."

"Shhh," she interrupted, and placed a finger across Dan's lips. "I'm not done. I also want you to know that I want you with me, I want you around me, I want you beside me. And . . . look at me, I'm shaking, I can hardly say it . . . I want you inside me."

FIFTY-SIX

· ·

The hike back from Turn Point was a blur for Dan. He held Allison's hand most of the way, stopped to kiss her twice, and tried to think. That was the hard part. He marveled at the male human's propensity for mental befuddlement when confronted with the honest expression of female desire. Allison's words had been so simple and clean, yet so devastatingly sexual. And of course it hadn't been just her words. It had also been her beautifully crooked little smile, the look of her hair blowing back in the wind, the trust and openness in those turquoise eyes, her placement of his hands on her . . .

Dan's shoe caught the edge of a rock and he tripped, lurching forward on the trail. He released Allison's hand to keep her from going down with him. To his embarrassment, he tripped again on an exposed root and ended up on his butt in a ditch beside the trail.

"Are you okay?" he heard Allison say from behind him. He guessed that she could see he was unhurt because there was an unmistakable element of mirth in her tone.

"Yeah, just being an idiot," he groaned, hoisting himself up and out of the ditch. "A bumbling fool in love, I think." He brushed the dirt off his pants and shirt.

Now Allison was laughing and Dan wasn't quite sure how to take it. "Kind of reminds me of that time in your waiting room—the day of my first appointment," she said.

"Yeah, what a klutz I was . . . am."

"You? I started the whole thing with my coffee, remember?"

"I'll never forget it. Hey, speaking of coffee and other things I'll never forget, do you have another one of those long, white T-shirts like the one you spilled coffee on this morning when I startled you?"

"Yes, but I think it's quite a bit shorter, and it might be black, and it might not be exactly a T-shirt. Do you think that'll be a problem?" Allison smiled.

"No, I, uh, don't believe that will be an issue. I really do not."

"Good."

They arrived at the trailhead by five in the afternoon and paddled back to the boat. Two curious harbor seals poked their heads up and followed at a distance. Dan reached the stern first, tied up his kayak and reached for Allison's line. He helped her aboard and, without a word between them, they headed up to the pilothouse to check for any new email that might have arrived in their absence. During Dan's few lucid moments hiking back on the trail, he had hoped they would find something conclusive, something that would signal the end of their flight.

There were eleven new emails, but none of them were of any relevance. It was as if email silence had been declared on the subject of Allison and Kane once they went missing. All communication had probably moved to closed-door meetings.

Dan looked up at Allison and could see the disappointment in her eyes. He racked his brain for other angles, other opportunities. How would they ever be able to gather solid evidence now? They had examined every email in detail, hadn't they? All except . . . hmm . . .

"Allison, do you think this Tim Johnson guy is from CRI, too?"

"I don't know. Wait, Dr. Kane did mention a friend in the IT department once. I don't remember if he used a name but, who knows? Maybe. But that email's encrypted, right?" asked Allison.

"Yes, but what if we were able to contact this guy and convince him to give us the key? And, come to think of it, the fact it's encrypted might be even more reason to go after it. It's obviously sensitive in some way."

"Yes, but wouldn't we be risking exposure just by contacting him?"

"Maybe," replied Dan. "Although I doubt that our satellite internet connection is easily identifiable, or at least not easily tied to our location at any given time."

"So, you mean just reply to Tim's email?"

"Yep, it could be as simple as that. Just reply and assume that he's with CRI and he's on our side."

"Okay, I'm willing to take the risk if you are. Why don't you compose it—you're the psychologist. I'll play chef and start that dinner we missed last night. How's that?"

"Works for me," replied Dan. He put together an email identifying himself, explaining how he came to have access to Nathan Kane's account, and expressing his condolences for Dr. Kane's tragic death—he actually used the word "murder." He then made the request for the decryption key, saying that he understood how trust might be difficult. He finished by saying that if Mr. Johnson felt that the contents of the encrypted mail might serve to convict the guilty and therefore also to protect Allison Walker and exonerate Dr. Kane, would he please seriously consider sending the key.

Just as Dan finished, Allison returned with two glasses of Malbec.

"To Dr. Kane." she said, and they clinked their glasses together.

"Here, have a look before I send this," said Dan.

Allison read the email, nodded her head, and Dan clicked Send.

The early evening temperature hovered in the low sixties and the sunset promised to be a glorious one as it reflected off a thin layer of stratus clouds, so Dan and Allison decided on the upper deck for dinner. It would have been difficult to imagine a more beautiful setting with the smooth water punctuated by craggy rock and the forested hills rising on three sides of the harbor. Seabirds settled on rocks for the evening and, as if in imitation, a few late boats drifted into the harbor with running lights on, searching for a mooring buoy or a choice spot to anchor.

As the sun completed its performance, Allison told Dan about the touching scene she had witnessed in the same harbor years before. She said that the look of the fading sunset brought the plaintive notes of the bagpipe back to memory as vividly as if she were actually hearing each one again.

Dan looked at her with concern.

"These are good tears, Dan. I'm very happy right now."

She snuggled into his arms and they watched the fading light together without speaking. Dan slowly stroked her hair and thought that he would be perfectly content to stay there, doing only that, for the rest of the evening.

But Allison apparently had other ideas and so, after fifteen minutes in the dark and comfortable silence, she looked up and said, "It's getting a little chilly up here, don't you think? Let's go below and get warmed up."

"You go ahead. I'll take care of the dishes and come looking for you after that. How's that sound?"

"Perfect."

One last look at the water below, then Dan began gathering up dishes and glasses. He noticed that his hand was shaking as he carefully picked up Allison's empty wine glass. Faint lip prints around the edges—no lipstick stains. Dan smiled.

It took two trips to get everything down to the galley, but ten minutes later the dishes were finished and Dan secured the hatch leading to the upper deck. Next he went to the salon's aft door and locked that as well. The sound of the diesel furnace was soothing as it warmed the interior of the yacht, and that seemed to ease the shakes a bit. *Maybe it was just the air*, he thought. *It is getting cold out there.*

Dan shrugged off the jumpy feeling and went below to his stateroom where he peeled off the day's clothes, washed up, shaved, and put on the only other things he had with him. A pair of cargo pants and an old long-sleeved, black silk shirt from Hawaii, open at the collar—these would have to do. *No need for shoes, right? How about underwear? No.*

Dan looked at himself in the mirror, ran a brush through his hair, and thought that he looked okay, still solid and nicely muscled. The years of California surfing certainly hadn't hurt. *Not too bad for thirty-three.* He took a deep breath and walked over to Allison's stateroom.

The door was closed. Dan took another deep breath, let it out slowly, and knocked.

"Come in."

When Dan opened the door, there was Allison, standing on the far side of the stateroom across the bed, looking back over her left shoulder at him. Her hair was down and looked softly brushed. She must have been gazing out the window at the water, Dan thought. Or maybe she was remembering this morning's moments in the galley. Her smile was as soft as her hair and Dan could tell that she wasn't intentionally trying to look sexy—she just was. The authentic tenderness in her face melted away any anxiety that Dan had left.

He closed the door and slowly walked toward her. True to her word, she was wearing a short black shirt, but it was much shorter than Dan had expected and had a row of lace at the hem. Dan didn't know what to call it, but it was definitely not a T-shirt. She wore nothing beneath, and the feminine curves and crevices of her body painted a masterpiece in Dan's mind.

By the time he reached the other side of the room, Dan had unbuttoned his shirt. Allison had not moved from her position and he came up behind her, kissing her neck and pressing his body against hers. She took his hands in hers and slowly moved them up under the front of her shirt. He cupped her breasts and felt her nipples rise to him. Hard and soft together. Hard and soft.

They moved together like this, slowly at first and then with building urgency. Allison turned to face Dan. As they kissed, Dan felt Allison's hands working the button on his pants. She seemed to realize that he too had decided to forgo underwear because he could feel her kiss widen and become a smile. His pants dropped to the floor and he stepped out of them. He pressed against Allison again. Hard and soft, together.

Allison pulled back from Dan and he saw her eyes upon him, upon every part of him. She pulled her only article of clothing up and over her head, letting it drop to the floor. Then she kissed Dan one more time, looked longingly into his eyes, and repeated the words she had last spoken at the lighthouse.

281

FIFTY-SEVEN

. . . .

D an woke to the faint sound of metal on metal. Or had it just been a dream? Allison's warmth and her slow, steady breathing worked as a sedative, enticing Dan back down into the cradle of sleep. Then, just as he had blissfully accepted the invitation, there it was again—subtle but unmistakable. More than a clink but not quite a clank.

Dan sat up in bed and tried to focus on the small clock on the built-in nightstand next to Allison. Two fifty-five: definitely the wee hours. Way too wee, even for Dan. The morning was very small indeed and Dan had no desire to engage with it until it had grown a bit more.

Dan heard the clink again. It reminded him of one he had heard aboard a sailboat long ago: a metal fitting on a halyard hitting the surface of an aluminum mast in the wind. But this boat had no masts, no halyards, and the stillness of the vessel in the water told Dan that there was no wind. But something had moved. Something had caused the sound that Dan now knew to be real. It seemed to be coming from somewhere in the direction of the bow. Moonlight gently painted the stateroom through a partly open curtain.

Quietly, Dan swung his legs over the side of the bed. He pulled on the cargo pants he found in a heap on the floor and looked around for his shirt.

"Hey you, early isn't it?" came Allison's muffled voice. Half of her face was pressed into the pillow and Dan had to smile at the sound of her words.

"Hey you, too. I just heard something up front and thought I'd better have a look."

"Something? What something?"

"I don't know. Metallic kind of sound. I'll go check it out. You can stay put."

But Allison was already tossing the covers off.

"Or maybe not," said Dan.

Dan moved out into the companionway and toward the VIP stateroom. It was all the way forward, and in a smaller boat it might have been called a V-berth because of its shape. But in this boat the area was big enough for a queen-size bed with walk-around space on both sides. At the head of the bed, behind the wood paneling, was a compartment holding the anchor chain—the chain locker. Once again, Dan heard the sound, only this time it was much more distinct and seemed to be emanating from the locker. He opened the compartment hatch carefully.

Nothing seemed out of place. The chain snaked down from the windlass above and into a neat pile below. Then, just as he was about to close up the locker, Dan heard something else. It took his brain a moment to switch contexts. A muffled voice had come from outside—the single loudly whispered word, "Damn!"

Dan turned his head as he heard Allison approaching the stateroom door. He placed a finger on his lips to signal the need for silence and carefully walked toward her. He motioned for her to follow him back out into the companionway and quietly closed the door behind them.

"There's someone out there," he whispered. "And he's doing something with the anchor chain."

"What? At three AM?" whispered Allison.

"Or any time," added Dan with raised eyebrows.

"Yeah." Allison rubbed her eyes. "What should we do?"

"I'm going to take one of the kayaks from the stern and go investigate. If I'm not back in . . . let's say ten minutes, then grab the other kayak and get away. Go to another boat nearby and get help, but get yourself out of danger first."

Allison nodded but Dan wasn't convinced that she would do anything of the sort.

"Are there any weapons on board?" he asked.

"Yes, there's a nine millimeter handgun. I think it's for dispatching sharks. The owner does some deep sea fishing. I'll get it."

"Wait just a sec. How about duct tape? Any of that?" asked Dan.

"In the engine room," said Allison. "I'll meet you at the kayaks."

Allison returned with both items and Dan checked the gun. Loaded, safety on. He shoved it into a front pocket, fitted the roll of tape tightly over his forearm, and got into a kayak. *What am I doing? I haven't held a gun in my hand since I was a teenager out in the canyon. And I was aiming at beer cans, not people. This is crazy.*

"Be careful, Dan."

"Yeah."

Dan paddled silently along the port side of the fifty-eight foot vessel until he was within a few feet of the point where the hull began to angle in toward the bow. From there he could see ripples fanning out in the otherwise smooth water ahead. He moved forward, staying close to the side of the yacht and watching for the source of the disturbance. Then he stopped. Dan silently cursed the fact that he was in a kayak. In the moonlight, the long bow of his craft would become visible to whoever was up ahead long before he would be able to see them. Not a good situation. *Damn! Hadn't thought of that.*

Dan sifted through the alternatives, searching for anything that made sense. He felt alarmingly like the proverbial sitting duck. *Turn around and go back? Okay, but then what? Keep going and hope that the intruder is facing away? Hmmm. Damn the torpedoes, full speed ahead?*

The last alternative seemed insane. It also seemed like the best choice. Whatever happened, Dan reasoned feebly, at least new opportunities would present themselves right away. Things would happen fast. Dan positioned his paddle for a strong thrust and was about to launch himself forward when he heard a short but unmistakable "pssst!" from above. He looked up.

There, about six feet above him, crouching at the rail of the yacht, was Allison. She was holding her right hand up, palm open and thrust toward Dan, clearly signaling him to stop. Then, when Dan nodded, she held up a single finger and crawled slowly forward, peering around the sloping edge of the pilothouse. Dan watched as Allison held her pose, appearing to track something with her eyes. After a few moments, she inched forward again, keeping that single finger up, staring ahead over her right shoulder into the moonlit night. Finally, Dan saw Allison's finger form into a crook. She turned her hand around and waved him forward.

Dan felt adrenaline surge through his bloodstream and was about to release his pent up energy into the paddle when he saw Allison's finger move to her lips. She mouthed the word, "quiet," and then made another forward waving motion, much slower this time, pointing off to her right.

Dan took a deep breath, trying to control his urge to charge ahead, then let it slowly out. He placed his paddle silently into the water and glided forward. Keeping one eye on his scout and the other on the water ahead, Dan slowly and silently cleared the bow of the yacht and peered off to his right.

About fifty yards ahead he spotted the dark outline of a small trawler. It had not been there when he and Allison had gone to bed that night, he was quite certain. The boat had no lights on, not even an anchor light. Approaching the stern of the trawler was a small inflatable dinghy, its V-shaped wake trailing behind and its skipper facing forward and away. From the back and at that distance, Dan could not make out the features of the person but it appeared to be a man. He seemed rather short, wore a dark sweatshirt with the hood up, but Dan could see little else. Whatever he might have been doing near *Grape Escape*, he was no longer doing it.

Dan felt his energy drain away as the cool air and the darkness closed in upon him. He was tempted to dismiss the whole thing and get back to bed. Maybe the man had just been setting or checking a crab pot nearby. Dan didn't see a telltale buoy or marker. Drunk and out for a 3AM ride in the dinghy? Seemed unlikely. Dan back-paddled to tuck himself in behind the yacht and think about what to do next, if anything. Maybe he was just being overly cautious. Even a bit paranoid?

As he passed directly under the bow, something on the hull just below the water line caught his eye, something that looked lumpy, gray, and out of place. *A big sea anemone of some kind?* Dan made a mental note to tell Allison that the bottom needed cleaning. Then he saw the thin twisted pair of white wires protruding from the lump and running close against the white hull.

His eyes traced the path of the tiny white wires in the dim light, white on white but making a subtle shadow against the otherwise homogenous surface of the bow. He moved the kayak closer. In spite of the wires, his mind still clung to the anemone explanation, as if the two objects—the gray growth just below the water's surface and the wires—were unrelated. He traced the strange wires up the bow, higher and higher, until they terminated, with some extra slack, at a little black box attached to the anchor chain a couple of feet below the bow pulpit. Only one wire was attached to a screw terminal. The other hung loose. It looked as though there was no screw for that one. Again, Dan searched for an explanation. Was this part of an anchoring system of some kind? No, that made no sense at all. The little black box was attached to the chain with a hefty-looking white zip-tie. There was no way it could pass through the anchor guide above when the chain was hauled in. It would be compressed or crushed or . . .

Then, with a shock, Dan's observations finally integrated. He back-paddled and looked up to catch Allison's eye. "Allison!" he hissed in a loud whisper. "Get off the boat now! It's wired with plastic explosives! Get the other kayak!"

Dan paddled quickly back to the stern of the yacht and met her there. Together they paddled well away from the yacht, putting it between themselves and the other trawler.

"Are you sure, Dan?"

"Positive. I don't think it can be anything else. I've never seen the stuff before, except in the movies, but what else could it be? A gray blob stuck to the hull just below the waterline with wires coming out of it up to some kind of switch attached to the anchor line?"

"Designed to detonate when we hauled up the anchor," Allison concluded.

"Yep, I'm afraid so. But the guy didn't finish. I'm guessing he dropped a screw in the water while trying to hook up the last wire. He probably went back to his boat to get another one."

"So . . . what now?" Allison asked.

"Well," said Dan, "the way I see it, we've got two options: we either get the hell out of here right now or we grab this guy and prevent him from finishing the job."

Allison nodded but Dan couldn't read her. She looked across the harbor into the darkness of the trees on the other side, then back to the yacht. "How sure are you about him not finishing?" she finally asked. She reached across to touch his arm as she spoke.

"About as sure as I can be. Ninety eight percent, if I had to put a number on it. I don't know much about explosives but I do know that there are two wires going into that plastic blob and only one is connected to the black box. The other one has a loop on the end of it like it was supposed to be attached to the other screw terminal but it isn't. It's just hanging there. And I heard the guy say 'damn' before, when I was checking the chain locker from inside."

"Okay," said Allison. "I vote we try to get this guy. If we leave him to finish, somebody is going to get hurt. If it isn't us it'll be someone else. And besides, he's evidence. We need him. We couldn't get very far in these kayaks, or on this island either. He'd track us down, or somebody else would."

"My vote, too. We've got to try, and we've got to get to him before he connects that last wire," Dan agreed.

Dan and Allison whispered together for another minute before paddling back. Dan headed for the stern of the yacht and Allison paddled ninety degrees off to Dan's left, directly to shore, where she tucked her kayak in behind some overhanging trees. The moon still shone into the cloudless night sky but it was now lower, hanging just above the hills behind Allison's chosen spot. The tall trees on the hill created a deep moon-shadow over half the harbor and Allison took full advantage of that.

When Dan reached the stern, he tied up the kayak and quietly walked aboard. He re-checked the gun in his front pocket: loaded, safety on. Next, he found a small flashlight in the engine room, stuffed it into his other front pocket, and made his way back to the kayak where he had forgotten the roll of duct tape. Now, as ready as he could be, he swallowed hard and climbed the stairs to the upper deck. There Dan crouched and moved slowly forward until he was able to see down across the bow and over the water.

He spotted a dim light moving around inside the trawler. A flashlight. The man must have been searching everywhere for a replacement screw or some other means of attaching the detonator wire. Finally, the light went out and Dan waited for the man to emerge from the trawler. Several minutes crawled by and they felt like hours. *Where is that guy? What is he up to?*

Finally, just as Dan was considering another tactic, he saw movement at the stern of the trawler. Now, both the trawler and the yacht were in the deep darkness of the moon's shadow and it was difficult to see any detail. But detail wasn't necessary. The little inflatable dinghy was moving away from the trawler and toward the yacht under power of a silent electric trolling motor. Dan made his next move. Crouching low again, he worked his way down from the upper deck to the stern, then around the port side of the vessel, using its superstructure to hide himself. Having gotten as far forward as he could risk, Dan peered around the end of the pilothouse. He waited until he saw the dinghy drift under the yacht's bow.

Dan knew that he had very little time, probably less than a minute, to do what he had to do. But he invested the first five seconds of that time talking himself into his role as fully confident psychotherapist. He was only marginally successful. *Therapist with a gun? Okay, okay, just breathe and go.*

Breathe and go. As stealthily as possible, Dan walked, then crawled onto the foredeck toward the bow pulpit where the anchor chain hung down into the water below. There he pulled the gun from his pocket and wriggled forward to the point where he could just see over the edge.

Dan had chosen a good moment because the man below was standing up in his unstable dinghy. He was holding a small flashlight in his teeth and was looking down at a length of wire in his hands. He seemed to be trying to fit a small machine screw into a loop in the end of the wire. He had pulled his hood back and Dan could now see that he was a short but solid-looking man with scruffy brown hair. He looked as though he hadn't shaved in a couple of days.

Dan rose to his knees, took the gun in both hands and aimed straight down. *Damn safety.* He pulled the gun back and clicked the safety off. But that must have been enough motion for the man below to detect. In the fraction of a second that it took Dan to re-aim, the man dropped the wire and was reaching into his pants for something.

"Stop!" Dan shouted. "Get your hands back up where I can see them! Now!"

The man hesitated. "What the fuck?" One hand grabbed the wire again.

"Get both hands up. Put 'em on the chain. Now!" Dan felt his own focus sharpen. His body, the gun in his hands, the man below—those things comprised the entire universe. He knew that the next few seconds would be crucial. *Control. It's all about control right now. One of us has to have it. It's got to be me.*

The man had frozen but his arms remained down. He was looking up with a squint, testing. Dan could now see his face in the dim light. He looked to be in his mid-thirties. A long scar ran from his left temple, outside his eye, and partway down his left cheekbone.

"Your hands—get them up! I *will* shoot. Don't tempt me." Dan heard his own words as if they had come from someone else.

"Yeah, sure. Right." The man brought one hand up to the anchor chain. The other remained down near his pocket.

"The other one! Up!" Dan saw that the man continued to hold the single white wire in his hand. A slight tremor in the hand. *Cold? Nervous?*

"All I gotta do is touch this to the chain and you, me, and your big-ass boat are history," said the man, looking down at his right hand.

Dan tried to hear anything in the man's tone that would communicate actual intent. He didn't hear it. He wondered if the technology even worked that way. The little box on the chain? Was it somehow tied into the boat's grounding system? It didn't look like it, but Dan supposed it was possible. Possibility was enough.

"But you don't really want to do that, do you?" asked Dan.

The man just laughed.

Dan waited. *Contact points. Personal contact.*

After a second, he tried again. "My name's Dan."

"No shit."

"Yeah, no shit. Yours?"

The man laughed again, a single guffaw. He shook his head. His right hand remained clutched around the wire. Finally, he spoke. "Where's your girlfriend?"

"She's not here. Left about fifteen minutes ago."

"You're lying."

Dan thought he detected more emotion in the man's voice. *Good.*

"No, I'm definitely not. She's gone."

"Your dinghy's still up there. I saw it," said the man.

"She took a kayak. By now she's probably aboard someone else's boat. On the radio."

Silence.

Dan decided to press the advantage a bit farther.

"Look, you can't finish what you came here to do. It's over."

"I can finish half of it," said the man.

"Not the half they're going to pay for, and you wouldn't be around to collect anyway. They don't give a damn about me or this boat, or you for that matter."

"Might as well go out big then, huh?" said the man with a twitch of his upper lip.

"Why go out at all?"

"No money, no life."

"Hmm, would you like to talk about that?" Dan winced internally at his automatic response. For a fleeting moment, he thought how similar that was to Allison's experience. The therapist part was coming out.

"What are you, some kind of shrink?"

"Yes. I'm a psychotherapist."

"Fuck."

"Maybe I can help."

"Naw. I went to one once. Got me thinkin' too much. Really fucked me up."

"That can happen. Maybe he wasn't the right guy for you."

"Girl. It was a girl."

"Oh, okay. Look, you've still got a lot of years ahead of you. You could turn things around."

"Not with no money."

"And why is that so important?"

"I don't want to talk about any of this, so shut up. Just shut the fuck up!"

Dan nodded and thought about the situation. This guy was clearly no suicide bomber. There was no ideology here, no grand mission. He might be a suicide *risk*, though. He was worried about money problems. Maybe big debt, probably owed to the wrong people. Still, no deep despondency. Fear and anxiety, yes. He was making an effort to get himself out of whatever mess he was in. Doing it in a lousy way, but still trying. Dan decided that there was room to push.

"Okay, we won't talk about any of that, but let's get realistic. I'm up here with a gun. You're standing in a dinghy below me. You don't want to die, neither do I. So here's the way out. You agree to let go of that wire and come with me. You haven't done anything yet, so you agree to testify against the people who hired you and I bet you get off easy."

"Or, how 'bout this, asshole? You do whatever it takes to get your girlfriend's pretty ass back over here—get her on the radio or whatever—or I blow this thing now. I really don't give a shit. Either way."

That push didn't get me very far. Dan decided that he didn't know enough and probably couldn't get there. *There just might be real psychosis here. He's not truly despondent, but not entirely rational either. Provide some clarity, some direction.*

"No. That's not an option. Here's your only choice, so listen to me." Dan was about to continue when he detected motion in his peripheral vision, behind the man and to his left. Allison was paddling toward them. *What is she doing?*

Dan kept his eyes off Allison's approach and focused on the man. "Let go of the wire and put both hands on the chain!"

Allison was now within twenty or thirty feet. Too close. At least she hadn't spoken or made any noise. *What the hell is she doing?!*

The man looked down at his hand, holding the wire. He placed the bare end of the wire between his thumb and forefinger.

Allison was now fifteen feet away and Dan could hear the faint splash of her paddle as it entered the water.

"Don't do it!" Dan shouted at the man, both as a genuine warning and to cover up the sound of Allison's approach. Allison was much too close now. Well within range of the bomb.

The man clenched his jaw and raised his arm. Dan followed the motion with his gun.

"I said, don't do it!" Dan repeated. He could see the decision in the man's eyes as his hand continued moving toward the chain. Dan squeezed the trigger.

The shot was good. The man jerked his hand away as the nine millimeter bullet ripped through his wrist. He sunk to the bottom of the dinghy, clutching at his wrist with his other hand. Blood spurted from the wound. The white wire hung free in the air, its exposed end dangling inches from the chain.

On exit, the bullet had evidently continued its journey because one of the pontoons on the man's inflatable craft was losing air rapidly. The little boat was beginning to list heavily to its starboard side. Dan could see the dark stain of blood spreading across the white bottom of the boat. It was growing alarmingly fast.

"Looks like you've got a patient," Dan said to Allison as she paddled up. "I think I might have hit an artery." He wanted to ask her why in hell she was there at all but decided that discussion would have to wait.

"Get the first aid kit, Dan! It's up in the pilothouse in a drawer on the port side," Allison said.

Dan considered doing something about the loose wire first, but it seemed stable, and one look at the man below told him that there was little time to waste if they wanted to take him alive. He ran.

When Dan returned, he tossed the kit down to Allison who busied herself with the patient. He was still conscious but slumped over in the little boat which itself appeared mortally wounded. She had evidently stopped the bleeding by gripping the man's arm hard above the wrist. Even in the starlight, Dan could tell that the man was as white as cake flour. He was no threat. Unless he died. Dan was taken aback by his own thoughts of self-preservation, his own needs. He needed this man to live.

While Allison worked with bandages and Neosporin from the kit, Dan leaned over with his flashlight to examine the black box on the anchor chain. He could see it easily but it was down the chain just beyond his reach. He ran back inside the boat, found a pair of wire cutters in the engine room toolkit and brought them back on deck. There he took one of the boat's heavy lines and tied it around his waist using a bowline knot.

Just like on the rocks in San Diego before I could afford a harness. He looped the other end around a cleat, wrapped it one more time around his waist, and rappelled down over the edge of the bow. He tied himself off and went to work. Cutting the single wire on the black box, Dan then reached down and clipped the exposed end off the other wire, just to be sure. He finished by cutting the zip-tie that held the black box to the chain. *Now to get back up.*

That turned out to be difficult. The inward slope of the smooth fiberglass bow offered no traction, and without that it was impossible to take the weight off the rope and shorten the loop. Dan looked down to check on Allison's progress. She seemed to be putting the final touches on the bandage. The man was now lying down at an awkward angle in his sinking boat. He muttered an unintelligible word or two. There was a startling amount of blood in his boat.

Dan abandoned the idea of using the rope to get himself up. It was smooth nylon and he couldn't climb it. Instead, he reached out for the anchor chain, grabbed it, and pulled himself toward it. Wrapping arms and legs around the heavy chain, he climbed up just far enough to grab the stainless steel anchor guide. He muscled up from there and swung a leg up and over the edge of the bow. He was up. He quickly untied from the rope and ran to the stern where he boarded the second kayak and paddled back to Allison.

She had apparently finished the job and was busy tying her kayak's dock line to the man's derelict dinghy. Dan searched the man's clothes and came up with a handgun and a small knife, both of which he stowed in his kayak.

"Can you tow him a hundred feet or so that way before taking him back?" asked Dan, pointing into the darkness. "Then I'll meet you back at the stern. Just want to be absolutely sure that the explosive can't do any harm. Oh, here, just in case." Dan clicked on the safety and tossed his gun over to Allison.

She caught the weapon, looked up as if she were about to object to something, but then nodded and paddled off into the night with her prisoner in tow.

When Allison and her charge were far enough away, Dan paddled over to the section of the hull where the gray lump of plastic material was stuck just below the waterline. The twisted pair of white wires coming out of it now lay in the water nearby. Dan had heard from a military client with PTSD that this kind of explosive, probably C-4, was extremely stable by itself. His client told him of soldiers burning the stuff in campfires to keep warm. It would only explode when violently shocked by another explosion—one from a detonator like that buried inside the particular clay-like lump that Dan now stared at.

Dan reached into the water and picked up the wires. Carefully, and with little force at first, he began to pull on them. He didn't want to break them and have to fish around inside the blob with his hand to remove the detonator if he could avoid it. The wires went taut and resisted. He increased the force, trying to sense anything beyond a stretch in the wires. Nothing. Wrapping a length of wire around his right hand, Dan exerted more force. Slowly at first, and then with a sudden release, a small red cylinder pulled through the blob's surface and presented itself at the end of the wires. Dan remembered to breathe again, stowed the detonator in the kayak and began paddling. The blob could remain on the hull for now.

When he arrived at Allison's position, Dan tied his kayak to their prisoner's dinghy, and together they towed him back to *Grape Escape*.

Getting the man out of the dinghy and up into the yacht was a chore, and not just because of his weight. Even in his severely weakened condition, he kicked a few times and tried to twist away from Dan's grip.

"Don't piss me off any more than you already have," said Dan, re-gripping the man's feet and giving them an extra yank. "Or I'll make you sit through a therapy session and talk about your feelings."

FIFTY-EIGHT

· ·

With Allison's help, Dan wrapped several layers of duct tape around the prisoner's ankles, then did the same with the man's good arm against his body. They left him on the teak floor of the cockpit and walked back up to the pilothouse.

"Dan, he's going to need better antibiotics, some blood, and probably some bone repair."

"So, you're saying we need to get him somewhere," Dan said. "Kind of puts us in another bad spot, doesn't it?"

"But we can't stay here anyway, right? Whoever hired this guy is going to want to hear back from him and when he doesn't check in they'll probably send someone else."

Dan nodded. *What a mess*, he thought. *I should've controlled the situation better. Never should've gotten to the point where I had to shoot the guy. Stupid.*

Allison looked up and smiled sadly at Dan. "I came back because I heard everything he said, Dan. Sound travels well over open water. I knew you'd never give me up, and the guy sounded seriously suicidal to me. I had to come back. I couldn't bear the thought of you . . . Anyway, I think it's my fault they found us here to start with."

"How could that be?"

"I mentioned this place in my last recorded session with Dr. Kane. He asked me to describe a peaceful place and time and I talked about Reid Harbor. I didn't think of the connection 'til now. Wish I'd thought of it before. I'm so sorry."

"Not your fault, definitely not your fault, Allison. You were in therapy. You don't expect that kind of discussion to ever go beyond the office."

Dan turned to scan the area around their boat. A few other vessels that were dark before had lights on now. People had heard things—certainly they must have heard the gunshot—but no one was coming to investigate. They needed to move quickly. But there was one other thing to do before leaving.

"Allison, I want to do a quick search on this guy's boat before we leave. We need all the evidence we can get."

"Good idea. He isn't going anywhere, that's for sure. I'll get our boat ready to leave. Oh, and get his boat's registration number if you can."

Dan paddled over to the dark trawler anchored nearby, towing the half-deflated dinghy with him. He tied it up there, then boarded and searched the trawler.

He returned to the yacht ten minutes later, smiling and carrying a cell phone. Allison was in the pilothouse staring at the computer screen.

"We got it, Dan," said Allison. "Tim Johnson replied with the decryption key."

"Excellent! Let's open up that email and have a look. And, you won't believe what I found," said Dan, handing over the phone. "Take a look at these text messages—direct orders to find us here and take us out."

The email from Tim Johnson was brief and contained an attachment, a compressed audio file. The text of the mail read:

Dr. Kane,

After we talked I decided to do a little sniffing on my own. I hope you're okay because there's bad shit going down. So bad that I'm out of here tonight for good. Going somewhere far away for a while. I'll check email once in a while. For now, listen to the attached file. Everybody thinks this place is so damn secure. What a crock. Dead easy to get into Carver's office audio system. He thinks that mike is just for voice control and intercom. Hah!

Be careful.

Tim.

Dan looked at Allison when they'd finished scanning the text. She nodded and he opened the attachment. For the next five minutes they listened to a recording of a short meeting in Carver's office. Allison recognized the voices of Carver and Hamilton but could not identify that of an older woman who seemed to be in charge. The discussions—mostly tirades and orders from the woman—were shocking in their callousness. The woman told the two men that the trial *would* succeed, that they *would* get FDA approval, and that nothing and no one would stand in the way. She mentioned Kane's "necessary removal" and said that they must now "clean up the rest." Then they proceeded to discuss opportunities and methods. Hamilton mentioned Allison's discussion of Reid Harbor in her last recorded session, and they decided to add a man to the team to cover the possibility that she would hide out there.

"I don't know if this stuff is admissible in court, but it's got to count for something, doesn't it?" asked Allison and then continued. "I think it's time to go to the police, don't you?"

"Absolutely. We've got the audio, the text messages, and the explosives, not to mention the hired gun himself. But I think we should go through your lawyer friend."

"Margaret."

"Yes, she'll probably know exactly who to talk to and how much to reveal."

"Okay, let's get underway first; then I'll call her on the SAT phone."

"At four-thirty in the morning?"

"Won't be the first time I've gotten her up."

With that, Allison started the diesels and Dan made one more kayak trip to remove the C-4 blob from the hull. When he returned and stowed the kayaks, Allison weighed the anchor. They idled through the harbor, out the mouth and into Spieden Channel. Daylight was just starting to glow in the east.

After some discussion, they decided on a destination. They would head away from the islands and make for Anacortes, a location much more easily accessible by law enforcement on the mainland. It would take them a couple of hours and at least they would be a moving target while they set things up.

Allison keyed in Margaret's home number on the SAT phone. A sleepy voice answered after two rings.

"Hello?"

"Margaret, it's Allie. I'm so sorry to wake you but I need your help."

"Allie! Oh, God am I glad to hear your voice." Margaret sounded instantly awake. "Where are you?"

"On a boat headed for Anacortes. Dan's with me and we've been targeted by CRI but managed to escape. We've got evidence and a prisoner. There's so much to tell you but I can't do it now. Can you get in touch with the police and have them meet us at Cap Sante Marina?"

"Yes, yes of course. Allie, I was so worried you might be . . . I'm sorry. I'm so glad you're okay. How long 'til you get there?"

"A little over two hours, I think. Dan's going to email you an audio file which you might want to listen to before calling the police."

"Don't worry, girl. I'll take care of everything. I love you."

"I love you, too. Thank you, thank you, thank you."

"So, I take it Margaret's on the case?" asked Dan from behind the captain's chair. He rested his hands on Allison's shoulders and lightly massaged them.

"Yes. I feel so much better with her coming up to meet us. Oooh, that feels good, too," said Allison, with a smile over her shoulder. "It's like, I don't know, it's like I can look at the future again, even if it still isn't clear. You know what I mean?"

"Yeah, I think I do. What do you see?"

"Is that a question from my psychotherapist?" Allison's crooked little smile made an appearance.

"I'm not your therapist."

"Good. Then I see you."

"Am I smiling?"

"Most definitely."

"Good. What else do you see?"

Allison's smile faded. She made a quick adjustment to the autopilot then swung the chair around to face Dan. "I want to do something with this gift or curse I have. I want to learn more about my past and then make some kind of positive contribution to research, to neurogenetics. But without the right credentials, well, we know where that goes." She swung the chair back around to face the open water ahead.

Dan moved to the chair next to hers and stared into the smooth dark water as the bow of the boat sliced through it.

"But you can get the credentials. You're more than capable of that, and I know just the guy to advise you."

"Your friend, Skip?"

"Yes, I'm sure he'd find a way to help."

"You don't think I'd be treated like a specimen?"

"By Skip? No way. Sure, he's got a vested interest in the research, but he's a good person, a caring person. I can't think of anyone better to work with you. And, he's confident enough in his developing theories of trans-generational memory to risk his academic neck. Trust me, there are very few people of his stature willing to take that kind of risk at the early stage of what will probably be a brand new field. You've inspired him. Now let him inspire you."

"I don't know; so much would have to change. I mean, there's my business, my nice quiet life; everything would have to change."

"And . . . you don't think that's already happened?" asked Dan with raised eyebrows.

Allison sighed. "Yeah, I know. But still, if Margaret can straighten things out legally, I could go back to being just me. Knowing who my Teachers really were, maybe I can control things a little better. Maybe I'll be less compelled to act, be less stupid."

"You're anything but stupid, Allison. And if you want my two cents—do you?"

"Of course."

"Then here's how I see it. You're not likely to feel any less compelled to act on your knowledge because it's in your nature to be helpful. And it *is* your knowledge now, not anyone else's. You said yourself, just a minute ago, that you want to contribute to the research, and I think you really meant it. But I think it goes beyond that. I think you want to practice medicine, to work with real patients. It's really pretty obvious. And pretty damn wonderful."

Allison nodded and smiled.

Their course took Allison and Dan just north of Orcas Island, south down Rosario Strait, past Blakely Island, and then east into the Guemes Channel toward Anacortes. About half way down Blakely they encountered a dense wall of fog, forcing Allison to cut her speed in half and rely almost exclusively on radar for the rest of the journey. So it wasn't until seven-thirty that they made the last of the turns into the marina.

Allison lifted the VHF microphone and broke radio silence for the first time in their trip. "Cap Sante Marina, Cap Sante Marina. This is Grape Escape."

"Grape Escape, Cap Sante," came the harbormaster's response.

"Cap Sante, we're currently entering the marina near B-dock, requesting transient moorage, side-tie for a fifty-eight foot vessel, sixty-four foot LOA. We're being met by law enforcement. Please advise."

"Grape Escape, Cap Sante. Officers are waiting for you at the end of P-dock, P as in Paul. Please tie up there and follow instructions from them."

"P-dock, roger. Grape Escape out."

As Allison gently swung the yacht into position against the end of P-dock, she spotted Margaret, dwarfed amidst a group of uniformed police officers.

Dan was on deck, tossing lines to the officers who tied up the boat and motioned up to the pilothouse for Allison to disembark. She wasn't sure whether to expect arrest, congratulations, or something else, but she felt certain about one thing: safety would be better than living on the run, no matter what kind of package it came in. She shut down the engines and made her way down to the dock.

The ranking officer introduced himself to Allison as Captain Joe Mendez, and when he offered to shake her hand she knew that all would be well. Mendez asked where the prisoner was, dispatched two officers to take him into custody, and then informed Allison they would need to speak with Dan and her separately before they would be free to go. Allison nodded but barely heard the words as she looked beyond Captain Mendez to find Margaret in the crowd which had grown to include several reporters and onlookers.

"Thank you, Captain. I'd like to speak with my attorney—who's right over there—if I could, please." Allison glanced over the Captain's shoulder.

"Of course."

The rest of the morning on the dock was a blur for Allison—hugs and quick advice from Margaret, delivery of evidence, questions from the police, and new information. Dr. Kane's attorney had received a delayed email from his late client the day before containing Allison's patient files and a long narrative detailing the gross mishandling of the Amethyst clinical trial. Doctors Carver and Hamilton had been picked up an hour earlier and were under arrest. They, along with someone named Cynthia Roth, had been charged with the murder of Dr. Nathan Kane, with conspiracy to commit murder, and with various other crimes including fraud and medical malpractice. If Allison would agree to testify against them, the remainder of her short sentence would be commuted. Dan would not be charged with the shooting of the would-be assassin if he would also agree to testify. The matter of the borrowed yacht was a bit stickier, but, with a couple of phone calls to Argentina, Margaret was able to turn that into a non-issue as well.

Allison readily agreed to testify in the upcoming trials, as did Dan, and within three hours the crowd had dispersed, leaving Allison, Dan, and Margaret alone on the boat.

"Margaret, I'll never be able to thank you enough. You are such an amazing friend," said Allison with a catch in her voice.

"It's going to be a whole new life, girlfriend. Oh, can I still call you that?" asked Margaret with a sly glance at Dan.

FIFTY-NINE

· ·

Three weeks later, Allison and Dan boarded a plane in Seattle bound for St. Louis. Allison had decided to visit her mother's gravesite as a way of attempting some closure on her troubled past, and Dan had agreed to go with her. Through recent phone calls to the records department at St. Louis University Hospital, Allison had learned that Dr. Kathryn Johansen had been buried in a small cemetery in the tiny town of Cedar Hill where she had rented an old farmhouse, about twenty-five miles southwest of St. Louis.

The past weeks felt to Allison as though they comprised a lifetime of their own. It wasn't that the time had gone slowly. It had practically flown by. It was just that so much had been compressed into those weeks. She and Dan had spent happy days together talking, hiking, boating, and trying to keep the coffee in their cups. And there had been passionate nights as well, most of them aboard *Far and Away*.

As Margaret had foretold, life had changed radically, and much for the better. At first, Allison had balked at the offer coming from Dr. Skip Hanover. He had asked if Allison would be willing to join a work-study program under his tutelage at the University of Washington Medical School in which she could fill in the gaps of her education with the intent of becoming a full-fledged medical student there within a year. The catch, if it could be considered one, was that she would spend her work time as the subject of Dr. Skip Hanover's controversial research on the new genetics of memory. The controversy didn't worry Allison. Quite the contrary. She knew, first hand, that his work would remain controversial only for a short while. And after that, the possibilities seemed endless.

What *did* bother her was the prospect of giving up Rain City Yachts. But, with ideas and offers of assistance from Margaret and Dan, Allison found a way to keep the operation going by adopting a new strategy. Her business would be intentionally small and highly selective—a boutique brokerage. She and her new partner, Margaret Yee, would build on Allison's reputation for excellence in client service. They would take on a maximum of three high-end listings at a time—two of which Allison already had—and they would agree to five or fewer active searches on behalf of carefully selected buyers. Margaret would assist clients with custom insurance, international transfers, establishment and dissolution of partnerships, and of course, closings. Allison would deal with showings and sea trials. Ultimately, they would plan to hire another sales person as Allison's academic schedule became too demanding.

All of this was fresh in Allison's mind as she watched Mount Rainier drift by the airplane window, its cap of snow still large and bright in the early summer morning. She gave Dan's hand a little squeeze and sat back in her chair so that he could see the mountain, too.

"Dan?"

"Yes?"

"There's something else I'd like to do in St. Louis. You're going to think I'm nuts."

"Oh, I think we've already established that, my love," Dan smirked.

"Okay, okay, I asked for that. No, remember that journal reference that I told you about? The one from the American Journal of Surgery that was stuck in my head even before I knew what it meant?"

"Uh huh."

"Well, I got to thinking more about it yesterday. The paper itself never seemed significant and yet I kept going back to it over the years to try to read something into it, something that would help me understand more about Kathryn, more about myself."

"And you found something?"

"No, I gave up. And the minute I gave up, I had this off-the-wall idea. Maybe the contents of the paper aren't significant at all. Maybe it's the particular physical copy of the journal that Kathryn actually read. Maybe that's what's somehow meaningful. Maybe she wrote some notes in it or something."

"Seems like a stretch to me," said Dan. "Doesn't seem likely that it would even still be around, does it?"

"No, but that's what I want to find out. I promise I won't spend more than a few hours on it. It's not the reason we're going, anyway. Just a wild thought."

"I love your wild thoughts," said Dan with a smile.

After landing at Lambert-St. Louis International Airport, they rented a car and Dan drove out of the city down highway 30 to Cedar Hill while Allison navigated. Once there, it was easy to locate the small but well-kept cemetery along the main road. It didn't take long for Allison to find the headstone she was looking for.

The epitaph was as plain as could be. It simply read:

Kathryn Johansen
January 4, 1950 — January 7, 1980

She was my age when she died, when she gave birth to me. Allison had not expected to feel very much. She had just wanted to see for herself that this woman had actually lived and died. But standing at the grave with Dan at her side, Allison found herself suddenly weeping. This was not just a woman who had lived and died. This woman had been her mother. A mother who, had she lived, would have cared for her, would have held her, fed her, clothed her, taught her, loved her.

Allison fell to her knees and cried while Dan held her. There were no words, and none were needed.

SIXTY

. . . .

That night, Allison and Dan stayed at a small hotel in St. Louis, used room service for dinner, and talked late into the evening. Allison told Dan more about her childhood, remembering things that she had kept locked away for years. Dan held her close and stroked her hair. They didn't make love that night but slept with warm skin on warm skin, holding onto each other for the sake of life itself.

In the morning, Allison awoke feeling much better. She said she felt lighter and used the word "whole" to describe a different sense she had about herself. Dan nodded, seeming to understand. After a light breakfast in the hotel restaurant, Dan drove them to St. Louis University Hospital where Allison asked for directions to the medical library. They took the elevator and walked a few steps down the hall to the library's entrance.

"Where would I find your archives?" Allison asked the librarian, a thin and graying woman who appeared to be in her late sixties. "I'm looking for an old volume of the American Journal of Surgery, one from 1977."

"My goodness, that does go back a ways, doesn't it," said the librarian with a kind smile. "About the time I started here." She seemed to drift into a memory, then came back to the present. "Are you new on staff here, dear? I don't remember seeing you before but you look so familiar."

"No, but my mother was, thirty years ago. Dr. Johansen. Kathryn Johansen."

"Oh, my." The librarian brought both hands to her mouth and stared back at Allison with a mist forming in her wide eyes.

"Are . . . are you okay?" asked Allison, not sure how to interpret the woman's reaction.

"Yes, I'm sorry. It's just that, well, you look so much like her. Beautiful, my dear, just beautiful. And those eyes."

"You knew my mother? She looked like me?" Allison said.

"Oh goodness yes, I knew her. She spent half her time in this library, it seemed. Quiet, mostly kept to herself, but very sweet. She always made an effort to talk with me—not like some of the other doctors, you know. It was so sad when she died. I cried for days, every time I'd think of her."

Allison nodded. Her lower lip quivered and she couldn't speak.

"Oh, I'm so sorry, dear. Here, come on back to my office and sit for a while. You, too, sir. My name is Marilyn Jamison, by the way."

She shook hands with Dan, who introduced himself, and then she turned back to Allison.

"And you would be Allison. I remember the name because, well, because I gave it to you. I visited the baby—I visited *you*, my dear—almost every day after Dr. Johansen died, down in the brand new neonatal unit. When you got strong enough, they would let me hold you. They called you 'Baby A' because you were the first patient in the new unit. But to me, you looked like an Allison, so that's what I called you, and it stuck. You were so tiny—six weeks premature, you know. And look at you now, all grown up." Marilyn stood back and smiled. Her eyes were wet.

Allison gasped for breath and nodded, trying to smile back through her tears. *All grown up.* She walked toward Marilyn Jamison and held out her arms. "May I?"

"Of course."

Allison fell into the arms of the woman who probably had made her feel loved at the very beginning of her life. And now, Marilyn was making her feel that way again, almost as if no time had passed.

After a long, silent embrace, Allison felt herself settle into something like peace. It was an odd sensation because it coexisted with a thousand questions. There was so much that Allison wanted to learn about her mother and yet it was hard to know where to begin.

"Marilyn, may I ask you something about my mother?" Allison daubed at her eyes with a tissue.

"Anything."

"Did she ever talk with you about personal things, problems she was having, anything like that?"

"Oh yes, little things, all the time. But there was this one time . . . I never quite knew what to make of that conversation. Kathryn, your mother, was very upset that day, which was unusual for her. She always seemed so even-tempered, you know."

"Why do you think she was so upset?" asked Allison.

"Well, I remember she said she was having trouble concentrating on her work. I think I asked her if her patient load was too heavy, if that was getting to her, you know. She said that her schedule was pretty tight but it wasn't that. It was the Teachers, she said. I remember being puzzled by that and asked her what she meant. She told me that she knew things she had no business knowing—things about her mother, her grandmother, and others. Then she sort of dismissed it, said she wasn't making any sense and that I should just forget about it. I tried, but I didn't succeed, did I."

Allison was speechless for a moment. Then, "No, but I'm glad you didn't. I wrestle with the same things. I guess it's my turn now."

"Does it make sense to you, dear?"

"Not yet, but I'm working on it, with a lot of help." She looked over and smiled at Dan.

They spent the rest of the morning talking in Marilyn's office while her assistant handled the business of the library. Eventually, the conversation slowed and came back around to Allison's original intent for the visit.

"Oh, that journal you wanted, Allison? We don't keep bound paper copies that old anymore, but everything's been digitized so if you want a particular paper I can pull it up and print it for you."

"No, I won't be needing it, thank you, Marilyn. I've read the paper itself. I guess it wasn't really the journal I was looking for anyway. It wasn't about the paper *or* the journal. It was about you."

Marilyn smiled and nodded.

About the Author

D on Thompson received a degree in Applied Physics and Information Science from UCSD in 1973. He enjoyed a career in software development, then left the corporate world in 2000 to pursue his love of writing. He is the author of the young adult *Stellar Woods* trilogy and now *Second Nature*, an adult thriller. Don lives with his wife Donna in Woodinville, Washington. They have two grown children.